To Sharon,
The very best of life —
Hope you'll enjoy this

Lee Martin
2015

www. leemartinbooks.com
678-478-6582

SOUTHERN PSALMS

LEE MARTIN

WESTBOW
PRESS
A DIVISION OF THOMAS NELSON

WestBow Press books may be ordered through booksellers or by contacting:

WestBow Press
A Division of Thomas Nelson & Zondervan
1663 Liberty Drive
Bloomington, IN 47403
www.westbowpress.com
1-(866) 928-1240

ISBN: 978-1-4497-8451-5 (sc)
ISBN: 978-1-4497-8452-2 (e)

Library of Congress Control Number: 2013902369

Printed in the United States of America

WestBow Press rev. date: 07/30/2013

Also by

Lee Martin

The Third Moon is Blue

Starbright

The Six Mile Inn

The Valiant

Ten Minutes till Midnight

Wolf Laurel

Provocation: Return of the Weatherman

A Hateful Wind

The Justice Club

ACKNOWLEDGEMENTS

My thanks to the Reverend Jim Crutchfield who served as my spiritual *and* scriptural advisor. Jim, a friend and brother in Christ, assured that the scripture used to support the foundation of the novel was both appropriate and complementary.

Southern Psalms, set mostly in Southern Louisiana, is dedicated to my special friends in the greater New Orleans area. All of you. You are good people.

In memory of the Honorable Joe Giarrusso and Colonel Ed Radford. Great friends who loved my stories. We miss you.

Although during the time frame of this novel, the King James Version of the Bible would have been used, the author chose to quote scripture from the New King James Version which hopefully will present as a more fluid and conducive experience for the reader. The author further asks the indulgence and understanding of the reader in regards to this technical point.

NLM

There are four especial ways in which God speaks: by the voice of scripture, the voice of the inward impressions of the Holy Spirit, the voice of your own higher judgment and the voice of providential circumstances.

For we must not overlook the fact that there are other voices that speak to the soul. There is the loud and clamoring voice of self that is always seeking to be heard. And there are voices, too, of evil and deceiving spirits who lie in wait to entrap every traveler entering these higher regions of the spiritual life.

Hannah Whitall Smith

Southern Psalms

Part One

He sits in the lurking places of the villages; in the secret places, he murders the innocent; his eyes are secretly fixed on the helpless.
He lies in wait secretly, as a lion in his den; he lies in wait to catch the poor when he draws them into his net.
So he crouches, he lies low, that the helpless may fall by his strength.

Psalm 10: 8–10

Chapter One

Inner Demons

In his dreams he usually found himself in some kind of trap, sometimes bound and unable to move, always unable to extract himself from the dream until he awoke in a fearful sweat, gasping for breath and heart pounding like a hammer. In this dream he was crammed inside of his daughter's dollhouse peering from its tiny windows, crying out with a silent tongue while the tiny playhouse was burning. But there was no one in his daughter's room. And if there were, no one was coming to rescue him. The fire that was quickly consuming the pulpwood box would soon eat him alive.

It had been over three weeks since he left. He had hopped off a train in Paducah, bagged groceries for a week at a Krogers netting only a few dollars, then slipped into a boxcar of another slow freight bound for Memphis. There, on the dock of the Mississippi, he asked for work as a helper loading crates onto the merchant ship *Mary Doone*. Even though the waterfront crew was totally unionized, the boss, finding himself short-handed, took pity on him and allowed him only three days work. Still moving south, errantly and without purpose, he found *no* work in Jackson. After two days of living at the Union Mission and accepting a couple of hot meals, he finally walked to the edge of the city and caught another train.

He wasn't sure whether it was the tickle of the roach crawling across his lip that woke him or the pungent smell of smoke from the dream's burning dollhouse. Anything that he had so vividly heard, seen, felt, tasted or smelled in his dreams had never before continued beyond his sleep. But even as he swatted at the roach and opened his eyes, now fully awake, the smoke still lingered. Why had it not dissipated, he wondered?

He had no idea what time it was. It was dark, not just inside the boxcar, but because it was also night. Even if he *did* have a watch, he wouldn't be able to see the dial. But then as he sat up erect against the side of the car, he suddenly realized that what he was smelling was smoke from a cigarette. Now he was able to pinpoint its origin. Someone was sitting across from him smoking. Each time the red glow brightened, he saw the man's eyes; then more smoke filled the car.

"Who's there?" the dreamer called out.

There was no answer...just another fiery glow that lasted maybe two seconds, after which a long plume of smoke drifted toward his nostrils.

"I said, who are you?"

Then a match was struck and applied to the wick of a small lantern. It took a few moments for the dreamer to adjust to the sudden brightness, which caused him to squint and shield his eyes. When he was finally able to make out the man's features, the lamp now sitting on the floor of the boxcar reflected light upward onto the man's face, creating a gothic, even sinister impression.

Finally, the second man spoke. "Ah, you don't recognize me?"

The dreamer's eyes, ever gaining their vision, saw that the man was dirty-looking, perhaps fifty, with long blonde-gray hair and an unkempt beard. A tattered, red flannel shirt was shoved inside the waist of frayed, soiled jeans.

"Should I? You're apparently just another tramp and nobody I ever recall seeing before."

The man grinned, showing a set of gnarly, yellowed teeth beneath the beard. "Yeah, just a bum like you." He then took another drag of the cigarette.

"Why would you think I know you?" the dreamer asked.

"I didn't say you knew me personally, but you know me just the same."

A sudden chill shot up the dreamer's spine. "And again, why should I?"

The hobo chuckled, which led to a raspy cough. "You may not have seen this face, but you know me all right. I have called your name many times, especially recently; and you have not only responded to me, but followed after me."

The dreamer was amazed that the derelict spoke so well... and with a degree of articulation. He narrowed his eyebrows into a frown and shook his head. "You're talking in riddles, mister. As a matter of fact I don't think you're all there."

The man laughed again. "So, you think me mentally ill?"

"Okay. This is nonsense. If you think you know me, who am I and where am I from?"

The man glared at the dreamer while crushing what was left of the cigarette onto the wooden floor with his shoe. "Let's just say we have been watching you all of your life and have been waiting for this chance, minister."

The dreamer pushed himself up with his feet and stood in a ready-for-anything stance. "All right. Either you're a nut case or telling me you've been stalking me. If you're trying to frighten me, you'll take note that I'm much bigger than you and in better shape. You don't want to tangle with me."

The tramp smiled, baring his loathsome teeth. "Temper, temper, Travis Marlowe. I know that you could best me... physically, that is. I remember watching you in the New York junior Golden Gloves when you were sixteen."

Travis was stunned...nearly to the point where he could not respond. But, then up-righting himself, he stepped into the man and snatched him to his feet by his shirt. After slamming him against the wall, he said, "Okay, out with it. Who are you? How do you know my name?"

The man was actually bigger than Travis thought, but considering he had to be twenty five or more years older and appearing as if life had taken a huge chunk out of him, Travis was even more convinced the hobo would be no match for him.

"Ah, there's that hostility coming to life, just as I've seen a thousand times."

Travis jostled the man again, pushing him hard against the wall a second time. "So, you know my name...somehow. Now, what's yours and what do you mean you've been following me?"

"If you will release your grip on me, perhaps we can then have a civil conversation."

Travis let go of the man's shirt and motioned for him to return to where he had sat by the lantern. "Then start talking. I'm all ears."

When the hobo lowered himself to the floor, he crossed his legs, took another cigarette from his shirt pocket and lit it. His eyes, now piercing, seemed to burn into Travis' very soul. "You will not recognize me by my face. Actually, you have never seen this man before."

"What do you mean *this man?*"

The hobo's yellowed eyes did not lose their intensity. "This body."

Travis actually laughed. "So, you're a schizophrenic, eh?" But quickly he lost his grin.

"Not a schizophrenic, Travis. At least *I'm* not. The man you see before you probably is. Actually, he's pretty much a nobody."

"Then, old man, you are just plain crazy. But that still doesn't tell me why you know my name and have followed me into this boxcar. And it doesn't make sense that you know I was a Golden Gloves champion. You're freaking me out, mister."

"You may not believe me, Travis. "But..." He took another drag off of the cigarette. "...you continue to believe *in* me."

Travis laughed. "You're pretending to be God, of course."

The man continued with his fixating stare and said nothing.

"Or maybe you think you're Satan."

"Satan? Ah, but you flatter me. Let's just say I am *of* him. In the flesh...literally. You see *me*...you see *him*. But, I can see you don't believe that."

For a moment Travis drilled his eyes into those of the hobo. Then suddenly a rush of fear came over him and he backed up against the forward boxcar wall. But after taking in a deep breath, his sense of reason reclaimed him.

"You're right...I don't believe it. If you *are* Satan...or *of* him...then prove it."

"He prefers Lucifer, you know. The brightest of all angels."

"And again, you think you're him."

"Ah, but you *know* who I am, Travis. I see the fear in your face. Just as you think you know your God, you equally know that we exist and are capable of taking any form. I can be a serpent as you read in Genesis. I can take the form of a beautiful, enticing creature. It was the Great One who sent the woman that caused your fall from grace and ended your marriage. It was he who took your ministry from you and had you shunned. You see, Travis, *we* became your God and caused the One you followed so faithfully to turn his back on you. You could ultimately say we are more powerful than the God you worship."

Because the man who believed himself to be one of Satan's disciples knew these intricate details about him, Travis' heart began to pound like a kettledrum. A catch in his throat prevented him from responding. How could the man know these things? Occurrences that even went back to when he was sixteen. He slid down the wall of the car until his buttocks touched the floor. The steady rocking of the coach on the rails caused the back of his head to thrash about against the wall. He swallowed hard and finally said, "No. I refuse to believe you. Either I'm still dreaming, and it is the most vivid dream I've ever had, or *I'm* the one who has gone schizo."

"You know neither is the case, Travis. And you know a worthless bum like this…" he then placed his fingertips to his chest…"would not be able to speak as I am doing nor would he know the things about you that I do. *I evah desuac uoy ot tbuod ruoy htiaf.*"

"What?"

"Figure it out, Travis. Play my words backwards in your mind as though you would play a record."

Travis was now shaking. "It's…it's not possible."

"Did your God not reveal Himself many times to the likes of Abraham, Moses and of course David, the man after His own heart? Who by the way was also tempted with the lovely Bathsheba."

"This is the Twentieth Century, not two thousand or five thousand years ago. It's some kind of trick. I can better believe you are a magician or sorcerer than the devil."

The man shook his head. "I know what you're thinking, my friend. You know in your heart I'm real. Stop trying to convince yourself otherwise. Stop trying to deny me."

Travis laughed nervously. "Okay, I get it. While I was asleep, you fed me some kind of pill...a hallucinogen. It's distorted my thinking."

The hobo shook his head and casually puffed away on his cigarette without reply. They were both silent for a few moments, staring at one another, studying each other's face. Then the hobo smiled and crushed the cigarette into his left palm. There was no wince or frown that indicated pain.

"So, my boy, here you are, sitting across from me with no life. No possessions, no money, looking for your next meal. Now that you have been literally run out of your village on a rail," he then chuckled, "I appear to be the only friend you have. The only being on this earth who cares about you. You've been abandoned by your wife and daughter, but most of all by the One you have worshipped for so long."

Slowly, Travis rose to his feet and then moved toward the door on the starboard side of the boxcar. Finding the handle and latch, he slid the door from right to left and stood at the floor's edge. The fresh night air of the Louisiana countryside suddenly filled his lungs. Through the dark silhouettes of the trees that flicked by, he caught occasional glimpses of lights appearing and disappearing again from the houses where families with simple, uncomplicated lives lived.

"Go ahead, Travis," the voice behind him cried out. "Make your choice. If you jump, you come with me and live in a world beyond your wildest imagination. If you don't, you remain here in this cesspool of a world for many days to come without all of the things you have valued and desired, but were never able to possess for real."

Travis stood for a long while at the door, then turned toward the man. If the bum was indeed a demon incarnate, Travis had finally reached bottom. To be speaking to Satan himself or one of his followers, although still not the least bit convinced, his sin had now taken him into an abyss from which he may not ever resurface. He truly believed he had lost his faith. If not his faith, then his senses. Even so, he did believe he was occupying the train car with some kind of evil spirit from which he must rid himself. And that spirit was occupying the body of someone the world would never miss.

Grabbing the hobo by the shirt, he then dragged him toward the open door. A smile broke out from beneath the man's scraggily beard.

"Ah, so this is what you'll do. An act of murder to add to your list of sins, Travis Marlowe. So many sins that your God will never turn His face toward you again. I like it."

"You're wrong, maggot. You know full well the capability of my benevolent God who through the blood of His Son Jesus forgave every sin I have or will commit. Jesus took on my sins eons before I was even born. However, if you are who you say you are, and you know any truth at all, you know *that*. And you know that you yourself are doomed along with your...*boss* to spend an eternity bound in chains in your own hell."

"And of course you believe these lies, these myths... written by misguided scribes."

"I believe this conversation ends right here. Now, get off and get out of my life." Travis then flung the man from the car and watched him slide and tumble down a slope. If he died from the fall, so be it. However, the way he fell and rolled, Travis did not believe he had killed him. Whether a devil or not, he was glad about that. His eyes continued on the man in the pale moonlight until he saw him right himself up and shake his fist. So, he did not die. Would the man now revert to being his mere hobo self again?

Suddenly, as the terrain flattened out, a highway running parallel with the tracks appeared. After the boxcar had reached the point to where the road ultimately crossed the tracks, Travis then caught sight of the lighted sign that read, WELCOME TO DESTINY, LOUISIANA.

When the train slowed a mile or so down the tracks to enter the switch yard near where the lights of the town began, Travis jumped off and rolled gingerly into a consuming field of kudzu.

Destiny. It had a nice ring to it. Maybe an omen. Maybe a place to end his journey.

CHAPTER TWO

THE BETRAYAL

IT HAD BEEN JUST UNDER THREE weeks before that night on the first Saturday afternoon in May, 1960, when Travis returned from the fields and found his wife, Sarah, a smallish, pretty brunette, sitting in their parlor, hands folded in her lap and weeping softly. The day had begun for him like any other…wolfing down a hearty breakfast of ham, eggs and hoe cake, then kissing Sarah on the cheek and stopping to give their daughter Rachael a bear hug. But being Saturday, that work day of tending their twenty nine acres of corn and soybeans would end a little early for him as usual, unlike the thirteen or fourteen hour days during the week he spent in the scorching Indiana sun. There was an ice cream social at Brother Daniel's house and the entire Amish community was expected to attend.

While Travis was still in the field earlier that afternoon, Sarah's life-long friend, Mary Holmgren, stood at the front door of the Marlowe two story board-and-batten house with a look on her face that Sarah had not seen before. A look that could have belonged to a Bassett hound that had just violated the floor. And from her eyes fell a bucket of tears.

"Can I come in?" Her lower lip was quivering. Her eyes were swollen and reddened.

Sarah opened the screen door. "Of course, Mary. What's wrong? Has someone died?"

"I wish," replied Mary. "And I wish it was me."

"Oh, darling, please come in and sit down. I will prepare us some lemonade." Again she asked, "What is it, dear?"

Mary followed her to the kitchen and sat down on one of the straight-back wooden chairs. Placing her head in her hands, she muttered softly, "I...I just don't know where to begin."

Sarah set a glass of the lemonade down and placed her arm around her friend's shoulder. "You can tell me anything, you know. Is it Robert?"

"No," she sobbed. "Robert doesn't know."

"Know what?"

"Just give me a moment."

Sarah sat down beside Mary and took her hand. "All right," she said softly. "Take your time."

Mary wiped her eyes with a napkin and took a sip of the tart drink. "It's...about Travis."

"Travis?" Sarah exclaimed and placed a hand over her breasts. "Oh, dear Lord. Has he been in an accident? Is he all right? I worry so much about him with the machinery."

"No. I'm sure he's fine. He hasn't been hurt...at least I pray not."

"Then what? What *about* Travis?"

Mary, who had been avoiding eye contact all the while, finally looked up at Sarah, eyes red and swollen. Her lips trembled to get out the words. "You and I...we've been friends for a lot of years."

"Yes, since we were seven, I reckon. But what does that have to do with Travis?"

"I love you, Sarah…like my own sister. I always have, and I never intended to do anything to hurt you?"

Sarah froze and narrowed her eyes. "Are you going to where I think you're going? You…and Travis?"

"Yes," Mary sobbed. The tears began again. Her breasts shuddered as she blubbered out the next few words. "I went to him for counsel…he being one of our ministers. It was about Robert and our differences. Travis was so sweet and kind… said all of the right things…prayed with me and consoled me. I went to him two or three times and then…"

"And then what?"

"I asked him to hold me. I…I just needed to be touched. I needed a man's arms around me. Something I hadn't had in maybe two years."

Sarah moved slowly to another chair at the table, but before she sat down, her knees gave away. She then wrapped her arms and hands around her own body as though she were suddenly cold. "And then that led to…"

"Yes."

Sarah closed her eyes and bit her lower lip. "Where?" she asked softly.

"At my house."

"Once?"

"No. More than once."

Sarah slammed her hands onto the table and shouted. "*Then how many times?*"

"Maybe three times."

"Maybe? *Maybe?* Is this not something you would know for sure?"

"Three times. After the first time, it seemed so easy…so right. Like a drug of some sort that we couldn't stop taking…"

Sarah suddenly sprung from her chair and stood over her friend. "Get out, Mary.

"Sarah, I...I'm so sorry. I just felt you had to know this. I had to get it off my chest."

"*Get out!*" Sarah demanded, now in a near scream. "Get out of my house now, Jezebel!"

"Please. I know you're angry and hurt. You have every right to be. And I don't expect you to understand. I don't even blame you if you hate me. But it was a matter of need for me."

Sarah leaned in further and placed the palms of her hands on the table in front of Mary. Her face was within inches of Mary's. "And what about *my* needs? My need to be a trusting wife who never had to worry about her husband's fidelity and a best friend that would take him to her bed."

Mary dropped her eyes to her hands, hands that were folded and wringing. "Yes. I know you won't forgive me right now. But I pray that one day you will. I love you, and..."

"No! You don't love me. You love yourself. And worst of all, you *made* love to my husband. I always thought of myself as a strong and understanding woman, but I will never forgive you. A person who is suddenly dead inside has no feelings... cannot forgive...cannot love a friend who betrayed her. Now, please leave before I say something I'll regret."

Mary nodded, wiped her eyes and gathered herself up with as much dignity as she could muster. There was no further word or look between them. When Mary closed the front door behind her, Sarah stood with her back to it, arms folded about her again, and then began to cry.

That afternoon when Travis came in from the field and Sarah did not spring to meet him with a hug and peck on the lips as usual, he was set to wonder if she was in the house at all or just didn't hear him. But when he entered the parlor, he first saw nine year old Rachael rubbing an orange crayon on one of the animals in her Noah's Ark coloring book. And then he saw Sarah sitting in a chair across from her, hands lying in her lap and eyes on the green rug beneath her feet. He thought at first Sarah may have just had a testy kind of day, maybe with their daughter, as she did not rise to greet him. But immediately, he knew it was more than that since Sarah neither rose nor even looked at him. To him the room seemed as cold and mournful as the parlor at Persinger's Funeral Home on a visitation evening.

"Go upstairs to your room, Rachael," Sarah finally said. "Your father is home and we have some matters to discuss."

When Rachael obediently and without word did as her mother instructed, Travis, who did not have a clue as to his wife's emotional malady, began probing.

"What's wrong, Sarah? Why so somber? I've never seen such a look on your face."

Sarah finally lifted her head and fixed her eyes on his. "I've *never* had cause to have this look on my face, Travis. Mary was by this morning. Would you like to know what we talked about?"

Travis' knees began to buckle and he sat down in a chair opposite his wife. It suddenly seemed to him that all of the air had been sucked out of the room. The blood began to drain from his face and his heart beat as though it would jump into his throat. He knew immediately that she knew. Although he had never lied to her, the affair itself was a lie. An unconfessed lie that had laid rotting and stinking in his very soul for too long. They said nothing for several long moments. Sarah's eyes were hurting, but stern just the same. *His* shouted of guilt.

"You profess to be a minister...more than that, a messenger of God. A man who stands before his congregation with a tongue that preaches against adultery. You, my husband, who I have loved, admired and trusted like no other, have not only betrayed me, but also our daughter and the good people of our order...people who have for so long trusted and respected you. You are worse than any sinner who has yet to know the Lord. Our people...our friends...will soon know what a hypocrite you are. I feel almost as sorry for them as I do for myself."

"So, she told you...everything," he said softly.

"In as many words. The details don't matter."

He looked away and nodded. "I guess it seems so cheap for me to tell you I'm sorry."

Sarah was quiet for a moment, but kept her eyes on his. "Do you love her? I know she is more beautiful than I am and I can understand why most men would be tempted. But do you love her?"

"No. At least not in the sense that you think."

"Then why would you have relations with a woman you do not love? I could better understand it if you did."

Travis leaned forward and placed his hands nervously on his knees. "Weakness. Carnal weakness. Giving into lust."

"Giving in to the devil, you mean."

He nodded again. "I suppose."

"No!" she shouted at him. "You *know* it to be so!"

Travis then placed his face in his hands and said nothing more for a lengthy time. In a scant two minutes, he had gone from a husband, so very happy to be home with his sweet wife, to a clump of clay with the knife of shameful discovery buried in his chest. Even before this moment, he had already experienced the guilt associated with his affair. And yes, Sarah had nailed it when she held the mirror to his face...the face of a minister standing before his people each Sunday preaching about the Christian's responsibilities to faithfully keep all of God's commandments. But now that the affair had been found out by the woman he loved like no other, a fiery adrenaline suddenly burned through his arteries, scorching his very heart. Was it more the shame and guilt over the matter or the fact that Sarah now knew that he had been intimate with another woman? His sin, now found out, seemed to be magnified ten-fold.

They sat not looking at one another, eyes filled with tears and pain, not knowing what further to say. Where would they go from here? Was it too soon to think about that? Would Sarah turn him out and would his people shun him? But then he soon realized that she was quick to decide. Slowly, she stood and with soft but accusatory eyes, she stared into his face…a face that went from a flushing red to a wanly white.

"You pack your things at once and leave this house. I will go on Monday to the elders and tell them that I plan to seek a separation. It will then be inevitable that they in turn will shun you."

Another surge of adrenaline struck him in the chest like a heart attack. "But Sarah, I beg you to at least take some time with this. Sleep on this. Consider Rachael…"

"I *have* considered her, Travis. She should not have to live with a father who betrayed her mother. It will be enough for her to experience the ridicule and scorn she will receive from her friends. Me? I don't care what people will think. But at least Rachael will know she does not have to sit across the dinner table from an adulterous father. The look in her eyes will bring pain to you both."

Travis shook his head. "Does that mean you're considering divorce?"

"You know full well that we Amish do not sanction divorce. But our order will require you to leave the house. You will do so today. You know you will have to face the elders before you go to confess what you have done. The

Ordnung requires it. They will then decide if you will remain in the order. But you also know they will not allow you to live here in this house...if they allow you to stay in our community at all."

He knew how head-strong she was. When she had made up her mind about something, one could sooner turn back a locomotive than stop her course.

"Okay. I'll do as you ask. But please, let's not tell Rachael anything at this time. She'll ask immediately why I have left and I ask that you just tell her I'm away on business."

"I will not lie to her, Travis. She probably already knows."

"Then you told her."

"No. But she is a young woman who I know can sense these things."

"She's still a child...not a woman. But look, Sarah, I will pray about this over the next few days...pray that your heart will soften to a point where you can forgive me."

"Better that you pray not for me, but for our daughter and for your own soul. You have left a stain, black as tar, on this house and the people who love you. And with that, you have to live. Now, pack your things and go."

"And where *can* I go?"

"That is up to you. You should have thought about the consequences of your adultery as you lay with my best friend." Sarah then broke again into tears and turned her head away. Still having enough grace and dignity to hold her head high, she then looked back at him and said, "I will go to be with Rachael in her room after you clear the house. I suggest you go to see Bishop Herrmann. You will then know what will happen to you. "

"Will you allow me to say goodbye to Rachael and tell her I'll be going away for a while?"

"It is best that you not do that. She will have questions about why, and you will lie to her."

"I will get a job and a place to stay in town. But, I ask that I be allowed to come here see our daughter."

"Your betrayal of our marriage and our family has caused you to forfeit that right. I am sorry, Travis. You will not be able to come back to this community at all and I do not want to see you again. Get your clothes and leave *now*."

He started to tell her that no one in their pacifist community would ever physically try to stop him, but then thought the better of it. He then moved forward to her and placed his hands on her biceps. She shook him off. After a moment, he turned and trod heavily up the stairs to their bedroom where he packed a small suitcase. When he had neatly placed his socks, underwear, toilet articles and folded shirts in the case, he snatched up his one suit from the wardrobe, then laid it on top of the other articles. When he passed by the closed door of Rachael's bedroom, he paused to knock. However, then thinking he should leave well enough alone, he returned downstairs, passed by Sarah, who was standing with her back to him, and left the house.

It somehow seemed to him that when he stepped out onto the front porch into the bright rays of the setting sun, every set of eyes in their order were upon him. Yet the next house in the community was at least thirty acres away. No one was watching. No one would see him leave. He knew that he had disappointed his lovely Sarah and when the word was ultimately passed throughout the community about his grave sin, he would be a disappointment to his adopted people. Especially, those that he had pastored. But, what was mostly going through his mind at that moment, besides the pangs of guilt and shame, was that he had disappointed the one Being who had known his every thought and seen his every move...the Lord God Himself.

CHAPTER THREE

MEIDUNG

HE HAD NO IDEA WHERE HE would go. Perhaps into Hurley where he could stay a few days on the thirty dollars he had taken with him. Maybe he would then go back home to see if Sarah had cooled down after sleeping a few nights on their predicament and then allowing him back into the house. They needed one another and Rachael needed a father.

Travis had decided he could not take either of their two horses as Sarah needed them for the farm and buggy errands. But she had not been in the fields for years and would have to hire someone to help her along with part-time hands Lars and Benjamin, the Albrichts' two strapping sons, who never missed a day of work at the farm.

Having walked less than half a mile to the north edge of his farm, he stopped to put his suitcase down and then sat on it, leaning his back against a fence post. Off in the distance along the horizon, he could still see his house. Though it was late May and warm, the house looked cold. In it were a broken-hearted woman and a nine year old girl who didn't quite know what was happening. But he was sure that before the night was over, she would. She would be hurt, like her mom…and disappointed in her father. Dropping his head in his hands, he closed his eyes and asked God a battery of questions. "What have I done, Lord? How could You allow this to happen to us? Why didn't You stop me with Mary?" Then he paused and shook his head. "What am I saying? I can't blame You. But please help me. Help *us*. I know I have to leave for a while, but please help piece us back together."

Travis sat against the post another few minutes and then stood to take one last glance back. Slowly, he retrieved his suitcase and turned back in the direction of Hurley. Now having covered more than a mile along the dusty Secondary Road 23, behind him he suddenly heard the clop-clopping of horses' hooves. Turning to look, he then saw two horse-drawn buggies approaching. In each were two men. The first driver sounded a 'whoa,' and when the buggy came to a stop, he said, "You seem to be going our way, Friend Marlowe. Climb aboard."

"I'm going into Hurley…and you?"

"It appears we are going in the same direction for the same reason," replied Nells Strubhar.

"What do you mean 'the same reason'?" asked Travis.

"I was earlier visited by Mary Holmgren who told me what she told Sarah. We have business with the bishop about it…and so do thee."

Travis paused for a moment and looked down. He owed the bishop as much. It was Herrmann who went to bat for him when Travis asked to become one of them those many years before. And anyway, leaving without a word to the bishop would be perceived as cowardly and disrespectful on his part. He nodded to Strubhar. "Then we will get this behind us quickly," he said as he slid onto the cramped seat.

Travis was the young neophyte minister in the Himmel community. In their order were fourteen families, pastored mainly by Minister Strubhar and associate minister, forty seven year old John Hovermund, who sat beside him in the carriage. Travis, who had been recognized by the bishop and these two senior ministers as a true, witnessing man of God, had been welcomed into the ministry by ordainment only the year before. The two men in the trailing buggy were also well-respected deacons in their order named Knepp and Petershwim.

It was an uncomfortable ten minutes for Travis…not only because they were jammed in like sardines on the buggy's seat, but during the time it took to cover the last mile of their ride, no one spoke. Upon arrival at the bishop's house, each of the men dressed in their traditional black suits, white shirts and either straw or cloth hats, dismounted and with solemn faces walked up the steps to the front porch. Hearing their shoes on the creaking stoop, Bishop Herrmann greeted them at the door. "My friends, please come in. What brings such a party of good Christian men to my door this Saturday evening?" He then led them into the small foyer.

"It is not a pleasant occasion that does, to be sure," replied Strubhar who quickly removed his straw hat. Travis looked down, avoiding eye contact with the bishop. He then noticed his shoes were covered with dust from the road. Taking a white handkerchief from his coat pocket, he wiped them clean.

"Would you have some lemonade?" called Herrmann's wife from the hallway. "Freshly made."

Each man shook his head. Knepp, whose chin whiskers had grown much fuller than the other men's, waved this way and that as he responded negatively. "We are here to speak about Minister Marlowe, Bishop," he said.

"Ah, young Travis. Thou hast been a genuine blessing these years to our community. I hear nothing but good things about thee. I am so pleased that we accepted thee in… what has it been a dozen years now?"

"Yes, Bishop. Nearly thirteen years since I landed in Hurley."

Strubhar scowled and broke in. "What we are here to discuss, Bishop, is not so pleasant. I will ask Friend Marlowe to explain to thee in the presence of this order of men why we are gathered."

As they were still assembled in the foyer, the bishop led them into the parlor and closed the door behind them. "Please sit, my friends."

When they had done so, Strubhar wasted no time. Sternly, he said, "Travis Marlowe, will thou now confess before God and to the bishop thy discretions?"

Travis now felt like he needed the lemonade to smooth out the catch in his throat. "Bishop Herrmann, I...am so very sorry to report to you that because of a relationship that developed between one of our married ladies and myself, I can no longer continue in the ministry to our people. I..."

Herrmann frowned and resettled in his chair. "A relationship. Does this mean it was physical?"

"Yes, Bishop."

Herrmann stroked his beard and bore down on Travis with searing eyes. "I must say that this grieves me more than I could ever have imagined. Although I ask that thee spare us the sordid details, how did it come to happen?"

"She came to me for counsel, sorely depressed, and as I was consoling her, feelings of want came upon us both. It is a sin that I deeply regret. I have prayed constantly today not only for God's forgiveness, but that Sarah will forgive me as well."

"It is bad enough, young Travis, that thee committed such a transgression, but thou hast violated the oath as a minister and counselor by taking advantage of a vulnerable one who was in despair. Thou hast done right by coming here with these men. And although thou hast asked to resign thy ministry, thou must realize your punishment does not end there."

"I know the consequences, sir, but I ask you and these good men to consider a relaxing of the law. I was going to stay in Hurley for a while and return to my home to ask Sarah to take me back in. Sarah had demanded that we separate and..."

"But thee cannot divorce and continue as a member of our order."

"I do know that," replied Travis. "I also know that if she does divorce me, she cannot remarry. She would have to leave the order as well. Our daughter will then not have a male influence in the home as she grows up. I am counting on Sarah to forgive me so that we can continue our marriage."

"It goes beyond that, Travis. The indiscretion thee committed as a minister of the Faith endangers thy continuation as Amish. And now thee must realize that thee are not guaranteed salvation. Our understanding of salvation is that God evaluates thy entire lifetime and record of obedience to the church. If thou art shunned, under the rules of meidung, thou wilt never see the kingdom of Heaven." He then turned to the assembly of brethren. "These men represent a forum that will vote along with me as to any future thee hast in this community...and where thee will spend eternity."

"I have never believed that. I have always believed that when one becomes a follower of Christ, he is saved forever. We all sin and it should not be the decision of men such as us as to whether someone goes to heaven or hell."

Stubhar shook his head. "This tells me we should never have ordained thee in the first place, Travis. You learned the tenets of our faith when we brought thee into the order. Thou hast received training and took an oath that thee understood our doctrine. Now thou tellest us thou doest not believe in it"

Travis nodded. "Yes."

There was silence in the room for a few moments and then Bishop Herrmann spoke. "I now ask that thee step out onto the porch while we together decide thy fate."

Slowly, Travis rose and without word left the parlor, closed the door behind him and sat down in a rocker on the porch. His fate. Although he fully understood the worst that could happen to him, he still relied on the bishop's and other ministers' compassion. He believed that in spite of the fact he had committed a horrific sin against God, against Sarah, and against his vow as a minister, the men, his brethren, still liked him. But whatever their decision, the only thing that mattered was whether the betrayal of his wife would ultimately prove fatal to his marriage. What the brethren actually decided meant little in comparison. As he sat watching the sun disappear over the tree line on the horizon, he was glad to have his day of confession behind him. His embarrassment before them had now been experienced. But whether or not they forgave him, he knew that God had already done so.

Less than twenty minutes later, the bishop stepped out onto the porch and motioned for him to come inside. When he went back into the parlor the bishop placed him inside the circle of the five of them.

"Travis Marlowe, we the elders and ministers of this community have made the decision to shun thee from the Amish order. The transgression thou hast committed is too grave for thee to continue among us." He then raised from his right hand a set of large scissors which at first frightened Travis. Then it was clear to him what would happen next. And he would allow it. Herrmann was the first to cut a section of jaw and chin whiskers from Travis' face. He then passed the scissors to each of the others who followed suit, each cutting as much off as they could. Thomas Petershwin was the last to cut the fullness of Travis' beard down to a mere stubble.

"Thou wilt no longer be a member of this or any other Amish community, English," said Strubhar.

English. The word the Amish referred to other Caucasian men not of German descent...an outsider. He was now 'English' again and not one of them.

"You may go now, Travis," said the bishop. "As thou hast asked forgiveness from the Almighty, I am sure He has heard thy prayer. He will evaluate your destiny. I am sorry about thy family. We will pray that God will bless Sarah and Rachael in their sorrow. But, thee cannot continue living in our community. And I cannot tell thee how much all of this grieves me. Now go with God." He then turned his back on Travis and the others in the council followed suit.

Travis stood for a moment looking down at the shorn, black scraps from his beard. Its remnant was an all too real metaphor of his shattered life. As beards were only worn by betrothed Amish men, not only was he evicted from the order, he was no longer associated with his wife. It was then that reality had set in. Having lost everything, he was now turned out into the world. Tears formed unexpectedly in his eyes and after pushing Knepp from his way, he quickly left the house. Retrieving his suitcase from the front porch, he then bounded down the steps, stumbling on the last one because of his tears and landing on his knees.

The dark seemed to come all too quickly as he could see the distant lights of Hurley beyond the tree line. But he would not stay there. It would be no use to wait Sarah out those two or three days he had planned. He had been shunned and banished from the Amish settlement. Sarah would abide by the order's decision. If he found a job in town, the fact that Sarah and Rachael were so close, yet so inaccessible, would eat away at him. In his heart somehow he knew they would forever be separated. Sarah and the ministers had made it so. No, he would not stay. He would leave Hurley...leave Indiana. Maybe head south.

It was now very quiet on the road, deafeningly so. In his head, it seemed a thousand voices were calling his name. Maybe Satan's chorus of demons, celebrating his despair, self-made as it was. He tried praying as he walked, but the words sounded empty and hollow. His faith had left him. He was now sure of it. It was as though a thief had entered his body that afternoon and had stolen it away.

As he walked along Route 23, the dust of the road kicked up by the tires of passing vehicles quickly consuming him, an excerpt of David's Psalm 22 suddenly entered his mind:

I am poured out like water and all my bones are out of joint. My heart is like wax; it has melted within me. My strength is dried up like a potsherd, and my tongue clings to my jaws. You have brought me to the dust of death.

Reverberating through the night air, somewhere on the outskirts of Hurley, he then heard the soft, distant blare of a locomotive's horn...calling, summoning him. His way south.

Chapter Four

Destiny

As the freight train began to slow in the switchyard, Travis pulled his suitcase up under his arm and jumped to the ground. After checking to make sure no brakeman or yard worker was nearby, he waited until the caboose had passed and then scampered across a half dozen tracks until he found the road that led into the town. A road that paralleled another single set of railroad tracks. Perhaps there was a YMCA or shelter that would take him in; but then again, he figured he wouldn't find one in such a small town.

Still in his weathered and worn collarless black suit, handmade Amish style, and his white shirt now yellowed with sweat, he caught a whiff of himself. He not only smelled of body odor, but fish and whatever was on the floor of the box car. He had worn the pants continuously while working in the grocery store in Kentucky and in Memphis on the dock. Even in the dark, he could see that the trousers with the buttons no longer matched the coat.

The walk into the town proper took about fifteen minutes and one of the first buildings he spotted was the depot. It was apparently closed since there were no lights on the inside. The clock on the side of the station read ten minutes past ten. Taking one of the two benches sitting close up to the wall, he stopped to rest and to ponder where he would go from there. When he closed his eyes, the faces of Sarah and Rachael formed in his brain. It might have been a day last week. It was evening. Dinner was done. Baths were taken. He was reading to them in the parlor a passage from his favorite book in the Bible, the Psalms. Sarah might have made oatmeal cookies and on the end table beside him was a cold glass of milk. Everything was right with the world.

His eyes still closed, he then imagined Sarah lying under the clean sheets of their bed, sobbing bitterly, lonely, aching inside. Maybe realizing for good she would never see him again. She might even wonder if she had been too quick to send him away. Maybe it was more so her hurt and anger that did it. But according to the Amish Ordnung and code, it had to be. Slowly, Travis felt himself drifting off to sleep.

No sooner had his head drifted back against the wall, a sudden, blinding light hit his eyes.

"You there. What are you doing here?"

Travis shielded his eyes, but was still able to make out the uniform and badge of a police officer. "I'm just stopping here to rest is all," he replied.

"Stand up and let me get a look at ya."

Travis did as ordered, but then said. "Can you please get the light out of my eyes?"

The officer lowered the light to Travis' chest. "Now turn around and place your hands on the wall."

"But why? I've done nothing and I don't have a weapon on me." Still, he obeyed the officer and put the palms of his hands against the station wall.

The officer ran his hands over Travis' body, then between and down the legs. Satisfied he was not armed he barked. "Okay, now turn back around. What's your name and where're you from? I know you're not from around here."

"Marlowe. I'm Travis Marlowe from Indiana."

"Then let me see some identification."

"I...don't have anything on me."

"No driver's license or other ID?"

"No, sir. I haven't owned a car in years."

"Then how did you get here...hitchhike?"

"I rode the train into town."

"Well, now, that's a lie, Marlowe. The passenger train doesn't stop here."

"I rode in a box car all the way from Shreveport."

"Which is against the law. Who do you think you are... Woody Guthrie? Maybe Clem Kaddiddlehopper?"

"Look, officer, I have just fallen on some bad luck, that's all. I didn't have the money to ride the Greyhound."

"So, where did you hop off?"

"The switchyard, about a mile out of town."

The officer toned his voice down. "Okay then, what *is* your story?"

"It's not a very pretty one, sir. All I can tell you is that I started out in Indiana a couple weeks ago, found a bit of work to put a little money in my pocket, and just told myself I was going as far south as I could."

"Uh huh. You know that vagrancy is against the law also. Where you plannin' to sleep tonight?"

"I haven't thought much about it. Is there a Y here?"

"No Y, but there is a cheap motel down the road a piece. There should be vacancy on a Sunday night. You got any money on ya?"

"Maybe forty dollars is all."

Once Travis had gotten his night vision back, in the light of a nearby street lamp, he took account of the officer. The man, appearing to be in his fifties, hair white as new snow and wearing a cap that seemed just a little too small for his head, likewise continued studying Travis.

"All right. My cruiser is over there by the curb. I'll take you down to the motel. You're gonna need a bath besides a bed for the night. So, what are your plans from here?"

"As you suggest, take a bath and settle in for the night. Tomorrow, I'll get some breakfast and maybe go look for a job."

"Then you intend to stay here."

"About as good a place as any, I expect."

"What kind of work have ya done?"

"Mostly farming, but I'm not stuck on that."

"There ain't many jobs open around here, fella. This is not a rich town. And if you ain't an established fisherman or trapper, you won't find a thing. That's what we do most around here. So, you want me to take you to the motel? If you don't , I'll have ta lock you up for the night."

"The motel will be fine, sir. I didn't catch your name?"

"I didn't give it...but it's Harold Presley."

"Presley."

"Yeah. Like Elvis. There's some speculation in our family that we're distant cousins with them Tupelo folks. But I guess if it was so, I'd be up there lettin' them know about it and not makin' twenty bucks a day as a police deputy."

Travis smiled. He didn't know who 'Elvis' was, but said nothing. The man looked like a nice enough character and with his weathered face and deep lines around his mustache, he reminded Travis of his grandfather back in New York, the man who became his father after his dad was killed in the war. Thinking about those days brought on a new sadness. Only a year after his twenty nine year old father was buried, his mother was struck and killed by a taxi on a New York street. And then after that, his grandfather lost his job and put Travis out. He just couldn't afford to keep him. Now, once again, his life was back in the toilet.

Harold Presley tossed Travis' suitcase in the back seat of his sedan and told him to 'git in.' A half mile down Route 173 he pulled into the parking lot of Shirley's Motel. On the building was a set of red, neon letters with a couple of letters missing that read V_ca_cy.

"Here ya go, Marlow. Good luck on findin' some work. But if you don't in the next day or so, you know you have to move on. The mayor's been on this binge about clearin' out any vagrants and bums on the street. If ya do find somethin', stop by the station on Main and let me know. Maybe we can get further acquainted. "

"Thanks, Officer Presley. I appreciate the ride." He then shook the man's hand, retrieved his suitcase and closed the car door behind him.

After he checked into the motel, besides spending fifteen dollars for the room, he purchased a small box of Tide and grabbed a banana and a large chocolate chip cookie that came with the room. After bathing, he refilled the tub and laid his suit and white shirt in the suds-filled water. Kneading the clothing with his hands, he rinsed them thoroughly and hung them over hangers he found in the closet to drip dry. They would still be wet in the morning, but would hopefully dry quickly in the heat of the morning sun when he hung them outside of his room door. He was sure the suit would shrink, but as he had lost weight in having little to eat the past few days, maybe the new sizes of both suit and man would balance out.

From his suitcase, he took out a T shirt and a pair of boxers to sleep in. The motel actually had a small black-and-white TV, so he sat on the edge of the bed and clicked the channel selector through the four network possibilities. The picture was snowy on all of the channels and it made him realize that those years in the community without ever seeing a TV…well, he didn't really miss anything. Jack Benny was bantering with George Gobel in a rather boring comedy routine on one program, and on another station, a woman named Loretta Young came out spinning in a taffeta dress announcing her show. Since to him it all wasn't much worth watching, he clicked the TV off.

Settling back on the bed, he found it felt good to his bones which had bounced around for a day and half on the box car's floor. But then, looking around the room and realizing his predicament, he knew that he was definitely at the low ebb of his life. And that included the year when he was seventeen, when both his parents were gone and his own grandfather turned him out into the streets. The room was disgusting. It smelled of sweat and stale cigarette smoke. Beside him on the wall was a nasty stain where it appeared someone had tossed a beer. On the ceiling over his head was probably the biggest roach he had ever seen. He heard tell that the south was full of them. People referred to them as palmetto bugs. For a while his brain just wouldn't turn off. It seemed a thousand thoughts had invaded his skull, forcing him to revisit and reflect on his sins of the past couple of months…the covetousness, lust, deceit, adultery… the betrayal to his wife and daughter. God was obviously furious with him. As punishment, He had banished him from his loved ones and community, tried and convicted him and sentenced him to something close to hell on earth. But it was his own behavior that had spawned the tempest.

When it came upon him that day, it was sudden, like a rogue storm. A storm of his own making. And just as a hurricane wreaks and destroys, leaving nothing in its path, he was now only left with his life and the clothes on his back.

It all made him wonder just what or who had caused him to fall away from his faith so easily. And that thought led him to ponder the man in the box car. Was he real or was what he had experienced a continuation of his dream? And if the man was real, how could he know so much about him unless he actually *was* Satan incarnate. Or at least one of his disciples. No man, especially an old coot with rotten teeth and smelling of nicotine, would even be speaking so articulately as he did. Was it all in his head or some kind of supernatural phenomenon? Travis knew that God was supernatural and had appeared thousands of years before to Abraham and Moses. But such things did not happen in 1960. He had heard stories that God and Mary had appeared to people throughout the centuries, but to him they *were* just stories. Unproven. Unwitnessed. However, that was before tonight. There was no explanation for what he experienced. And allowing the experience to haunt his mind as it did, might just keep him awake for the night…even as tired as he was. But after downing the cookie with some water and then getting back up to empty his bladder, he slid between the clean sheets and turned out the lamp. Although having good intentions of saying his prayers, he fell almost immediately into a deep sleep.

CHAPTER FIVE

SMOKEY'S PLACE

AROUND SIX THE NEXT MORNING, HE woke, stiff and sore, and hardly able to move. The roach on the ceiling was gone and he wondered if it had accompanied him in bed during the night. Throwing his legs over the side of the bed, he was glad that he had the strength to stand on his feet. Just as he expected, the suit and shirt were still damp, so he opened the door to his room and hung the garments on the outside light fixture by the door. In less than forty five minutes, the sun which had already peeked over the horizon began drying them out. By the time he had finished shaving, consumed the banana and read Psalm 42, the clothing was ready to don. The suit may have been clean, but was hopelessly wrinkled and misshapen; however, it would have to do. If he was going to find a job, the pair of dungarees and blue shirt which were also soiled, reeking from his dock work and never washed, would most certainly give people in the town the impression he was merely an itinerant tramp looking for a handout. Still, as he looked at himself in the dresser mirror, he hardly recognized his thirty one year old image. At six feet one, and lean anyway, losing the ten or so pounds made him appear gaunt. And did he see a few premature gray hairs or was it the sunlight streaming in between the venetian blind slats, casting its rays upon his black head of hair?

His stomach still gurgling from not having eaten anything substantial for more than two days, he grabbed up his suitcase, closed the door to his room for the night and walked about three blocks down on Main to where the town proper began. Maybe a biscuit and some eggs in a diner somewhere down the street. It was a sleepy town and as Officer Presley had indicated Destiny's mainstay of commerce was seafood, the boats and fishermen had long been out on the water. He would be fooling himself to think he could get a job on a shrimper. He knew nothing about fishing and had actually never been on a boat in his life. Maybe he could find a clerk's or janitor's job at one of the stores, taking note of the Western Auto and the Montgomery Ward storefronts he passed by. Of course, at seven o'clock none of the stores would be open, so he continued walking until he reached the corner of Main as it intersected with Beauregard Street where he found the large, rather shabby-looking board-and batten building called *The Old South Diner.*

Even thirty feet away from the diner, the inviting aroma of bacon on the griddle and brewing coffee filled Travis' nostrils. It reminded him of the smell that came from Sarah's kitchen every morning...the smell of a hearty breakfast waiting for him before he went into the field. But another odor reeking from the diner...that of cigarette smoke...would never be smelled in any Amish house of the old order. That was not to say a few of the young men in the community didn't light up a little corn silk whenever their fathers weren't around.

No sooner had Travis entered the diner, more than a dozen heads and sets of eyes turned toward him. Had he been one of the town folk, he may have received some nods or 'heys,' but being a stranger in an even stranger-looking suit, the eyes stayed on him as he made his way to the counter. As nearly every seat was taken at the breakfast counter, he only had his choice of two stools. Sliding his suitcase between two of the red and chrome stools, he sat down between two men, quickly catching the eye of the man on his left. He was an older gent in a green feed and seed company cap and a gray work shirt. It appeared he had just finished his breakfast and was now stirring some cream into his mug of coffee.

"Hain't seen you in town before. You visitin'?" he said with a degree of brusqueness.

"Passing through, I expect. But I *am* looking for a job."

"Good luck, I'd say. Jobs are hard ta come by." He then turned his head back to his coffee.

Travis then noticed a young Black woman behind the counter, perhaps twenty-three to twenty-five, humming and pouring fresh hot coffee into a few of the customers' cups at the bar. She then laid a menu in front of him and said, "Moanin', suh. You want coffee?"

"Yes, ma'am. Thanks."

"We got a special on tap this moanin.' Ham, eggs, toast and grits for a dollar. "

"Hey, girl," bellowed the man beside him. "How about fillin' up *my* cup. You went right by me."

"Yes, suh." She gave him a faux salute. "Right away, *suh*."

"Now don't get briggity with me, girl. Don't need no lip from the likes of you."

Travis glared at the man and then turned back to the waitress. "Sounds good, ma'am. I'll have that special, then.

The man in the cap then nudged Travis with his elbow. "Why you callin' that girl *ma'am*, son? You definitely ain't from around here, air ya? We don't refer to the colored as ma'am and sir."

Travis looked at the man, but didn't respond. He knew the woman had to hear him, but she just kept humming and busying herself.

"So," continued the man. "If you ain't from here, where're you from?"

"Indiana," said Travis.

"Indiana. That's where they have that big car race up there."

"The Indianapolis 500."

"Yeah, that's it. You seen one of 'em?"

Travis shook his head. "No. I live in a different part of the state. Never got there."

"And you're thinkin' of getting' a job around here."

"Maybe," replied Travis. "If people are friendly, I'll stay. At least for a while."

"Oh, I 'spect you'll find us friendly enough. Good God fearin' town, we are."

"So, tell me, Mister…"

"Boucheau. Marty Boucheau."

"…Mr. Boucheau. I get the impression that people of color are treated a little differently than white people in this town."

"I get the impression you don't know that's the way things are."

"In this town?" said Travis.

"In the entire south, man. You don't know much about the colored, do ya? We fought a war over them people."

Travis smiled. "The Civil War. *We*, meaning you, me and everybody else in this country didn't fight that war. But it sure seems like people are still trying to fight it in their minds."

Boucheau then elbowed the man on his left, grinned and winked. "Ya hear that, Eddie? This Yankee boy don't understand…"

"I understand perfectly, Mr. Boucheau. I'm not so sure this is that friendly of a town, after all."

"You know, Eddie, I think my breakfast is startin' to sour in my stomach. I gotta get out of here." Boucheau then slapped down a dollar by his plate and whirled around on his stool. Before leaving, he touched Travis on the shoulder and said, "Son, if you're gonna get along here in the south, you better educate yourself about the way it is between the Whites and Coloreds. We ain't all the same. It's the natural order of things. God made us different from them."

"Yes, Mr. Boucheau. He made us different, but equal. And God expects that we all treat each other equally."

Boucheau smiled, looked back at his friend and shook his head. "Goodbye, Yankee boy. Education. Better get some of it if you want to stay around here."

When Travis turned back around, he saw that the waitress was placing his plate of breakfast in front of him. She smiled as she freshened his coffee cup. "Your breakfast, suh."

"Thanks," he replied.

Travis then dropped his head, said a blessing over his food and dove in. It was a huge plate of food. Could he eat it all, considering his stomach seemed to have shrunk from not having eaten for two days? However, ten minutes later, he was swabbing the remainder of his egg yolk with what was left of his toast. It appeared that hunger overcame space.

The waitress was now back, pouring in more coffee. Travis held up his hand and said, "Oh, please. I think I've had enough for the morning. But it was all good, though. Thanks." From his pocket he pulled out a dollar bill and a quarter for a tip, laying them beside his plate.

She leaned into him and whispered. "No, suh. It's on the house. My treat. Thank you for standin' up for me *and* us coloreds."

He smiled at her. "Please take it. I have a feeling it might come out of your wages if you don't. By the way, does everybody who comes in here have a bigoted attitude like that guy?"

"Naw. Just a few. Most people don't mind havin' a Black person wait on 'em. A couple of women that come in do… and people like old Boucheau there. Seems like the more uppity people are, the more prejudiced they are."

"What's your name?"

"Everybody calls me Sissy. Had that name since grade school. But my given name is Harriet. Never liked it."

"I'm Travis Marlowe, Sissy. Good to meet you." He then held out his hand and she shook it.

"Good to meet you, Mr. Marlowe. Did you just move here?"

"Call me *Travis*, Sissy. I've never been a *sir* my entire life. And I'm probably the same age as you are. No. I just came in last night. I'm thinking about staying a while, though; so I'm desperately in need of a job."

About five-five and a hundred ten pounds sopping wet, Sissy was a pretty soul with an infectious smile that came with a perfect set of brilliant white teeth.

"So, what kind of work you lookin' for?" she asked.

"I don't know. I've worked in a general store and have been a farmer. But I'm not proud. I'll dig holes in the ground, wash dishes, clean bathrooms."

"But listenin' to you, Travis, you sound like a smart guy. You could do better than that."

"Do you know of a better job that's open?"

She shook her head. "No. Reckon not. But did you see the sign in the window when you came in here?"

"No."

"Smokey…the owner. He be lookin' for a bus boy… somebody to clean off tables and wash dishes like you mentioned. I can go back to the kitchen and let him know."

Travis looked down at his folded hands and said, "That might work out all right; but you see, I have one slight problem. I don't have any place to stay yet. I don't have enough money on me to stay one night anywhere. I'd have to make some money to get stabilized. Also, I have a little girl back in Indiana and because I'm no longer there to work, I'll have to make enough to send there."

"I ain't pryin'," said Sissy. "It's none of my business how you got here, but is there a mama?"

"Yes."

"How old is your girl?"

"Nine."

"Well, I got a little girl, too, only she's eight. I know how tough it is to make ends meet." She then frowned. "Were there no jobs back in Indiana?"

He felt himself flush. "There...were problems. Between her mom and me."

"Oh. I think I did pry too much."

"Don't worry about it, Sissy. I did something I'm not proud of and had to leave. Now I have to get my head on straight and set things right with God."

"You been arguin' with God?"

"Something like that."

"Well, better take care of that right now. You can't fight God. You don't want to fight with God. You can't beat Him."

"I know that all too well, Sissy. The problem is, I turned my face from Him and He did the same."

From the kitchen a voice suddenly bellowed. "Sissy! Pick up! What're you doin' out there?"

Sissy smiled and patted Travis' hand. "No suh. He never turns His face away. He's always standin' up there beckonin.' He does that even when we don't do what He wants. I gotta go. I'll mention somethin' to Smokey if you want. Smokey Woodruff's a good man."

"Okay."

As another patron slid in beside him on the stool to his left, Travis closed his eyes and took a deep breath. Within the past twelve hours, he had come face-to-face with a man who could have been the devil and a young angel who had just served him breakfast. Was there a reason he had landed in Southern Louisiana? Had God sent him there or had God simply exiled him?

Chapter Six

A New Beginning

Travis sat for a while as breakfast patrons came and went…mostly blue collar workers in coveralls and ball caps. But there were also a few more stylishly-dressed men and women who likely had jobs in the stores and were catching a wholesome breakfast before commerce began around nine. Two ladies who appeared to be in their upper sixties had remained in a booth close to the counter for over an hour. Suspecting they were the cream of the town's society, Travis noted their hair was fashionably coiffured and manner of dress, colorfully stylish. He couldn't help overhearing their incessant dialogue which consisted of everything from the latest gossip to what they believed was the decay of American culture. There seemed to be more vandalism and boozing going on with the young crowd and what was it with this beatnik movement? Two of the town's teens from very affluent families had grown mustaches and chin whiskers and wearing those stupid looking beret things. And to beat all, one was the mayor's son. If he allowed such a thing with his own boy, then maybe come election time, he won't be such a shoe-in like he'd been for all these years.

Travis smiled, wondering what they might think of the beard *he* had for twelve years...if he still had it. The smile quickly faded when the memory set in of how the brethren had encircled him to shear his beard in disgrace that day he left the community.

Smokey Woodruff, having just finished splitting the rack of ribs he was about to throw on the cooker at the rear of the diner, came out of the kitchen wiping his bloodied hands on the full-length apron that covered his bib overalls. Travis was still sitting at the counter when he saw the short, rotund man approaching.

"You the boy Sissy was tellin' me about?" Smokey asked in a rich Cajun brogue.

"Yes, sir," replied Travis.

"Then follow me out back and talk to me whilst I'm workin'," he bellowed gruffly.

As Travis trailed him down the hallway and out the rear door, Smokey said, "So, you lookin' for a job, eh?"

"I am."

When they reached the cooker, Smokey lifted the rusted door and began stoking the hickory. "What are you, about thirty? You look like you got some smarts. I can tell a lot about a man by lookin' him in the eyes...whether he's tellin' the truth, if he has any guts about him and if he's a worker. What do your eyes say, boy?"

"I will always tell you the truth and anything I set out to do, I'll finish it."

"She said your name's Travis. Okay, Travis, you come here dressed in some kind of goofy-looking suit...it makes me wonder if you're expectin' something more than bein' a dish washer. I've had a great many of 'em. They be here a few days and get some change in their pockets, then move on to somethin' else better. Is that the way it'll be?"

"One thing you'll learn about me, Mr. Woodruff, is that when I make a promise or commit to something, I stick with it." No sooner as he had said the words, he thought about Sarah and the vows he had made to her a dozen years before. He had reneged on the most important commitment of his life. And because that thought was rattling around in his head, he missed the next thing that Smokey said.

Smokey, who had been seasoning the ribs with a dry rub, looked up at Travis and said, "Well?"

"Well what, sir?"

"Do you want the job or not?"

"Yes...great. When do I start?"

"How 'bout first thing tomorrow. A buck fifty an hour and you can eat your three squares here. Can't beat that deal, can you?"

"No, sir. Thank you."

"Only a couple of things. You gotta be here every mornin' at five thirty, Travis. You work hard and clean this place up, washin' up the dishes and silverware, and then sweepin' out after nine at night when we close. Officially, we serve breakfast from six till nine AM. We shut our doors about nine-thirty after we kick the last customer out. Because we have just the few of us, it allows us to catch up and prepare the next meal. We let 'em back in at eleven-thirty and close the doors again at two. Then our suppertime is from four till nine. Long hours, boy. Maybe fifteen a day, six days a week. We's closed on Sundays. Don't disappoint me; that's all I ask."

"I won't, Mr. Woodruff."

"And do me a favor...call me Smokey. Everybody does. Ain't no Mr. Woodruff 'round here no more since the old man is gone."

"I have just one concern, Smokey."

"Oh, Lord. Here we go. What is it?"

"I'm looking for a place to stay. Do you know of anybody who rents rooms in town for a reasonable price?"

"Mmm, let me think. I know Julia Grace took on a boarder about six weeks ago, but I think he's still there. She only has the one room. But, tell you what. If you don't mind sleepin' in my store room, I got a cot back there. And a shower stall for when I need to spray off from time to time. It's pretty small and you might see a rat or two. I won't charge you for it."

Travis smiled. "The price is right."

Smokey chuckled. "You ain't *seen* it yet. One thing, though. Can you handle a gun?"

Travis' eyes widened. "I guess. Why do you ask?"

"Well, every once in a while, we get broke into. Seems like more so the last couple of months. The cops drive down the alley back there a lot, but the crooks are smart and break in after the tail lights disappear around the corner. You sleepin' back there with a .38 close by…well they might break in once, but you put a bullet in somebody…that'll stop it for good."

Travis looked down and kicked away a piece of gravel. "I don't know, Smokey. I don't think I could shoot anyone… maybe fire a round past them. That'll sure as heck put a scare into them."

"All right. Good enough. Now, why don't you get yourself set up back there today, sleep there tonight and we'll start in the morning.' If you need soap and towels, there's plenty around."

"Actually, Smokey, if it's all the same to you, I can start right away."

"Fine with me. Why don't you stick around me today and I'll teach you somethin' about cookin' and cleanin' up. I'll make a woman outta ya." And then he chuckled. "We'll start with the ribs and then I'll show ya some ways to prepare crawfish."

"Crawfish. I've heard about them. They look like large red roaches if I remember."

"Hey, boy. Don't be talkin' about 'em like that around here. They's our staples here in Louisiana. *You* could end up bein' the one who gets yourself shot if you start puttin' them little critters down."

"I'll remember that."

"And a couple other things. That Sissy gal will talk your leg off, so don't socialize with her much. Neither of you will get nothin' done."

"Is she the only waitress? If you serve breakfast, lunch and dinner, she'd be here as long during the day as me."

"No, she works mornins' up till two and then Dreama comes in at three. Dreama works till we close up. And that's the other thing. She's a mighty good lookin' woman. Blonde... great body. Now she can be trouble, so stay away from her. She's on the prowl and a handsome feller like you might get on her radar. She buried a husband maybe five years back."

"How did he die?"

"He just up and died in bed one night. He was only forty or so. Bad heart, I guess." He then winked. "All kinds of insinuations about that deal...if you get my drift."

Travis nodded. "Let me ask you something else, Smokey."

"Shoot."

"You didn't quiz me on where I was from and what my story is."

"I ain't interested. I know you's not from around here, 'cause you don't talk like us. And unless you're an escaped fugitive...which lookin' at you, I couldn't believe...your story you can keep to yerself. I don't have time for any soap operas. You just do yer job and we'll git along."

"Fair enough. Thanks."

The remainder of that Monday morning, Travis spent about half his time observing Smokey's artful preparation of the ribs and chicken, three or four different ways to cook the crawfish and sauté shrimp fresh off the bayou. Not far into the lunch crowd, Travis began performing his bus boy duties, clearing the plates from the table, disposing of the garbage and chaffing his hands in the scalding dishwater until they looked like beets. Just working those six hours until the lunch bunch finally cleared out gave him a good bit of vision as to how long and exhausting a day could be. But, he was used to hard work and long days in his fields. However, it was a different kind of work…work that would send him to bed with dishpan hands.

The diner was nearly emptied out at two-thirty, when two uniformed police officers came through the door. One of them was Harold Presley from the night before. The other appeared to swagger with a higher degree of authority. Travis was wiping down a table as Sissy was taking money from the last customer at the cash register. Smokey, who was standing at the grille, turned and nodded to the officers. "Chief. Harold. Need some coffee?"

"We're good for now, Smokey," said Chief Couture.

Presley then pointed at Travis. "That's him over at that table, Joe."

"You…fella. We need to talk to ya. Come over this way," Couture called.

"What's the problem, Chief?" asked Smokey , stepping out from behind the counter. "That's Travis. I hired him today."

"You hired him, eh? You know anything about the boy?"

"Enough, I reckon. What's goin' on?"

"We just want to question him, that's all." The officers sat down in chairs at a table near the door. "Come over here, Marlowe, and take a seat," said Presley.

Travis did as ordered. Scooting the chrome chair with the red padding up to the table, he interlocked his fingers and placed his hands in front of him. "What can I do for you?"

The Chief looked down at Travis' reddened hands and commented. "I can see you were hired as the dishwasher."

"Yes, sir."

"I'm Chief Joe Couture. Officer Presley told me he ran into you last night, just having hopped off a train over at the switchyard."

Smokey leaned into the counter on one elbow, deciding to take in the conversation. After paying his tab, the customer then gave Travis a quick look and left the diner.

Travis squirmed a little in his chair. "Yes. He and I talked about that. I then took a room at Shirley's. Is that what this is about? I know it's illegal to…"

"It's not about that, Mr. Marlowe. About a mile from where you said you jumped off, a man was found dead."

Sissy, who could not help but overhear, picked up her purse and shot Smokey a furtive glance. Her eyes were as large as brown and white shooter marbles. "I 'spect I'm done for the day."

"Yeah, go on home, Sissy. See you in the morning.'" Smokey then settled in on one of the counter stools and pulled out a pack of Winstons from his pocket.

Travis' face revealed a look of amazement. "A man…dead? How did he die?"

"Tortured and murdered. Lyin' in a field."

"What?" exclaimed Travis.

"I'll ask you an official question, now, Marlowe," said Couture. "When you were either in that box car or when you got off the train, did you run into anybody?"

Travis felt himself flush. It was something he couldn't lie about. "There was another older man in the same box car with me. I didn't notice him at first. He must've gotten on somehow while I was sleeping. I woke up and found him there."

"And what did that man look like?"

"He was about fifty-five or sixty with a mostly white beard with a little red-blonde in it. I think he was wearing a red plaid shirt."

The Chief looked at Presley and then back at Travis. "Marlowe, I believe you just described the dead man. So, was he still on the train when you got off?"

"No, sir."

"Then he jumped off before you did."

"Not exactly."

"Then how exactly *did* he get off?"

Travis shuffled again in the chair looked down at his hands. He saw they were shaking. He then looked back into Couture's eyes. "He provoked me and we scuffled a bit."

The Chief raised his eyebrows. It was something said that he did not expect. "Explain."

"I don't know how we got to the point of discord except that he kept slamming insults at me and then laughing. Look, sir, I've had a rough couple of weeks and when somebody out of the blue starts needling me…"

"You have no recourse but to kill him and dump him off the train."

"No. No sir! Like I said, we scuffled and then I just tossed him out of the box car. The train was moving very slowly and I saw him land in the dirt. When I looked back at him, he was shaking his fist and cursing me. I did not kill the man. Anyway, I got off the train and came immediately into town. I didn't go out into any field." Travis then glanced back at Smokey whose eyes he felt on him. What he must be thinking. Travis guessed his newly-found job was all but gone.

"You want to know how we found the man?" asked Couture. "His shirt was hangin' off him and there was what they call a pentagram carved in his chest. And, oh, his eyes were gouged out."

"Good God!" Travis exclaimed. "What kind of person would do something like that?"

"I'm thinkin' you might know, Marlowe."

Travis looked at Smokey again. His expression hadn't changed.

"How could I?"

"Well, let's see. You were the last to see him alive. We've never had anybody carved up and murdered like that in these parts. And you're somebody we don't know. So, what do you have to say to defend yourself?"

"Let me explain something to you officers. It sounds to me like the man was killed in some kind of sacrificial way by some kind of voodoo cult...maybe devil worshippers. And you are insinuating I was involved. Do *you* ever have the wrong man. Yes, I've been something of a vagrant the last few weeks, but if you check me out, you'll find that I am a Christian man who is from a community of Amish near Hurley, Indiana."

"Amish," repeated Presley. "Ain't that some kind of cult in itself?"

Travis scowled. "You obviously don't know anything about our people."

"Maybe not so much, Marlowe," replied Couture. "But if you are, why are you travelin' as a bum comin' all the way down here?"

"I ran into some adversity back there...but not because of any crime. It was a domestic situation with my wife that compelled me to leave. I could never fathom harming or killing another human being like that."

"You admitted beatin' up the man on the train and throwin' him out of the car. I'd say that was pretty hostile."

"No. It was more like self-defense," replied Travis. "And I didn't beat him up. I actually only had hold of his shirt. What I've told you, I will swear to."

"To God...on a stack of Bibles?"

"If it came to that."

"It just might do that, Marlowe. I think you'd better start fillin' in the blanks."

"So, are you arresting me?"

The Chief settled back in his chair and looked across the room at Smokey. "So, what say you, Smokey? You hired this guy. Does he now not look like the killer type to you?"

Smokey tamped out his cigarette and looked at Travis. "I'm a pretty good judge of people, fellas. You know that. And I've sized Travis up pretty close today. He ain't no killer. No way."

"Psychopaths have a way of foolin' people, you know. Some of 'em have what they call dual personalities."

"Now Joe Couture, just what do you know about psychology? You're just a small town policeman who gets elected every year. You ain't got no case against this boy. I think I know more about people than the two of you put together. Let Travis be. He's workin' for me and I'm good with him. Don't worry...I'll keep an eye out."

"Smokey, the man has no identification on him," Presley remarked. "No license and doesn't drive, he says. A man that looks and talks like him oughta have a car, I'd say. And how do we know he's who he says he is?"

"If he's from one of them Amish communities, genius, he's not gonna *have* a car. His house won't even have 'lectricity. And as I 'spect he's a good and decent man, I'm gonna believe him."

"Unless he *is* one of them devil worshippers," replied Presley.

"Oh, you fellas go on and git. Leave the boy alone." He then paused. "The coffee offer still goes if ya want some."

"All right, Smokey. He stays here with you and you watch him like a hawk," said Couture. "And maybe we *will* take a couple coffees to go."

Travis stood, eyed the officers a moment without word and then walked back to where Smokey was standing. "Thanks, Smokey," he said in a low voice.

"Just don't disappoint me, boy," he replied in an even lower voice. He then nodded to Couture and Presley. "I'll get them coffees."

Chapter Seven

Dreama

When the officers left the diner, Smokey said, "Dreama will be along in a short while. Why don't you get your bag and go get settled back in the store room. Might wanna freshen up to be ready for the supper crowd about four. Your day prob'ly won't get done till after ten. Mine either."

Travis was beyond grateful. Sissy was right. Smokey *was* a good man…and a trusting one at that. He had taken in a stranger, given him a job and meals and a place to sleep without knowing the first thing about him. And even after hearing the insinuations about him possibly having killed the man on the train, Smokey stuck with him. As he lay down on the store room cot, he interlaced his fingers behind his head and allowed the face of the dead man to enter his brain. Travis guessed the man was just a bum, but someone who somehow had become possessed with a satanic spirit, if that was possible. And then to end up tortured and slain like he was, had to be the work of some other evil being or cult. The evidence, though immensely circumstantial, could easily point to a nomadic stranger in town who fought with the man only hours before his body was found in an open field. He could hardly blame the police for their suspicions.

It wasn't five minutes after Couture and Presley left that Dreama came on duty. "Sorry I'm late, Smokey. I was on the phone with my mom in Shreveport for over an hour. She went on and on about the gawd-awful blue rinse her hair dresser put in her hair. She…"

"I don't wanna hear any of that stuff, Dreama. You know how I am about your soap operas. Why should your mom's butcher job at the beauty shop interest me?"

"Well, she was more upset than I have heard her in years."

He threw up his hand. "Yeah, yeah, yeah. Spare me the details, gal. By the way, I hired a new dishwasher today. "

"Another one? How many does this make…three in the past month? How long will this one last?"

"Longer'n you might think. He's back there takin' a break in the store room. 'Spect he'll be out in a while."

"Well, what's he like…sixteen or sixty, Negro, White, what?"

"He's a Yankee boy from Indiana, I'd say 'bout your age. Says he might settle here. Nice lookin' kid, so don't get any ideas about latchin' your claws onto him. I don't want him runt off."

"Oh, give me a break, Smokey. You'd think I was a Mata Hari or something."

"Already he's doin' good work. Cleaned the place up nice after the breakfast crowd and had the dishes, pans and everything spic and span in no time."

"Well good. It's about time we got some good help around here. Now, when are you going to open up your wallet and hire another waitress for each shift?"

"You two're doin' all right. We only got the three booths, a handful of tables and the counter. You gals can cover it. Anyway, more tips for ya."

"Yeah, a dime here, a quarter there…I'll be able to retire soon."

Smokey winked and chuckled. "Don't forget about your fifty dollar Christmas bonus I give ya every year."

Dreama merely rolled her eyes and dismissed him with the flick of her hand.

Travis spent his hour in the store room washing his only pair of pants, except for the suit pants he had on, and his two white shirts, under wear and socks in the deep utility sink that sat in one corner of the room. After scrubbing the clothing in water that contained a cup of Tide, he rinsed the items several times and hung them over a makeshift clothesline that ran between the shower and far wall. It was for sure he needed more clothing and figured after his first paycheck, he would run down the street on a break to purchase a couple more shirts and pairs of trousers. A large wooden crate sat by the cot on which he placed his Bible. A naked light bulb, the only light in the room, hung over the bed and from its fixture dropped a chain that could be reached even as he lay on the cot. However, in a storage closet he also found a flashlight which he would keep on the crate beside the Bible.

Promptly at four, he left the room and walked along the hallway to the dining area where he found the attractive, blonde waitress, Dreama, already serving two tables of the early customers...an older couple having Swiss steak and fried chicken plates and a very large middle-aged man resembling a lumberjack devouring the remainder of the day's ribs. Smokey cooked and prepared anything and everything. Marvelous gumbo, po' boys, burgers and steaks, crab cakes with remoulade, the Louisiana staple red beans and rice sauce, and black bean cakes with Coriander sauce. And then there was that scrumptious bread pudding. A considerable variety of food for such a small restaurant. That's why Smokey worked from before dawn to ten or eleven at night. From hearing some of the customers talk earlier in the day, Travis learned the Old South served the best food in town...maybe in the entire parish.

"Travis," Smokey called. "Until it's table cleanin' time, I'd like you to stand with me at the grill. The place will be packed in an hour and we be servin' up everything from burgers to craw daddies. A lotta catfish eaters, too, so when I tell ya, you take them breaded cats there and get ready to put 'em on the fish grill."

"Yes, sir."

"Did'ja meet Dreama yet?"

"No. She looked pretty busy, so I didn't talk to her."

"No matter. Hey, Dreama. Shake loose there and come over to meet Travis."

Dreama locked up her conversation with the elderly couple, then moved to the counter where Travis stood.

"So, you're my new diner mate. Welcome." She put out her hand and Travis shook it. "You're right, Smokey. He *is* a great looking guy...but not much of a dresser. Have to do something about that, Travis."

His eyes reflected his embarrassment. "I plan to, once I get settled."

"Well, maybe after the supper rush, we'll have a moment to get better acquainted."

"Don't be keepin' Travis from his chores, Dreama. That'll be when he's most busy."

She smiled. Her teeth were perfect and her eyes dazzling... so Travis thought. A very fine-looking woman indeed.

"Okay, Smokey," she replied. "We'll chat later, Travis."

'Suppertime', as Smokey referred to it, was the longest meal period...and the busiest. Although Dreama tended all of the tables, booths and counter herself, when Smokey's watchful eyes saw that she was becoming inundated, he would either bring the food out from the kitchen to the tables or if Travis did not have his hands in the dishwater, summon him to help out. Nonetheless, the hours passed quickly.

Dreama was poetry in motion while she served, Travis thought. It seemed like every movement she made from table to table with the sweet tea pitcher and back to the kitchen for the next ready plate of food was choreographed. She was good at what she did and the customers loved her. She spent just the right amount of time with them, listening to their small talk and showering the old men with her southern charm. Her voice, slightly smoky, but always velvet, had just the faintest of southern brogue, which told Travis she either hadn't lived in Southern Louisiana all her life or perhaps was educated a few latitudes to the north. He often found his eyes on her that first night, not for reasons of lust or the appreciation of her beauty; but, for some reason he just found her fascinating. Perhaps it was because she was so full of life and genuinely friendly to everyone.

At around nine-twenty, Dreama coaxed the last two men out of the diner. They had spent another hour after their pie was gone, smoking and joking, likely delaying going home to their wives as long as they could. At least that's what Dreama said.

She helped Travis clean the rest of the tables and then placed the chairs on top of them so that he could mop the floor. Although her shift was officially done at ten, she waited until Travis was winding down and then plopped onto one of the counter stools.

"Take a break, Travis. Come sit and tell me about yourself."

Smokey, still in the kitchen cleaning the grills, shook his head and said under his breath, "Leave the kid alone, Dreama."

Travis took the stool on the left next to her and leaned his elbow on the bar. "I don't mind telling you, I'm whipped. And I didn't even work the full day."

"Well, when there's only one of you to work all those hours, you won't have much down time in between. Six days a week, my friend...and Saturdays are especially challenging."

Travis smiled. "Can't wait."

"So, what's your story, Mr. Marlowe? Smokey said you're from up north."

"Not much to tell. I was orphaned in New York, landed in Indiana in my upper teens, worked in a store for a while and then worked on the farm the rest of the time."

"So, you got tired of being an Indiana redneck and decided to become a southern one."

"The only things that are going to be red on my body are my hands."

"Yeah, I see." Then to his surprise, she took his hands in hers and massaged them. "Not only reddened, but rough and callused. I guess you *were* a farmer, huh? You'll have to put some cold cream on them tonight. I've got some good stuff back there in the kitchen. But, hey, use the rubber gloves when washing the dishes, okay?"

Smokey looked up from the grill and shook his head again. "Hey, Travis," he yelled out. "I need you to help me out here. Can you break away from Mizz Van Horne there?"

"Be right there, Smokey," Travis replied, releasing his hands from hers. "Maybe I'll catch your story another time."

"Well, I'm not through grilling *you* by a long shot. I know there's more of a story to you than you gave me." She then called out to Smokey. "See you tomorrow, boss man. Don't work our new guy to death. And hire some more people, cheapskate."

Smokey waved his arm at her a couple of times. "Yeah, yeah, go on home, trouble lady."

"Welcome to the family, Travis Marlowe," Dreama said. "Don't take any junk off that old man."

Smokey pointed to the door. "Out, girl! And don't be late tomorrow. Say hello to your mama for me."

When Dreama had gone, Travis asked Smokey what it was he needed help with.

"I was just tryin' to do ya a favor, son. Like I said she would, the girl had you already in her clutches. Liter'ly. What was with the hand holdin'?"

"She was concerned about my hands getting scalded all day in the dishwater."

"Hmm, yeah. They do look pretty rough. You ain't washed many dishes, have ya?"

"Not really. Not on this scale," said Travis.

"I guess I shoulda told you this, but we got rubber gloves back there by the basin. You s'pose to wear 'em when you're putting hands in scaldin' water. I thought you mighta figured that out on your own."

"I sure as heck know now. Dreama told me the same thing."

"Well, it won't be the first or last thing you'll learn around here. Okay, I'm finishin' up for the night. You go get you a good night's sleep. Five o'clock comes early around here. Seems like you blink and it's mornin' again."

"All right, Smokey. I am a little tired. See you bright and early."

"It'll be early, but danged if it will be bright. Won't get light till six-thirty or seven."

"Good night, Smokey. And...thanks."

"Don't mention it. Harder days is comin.' You'll see."

That first day of abbreviated hours was still long and arduous for a man not used to such tasks. But it was good, honest work, where he didn't have to set fence posts, till the fields, milk the cows and spend seemingly endless hours on the combine. Not that farming was less than honest work. It was good, wholesome work. But he wasn't there anymore... and he missed it. It had been his family's only source of income for eight years since he and Sarah sold her father's store. And even though he knew the Amish community would come out in force to help manage the farm, he still wouldn't be there to run the operation. He was good at what he did and knew how to make the farm profitable in spite of dry Indiana summers and harsh winters. No doubt he would have to send much of the money he made at the diner home to supplement the household income. Sunday, his day off, he would start writing a letter. He would have the rest of the week to ponder what would go into it.

Maybe the diner job would not last that long, although he *had* committed himself to Smokey. Maybe give it three months. Maybe try to get a job on a shrimper. Earlier that morning and during the dinner hours, he had heard the shrimpers and crabbers talking about their businesses and the gulf's bounty they had pulled in the day before. It sounded adventurous. He knew he was in as good or better shape than most of the men who either captained or worked on the trawlers, pulling in tons of oysters, shrimp, crabs and baskets of crawfish. He'd like to try that. There definitely would be more money in it. Perhaps one day.

His bed he found less than comfortable, but it served his tired frame considerably better than the hard, dirty floor of the Illinois Central box car. Sometime during the afternoon, Smokey had pulled out the Smith and Wesson .38 and placed it on the crate alongside Travis' Bible. Obviously, Smokey was serious about Travis stopping intruders. He picked up the gun and massaged the barrel and cylinder. Could he ever shoot anyone if it came to it? And if he did, would God then add another black mark to his record?

As he lay back on his bed and before the light went out, he ran his thumb along the golden edges of the pages of his Bible until he stopped nearly halfway through at Psalm 4. As he devoured the words of David, excerpts from the text seemed to resonate in his head, appropriate to his day at the diner and now the night.

Hear me when I call, O God of my righteousness. You have relieved me in my distress; have mercy on me and hear my prayer. You have put gladness in my heart...I will lie down in peace and sleep; for You alone, O Lord, make me dwell in safety. (1, 7, 8).

CHAPTER EIGHT

ACTS OF KINDNESS

FIVE THE NEXT MORNING WAS LITERALLY an hour of rude awakening for Travis when he first heard Smokey Woodruff scurrying about, having just entered the back door of *The Old South*. He might have been the owner, but he still worked just as hard as any of his employees. And as he was obviously a demanding employer, it was likely the reason he couldn't keep anyone, except Sissy and Dreama, who had stayed with him these years. If Smokey expected his bus boys to work the hours that he did, no wonder he couldn't keep anyone.

Quickly, Travis rose, waited for the water from the spigot in the wash basin to heat up, then washed his face. After shaving with the straight razor that was in bad need of sharpening and brushing his teeth, he threw on his hopelessly wrinkled shirt and pants that he had washed and hung the day before, and began his first full fifteen hour day.

"Well, good afternoon," said Smokey, when Travis appeared in the kitchen. "I wondered if you were gonna sleep all day."

"But, it's only ten after five. I..."

"I'm just yankin' your chain, boy. All right, now, here's what we do first thing in the morning. I fire up the grills and the smoker out back while you cart in from the cooler room the eggs and breakfast meats. Then whilst I cut up potatoes and onions to make the hash browns, you whip together the grits and slice up some bread to make the toast. Also, in the cooler you'll find the pancake and biscuit mixes I made up last night. Need to set the oven to three seventy-five, measure out two dozen biscuits into clumps 'bout as big as a large egg and shove 'em in for thirty minutes, no more, no less. And that's just for starters. Sissy will be along soon ta hep ya do it. You good with all that?"

"I think so, I've never done much preparing food and cooking it. But I do have one question: how do you whip up grits? I'm not sure what they are."

"They don't eat grits in Indiana? I thought for sure you workin' a farm, you'd know about grits. It ain't just a southern thing. I got a cousin up north in Virginia who won't let a mornin' go by without grits."

"Virginia's part of the south, Smokey."

"Yeah, I guess it is. It hain't been completely taken over by northerners, although people are still mighty upset about the Yankee gov'ment takin' over Robert E. Lee's Arlin'ton house."

"Seems they're still fighting the Civil War down here. Doesn't anyone realize things ultimately got reconciled?"

"Yer down in the heart of Dixie, Travis. We love our women, redeye gravy, sweet tea and pick-up trucks. We fly our rebel flags right along with Old Glory. And every breakfast platter that don't have hash browns on it, got grits on it. Got a lot to teach you, if you plan to be around here long."

"I'm a quick learner."

"And the good ol' boys that come in here don't rightfully cotton to northerners. You found that out with old Boucheau yesterday I hear."

"I guess I heard his message loud and clear where it comes to the Negroes."

Smokey placed his bear-like paws on the counter top and leaned into Travis. "Look, son. That's the way things are here. I love Sissy like she was one of my own and some of the customers don't like that. Most people don't think like I do. They've carried on this thing about the Coloreds for generations. A right smart number of people had grandfathers who fought in the rebel army. That statue over there in the square of the Confederate soldier is probably the most worshipped thing around. It weren't long ago that old Marshall Loudermilk, who actually fought in the war, up and died at a hun'ert and two. Biggest funeral in these parts since the Kingfish died."

"The Kingfish?"

"Lordy, boy, you ain't even heard of the Kingfish? You *have* been livin' under a rock up there in Indiana for sure. Tell you what…just keep your mouth shut and don't run any of my customers off with your yankified tongue. And whatever you was doin' playin' hands with Dreama last night, don't let her get her clutches on you."

"She was only checking out my scalded hands, that's all. So, why do I steer clear of her?"

"She's on the make ever since she became a widow. A good-lookin' boy like you is a rarity around here, dish washer or not. She's just lookin' for male companionship and a man like you might end up like a fly stuck to flypaper."

Travis nodded. "Not to worry about Dreama, Smokey. I have a wife and daughter back in Indiana and they're the only women in my life."

"One day, I won't mind sittin' down with you and hearin' about them; but today, we got work to do. There comes Sissy now."

"Moanin', Travis," she greeted. "You came back, I see. Well, Smokey, might be you won't run this one off with your slave hours and wages."

"All right, none of your sass. And don't be talkin' his ear off like ya did yesterday. Now, both you all git to work."

She smiled her toothy grin, but still had to have the last word. "Yes, boss man."

From six until just before nine-thirty when Sissy closed the front door on the last customer, Travis did not stop for even a bathroom break. He did learn a little about cooking by watching Smokey in between clearing and wiping down tables. He also managed to capture a number of smiles and nods cast in his direction by the friendly faces he would soon get to know. Breakfast was generally the biggest draw of the day, except for Friday nights, which was the catfish special, and Saturday nights that featured Smokey's low country boil.

During the short break between breakfast clean-up and preparation for the lunch crowd Sissy sat down at the counter with Travis to sip on a Coke.

"I was kind of worried about the law cornerin' you in here yesterday. You not in any trouble with them, are you?" she asked.

"I don't think so. It seems a vagrant was found dead out in a field near the switchyard and since I'm the only stranger in town, they had questions."

A furrowed expression formed on Sissy's brow. "I heard about that. Word is some devil bunch got hold of him. Bad voodoo stuff people say."

"It could be that the killer was just some crazed psychopath and not connected to any cult," replied Travis.

"Psycho what?"

"A guy who is off his rocker...or maybe on some kind of drug."

"Well either way, somebody from around here that would do sumthin' like that makes me want to go hide under my bed."

Smokey's voice then boomed out from the kitchen. "You all don't be listenin' to stuff like that. You know how people speculate around here. Why last week, old Mrs. Jennings was sure the lights over Bear Town was from an alien spacecraft and it turned out to be nothin' but swamp gas. It started people thinkin' they was seein' aliens walkin' down the street."

Travis laughed. "I've come to think that the only alien that people will be talking about will be me...you know, the Yankee boy."

"We ain't *that* bad around here. May not cotton to northerners, but once people git ta know ya, you'll fit in all right."

After Sissy had left for the day, Dreama came in at five minutes before three...actually early for her.

"Either my watch must be broke or I'm in The Twilight Zone," remarked Smokey, tapping it several times.

"Oh, funny, Mr. Woodruff. You should take your comedy routine on the road," Dreama replied.

"Anytime I can get five minutes more work outta ya, I'll take it."

Dreama shook her head and then turned her attention to Travis. "What's this I hear about the cops grilling you in here yesterday? You didn't tell me that when we talked."

"There really wasn't anything to talk about. I'm a stranger in town and the very night I get here, a tramp ends up dead."

"So, naturally you killed him. How did he get dead?"

"Speculation that some voodoo cult did it."

"The people who practice that stuff generally don't kill people. They deal in black magic...maybe sacrifice a bird or a goat."

"Could also be some Satan worshippers as well," said Travis.

Smokey jumped in to break up the dialogue. "I don't pay you people to stand around talkin', you know. And we 'specially don't want any more talk about the devil or voodoo-ism in here. So, get busy doin' what yer paid for."

"I guess I'm officially on the clock, now that it's a minute past three," Dreama said. "Travis, we'll talk later. Maybe you'd like to accompany me after work down to Barnacle Bill's for a nightcap."

"Thanks, Dreama, but I guess I won't. I don't drink, anyway."

"Maybe a cup of coffee?"

He shook his head. "Not tonight. I have to hit the floor at five in the morning. I'd like to do that with some sleep behind me."

"Okay. Rain check, then?"

Travis nodded. "We'll see how the week goes."

"That's good enough for me. I'll hold you to it."

At ten-thirty, a half hour after the last customer left, Travis and Dreama finished wiping down the counter, sweeping the floor and drying the last of the dishes. Smokey threw out what was left of the garbage in the dumpster behind the diner, mixed the batter for tomorrow's pancakes and biscuits and scoured the large griddle. He then made up a plate of meat loaf, string beans and corn and set it aside.

"Is that to take home to your wife, Smokey?" Travis asked.

"Got no wife. It's for Dummy."

"Dummy? Who or what is that?"

"The old bum who sits out on the bench in front of the diner 'bout this time every night."

"Do you feed him every night?"

"Most nights, except if he gets enough change for a bottle of rum. He'll be layin' in the alley out back. Then I find him in the mornin' and give him some eggs and toast."

Travis smiled. "I knew you had a good heart, Smokey, but didn't know how good."

"He'd give the store away if Sissy and I let him," said Dreama. "And Dummy's not the first or last that will sit somewhere close by looking for a handout."

"Hey," Smokey grunted. "Dummy's been around here for twenty-five years. He's a town feature."

"So, why do you call him *Dummy*?" Travis asked.

"Cause he don't talk. Never has. Just sits there and grins, showin' nothin' but gums. That's why I don't give him steak or shrimp. He can't chew it."

"Do you mind if I take the food out to him?"

"Good with me. I got stuff to do anyway."

Dreama shook her head. "Don't get sucked into this, Travis. One bleeding heart in this diner is enough."

"Ah, Dreama. It is said: *For the needy shall not always be forgotten.*"

"Sounds like some kind of Bible quote. Or is that something you came up with?"

"A man named David said it a long time ago."

Dreama threw up her hand. "You're too deep for me, Mr. Marlowe. Anyway, I need to get on home. Enjoy your new friend out there."

"You're all heart, Dreama," Smokey said on his way back to the kitchen.

Travis and Dreama then walked out together.

"Toodle-loo," she said walking toward her car.

"Good night, Dreama."

For a moment, he didn't readily see the man on the bench as he was hidden in the shadows of a nearby oak. But then he saw the slightest movement. Moving toward him, he said, "My name is Travis and I work here with Smokey. He prepared this plate for you."

The man stood, folded his hands and gave Travis a slight head bow. Dressed in a dingy white tank top, tattered Bermudas and street-worn ankle length boots, he appeared to be sixty or sixty-five. As he moved from the shadows into the brightness of the street light, Travis could then better see his face. His short beard and long hair were as white as a snowy egret and his deeply wrinkled face revealed a lifetime of merciless southern sun and hardship. He was grinning, just as Smokey said he would be. There wasn't a tooth in his mouth. Quickly taking the food from Travis' hands, he then nodded again and returned to the bench.

"I don't quite know what to call you as Smokey didn't give me your name. He said people refer to you as Dummy, but I can't bring myself to calling you that."

The man ignored Travis' comment, unwrapped the cellophane from the plate and began to dig into his food ravenously with his fork.

"I'm also unsure how to communicate with you since you don't speak."

The response came in the man's eyes. Even in the shadows, they glistened with appreciation. He also stopped chewing for a moment and grinned.

"Well, I guess that's it. I'll be going back in, now. I suppose you can leave the plate and fork at the door when you're done. Good night."

The man nodded again and continued devouring the food.

Travis then returned inside, locked the door and went to the kitchen where he found Smokey wrapping up his work for the evening.

"You get him taken care of?"

"Yes, sir."

"Dummy's all right. He don't get out there on the street and hustle people. Mostly just sits over by the post office with a paper cup and people drop in a few coins. He might get a ben-yay and a cup of coffee in the mornin' from the place down the street, or he might just get a bottle at the A-B-C store. Shows up here most nights. I kind of slip out to see if he's there around nine or so."

Travis nodded, keeping his eyes fixed on Smokey in admiration, but didn't respond.

"You did a fine day's work, son. I think you gonna work out okay here. It's good to see a man like you that don't have a lazy bone in his body."

"Again, thanks for taking me in, Smokey. For putting your trust in me."

"Don't get all soapy on me, boy. Just do your job and I'll have no cause to git on yer case."

"Yes, sir."

"And like I said...watch out for that pie-ranna Dreama. Oh, she gives me the devil about tryin' to be charitable and all, but I've seen her with the customers. I know she's slips old Mizz Persinger a piece of pie or cake when she don't have the money for it. And she's let people out of here without payin.' She's all talk, but a good woman down under. Well, I can't jaw anymore with ya. Go on and take the garbage out to the alley dumpster. Then you better git on to bed. I'll be lockin' the door behind me in a couple minutes."

"Okay. Good night, Smokey."

Smokey nodded and went on about his work. He would wrap up his nightly routine in less than five minutes and shortly after be out the back door.

CHAPTER NINE

INTRUSIONS

AT JUST AFTER ELEVEN, AFTER HIS first really long day into night, he took his shower and lay down in nothing but his boxer shorts on the bunk. He had found himself uncomfortably hot and sweaty during the day, mainly because Smokey only had two overhead and three window fans to circulate the warm air that quickly filled the diner somewhere around ten. Even though it was early in the summer, he would find Southern Louisiana to be sweltering compared to Indiana. What would July and August be like?

The bold, naked overhead bulb was sufficient light for him to read the scriptures. Reading God's word was not only his nightcap before turning in, but his breakfast before beginning the next day. He loved Proverbs and the Psalms of David. But then, many mornings he feasted ravenously on the loving, instructional words of Jesus Christ which gave him the sustenance to get through the day.

This night he read from Psalm 63: *Because Your lovingkindness is better than life, my lips shall praise you. Thus I will bless You while I live. I will lift up my hands in Your name...When I remember You on my bed, I meditate on You on the night watches. Because You have been my help; therefore in the shadow of Your wings I will rejoice.*

After he had read this Psalm, Travis closed the Bible and kissed its cover, as he always did, and set it aside. Then after pulling the chain to the light, the room immediately became blindingly dark…as though he had just stepped into a cave. There was no window in the interior room to provide even the faintest of light. He then lay spread-eagle on the bed with his hands between the pillow and his head, hoping he would soon cool down to go to sleep. It was then he remembered that he had not started his day with his constitutional prayer, having been awakened at five. Many times he had told his Amish congregation that it was the only way to begin one's day…having a conversation with God. Else there would only be scraps left over for Him at night.

And so he began. "Holy Father, hallowed be Your name…" And there is where it stopped. Like the gears on his combine had frozen up and he could not continue. Had he no words for God? No prayer for his family? No prayer of remorse over his sins? No prayer for forgiveness? Thanksgiving? Nothing. It was as though that same *thief* who had stolen his faith and morality, and who tried to steal his soul, had now stolen his words. How deeply into his sinful abyss had he fallen to where he could not climb out? The tears then came. He could not remember the last time he had wept. Maybe at his mother's funeral. Several times over the last three weeks he had felt he might well up over being sent away by Sarah and the order of brethren. But his anger with himself over his heinous acts of sin had each time overcome and squelched his tears. And because he had wrongly imputed some of that anger back to Sarah and the order, he had become even more deeply angry and frustrated with himself.

Well past midnight he lay awake. As tired as he was, his brain would not turn off...the same brain that could not find any words for God. But, as sleep is apt to do, it finally overtook him without warning. And then it seemed like it was only milliseconds that the dreams came again. First, he saw the man in the box car, sitting across from him in the lamp light...except the man did not have the devil's tongue. But then, smoke began to filter out from the man's eyes, subsequently taking on a red-orange glow. Then the eyes turning quickly to two lumps of coal fell out onto the floor of the car, leaving two cavernous holes in his head. The scene then changed and the man was lying in a field near the ruins of a house where only the chimney stood. Dancing around him were figures dressed in black cloaks with hoods covering their faces, chanting in diabolical tongues. In their hands were gleaming daggers, the blades reflecting the light of the full moon just before they were thrust into the man's chest.

Travis forced himself to open his eyes so that the nightmare would go away. He would then know that it was only a dream and would not carry into his consciousness. Although his body had finally cooled down before he fell asleep, he was now once again drenched in sweat. The killing of the man from the train had invaded his dream. Even though he was not in that field two nights before when the murder occurred, he had been given the opportunity to witness it. Who was it that planted the dream in his head? And why?

Suddenly, there were noises. A click at the back door and then footsteps in the hallway. "Drats!" he thought. "Five o'clock already?" How long had he slept, four hours? It seemed like four minutes. He didn't know how Smokey got by on his few hours of sleep. But then Travis heard voices...none of which belonged to Smokey. It did not take him but a short moment to realize someone, actually more than one, had broken in.

Feeling for the .38 Special on the crate, he then remembered he had stuck it under his mattress the night before. Now finding it, he threw on his pants and eased his way to his closed door to listen further. After hearing the door to the freezer room shut, he quietly opened his door slightly to peer up and down the hallway to see if anyone was left to keep a lookout. There was just enough dim light filtering into the store front from the street light on the road for him to see there was no one standing guard. Then assuming that all of the burglars were inside the freezer room, he walked barefooted with a degree of stealth toward the freezer door to listen. Although the door was made of heavy metal, he could hear their muffled voices...two, maybe three of them. Boxes that he knew were full of chicken and pork were being scooted across the floor. And the closer he edged toward the door, he thought he heard them talking about how they would carry the large slabs of beef that were hanging from hooks.

Standing there waiting, he wondered how he would capture them. He could rush in and get the drop on them, but they may also be armed. Even if they weren't, he couldn't both hold them and go to the phone to call the police. But then he saw that the door had a latch. Remembering that there was a padlock with a key in it in the storeroom on a shelf, he returned to secure it. After snapping it in place on the hasp, he smiled. They shouldn't freeze to death before the police arrived.

Travis then went to Smokey's small, untidy office and found a number on a piece of paper on the wall that read 'police,' and dialed the number. As it was ringing, he noticed the clock on Smokey's desk that read one-thirty five.

"Police Department. Officer Presley."

"Hello, Officer Presley, this is Travis Marlowe out at The Old South. You or someone needs to get out here. The place is being robbed."

"What? Are you there now?"

"Yes. I've locked them in the freezer room."

Travis heard him laugh and then reply, "You captured them and put 'em on ice?"

"They went in and I put a lock on the door."

"Well, I'll be a..." Then he said, "Just a moment."

Travis heard him on the radio talking with what appeared to be another officer on duty.

"Okay, Marlowe. You stand by. I have Officer Sam Burnett on the way."

Travis then found Smokey's home number, also stuck to the wall. After dialing the number and hearing it ring three times, a coarse, groggy voice answered, "H...hello."

"Smokey. Travis."

"What in tarnation you callin' me for for at...at a quarter till two in the mornin'? This better be good."

"You need to get down here, sir. I caught somebody trying to rob your place."

Smokey coughed a couple of times. "I hope you shot him daid."

"No. I didn't have to use the gun. I just locked several of them in the freezer where they were trying to make off with some goods."

"Ah, good boy. I knew there was a reason I letcha stay there. Be right down." Travis then heard the hang-up click.

While the officer was en route, Travis then heard the burglars getting excited. When he edged closer to the door, he then knew they had tried to open the door with no success. "The door weren't 'sposed to lock when we came in. Try it again," someone yelled.

"It's no use. It's stuck or something.'"

Someone else said, "We gone freeze to death 'fore anyone finds us."

Travis smiled again and then returned to the store front where he saw the red flashing light of one of Destiny's patrol cars.

A large set man in a cap with a gun in his hand exited the car and quickly moved toward the door. A now fully-dressed Travis opened the door only to stare into the muzzle of the officer's revolver. Thinking Travis might be one of the burglars, Sam Burnett yelled, "Hands in the air. What's your name?"

"Travis Marlowe. I work for Smokey and sleep here."

"Okay, I was told you'd be here. Where are the perps?"

"The what?" Travis wasn't familiar with the term.

"The burglars, man."

"Back there in the freezer room. When I heard them break in and go inside, I put a lock on the door."

"How long ago? I'd hate to find some honest-to-God stiffs in there."

"About fifteen minutes ago. Just a minute ago, they realized they were locked in and started raising a ruckus trying to get out."

Travis then led Burnett to the freezer door and placed the key in the lock to open it. He then turned on the hallway light.

"Step back, Marlowe, in case there's any gunplay."

No sooner had that been said, the weight of the men pushing against the door caused it to swing open and crash violently into the wall. Three men, none of which expected the door to give, fell sprawling into a heap on the floor at Officer Burnett's feet.

"Stay down where you are and put your hands on top of your heads."

The three men, all appearing in their mid-twenties, did as ordered. No one wanted to argue with the forty-four magnum in Burnett's hand.

"All right, Marlowe, I need your help here. Frisk them for any weapons."

"Me?"

"I don't see anyone else standin' here named Marlowe. I called the parish sheriff, but nobody's here to help me yet as you can see."

While the men sat still, hands on top of their heads, Travis carefully checked their pockets, belts, boot leggings and jackets. He found a hunting knife in one of their pockets and a small Barlow knife in the jacket pocket of another. No guns.

At two-fifteen the back door swung open and a rather haggard-looking Smokey Woodruff appeared in the hallway, shotgun in hand. He took a look at the solemn faces on the burglars sitting on the floor and then said, "So you did git 'em, eh Travis? Good boy. Hello, Sam. Need some help runnin' these maggots in?"

"Naw. Sheriff Lawton will be here in a few minutes. They like your cooler so much, now they'll wonder how the parish cooler will feel."

Smokey then slapped Travis on the back. "I knew it was gonna work out, you stayin' here. Now you take the mornin' off and catch up yer sleep. I'll take up the slack."

"If you're staying, then I'll stay up. We'll get a jump on the day."

"No, boy. I'm used to it. Sometimes I only get two to three hours sleep anyway. My si-atica acts up and I might as well be workin.' Now you git some sleep. You'll be busy later. But, I want ya *alert* and busy."

Just as two sheriff patrol vehicles pulled up in front of the diner, Travis reluctantly agreed. "All right, Smokey. I do need some rest. But I'll be up for the breakfast crowd."

† † †

Joubert

After the parish sheriff deputies had loaded up the three intruders, who they learned were from neighboring Patterson, Smokey began his day that Wednesday at three-thirty instead of five as quietly as he could. Travis had not bothered to even take off his shirt and pants before caving onto his bed and immediately falling asleep. No dreams this time.

Though he had no idea what time it was, at just before seven, he was awakened from his sleep by a high-pitched voice he quickly recognized as Sissy's. But as the store room was closer to the diner's rear door than the kitchen, he was sure her exclamations were coming from the alley and not down the hallway. Suddenly, she began shouting and her voice projected the alarming ingredients of both fear and anger. Quickly bounding from his bed, he slipped his feet into his shoes and made his way into the hallway and out the back door. The first thing he noticed was the green sedan parked on the narrow street with a tall, muscular Black male leaning against the driver's door, arms folded. But then to his right, squatting against the diner wall with her arms pulled around herself he saw Sissy. She was sobbing and shaking. Blood was dripping from her lower lip onto her white blouse.

"Hey!" yelled Travis. "What did you do to her?"

The man shouted back, "None o your biz-nez, peeshwank," the man replied. "You best passe' dog or you git the same as she got."

Travis didn't quite understand some of the man's words, but fully discerned his threatening tone. He then reached down and pulled Sissy up by the arm, opened the diner's back door and coaxed her inside. Pointing his index finger sternly at the man, he said, "I *will* find out what this is about and *make* it my business."

"Don't be messin' where you best not, peeshwank." He then turned and entered his car. After giving Travis another menacing glare, he sped away.

When Travis returned inside, he found Sissy leaning against the hall wall and still crying.

"Are you all right?"

She nodded quickly and snuffed back the mucous that had formed in her nostrils.

"Who was that, your husband?"

"Yeah, but we don't stay together no more. He left last month and took up wif somebody else. Now he wants to come back and I tell him 'no.' But he won't stay away from me."

"Have you called the police on him?"

"Yeah, but they won't come. They say they don't mess in Black folks biz-ness."

"Come into the store room. We'll need to put a cold compress on your lip to stop the bleeding. I think I saw some peroxide in there, too."

While he was tending to her injury, Travis asked, "Do you want to talk about things? I've got a pretty good ear."

She smiled and then winced from the pain in her split lip. "You not like most White men, are you? Most men either ignore us or talk down to us like we nobody. Why do you care?"

"You're a young woman in obvious trouble and I definitely don't like it when men beat up women, husband or not."

Her eyes welled up again and she touched her lower lip with the cool, wet rag to assure she was not still bleeding. "Thanks, Travis, but it be best you stay out of this. Joubert is a bad man…dangerous man. I done seen him hurt people. You don't need to get yo'self hurt by the likes o him."

Suddenly, Smokey appeared in the doorway to the store room. "What's this? 'Bout time you got here, Sissy. Where you been? I had to do everything this mornin' include wait the tables."

She then turned her face to him and he saw her swollen lip. Closing his eyes and clenching his fist tightly, he said, "Not again. Tell me that bum of a husband did not hit you this mornin'."

Sissy dropped her eyes and didn't reply.

"I better not find him within fifty feet of this place or he'll sure fire git a dose of my buckshot. If you want ta go back home, Sissy, that's all right. Travis and I will manage breakfast. I'll also call Dreama in for the lunch people."

"No. I be fine, Smokey. I want to start work now."

She then walked from the room to the kitchen to put on her apron. Smokey looked at Travis and shook his head. "Happens every few days, it does. That bum he's gonna end up missin' someday if I have anything to do with it."

As bad a character as Joubert was, Sissy thought he might be somewhat afraid of Smokey. Although short, Smokey was robust with the arms of a lumberjack. And he was prone to toting his twelve gauge when driving around in his pickup. Combined with his fiery temper, he could be a force to be reckoned with. He and Joubert had previously butted heads a few months before when Sissy's husband had beaten her within an inch of her life. Smokey actually took his shotgun and went looking for Joubert who smartly went into hiding with some of his street friends. But then Smokey cooled off in a couple of days, which was a good thing when he ran into the man as he came out of the A-B-C store. It was then he pinned the much taller man up against the wall with a massive hand around his throat.

"You're Mister Big Time, aint-cha, beatin' up on a little thing like that. It happens again and you'll find out what a real beatin' feels like. Ya hear me, boy? They'll find what's left of yer carcass in the swamp after I feed ya to the gators."

Joubert apparently said nothing in return and quickly turned heel.

Smokey was one of those bigger than life figures in the community. Respected by both the Blacks and Whites for his fairness and generosity, he had on many occasions forgiven a meal ticket when a man had lost his job and could not afford the three dollars for his supper. When a Black man might knock on the back door after hours looking for a handout, he would always have some leftovers. Blacks were forbidden to eat at the city's eating establishments. It was not only the law in Destiny, but throughout much of the south. In those days, Blacks ate at their own restaurants, attended their own schools and used the public toilets designated for the Colored. Some of Smokey's women customers would not use the ladies room at the Old South because they knew Sissy used it. And the fact that Smokey had a Colored woman helping to prepare food and then serving it to Whites, did not set well with some of the patrons, even though the more affluent customers may have had Black servants in their own homes. But, as the food was the best in town, some said throughout the entire parish, his business would not suffer. There might be some bigoted, even scornful looks cast in her direction, but Smokey would never condone any racial slurs or words of scorn to be leveled directly at Sissy. Those who didn't like his rules didn't have to eat there. He would not miss their business, he always said. The sign he had in his window, *We reserve the right to refuse service to anyone*, was directed especially at them...not the Blacks.

Chapter Ten

Saturday Night

It had been an eventful three days at The Old South Diner for Travis. Smokey had taken him in, giving him a job and a place to sleep; he was questioned by the town police about what was probably a murder committed by devil worshippers; he met not only an interesting but very attractive woman from whom he continued to receive vibes; he caught three burglars, literally stopping them cold; and he kept a sweet little Negro woman from further assault by an estranged brutal husband. The remainder of the week would be rather uneventful.

He did take food two more times out to the man called Dummy, still trying to find out his real name which no one seemed to know. The man was always appreciative, placing his hands together in gratitude and returning the kindness with a slight bow.

Joubert did not reappear and by Friday, Sissy's nerves had calmed. However, she was still vigilant when she left for work in the mornings and returned home in the afternoons.

And Dreama continued her little flirtatious small talk with Travis here and there, which he decided to let roll off him. She was definitely a lovely, exploitive being, but his mind was on the one woman who was indelibly etched in his heart...the woman to which he would sit down and write a long letter on Sunday when it was quiet...at such time he was alone and could think of the right words to say to her. Words of love and desire. Words of remorse. Pleading words that might just convince her to let him back into her life now that nearly a month had lapsed.

On Saturday night, after the low-country boil and the shrimp po'boys were all gone, the doors closed at nine. By nine thirty Dreama had the place spic-n-span. Travis had the last of the dishes washed and garbage taken out to the dumpster while Smokey had cleaned up the grills and food preparation areas.

"Coo-yee," he said in his Cajun brogue. "This was the week that was, eh? It's time we all went shah cat!"

"What did he say?" Travis asked Dreama.

"He said *shah cat*, which means get out of here. You're going to have to learn a little Bayou talk if you want to get by around here, sweetie."

Smokey then came out with cash in his hand to pay both Dreama and Travis. "Here ya go, my boy. A little somethin' extra for savin' my bacon last Wednesday morning.' I'll be givin' you some time to go buy some different clothes next week down at the Monkey Ward."

"Monkey..."

"That's the Montgomery Ward store," remarked Dreama. "Everybody around here just says Monkey Ward."

Travis didn't count the money and just shoved it in his pocket. "Thanks, Smokey."

Dreama did count hers and in a sassy tone said, "Now I have enough to put gas in my car and buy a six pack of Black Label."

"Hey, gal. I saw the tips flowin' yer way this week. You made out all right," Smokey said. "Well, anyway, I'm goin' home. Lock up when yer done. You got yer key, right, boy?"

"Yes," said Travis.

"Then you go have a nice evenin' and find ya a church ta go to tomorrow."

"I noticed a church when I walked into town last Monday down on Main and I think Magnolia. Do you know anything about it?"

"Yeah, that's Trinity Methodist, Reverend Drake Moreau's church. It's a good'n and he does preach the gospel. You'd think you was in a hell-fire Baptist service. But if you don't want to have yer toes stepped on, maybe you oughta go down to the Episcopal on the south end of town. That man's as dry as a bone."

"Where do *you* go?"

"I go over to Houma where my brother and his family are. Then I have Sunday dinner with them. Let somebody else cook for me for a change."

"I guess I'll try Trinity. Thanks for the information."

"Don't mention it. Okay, then, good night you two."

When he had left out the back door, Travis remarked "*He* sure took off in a hurry."

"It's Saturday night. He's picking up his girl friend and heading to Baton Rouge. There's a country bar there they go to every week."

"So, he's not married. Was he ever?"

"Yes. A long time ago. His wife of fourteen years said she was tired of sharing Smokey with his mistress, then up and left."

"He had a mistress?"

"Yeah. You can call it that. The Old South Diner. *You* see the hours he works. This might be his bread and butter, but I wouldn't put up with a man being gone from my life seventeen hours a day, six days a week." She then sat down at one of the booths by the window and lit up a cigarette to have with her coffee. It was her usual wind-down ritual most evenings, especially on a Saturday night. Travis slid in to the seat across the table from her.

Dreama took in a drag, lifted her head and then blew smoke rings into the air so that it wouldn't end up in Travis' face. "It's Saturday night, Travis Marlowe, and you and I have got to stop a crime from being committed."

"What do you mean?" he replied.

"Being lonely is a crime, you know. So, why don't I place you under citizen's arrest?"

Travis smiled. "Which means what?"

"Which means you and I ought to go out dancing or something."

His smile remained, but he shook his head. "Dreama, I'm not much of a dancer and it's been years on end since I've done any socializing."

"Why is that? Are you married or something?"

"Something like that."

"Well, you either are or you aren't. Which is it? Married or single? You fell off a freight train, landing here in Destiny all by yourself. What gives?"

"I'm…separated from my wife. No divorce."

"Ah. Well, that says you're somewhere in between, then. Why don't we go somewhere and let me help you unload some of that baggage?"

"I think I just need to stay here and get some sleep and read some. It would finally be good to get more than five hours of sleep."

"You can get all you need tomorrow. I just think the best medicine for what ails you is to let your hair down a little and kick up your heels."

Travis shook his head again. "That is what I *don't* need. I'm not good in crowds. I wouldn't mind sitting here and talking a bit more if you don't mind. But *you* might want to separate from this place after a long week."

Dreama took a sip of her now cooled coffee and tamped out her cigarette. "Sounds to me you just need some excitement in your life. You're probably coming out of a boring marriage...boring for you both. And you got tired of each other. Am I right?"

Travis turned his head toward the plate glass window and watched a car go by. "I don't really want to talk about that. There's a lot of pain I'm feeling right about now, mostly because I miss my daughter. She didn't ask for what happened between her mom and me."

Dreama then placed her hand on his with the lightest of touches. "Hey. I used to be a hairdresser, which is much the same as being a divorce counselor. I'm a very good listener, so feel free to unload. Maybe you need to talk it out with somebody instead of just stewing about it."

"Dreama, my story would not be of much interest to you; but, if you really want to talk about something, tell me about *you*."

Dreama rearranged her position on the bench seat. "Fair enough. It won't take long, though. It's me that's not had a very interesting life. I was born and raised here. My mom lives up in Shreveport, but my dad drowned on Lake Coosawamee when I was five. Graduated high school and went on to cosmetology school in New Orleans. People around here thought it had something to do with astronomy, not realizing it had nothing to do with the cosmos. I met a guy in the Big Easy and had a fling. We got married when I was twenty-one and two years later he was dead of a heart attack. I came back here and worked as a hairdresser, but started losing my customers when Old Lady Gardner's hair started falling out after I put a new rinse product on it. She sued and the word got around. So, I closed shop. About four years ago, Smokey offered me a job here and the rest is history."

"So, how about your social life? You indicated earlier that you were lonely, yet you seem to have a lot of friends. Some of them came in here this week and it appeared they were more interested in socializing with you than eating."

"Well, I do have some friends...even a few male friends, but there's not a huge selection of good men around here. I go out with a lawyer every once in a while. Other guys? Well, I'm not at liberty to talk about. At least to someone I've only known for a week. But no, I do keep myself from getting lonely. And I do it up right, if you know what I mean."

As it seemed the conversation began to get a little too personal, Travis decided to change the subject. "As you heard me talking to Smokey about where to go to church, maybe you could accompany me to Trinity tomorrow morning."

Dreama laughed. "Me? Go to church? I'd be afraid the roof would fall in on me."

"So you're not a believer."

"A believer...in what?"

"In God, of course, and Jesus, His Son and the Holy Spirit."

She smiled. "Travis, I've never given that religious junk any thought whatsoever. What I believe in is three other beings...me, myself and I."

"Maybe you'd like to talk about it. You sound like you don't believe God exists."

Dreama was now obviously uncomfortable about the conversation as she began squirming and changing her position again. She then diverted her eyes to the street light at the curb. Looking back at Travis, she said, "What a thing to talk about on a Saturday night. So, let me ask *you* a question. Are you some kind of Jesus freak?"

"I'm somebody who cares enough about you to tell you about salvation. God is pleading for your soul. Believe that. I can give you all the information…"

"Travis, Travis, stop. My soul, dear man, belongs to little ol' Dreama Van Horne and the Old South Diner."She then picked up his hand. "Why don't we get off this subject and talk about you. I unloaded, so let's hear your story. You need to unwind that spring inside your head, lover. I've watched you around the diner this week and you don't talk or socialize. You're stiff as a board."

"I'm new here, Dreama. Don't know anybody and don't care to do anything but my job."

"Come on, now. Quit being so serious and…well, boring. Relax and have some fun. People might take you for being down-right unfriendly. Everybody loves having a good time in this town. We don't have a Mardi Gras atmosphere here, but we're fun-loving people in Southern Louisiana just the same."

He smiled. "I guess you're right in a way. But this is only my first week and I've been wrapping myself up in my job."

"A meaningless job."

"A job, just the same. It took me off the street."

"Poor poor Travis. You know what you need right now is to get out of this old place. I didn't tell you, but I'm also a pretty darn good artist, a painter if you will, and I'd like you to see what I do when I'm not waiting tables. My house is only about five miles from here." She then slid out from her seat. "Come on. You'll appreciate my work."

"I don't know Dreama. It's after ten and…"

"And your big daddy Smokey put a curfew on you for eleven."

Travis laughed. "Okay. What's the harm? If you're that close, then yes, I'd like to see your work. But, I need to get back to my fine little apartment and hit the sack. I'm pretty drained."

"Okay, Cinderella. I'll have you back by midnight."

After checking the back door and turning out the lights, Travis closed and locked the front door, then followed Dreama to her car parked at the curb a half block down. When she went around to the driver's side, he opened the door for her and allowed her to slide in under the wheel.

"It's nice to be out with a gentleman for a change," she said.

After closing her door and rounding the rear bumper, second thoughts…guilty thoughts…nearly stopped him from getting in. He was going to a young attractive woman's house on a late Saturday night, knowing full well she was attracted to *him*. He had felt it. If the situation were different…if he wasn't still legally married…he could easily garner the same feelings for her.

"Well, come on," she called out. "Has paralysis set in? I'm waiting."

After pushing any manufactured pangs of guilt from his mind, he then opened his door and planted himself on the seat beside her.

"What kind of car is this?"

"Fifty-six Chevy. You like it?"

"Very stylish."

"As ugly, blue four-door sedans go, I guess. But I do keep it in good shape. I take care of it…it takes care of me. You ready to roll?"

Travis nodded.

She smiled and then started up the engine, yanked the gearshift down into low and pulled away from the curb.

CHAPTER ELEVEN

TEMPTATION

AS SHE DROVE OUT MAIN STREET past the storefronts of McCrory's Five and Dime, The State Farm office, Marianne's Dress Shop and Harry's Bait and Tackle, the town was already dead. On their left about halfway down loomed the impressive parish courthouse with its lighted clock and ornate architecture. Another light shone on the Confederate soldier still standing guard, standing proudly above the engraved based that read *He Gave All for the Noble Lost Cause.* The clock was obviously broken as it still displayed the same time it did the morning he walked into town, three forty-three. It reminded him of another clock...the clock on the town hall in Hurley, Indiana, which also seemed to stick from day to day. And that conjured up more guilt. Only three miles from that clock lay Sarah and Rachael, by now tucked into their beds of freshly-laundered sheets, lonely and perhaps even still awake. He envisioned that Rachael may have cried herself to sleep from missing him.

"Maybe this was not such a good idea, Dreama."

She took her eyes off the road to look over at him. "Why not? You're not afraid of me, are you?"

"No."

"Then what?"

"I don't know that I feel right about going to a woman's house like this late on a Saturday night."

She laughed. "You're a pill, Travis Marlowe. I think you *are* afraid of me. You might just be the most pure but naïve man I ever met. You're just too, too nice. You treat me very respectful like a lady ought to be treated, which I like; but then you end up trying to save my black soul like I'm some kind of missionary case. And I know you're still mooning about a woman you split up with. But don't worry about being with me. I won't bite you. Let's just enjoy each other's company tonight."

She turned off the main road about a mile from town, actually not far from the railroad switchyard, and then continued on a narrow secondary road that appeared to be completely engulfed by large oaks on both sides of the road. Ghostly Spanish moss hanging low from the overhead limbs appeared in her headlights as masses of gray hair from the heads of old crones.

About a mile further on the left she slowed at a mailbox with a reflector on it and turned into a gravel driveway. The headlights then picked up the small, but attractive and well-maintained house with a wide front veranda on which sat baskets and pots chocked full of red petunias. Standing stately to either side of the house were two huge magnolias plastered generously with large, white blooms…a glorious spectacle indeed. Between the house and the magnolia on the left loomed a three-quarter stage moon filtering through the fog that helped illuminate the night. Had it not been for the moonlight and the car's headlights, the night scene would have been pitch black.

"You live way out here alone?" Travis asked. "I didn't see any other houses on the road coming in."

"I like it that way and I'm far from being a scaredy cat. There are a few other houses along the road. But they're set back a piece where you can't see them."

She then led him down a broken sidewalk at the end of which were three steps leading up to the veranda. The pale light of the moon caused two large blue hydrangeas nestled up against the house to give off a haunting aura. He was sure this was even more picturesque in the daylight.

But ascending the steps in front of him was an even more lovely sight…a young, provocative blonde woman wearing a light gingham dress and white shoes leading him deeper into her personal life. All the while, it was feeling wrong to him; and at the same time, he was feeling a surge of excitement and anticipation coming from some debauching source that continued to egg him on.

After Dreama had flicked on the house lights, Travis took account of the *woman's* touch immediately. It was obvious that her taste was refined and cultured, even to the eyes of one such as he who was décor-ignorant. The colorful furniture with the flowered patterns, silken drapes and ornate vases on pedestals were obviously expensive. A large painting of a beautiful Dreama Van Horne lounging in a long, flowing blue dress hung stately over her fireplace. There was enough money in furnishings alone for Travis to wonder how a waitress and former hair stylist could afford such a lavish interior. Perhaps it had come from family money…old money; however, for some reason, he thought differently. Perhaps the money came from the men she was 'not at liberty to talk about.' But then again, he felt guilty and angry with himself in thinking the worst about her.

"So, what do you think?" she asked.

"Nice. Very, very nice."

"Can I get you something to drink?"

"Maybe a Coke, if you have one."

"I have some mighty good Scotch in the cabinet. Me? I prefer wine."

"No. No Thanks."

"Of course. You don't drink. I remember. Well, just what *do* you do to loosen up after a long day?"

"I used to play board games with my daughter and read Bible stories to her before she went to bed."

"Hmmm, super exciting. I don't mean that to sound disrespectful or to poke fun. I just meant that you obviously need to experience a different kind of fun in your life." She then approached him slowly, put her arms around his shoulders and kissed him on the lips.

Travis took in a sharp breath and gently pushed her away. "That...is not supposed to happen."

The rejection did not seem to hurt Dreama. She merely smiled and leaned her head to one side. "Okay, that was a little out of line, I admit. Nice, but inappropriate. Let me go get that Coke."

In a flash she was back with a carafe of wine in one hand and his Coke in a glass made of cut crystal in the other. He took a sip and continued looking around. "Where are your paintings?"

"Check out the wall behind my couch and let me know what you think."

Travis walked over to the edge of her sprawling red and yellow patterned couch and viewed a collection of a half dozen landscape paintings, masterfully presented in rich, brilliant greens, golds and browns. One of paintings was of a Bayou scene with a line of trees in the background underneath a glorious blue sky. Another appeared to be the skyline of New Orleans with a steamboat docked at the levee on the Mississippi.

"I set up my easel in the little park that jutted out from the levee to capture that scene," she said. "So, what do you think?"

"Magnificent," he said. "You are very good...even professional."

"And this is what I do in my spare time...besides a little flower gardening."

"I especially like this one. The moon rising over the water is so...it's almost like I'm standing and looking at the real thing out the window."

"Thanks. I call it *Moon Over the Bayou*. I put my soul...you remember that dark soul...into all these paintings. I see the beauty of the world, try my best to capture it on canvass and then it's mine forever. The fleeting beauty I see in person I might never see again except in my works. And I can enjoy it again and again anytime I want."

"That's a very lovely sentiment. I can only try to keep something so beautiful in my mind as long as I can, but then find it is never quite as vivid as it was when I experienced it. Right now I'm trying to recall an image of my house sitting on rich, green farmland, but the image somehow seems faded." He looked at the painting again. "It is...simply glorious, Dreama. You have a keen eye for beauty and a wonderful touch with the brush."

His eye then caught a more curious painting. "What is this one about?"

"It's just a picturesque place further out in the parish that has a lot of meaning to me. I go there sometimes with my friends."

As he studied it, for some reason he found it familiar, although he had never been there. "It's a beautiful setting. Is that a chimney in the distance?"

"Yes. A house used to be there, but it burned down years ago before I was even born. A couple of my girlfriends and I used to go there and sit by that chimney to have a picnic lunch on a Sunday, making up stories of the family that might have lived there. There's a spring nearby as well. Sometimes we took our transistor radios out there and some wine. We just had a good old, spiritual time."

"Spiritual, huh? Does that mean there's a shot at getting you inside the church house?"

She laughed. "I think not, Mister Goody Two Shoes."

They sat on the couch for another twenty minutes or so, talking mostly about her school years and that short marriage. But try as she did, Dreama could still not get Travis to open up about his life, his marriage and just who he was, other than being the bus boy at The Old South Diner. During their conversation, he noted that she had consumed nearly the entire carafe of the red wine.

"Come on," she said. "I'll show you some more."

After they rose from the couch, she led him through the kitchen, where she poured the rest of the bottle of wine in her carafe, and then down her hallway, stopping at her bedroom door. Seeing her queen sized bed against the wall caused him to stir inside for the wrong reason. She entered the bedroom, but he did not follow.

"Oh, come on in here," she said. "Quit being such a scaredy cat with me. I want you to see these two paintings."

The paintings toward which she pointed above the beds were not landscapes. One was of a man about thirty standing with his foot on the running board of a car Travis thought looked like a Model T he had seen on the road back in Indiana. The other painting was of an older woman sitting in a chair by the same fireplace in Dreama's living room.

"The man was my dad. I painted it last year from an old black-and-white photo I found in our family album. This would have been about two years before he died. The other is of my mom as she looks now. I painted it last fall."

"You do have a real talent for capturing life, Dreama, whether it's nature or the human expression. It almost makes me think I know them. You're actually good enough to make a living from this."

After she took two more successive gulps of the wine, Travis noticed that her words were starting to slur. "Naw. There're plenty of starving arstice...artists out there even better'n me. I've resigned that all I'm ever going to be known for is Dreama the waitress. I get more money in tips than I'd ever make selling one of my paintings. You'd be surprised what a wink and a little sugar talk can get you." She then gave Travis one of those winks and threw her arms around him, dropping her glass on the floor. The faint aroma of her perfume still lingered on her neck. He felt paralyzed as she pulled him down with her on the bed.

"Dreama, no. You need to take me back to the diner. Come on."

She continued her grip on his neck, refusing to let go. But then after a moment she released her hands and began taking her clothes off. Her words were even more slurred. "Make me haaa-py, Travey. Stay and love me..."

His shoulders and arms wouldn't move. It was as though something or someone was holding him down on the bed. She then began to unbutton his shirt. His arms suddenly shook violently and his hands began to touch her body. Finally, with every ounce of will he could muster, he was able to release himself not only from her grip, but the force that seemed to be holding him to her.

He then stood and re-buttoned his shirt. Dreama continued to lay on the bed with a hurt look on her face. She seemed incapable of moving. "Why, Travis? Why can't anyone love me?"

For a moment he didn't reply. He just looked at her as her words reverberated inside of his head. He then looked above the headboard at the images of the two people she had lovingly transferred to canvass. "They love you, Dreama, and God loves you."

He looked back at her, but apparently she had not heard him. The wine had consumed her and he saw that she had passed out.

"Dreama," he called. But she was deep in a kind of alcoholic coma.

Travis pulled the bed spread over her, turned out the light and left the room. What would he do now? She would not awaken until morning. Even if she did, she was in no condition to drive him back. He could sleep on her couch and then get her to drive him to the diner whenever she did wake. But what time would that be? He had plans to go to Trinity for morning worship.

As he sat in her living room, he took account of how quiet it was in the house. The only sound was the ticking of the mantle clock. It read twelve-fifteen. He stood back up again and looked at her paintings. She *was* good. Very good. He could see her passion in the creation of her masterpieces. He saw her love for life and nature. But then he again placed his eyes on the painting of the field with the lonely chimney against the horizon. Suddenly, as though a knife had penetrated his chest, a fiery shot of adrenaline tore through his arteries. He now remembered where he had seen the image in the painting...in the dream he had on Tuesday night. This unnerved him. Just as in his experience with the satanic spirit, if not the devil himself, on the train, he was continuing to be the victim of unexplained, supernatural happenings. How could he have dreamed about a place he had never been? And who put the dream into his unconscious? Was it God Himself? And was it a forewarning?

As Dreama would be out cold the remainder of the night and he wanted to get back to the diner, he felt he had no choice but to walk. He knew it was a good five miles, but as the road that Dreama lived on made a right turn onto the highway that took him into Destiny proper, it would be easy to navigate.

Closing the door behind him, he then walked back down the gravel driveway until it ended on the road. The night air was still heavy and warm. The moon had now disappeared over the triple canopy of oaks to a point where its light only dimly illuminated the roadway. But he could still see enough to keep him on the road. After coming upon a chorus of frogs, they ceased their song until after he had passed. But in his head it seemed that a thousand demonic voices suddenly began chanting and mumbling, trying to get his attention...trying to frighten him. It was working. But was it from some kind of psychological self-induced fear and apprehension...or was it real?

"Stop it!" he yelled out. "Apparently, his voice frightened an animal in the brush just off the road. And as he remembered that Dreama's headlights had earlier picked up a bog just off the road on curve, he wondered if there were alligators or snakes in the marsh. He had heard talk of the venomous coral, cottonmouths and rattlesnakes that were prominent in the southern wetlands. This thought even more so heightened his anxiety. He imagined a hundred deadly, hungry eyes on him as he then quickened his pace. Almost in a dead run for over five minutes, he finally came up on the main highway.

"Lord," he said aloud. "I ask that you deliver me back to the diner safely. In remembering David's prayer to you, please accept his words as being mine. *You have tested my heart. You have visited me in the night. You have tried me and found nothing. I have purposed that my mouth shall not transgress. Concerning the works of men, by the word of Your lips. I have kept away from the paths of the destroyer. Uphold my steps in Your path that my footsteps may not slip.*"

After crossing the road so that he could walk facing the traffic, his adrenaline then calmed and heart settled down. There were still a little less than four miles to cover. But then after only walking about five hundred feet, a car approached from the opposite side of the road behind him and then slowed. When it came even with him, a blinding beam of light from the car hit his eyes.

"You there. What are you doin' walkin' out here on the highway?" Harold Presley. "Marlowe?" he called. "Is that you again?"

"Yes, sir. I was just walking back to the diner."

"And why are you out here in the first place?"

"If you're going into town, can I get a ride with you? I'll explain."

"Hop in," Presley said with a sigh. "This is gettin' to be a habit with you."

On the way into Destiny, Travis explained that he and Dreama had gone to her house for a short while and then she was to bring him back. However, she had gotten too intoxicated and passed out. As he didn't want to stay the night there and risk missing church, he decided to walk back to the diner. At first, Presley acted like he believed Travis was just feeding him a line, but then realized after observing his earnestness, that he was indeed telling him the truth.

"Don't know that Smokey would approve you goin' out there drinkin' with that girl. He went to a lot of trouble with you and put his neck on the line in takin' you in."

"I know. It was not my intention to go there, but she wanted me to see her paintings."

"I expect she wanted you to see a lot of things, knowin' her. Smokey oughta have warned you about that barracuda."

"I'm afraid he did. But, she's really not like you might think. She is a very caring person, only she's obviously had some difficulties in her life. I've enjoyed talking with her to this point. From here on, though, I'll be careful not to do things like this again."

"So, what *is* your story, Travis? You seem like a nice young man and told us you were some kind of religious man up there in the Amish country."

"That's pretty much it. As you know, I also fell on some bad times a month ago, but I'm working toward remedying that. I have a wonderful wife and a daughter I love like no one else. And in the not too distant future, hope to get back to them."

"Well, son. I'd then suggest that you keep a lower profile around here. There's some screwy stuff happenin' and bein' a stranger, you might get looked at more easy than anyone else."

"Yes, sir. I understand."

"Well, we're here at the diner. Go get yourself some sleep so you can get to church tomorrow. Don't let me be pickin' you up again. I just might let you try out our bunks at the station." He then chuckled.

Travis shook his hand, thanked him for the ride in and shut the car door behind him.

He showered, brushed his teeth and sat for a few moments reading the Savior's words from Luke 8: *Those by the wayside are the ones who hear; and then the devil comes and takes away the word out of their hearts, lest they should believe and be saved. But the ones on the rock are those who, when they hear, receive the word with joy; and these have no root who believe for a while, and in time of temptation fall away. Now the ones that fell among the thorns are those who, when they have heard, go out and are choked with cares, riches and pleasures of life and bring no fruit to maturity. But the ones that fell on the good ground are those who, having heard the word with a noble and good heart, keep it and bear fruit with patience.*

After he had digested the Word along with an apple that he had pulled from the cold storage room, he said prayers for Sarah and Rachael, their good health and safety, and then finally for Dreama, that she would ultimately accept the message of salvation. He would do his best to bring that message to bear.

When Travis blinked open his eyes, he thought it was still dark outside, but then remembered there was no window in the store room to let in the light rays of the morning. As he did not own a watch, nor had ever had one since before he came into the Amish order, he threw his legs over the side of the bed and went to the dining room to look at the wall clock. Eight-forty.

After preparing a small pot of coffee in the kitchen, he returned to the dining room with a steaming cup of the brew and a donut, then parked himself at the same booth where he and Dreama had sat the night before. The sun, now fully risen over the scrub oaks, cast its rays through the plate glass window and painfully into his eyes, compelling him to shield his face with a lengthy hand salute. He thought about Dreama again and whether she was finally awake, nursing one of her worst hangovers ever. What would they say to each other on Monday afternoon? Would they even be able to look at one another? But, as badly as *she* might feel about her behavior, *his* conscience was clear. Although he did feel guilty about placing himself in last night's situation, he had resisted temptation. Still, he had lusted. And in the heat of that alluring moment how easy it would have been to submit to her. That in itself was a sin.

At just after nine, Travis cleaned the coffee pot and returned to his room where he shaved and put on a freshly laundered shirt, the better shirt that he had sent out on

Wednesday for cleaning along with his old suit. Smokey had surprised him by paying for it when he picked it up. Until it was time to leave for church, he sat in the dining room which today would be his living room, turning the pages of Psalms seeking...seeking counsel, seeking comfort. He finally stopped on Psalm 92: *It is good to give thanks to the Lord and sing praises to Your name O Most High; to declare Your lovingkindness in the morning, and Your faithfulness every night.* As he continued reading, he found it to be the spiritual nourishment he needed that filled his morning.

At ten-thirty, he began walking the six blocks down toward the towering white spire that could be seen from anywhere in Destiny. In the morning sun, the cross on the spire's apex projected and gleamed against the deep blue sky, welcoming any and all, no matter what their sin. Before entering the church, he paused to sit on a bench at the corner across the street at Main and Magnolia to watch the families exit their Hudsons and Valiants...men in their hats and black suits, women wearing colorful dresses, white pumps and stylish hats and children in their Sunday best. They walked together with a sense of dignity as a family; but perhaps the children might then break off, to chase and tease one another, only to be corralled and lovingly chastised for their behavior before entering the sanctuary. And it was after following that perfect picture of a family with his eyes and listening to the chimes play *Fairest Lord Jesus* did Travis become emotional as he conjured up memories of those days in 1947 Hurley, Indiana.

SOUTHERN PSALMS

Part Two

Trust in the Lord and do good; dwell in the land and feed on his faithfulness. Delight yourself also in the Lord, and He shall give you the desires of your heart.

Psalm 37: 3-4

CHAPTER TWELVE

IN THE BEGINNING

It was that Saturday of Labor Day weekend in 1947 that eighteen year old Travis Marlowe's flat head Ford blew its engine. Earlier in the week, he had bought that 40 Ford for fifty dollars, banking on the used car salesman's promise that it was in the finest mechanical condition of any car on his lot. Travis had been working at a warehouse in the Bronx that summer…that same summer of his eighteenth birthday. And it was two days after his birthday that his grandfather, the sole surviving member of his family, turned him out in the street.

"You're of age now, boy, and you need to get out on your own. I can't afford to keep you no longer."

That's when Travis moved in with his childhood friend, Billy Caniff, and his family, paying them nearly everything he made as a forklift operator for room, board and supper. No sooner than he had saved enough to buy the Ford, he announced to Billy's family that he was setting out for Colorado the next week, hoping to find both job and adventure, perhaps in the mining industry. He was tired of the city life…the crowds, the high cost of living, the fumes and that walled-in feeling that New York gave him. There had to be a better life somewhere out west. A life of open spaces where he could breathe pure air and maybe not see another person for days.

But his old Ford dealt him a bum hand that Saturday on the outskirts of a place called Hurley, Indiana. With twenty-seven dollars in his pocket and a car not worth repairing, he found himself stranded on a rural route by a mailbox that read Noffsinger. After pushing his junker off the road into the ditch, all he could see was flat farmland. From the mailbox, he followed with his eyes the long dirt path that led to a plain white farm house with a red tin roof. Off to the right side of the house, was a barn and beyond that a silo. It was quiet. Almost deafeningly quiet. A slight breeze kicked up every few seconds, ruffling his black tuft of hair. The stench of cow manure and urine was magnified with each puff of wind. He remembered that day he told himself he wouldn't mind not seeing another person on any given day…and here was that day. Only he wasn't in Colorado.

He did see a sign about a quarter mile back that read *Hurley 1 Mile.* Civilization. Grabbing his suitcase from the trunk, he then began walking. It *wa*s a nice day, maybe seventy and blue sky, meaning low humidity. Whoever wanted the car could have it.

Suddenly, behind him he became aware of the clop-clop-clopping of horses' hooves on asphalt. Turning to look, he was amazed to find a black buggy of sorts being pulled by a beautiful roan. Driving the carriage was a man in a white shirt and large brim black hat. He had seen such a man and rig not only in pictures, but on that day two years ago when he found himself in Central Pennsylvania. The word *Amish* came to mind. When the horse came even with Travis, the driver pulled on the reins.

"Good day, friend," he said. "I take it that is thy car back there."

"Yes. You can have it if you want."

Travis thought he saw an attempt at a smile on the stern man's bearded face. "I would have no use for it. This is my mode of transportation. Never breaks down."

Travis did smile. "And I could use such a mode right about now."

"Thee would be heading into Hurley?"

"Some place I can stay for the night and have a meal, all for twenty-seven dollars. And after that's gone, I guess I'll hitch-hike to Colorado."

"Colorado is a long way, friend. And thee will have to eat along the way. If thou wilt climb aboard, I can take thee as far as my store. It is perhaps a quarter mile from the town."

"Thank you. I'll take you up on it."

After sliding onto the buggy's seat beside the driver, Travis shoved out his hand and said, "My name is Travis Marlowe."

"Ah, and a strong Christian name it is. I am Jacob Oberhauf." He then shook Travis' hand. "I hope thee finds what thou art looking for."

"So do I. This is just a bump in the road, I hope."

As the horse chugged along, Oberhauf had little else to say. But, when they pulled into the parking lot at Oberhauf's General Store, he said, "This is my place. Thou art welcome to come in and get something cold to drink."

"Thank you, I will. And thanks for the lift."

Oberhauf touched the brim of his hat and stepped from the buggy. Travis followed him inside and then he set his suitcase down to look around the store. It had nearly everything. There was much more than just fresh fruits, vegetables and cheeses. He saw rockers and tables, shirts, pants and simply-made dresses. And an entire section of fruit and cream pies, candies, molasses chews and chocolates of every sort, and cookies galore. A large sign on the wall read *All things handmade made by God and the Amish people.*

Jacob Oberhaus then went directly behind a counter where a young woman about Travis' age was tending the customers. Wearing a plain light blue dress and a white linen cap of sort, she might have had the most beautiful face he had ever seen. Even without make-up, her features were impeccably perfect. Once, she looked his way and smiled, which caught him a bit off guard. It prompted him to approach Mr. Oberhauf who was standing within a dozen feet of her and ask, "Can you tell me that girl's name, sir?"

"It is Sarah, friend. She is my daughter."

"Forgive me for being so abrupt, but she is beautiful... absolutely beautiful."

Oberhauf's eyes then bore down onto Travis like two hot pokers. "She is beautiful inside as well. Do not look upon another by the way she looks outwardly."

"I...I didn't mean to..."

"No need to stutter, English." And then there was that slight smile again. "She takes after her mother in looks."

Sarah was standing so close to them, she could not help but overhear their conversation. Travis saw her face flush and then she turned her eyes back to a lady customer. When she had finished serving the woman, her father then said, "Sarah, I believe this young man standing here with his mouth open intends to make thy acquaintance. His name is Travis Marlowe, passing through our community on his way to Colorado."

She smiled again and then dropped quickly into a slight curtsy. "Good afternoon, sir. Welcome to our store."

Returning her curtsy with a rather clumsy bow, he shifted his feet around nervously, replying "I apologize for staring earlier, but you are...well drop-dead gorgeous."

It was a brash line straight from the streets of New York that obviously did not set well with Oberhauf. "I think Mr. Marlowe might like a sample of some blueberry pie before he moves on, Sarah."

"Yes, of course," she said, continuing to blush. "And I thank you for your compliment." She then severed a small piece of the pie with a serving knife, placed it on a small paper plate and handed it to him.

Travis immediately recognized upon hearing her talk that she did not altogether adopt the Old English Amish manner of speech. There were no thous, thees and thys.

It had been nearly eight hours since his breakfast of a muffin and coffee and he tried not to devour it like a ravenous animal in front of them. "Wow. This is fantastic. The best I've ever tasted."

"It, along with other of the fruit pies, was made by the Yoders who live close by. Do you want to take a pie with you? Only seventy-five cents."

He shook his head. "I'd probably eat the entire pie in one sitting. Better that I save my money for supper in Hurley."

"Will you stay in Hurley long?"

"Actually, I intended to only spend the night and make my way on to Colorado. The gold-filled streams await me. I'm not so sure now."

She assumed from his leering eyes and dialogue that any delay of his travels might be on her account. It caused her to turn her head away. But then she said, "I hope whatever you decide to do, God will keep you safe."

"Thanks." He then grinned, however, keeping his eyes on her.

Oberhauf then broke in, sensing that Travis may be getting a little *too* acquainted with Sarah for his liking. "Then thee will be off now, English."

"Yes, and thank you for the sample of pie. It was good meeting you both. Again, I appreciate the ride here, Mr. Oberhauf."

He nodded, but did not reply.

With suitcase in hand, Travis continued his walk along the road that last quarter mile before he came to the sign that read *Hurley pop 4000.* Below the sign were smaller attached icons of the Lions, Kiwanis and First Baptist Church. After walking some long blocks within which sat a variety of houses, some small and neat, but a couple of stately Victorians as well, the road finally took on a more commercial aspect that included a gas station, a hardware store and a feed and seed. Deeper into the Town of Hurley on that main drag, he then came upon a Sears, Roebuck with large panoramic windows covering the entire front of the store. Displayed on mannequins were the latest in men's and women's wear which included seersucker suits, saddle oxfords, and flower patterned, cotton dresses accented with stylish wide brim hats. But then also staring back at him in one of the windows was a sign. *Experienced warehouseman needed.*

Popping his fingers, he exclaimed to himself, "Yes. Why not? Why the heck not?" Having no means of transportation, very little money and a future of uncertainty, why not get a job in Hurley, Indiana, work a while and make enough to refinance his way on to Colorado? It seemed like a nice enough town, even though a bit hokey compared to New York City. Maybe he could rent a room in a boarding house for a month or so until he was settled. But, it would only be a temporary arrangement, mind you. He would not abandon his dream of making it big in Colorado.

It was drawing on six that evening and the Sears business office was closed. But, he would be there at nine the next morning when it opened, pining for that job. As he walked further into the downtown, he stopped at the Hurley Inn, a small, but clean-appearing motel just one block off Main. Six ninety-five a night, a window fan and breakfast. It was a good deal, but he knew that tomorrow he would have to find another place that he could rent for a week or a month that didn't require much of a deposit...or in two days all his money would be gone.

After snagging a hamburger and a Coke at the Tasty-Freeze, Travis returned to his room at the Hurley, showered and lay back on his pillow listening to the radio as Frank Sinatra crooned *Serenade in Blue* and Rosemary Clooney belted out *Old Devil Moon*. And then when he closed his eyes, the angelic face of sweet Sarah Oberhauf appeared, smiling, blushing, diverting her beautiful eyes away from him. If he stayed, he would be frequenting the store as much as he could. Would he have a chance with her? Probably not. He didn't know much about the Amish, but they were a deeply religious people and only socialized within their order. *That* much he knew.

It seemed like no time at all until the morning sun found its way between the blind and window edge and planted a spear of bright light on the wall next to his bed. Checking his watch on the nightstand, it read eight-fifteen. In forty-five minutes the Sears business office would be opening. Hurriedly, he shaved, brushed his teeth, put on his Madras shirt with the fruit loop in the back, black slacks and oxfords, and then grabbed a boiled egg and piece of toast with a cup of coffee in the dining room. He would be back to check out before noon.

Promptly at nine, he stood at the door of the business office with two other chaps behind him and waited until a large set woman let them in. After giving each of them an application, she sat down at her desk and continued eating one of two donuts that lay on a saucer on her desk. The first one to complete the application would be the first to interview.

Travis found that he was not the first or second applicant to complete the form. Although he definitely had the experience from his summer job in the Bronx, he became stuck when he had to fill in the address block. He had none. If he put in his grandfather's address, that wouldn't fly. Could he not just put in a fake address somewhere in Hurley? But that would be a lie and he was not going to start his new life on a lie. So, he left it blank. Of the other two applicants, the kid his age may not have had his warehouse experience. The older man may be competition, though; he might have had enough similar jobs in the past to make him a shoe-in.

When both of the men had interviewed and departed, he heard the woman call, "Travis Marlowe."

Travis took into the office with him his application and then handed it to a thin man with a bald head and spectacles and who was wearing one of the new seersucker suits with a red bowtie he saw the evening before in the window.

"Good morning, Mr. Marlowe. Please sit down. I'm Maxey Kauffmann."

Travis did as requested, making sure he was sitting upright and not slumped.

"Hmmm, you didn't put your address on the application."

The truth was all he had. "Correct, sir. You see, I just came here fresh from New York yesterday afternoon. I was on my way to Colorado, but broke down here in Hurley. I was befriended by Mr. Oberhauf in the Amish community and in getting acquainted with this area yesterday evening, thought perhaps this might be a good place for me to settle. I plan to rent a room somewhere in town when I leave here today."

The man looked over the top of his wire-rimmed glasses and said, "I see." He then looked back at the application. "So you have experience in stocking, loading trucks and have a license to operate a forklift."

"I do, sir."

"So, why should I take a chance on a youngster like you who doesn't yet have his feet on the ground?"

"I can understand your concern, Mr. Kauffmann. All I can say is that I'm a hard worker and trustworthy. I will give you my best every minute of the work day. That's all I can promise."

"The two candidates that just left here have been in this town for several years. The boy has done stocking in a grocery store and the man has not only worked construction, but been a part of a lumber yard crew and had a variety of other jobs. How do you stack up against them?"

"I'd say the guy my age doesn't have the experience and probably never ran a forklift. The older fellow seems like he's flit around a lot to different jobs. I'd say I stack up pretty well, sir, all things considered. The difference with me is something you might not have with the other two... dependability."

Kauffmann settled back in his chair and flicked a pencil through his fingers, all the while studying Travis. "I think I like you, son. I'll tell you what. You go out and convince someone to rent you a room, then come back here with an address and a rental agreement. Then you'll have the job. Twenty dollars a week. I'd like to *take* that chance on you. You seem like a nice kid and a straight shooter. That goes a long way with me."

Travis stood and thrust out his hand. "I appreciate your confidence in me, sir. Thank you. I'll be back before you know it."

After leaving Sears, Travis stopped at a newspaper rack, stuck in a nickel and pulled out the day's copy of the *Hurley Times*. Finding a bench near the courthouse, he quickly leafed through the pages until he came to the Classifieds. As he moved his finger down the column, he stopped on *Rooms to Let*. Five listings. Two required references, so he focused on the remaining three. One listing in particular caught his eye. *Victorian on Main near downtown. Two units with shared bath. No cooking in room. Must be of reputable character. BR8-1001.*

In the back of his mind, he thought he remembered seeing the house as he walked into town the evening before. It was located about halfway between Oberhauf's and the Sears store. Maybe he saw the sign in the window, but as he wasn't looking for one, he didn't read it. Travis then took the paper to a phone booth, dropped in a nickel and called the number. A woman's voice answered.

"Hello. This is the Stanley residence."

"Hello, ma'am, my name is Travis Marlowe and I am interested in one of your rooms. May I come by to speak with you about it?"

"That would be fine. I don't conduct business over the phone anyway. Do you know where I am?"

"Not exactly, ma'am. I was wondering if you were on Main Street about eight blocks from downtown near the Sears? I think I may have seen your house."

"Yes. That's the house."

"Good. May I come by now?"

"That would be fine. I'll expect you within the hour."

No sooner was he off the phone, he turned heel and made his way back to the east on Main where he began walking at a brisk pace. In less than fifteen minutes he stood in front of the grand Victorian. The house was constructed of dark red brick, but boasted two large wooden turrets on either side.

On a huge, inviting veranda that spread completely across the front of the house, sat four rockers and large urns of red and white flowers. After he had climbed the four steps and set foot on the porch, he saw the wooden historic plaque by the door. *Stanley House, circa 1829.*

No sooner than he began tapping with the brass door knocker in the center of the door, a smallish, frail elderly woman opened the door to greet him.

"Mrs. Stanley? I spoke to you on the phone a few moments ago. I'm Travis Marlowe."

After she had looked him up and down, she motioned him in. "You sounded much older on the phone. We'll sit in the parlor."

As he scanned the foyer over which hung a very ornate chandelier, he followed her into the parlor. The drapes were dark green and a bit gothic, but the bright pink and white wallpaper tended to brighten up the room. Over the fireplace mantle hung pictures of ancient people with hard, prairie faces taken in the late nineteenth and early twentieth centuries. The furniture appeared to be of museum quality perhaps from the 1900s, but was in very good shape. It reminded him of the kind of furniture he had seen when his junior high school class took a trip to FDR's home on the Hudson.

"Please have a seat, young man. Would you like some lemonade? You look as though you've wilted from the warm sun."

"No ma'am. Thanks," he replied, trying to be as mannerly as he could.

"How long have you been in Hurley, Mr. Marlowe?"

"Exactly," he then looked at his watch, "eighteen hours, Mrs. Stanley."

"Have you taken a job here?"

"Yes, ma'am. At the Sears store. Mr. Kauffman hired me." He then thought that information might be a little premature. He hadn't landed a place to stay as yet.

"Maxey, yes. Fine man. And from where do you hail?"

"New York City. I stopped here on my way to Colorado and liked the town so much, I decided to stay and work here." It wasn't exactly the truth, but it seemed it was now in his plans.

"Is there anyone you know here?"

"As a matter of fact, yes. I have become acquainted with Mr. Oberhauf and his daughter, Rachael."

"You've been here eighteen hours and done so already?"

"Yes. On the way in."

"I do admire Mr. Oberhauf and his Amish people. I shop there occasionally for their good cheeses and pies. His people made the rockers on my veranda." She then formed a wrinkle in her forehead. "But what concerns me, Mr. Marlowe, is that you are not established here. I know nothing about you or your reputation. I suspect you do not have references."

"I imagine I could get Mr. Oberhauf or Mr. Kauffmann to vouch for me."

She chuckled with a degree of dignity. "I hardly think so. They couldn't have learned anything about you in such a short time."

"No ma'am."

"How do I know you're not a serial killer and you go from town to town doing away with older ladies like me?"

Travis *wanted* to laugh, but stifled his smile with his hand. "I suppose. Mrs. Stanley, you'll just have to believe in me."

She sat for a while and stared at him as though she were dissecting every molecule in his body. "I'm a very good judge of character, Travis...if I may call you that. I see goodness in you. I also see in your eyes a hard life to this point. You remind me of my grandson up in Indianapolis. Can I depend on you to pay me each week, to not have young girls in here and to not burn my house down?"

"Most definitely, ma'am. All I want to do is work and live a good life in this community. I am also good with my hands, having for a while worked as a carpenter's apprentice, and will help you any way I can to maintain this lovely home."

"The rent is ten dollars a week and I require a month's deposit."

Travis dropped his eyes and nibbled on his lower lip. "That...will be a problem, Mrs. Stanley. After I pay my motel bill, I will have less than twenty dollars on me."

She sighed and looked away. Then she replied, "I support several charities in this town, Mr. Marlowe. I don't need another one."

"Yes, ma'am." He then stood and said, "I thank you anyway for your time. I did enjoy the conversation. "He then turned and added, "I wish you well and hope you will find a suitable boarder." He had already entered the foyer when she called out to him.

"Mr. Marlowe, I didn't say I wouldn't take you in. I'll tell you what. You pay me ten dollars and you can stay a week. When Mr. Kauffmann pays you your first check, I will expect the rest of the deposit."

Travis smiled. "Thank you, Mrs. Stanley. Thank you for giving me your bill of confidence. I will not let you down." From his wallet, he then pulled a ten dollar bill and handed it to her.

"I'll be watching you, Travis, to see that you don't."

"If I may ask, will you make up a rental contract to close our agreement?"

She nodded. "Of course. Well, already I see a hint of business responsibility in you."

From there, Travis raced first down to the Hurley Inn to check out and retrieve his suitcase, then returned to the Sears store to meet again with Maxey Kauffman. "Mildred

Stanley's place, eh? I'm surprised she took you in without knowing you or checking references."

Travis smiled. "She's a good judge of character, sir." Which made *Kauffman* smile.

Chapter Thirteen

Sarah

Travis wasn't sure he decided to stick around in Hurley because he was at the end of his financial road or because he wanted to see more of the lovely Sarah Oberhauf. But he would be kidding himself with her, anyway. She was Amish and ingrained in her way of life. He was a drifter…English, as her father called him. Oberhauf would never allow it even if Travis *did* have a chance with her. And even so, he had only seen and talked with her for less than ten minutes. What made him think she would even want to have anything to do with him?

His room at Stanley House was small, but neat and well-furnished with a dresser, wardrobe, desk with a radio on it and a very comfortable four poster bed. Better accommodations than he had had at any point in his life. As he was making only twenty dollars a week, ten would go for the room and ten would go for food. He would have nothing else left for a while. He still had the remainder of the deposit to give Mrs. Stanley. It would be tight, but he would make it work.

There were no real rules to living there, except he would have access to the parlor, but not the kitchen in the back or upstairs where Mrs. Stanley lived. He would be quiet and not play the radio loudly. He would eat his meals out or could bring foods that did not require cooking into his room. As far as the widow, Mrs. Stanley, was concerned, she would hardly know he was there.

Travis started work that next morning at seven. His hours would actually be seven till three. A truck arrived every weekday and parked in the alley at the loading dock where Travis and two other men were to unload clothing, furniture, appliances and even candies that the store sold at the glass counter. All three men were skilled on the forklift, but most items were carried into the store by hand truck.

And that first day, that Wednesday, when Travis left work, he hustled back to Stanley House where he took a bath, put on a fresh shirt and slacks, and walked past the town entry point to Oberhauf's General Merchandise so that Sarah, the proprietor's daughter, would be fully aware that Travis Marlowe did decide to stay in Hurley. If things went *his* way, he and Sarah would become friends. Maybe even more than that.

As soon as he entered the store, she turned and looked. As she always did take immediate account of any customer coming in, this time her face actually broadcasted her surprise to find the same handsome young man she spoke with two evenings before. He could not help but notice her eyes...the eyes that gave away her delightedness to see him again. He smiled and she returned it. For a few moments he fumbled about the store, picking up apples and wrapped candies, as she waited on her last customer at the counter. When the patron had left the store, Sarah approached him. Her cheeks were slightly flushed again and her smile remained.

"Travis, isn't it?"

"You have a good memory. But so do I, Sarah."

"You didn't leave town yet."

"And I don't plan to. I've got a job at Sears and am staying at an inn on Main called Stanley House."

"I know the place. Mrs. Stanley is a sweet lady."

"I hope you don't think me forward, but I actually came here hoping to see you again."

Her smile was radiant. "You purposely came back here to see me?"

"Yes. I hope this doesn't embarrass you, but I told your father that I thought you were the most beautiful girl I had ever seen."

And then he could see that she *was* embarrassed.

"Thank you. You're not so bad looking yourself," she replied.

"I'll take that as a compliment...I think."

At that moment, Jacob Oberhauf appeared from a back room. His eyes reflected his misgiving about Travis communing with his daughter.

"Young Marlowe. I believed thee to be long gone."

"I've taken up residence in town. Have a job and everything."

"I see. Thou art here to shop then."

"Well, sir, to be perfectly honest, no. I won't get paid until Saturday, but since you all were so nice to me when I came into the community a couple days ago, I thought I'd stop by to get to know the Oberhaufs a little better."

"We do not socialize in the store, Marlowe. It is a place of business and we must tend to our real customers."

It was a statement that sent a shard of adrenaline through Travis' system. Now he knew that it would be difficult getting around Oberhauf, especially if the man realized

Travis had designs on his daughter. And thus, it wouldn't be easy cementing a friendship with Sarah. He then saw a new expression in Sarah's face besides a deeper embarrassment...a flash of ire.

"I'm sorry, sir. I don't intend to loiter or keep Sarah from her responsibilities. I...just don't know anyone and thought she could key me in on what's happening in the area."

"It is not my intention to be rude, Marlowe, but she would only be aware of happenings within our own society, not that of the English in Hurley."

"I understand, sir. I guess I need to go. But rest assured, the next time you see me I'll be a paying customer."

"I would welcome that."

Giving Sarah a final look, he saw her smile return. But it was a smile mixed with seething eyes that fell onto her father. Travis knew she might just have a few words for him after he left the store. 'Thou art a hard man, Jacob Oberhauf,' Travis said to himself.

At noon that Saturday, Sears paid Travis before its business office closed. Unfortunately, because he had started work mid-week, it was just enough for him to hand Mrs. Stanley another ten dollars and put six more dollars in his pocket to buy food for the next week. What he didn't plan to eat on in the town's restaurants or fast food stands, he would purchase at Oberhauf's to take back to his room.

At just after four, he was back at the store...this time as a paying customer. Their eyes met blissfully the moment he came in. Sarah was busy, but Travis whiled away nearly a half hour collecting a few groceries at a time until the patrons thinned out. She then motioned for another employee to take the sales counter while she tended to the one customer she hoped would come back again and again.

"Hi, Travis. So, you're really going to buy something today." She saw that he had already collected a loaf of bread, some cheese and bologna, peanut butter and jelly, several apples and a blackberry pie.

He laughed. "Well, I can't cook in my room, so I have to make do. I can get a cup of coffee at work along with a donut before I start up in the mornings. Then I guess it's sandwiches for lunch and supper."

"Hmmm. All very nutritious, I'm sure," she commented. "How are things at the Stanley House?"

"I don't see much of Mrs. Stanley. I leave early in the morning and when I get off work, I clean up and...well, come here."

"To shop for peanut butter?"

"To see you."

That caused her to smile and blush. "My father will be watching you closely, you know. You'll have to buy something each time you come in."

"If I have to spend everything I make to come here, I'll do it. By the way, where is your father?"

"He's helping his brother at the farm. You just missed him."

"He doesn't like me very much, does he?"

"I think he doesn't dislike you. He just doesn't want guys paying attention to his only daughter."

"And I'm sure there are a lot of guys doing just that."

"A few. But I just ignore them."

"But you're not ignoring me."

She laughed. It was a sweet, giggly kind of laugh. "You noticed."

Travis then looked down and shuffled his feet, timorously. "Maybe sometime we could do something together...like take a walk or have a picnic."

"My father would plant you along with the corn. Anyway, you see that he has me working in our store six days a week."

"How about on a Sunday?"

"We have services on Sunday mornings and the remainder of the day it is our custom that families spend time together, talking and praying."

"No time for troublesome English boys like me."

"We'll see." She smiled again. A smile that lit up his face. "I have a few minutes and there seems to be a thinning out of the customers. I can go outside to talk some with you if you'd like. There are some benches near where our people park the buggies."

"I'd like that."

The afternoon air was refreshing, considering a cold front had come through earlier and quelled the heat. He allowed her to sit and then he parked himself beside her. A slight breeze caused a wisp of her chestnut hair from beneath her headdress to flicker.

"What do you call the little hat you wear?" he asked her.

"It is a prayer cap. All the women wear them at certain times. Other times we wear bonnets."

"None so beautifully as you, I'm sure."

The smile was back. "You are somewhat bold with your tongue. Are all English men as candid as you?"

"Some worse, I'm afraid. I guess you don't get into Hurley very much, do you?"

"No. The only time I see the English is when they come to the store. But I'd like to know more about you. My father said you are from New York."

"Yes."

"I've studied about the city. It sounds exciting. I'd probably get run over by cars *and* people if I ever went there."

"It doesn't slow down; that's for sure."

"Do you have family?"

"Not anymore. Both of my parents are deceased and I'm an only child. I lived with my grandfather who took me in when I was fifteen. He continued to pay for my education at a parochial school where I went until I graduated and then he turned me out."

"Into the street?"

"I'm afraid so. I got a job, though, and then one day after the summer was over, I just decided to set out on my own."

"You were going to Colorado. Do you still plan to do so?"

"I'm not sure, now."

"Why do you say *now*?"

"Do you not have a clue?"

She grinned. "You mean…"

"I just want to get to know you better."

To his amazement, she laid her hand on his. "That would be difficult you know."

He turned his hand over and interlocked fingers with her. "Because of your father."

She nodded. "And our way of life."

"I'd always be an outsider."

She nodded again, but didn't reply.

For another two or three minutes, they sat without further word…her hand in his. It was a tender moment. Nothing really sensual. Just a nice feeling. He knew it would not take but a few more such moments with her that he would fall in love. And he somehow knew she might feel the same.

"I have to go back in," she said. "Will you be back next week?"

"Every chance I get."

She then squeezed his hand before releasing it and said, "I will look for you. But now you need to come back in and pay for your food. It's still sitting in you basket."

He laughed. "I actually forgot about it."

Travis followed Sarah back inside. In her dark blue pastel dress, gliding with more grace than he had ever seen in even the most refined and cultured of New York ladies, she was poetry in motion.

Sunday morning he slept late. At ten-thirty, he heard the chimes of a church bell somewhere in town playing a hymn he remembered from that parish church where his mother took him the day she received the news that that his father had been killed somewhere in France. *Great is Thy Faithfulness.* Tears began to form in his eyes. But, he shaved and dressed, then took a pastry he had bought along with a glass of the grape juice to the parlor. Just minutes later, he heard Mildred Stanley's footsteps on the creaking wooden stairs.

"Oh, Mr. Marlowe. I didn't hear you. Are you not going to church?"

"I...I didn't plan on it, ma'am."

"But you must. It is not enough for us to sustain ourselves physically...we must have the spiritual bread of life."

"Yes, ma'am. But, I don't own a suit."

"Then you will just have to get you one at the Sears store so that you can go next week."

"I'm not sure I can afford it, ma'am."

"Oh, pshaw. Don't you worry about that. I'll tell you what. Instead of that deposit you owe me, you take it and buy yourself a suit. You can still pay me from week to week."

"But, I..."

"I insist on it, Mr. Marlowe."

"Thank you, Mrs. Stanley. You're very kind...and trusting. I wish you would call me Travis, though."

"All right, Travis. And go on to the kitchen and have yourself some coffee I made this morning to go with that pastry."

Travis was moved. "Yes, ma'am. Thanks again."

"And oh, by the way. You said you were handy about the house. Perhaps you could fix the loose banister on the stairway there. I don't want to lose my balance and break a hip one day."

"I'll get right on it."

"Not today, though. It's the Lord's day. A day He rested and so should you. Next week will be fine."

"I'll be glad to do it."

She smiled and nodded gratefully. She then noticed that as he stood with his hand on the mantle, he had been perusing the photographs in frames of all shapes and sizes that were arranged neatly all the way across.

"That one is of Mister Stanley when he was maybe thirty. We were freshly married and shortly after, bought this house. That was in 1901. He's standing with our mare in front of the barn where the garage is now. He was very handsome, you know. Been gone nearly ten years now." A tear suddenly formed in her eye.

"And are these your children?" he asked. He was holding a photo of a teenage boy and girl.

"Yes. That's Polly and Matthew. When I first saw you, Travis, I thought you reminded me of my boy. Your dark hair and square jaw."

"Where are they now?"

"Polly's in Ann Arbor and Matthew…he just keeps moving around. A real free spirit, he is."

"They have good faces, Mrs. Stanley. I'm sure you're proud of them."

She smiled again and then her eyes moved to the grandfather clock in the corner. "I suppose I must get going, Travis, so I will bid you good morning. I will be going to my friend Beatrice Collier's house for Sunday dinner and will not be back until midday."

"I hope you enjoy your day, Mrs. Stanley."

He watched her as she descended the four steps from the porch to the sidewalk. She was indeed a kind lady. She reminded him in appearance of an elderly lady that lived below his grandfather's apartment in the Bronx. Except, that lady always seemed angry about something, especially about him making too much noise when he climbed the stairs over her flat or played his music too loud.

Chapter Fourteen

Mildred Stanley

Although tired from Monday's full day of work, Travis found in a tool shed on the rear grounds of the residence an electric drill, some screws, wood filler and several varieties of stain, and then set about to repair the banister on the stairs leading to the upper floor of the house. Not only had the ornate bottom post come loose from the floor, but the railing was wobbly all the way up. No sooner than he started in on the project, making a fair bit of noise, Mildred Stanley appeared on the top stoop.

"What are you doing down there?"

"Repairing the banister as you asked me to do, ma'am."

"I asked you to do that?"

"Yes, ma'am. Yesterday, on your way to church."

She looked puzzled for a moment and then smiled. "Yes, I think I remember that conversation. Go on with what you're doing."

A furrowed crease formed in Travis' forehead as he thought about the conversation and then he continued on with the repairs. By five-thirty he was done. Satisfied with its sturdiness, he then put the tools back in the shed and went to his room to take a bath. At six-fifteen he came out refreshed and settled into one of the sofa chairs in the parlor.

Momentarily, Mrs. Stanley came out from the kitchen and announced that supper was ready.

"But, the agreement was that I would take care of my own meals and not go to the kitchen and dining area."

"Pshaw," she said. "Come on in here and eat. I fried up some Swiss steak and gravy."

"It smells good. Are you sure?"

"Of course. Now, you've washed up haven't you?"

"Yes, ma'am. I've bathed and everything."

"Okay, then. Dinner is on the dining room table."

It was the first real meal Travis had had for a week. Burgers at the Tasty-Freeze, sandwiches in his room and donuts in the morning...all of that had gotten old. Besides the steak, Mrs. Stanley had mashed potatoes, green beans, hot buttered rolls and peach cobbler for dessert.

"Wonderful," he said. "Thank you for this invitation. You're treating me like a prince."

She smiled and waved him off. Then she started a dialogue about people around town like her friend, Mrs. Collier, and poor old Jimmy Houchkins who got polio like Mr. Roosevelt did when he was about his age. She mentioned Aunt Penny in Ann Arbor who was much too old to travel now and she knew she would never see her again. And then there was her daughter, Polly, who lived near Aunt Penny and was obviously too busy with her boys to where she hadn't been to see her in months. As she rattled on incessantly, Travis found that he had long since finished his dinner, but he thought it impolite to just get up and leave. However, as though she had suddenly turned off a spigot, she stopped talking and just sat staring beyond him out the window for several moments.

"I'll tell you what," he said. "If you don't mind, I'll clear the dishes and start washing them."

She then turned her attention back to him and replied, "Nonsense. It's woman's work. No man of mine ever spent time in the kitchen. Now you go on back to your room and enjoy the evening."

"But…"

"Go," she said, pointing an arthritic index finger in the direction of the hallway.

"Yes, ma'am. Thank you again for dinner."

"You're such a mannerly boy. I wish I had more like you."

Travis went back to Oberhauf's the next afternoon again after he had cleaned up. It had been since Saturday that he sat with Sarah, holding her hand on that bench. His feet couldn't carry him fast enough down Main and out of town. It was a good little walk and he thought maybe he should get one of those new Schwinn bikes Sears had put on sale that week. Maybe when he had built up his cash.

When he entered the store, he didn't readily see her. Perhaps she was in a back room. Picking up a basket, he rummaged through the store to see if there was anything he needed to take back to the room. Suddenly, behind him he heard the deep voice of Jacob Oberhauf.

"So, thou art still around, Mr. Marlowe."

"Ah, yes. Settled in at the Stanley House and working at Sears."

"Good. That tells me thou art a responsible man and no longer the drifter I perceived thee to be a week ago. Doest thou need help with anything?"

"I thought maybe I'd pick up a bag of fruit and some more cheese."

"The cheeses are over in the case. Mrs. Schlappach will slice what thee needs. Anything else?"

"Well, I don't see your daughter anywhere. I thought maybe I'd say hello."

He scowled. "She is helping her mother with canning today."

"Would you then tell her I asked about her?"

"I assume thou art asking me to do that to be polite."

"Er…yes. I'm not sure what you mean, but I don't mind telling you I enjoy talking with her when I'm in the store."

His scowl deepened. "I do not like it when she is distracted from her duties, English. I sense that thou art taken with her, but do not waste thy time. She is eighteen, an Amish maiden and forbidden to…date, as you call it…outside of our order."

"I'm sorry to hear that, Mr. Oberhauf. I would still like to be her friend and am sure mere friendship is not forbidden."

"I think that thee should concentrate on happenings in your world, English. Yes, we allow friendships to develop outside our order, but we do not encourage our children to get too close to your world. There is much influence that the impressionable young mind cannot always resist. It is the duty of the parent to keep the children focused on our faith and our customs."

"Sarah is not a child, Mr. Oberhauf. She is old enough to decide who her friends will be, inside or outside your order."

"Mr. Marlowe, I like thee. I like thy spunk and thy perseverance. But I must caution thee to not meddle in our family's business. If thou wants to stay on the good side of me, please respect my wishes."

"And I do, sir. I appreciate what you're telling me about your family. I wish my parents were not dead and I still had kin to be around. Family is most important and I would do nothing to interfere in the Oberhauf family."

"I thank thee. And I believe that."

Travis smiled. "Still, if you would be so kind to tell Sarah I asked about her."

He thought he caught a slight smile beginning on Jacob Oberhauf's face. Had it fully developed, Travis surmised that the man's face would crack open like a glazed donut.

Travis did not go back to the store for a couple of days, but told himself he would do so on Friday. For now, he would bundle himself up in his job, then either go back to his room to relax or walk around in downtown Hurley to get acquainted with the layout of the area. Actually, on Thursday afternoon, he did both.

Around ten on Friday morning, a clerk from inside the Sears store appeared at the edge of the loading dock and called out Travis' name.

Travis, who was helping another worker load a refrigerator onto the truck for home delivery, yelled back "That's me."

"Stop by the Men's Department before you leave today," the man said.

"What for?"

"Your suit."

"I didn't buy a suit."

"You must have. It has your name on it. My name's Wilson. I'll be there till five."

When he finished up on the dock at three, Travis went inside and found Wilson waiting on a customer. "Be with you in a moment, Marlowe."

Travis had no idea what the clerk was talking about. He intended to one day look at a suit, but that day was months away. Within about ten minutes, Wilson wrapped up his business with the customer and then approached Travis.

"So, what do you mean you don't know about picking up a suit?"

"Like I said, I didn't buy one."

"Well, somebody did. Only it has your name on the ticket."

"Let me see the invoice."

When the clerk handed Travis the ticket, he saw that the paid amount was $22.50. The signature at the bottom belonged to Mildred Stanley.

For a moment, Travis just stood looking at the invoice. Tears formed in his eyes. She knew he couldn't afford the suit, so she bought it for him.

"For this amount, you can choose any of these suits on this rack. There's a nice gray tweed there and an all weather black with a faint pinstripe in it. Pick one out and we'll alter it. It'll be ready for pickup tomorrow afternoon."

"I don't know what to say."

"Obviously, somebody out there likes you. Your mother perhaps?"

"No. Just a sweet, generous old lady."

Travis selected the black suit and Wilson then stood him before the set of mirrors to chalk it. He could not wait to get back to Stanley House to thank his house mother.

When Travis arrived at the inn, he stood at the bottom of the stairs and called Mrs. Stanley's name. There was no answer. He thought perhaps she was out or maybe even taking a nap. If she was out, she must have walked somewhere. Her Pontiac was tucked inside the garage at the side of the house. He called again, then gave up. He would catch her later.

Travis bathed and then took a walk to a restaurant about eight blocks further into town to take advantage of its Thursday night fried chicken special for $2.00. After his dinner, he went across the street to the courthouse and sat for about an hour on a bench that was nestled under some huge poplars. The sun had now set and the temperature of the evening was pleasant. Around seven-thirty he walked back to the inn where he found Mrs. Stanley sitting on the veranda in one of the Amish rockers.

"Good evening, Mrs. Stanley," he greeted after starting up the steps. "I came home about four and didn't find you. Didn't know if you had gone out."

"Well I've been right here all afternoon in this rocker," she replied. "You must've walked right by me."

Travis knew she had not been there and was probably up in her room taking a nap. "Anyway, I wanted to thank you for arranging purchase of my suit down at the store. You shouldn't have done that. I'll pay you back though, I promise."

"I have no earthly idea what you're talking about. A suit?"

Travis grinned. "Ah, Mrs. Stanley. You're the sly one, pretending you didn't have anything to do with the suit. I saw your name on the invoice. I'll not be forgetting your kindness."

She looked at him and smiled. "Are you hungry? Did you get yourself something to eat?"

"Yes, ma'am, I did. Thanks for asking."

"You're such a polite boy. You always have been."

That comment seemed a little strange, he thought.

"There's a chill in the air now. Do you want a shawl or to go inside?"

"I believe I will go inside. I *am* a bit cold."

He helped her from the rocker and held the door for her to enter the house. "Well, you have a good evening, Mrs. Stanley. I think I'll listen to the radio a while. There's a big band special on tonight with Tommy Dorsey and Frank Sinatra."

"I always liked those boys," she said. "Well, good night."

"Good night, ma'am."

As he had planned, Friday afternoon he walked down to Oberhauf's store, peering inside before entering to first see if Sarah was behind the counter and secondly, if her ogre dad was anywhere near. He was pleased to see only Sarah's sweet face.

When he stepped through the door, her eyes lit up. They had not seen one another for nearly a week and both had been ravenously anxious to do so. She waved to him and he flicked his fingers back at her.

"Mrs. Schlappach, would you take over for me at the register, please? Thanks."

Sarah wasted no time rounding the counter, walking to where he stood in the bread section. "I was hoping you'd be back soon," she said. She took his hand and squeezed it.

"I did come last Tuesday, but you were at home."

"Yes, my mom needed help. But, my father actually gave me your regards."

"Good. Well, do you have a moment?"

"Sure," she replied. "Let's stand outside for a while. I do need some air. As you can see, we're very busy, but we have two other employees helping customers."

"Your dad?"

"He's not here, but said he'll be back shortly."

In the parking lot were about two dozen cars along with three Amish buggies and horses. Travis and Sarah slipped to the side of the store beneath a large oak.

"I still want to get to know you a little better and don't know how or when we can have some time together," Travis began.

"Our farm is more than a hundred acres and there are nice little groves and streams on the north end. It is in the Amish settlement of Himmel. There are three such communities in our district overseen by our bishop. Maybe you can come visit our home sometime and I'll show you those groves."

"Your father would allow that?"

"You let me worry about my father. He might come on strong with other people, in and outside the order, but he turns to butter where I'm concerned."

"I would like to see how your people live from day to day and learn something about your customs and traditions. It's all very interesting to me."

"Maybe to you, but it's a hard life and when I see all of the conveniences out there in the world, I don't mind telling you I get a little envious. Of course, I'd never let my parents know that."

"So, you never intend to leave the Amish way?"

"No. It's my life and my heritage. And it's not just about our traditional values; it's also our *spiritual* values. We are deep into our religion."

"Christian, right?"

"Yes."

"I was raised Christian as well...actually Roman Catholic. But I guess I fell away from it all a couple years ago."

"Perhaps you will recommit yourself to God one day soon."

Travis nodded. "So, how could we make this happen? My visiting sometime."

"Let me approach my mother. I know she will like you. Then I'll go to my father and ask that you be allowed to visit. If he gives me any trouble, she will handle him. She can be very firm with him."

"Well, I sure don't want to cause any friction, but I really want to spend some time with you."

"And I with you."

"Do many of the young guys hit on you?"

"What do you mean hit on me?"

"Ask you out or make goo goo eyes at you."

She laughed. "One or two in our order. Sometimes an English guy like you tries to talk to me, but I pay him no mind."

"Then why are you paying me some mind?"

"I don't know. I think I saw something in your eyes I like...something different."

"I saw something in *your* eyes I like, too," he said. "Dazzling beauty."

Sarah laughed and he thought it made her eyes sparkle all the more. "I must get back. You are staying at Stanley House, correct?"

"Yes."

"I know the place."

"Come visit *me* sometime."

"I would not be allowed to do that. Even my mother would object. We don't visit with the English."

"Okay, then. Will I see you tomorrow afternoon?"

"I will be teaching the small children tomorrow and won't be in the store."

"You are a teacher?"

"Many of us are teachers. We hold classes in everyone's home just as we take turns holding our religious services in the home."

"You have no churches?"

"No."

"Interesting."

"Not really."

"Well, I'll see you again soon, Sarah. It was great spending time with you."

She took his hand again, looked around the exterior of the store and then leaned in to give him a kiss on his cheek. He had been kissed by a lot of girls in his teen years, but never felt anything like she had just made him feel.

"Goodbye, Travis." And then she went back inside.

He stood in a near stupor for a while, trying to digest that magical experience. As he walked back to the inn, he was within a block when it dawned on him that he needed some more bread and forgot to get it.

Travis picked up his altered suit on Saturday afternoon and brought it back to show Mrs. Stanley. She was sitting in the parlor staring out the window when he came in.

"My suit, Mrs. Stanley. What do you think of it?"

She turned toward him with a lost look on her face. "Why do you insist on calling me Mrs. Stanley?"

"I know your name is Mildred, but I can't call you that. What would you like me to call you?"

"What you've always called me, Matthew…Mom."

Travis was so shocked that his suit nearly slipped from his hands. "But Mrs. Stanley, you are not my mom. And my name is Travis."

"Don't be silly, Matthew. Where did you come up with such an idea?"

He didn't respond. Laying the suit aside, he went to her and picked up her hand. "Mrs. Stanley, do you not know who I am? I am your boarder who pays you for me to stay here. And out of the goodness of your heart, you bought this suit for me at Sears."

"Of course I did," she replied. "Why shouldn't I buy your clothes? You're my son."

Travis knew now that her mind had slipped and he didn't know what to do about it. Who would he call? He had no information on her family. She needed help.

"Who is your family doctor...Mom?" he asked her.

"Why Doctor Chisholm, Matthew. You know that."

"Do you have his number?"

"Of course. Why do you need it? Are you sick? If you are sick, son, we must call him."

"No, I'm not sick. I just want to have it in case I need it." He then paused. "How old am I, Mom?"

She laughed. "You're just trying to get my goat today, aren't you? Well, I'll humor you. You're fifteen, honey."

"Would you like to lie down now, Mom?"

She placed her fingers on her forehead and nodded. "I *am* a little tired. I think I will."

"Then let me help you up to your room."

She stood up and he noticed she was a bit wobbly. But she protested. "Do you think I'm an old woman? I can manage on my own."

Travis allowed her to ambulate, but he stayed close behind her all the way up the stairs in case she fell. Once in her room, she laid down on her bed and he slipped her shoes off. He then took the other half of the bed spread and covered her up.

"I'm okay now, Matthew. Let me sleep."

Once she closed her eyes, he hustled down the stairs and went to the phone in the hallway. In the small secretary against the wall, he found the Hurley phone book.

"Chisholm...Chisholm," he said in a low voice as he ran his finger down the names. "Byron Chisholm, M.D." He then dialed the number.

He heard four rings and then a woman's voice answered. "Hello, Dr. Chisholm's residence."

"Hello. My name is Travis Marlowe and I am renting a room at Mrs. Mildred Stanley's house. Is the doctor there?"

"Yes, but as it's Saturday, he doesn't take patients. Is there something wrong with Mildred?"

"I'm afraid there is. Her mind has left her, I think. She's calling me Matthew, her son."

"Oh, we were afraid this would happen one day. Even though my husband has treated her for years, she's been my friend for even *more* years. We play cards a lot and the last couple of months I've noticed she is awfully forgetful. Sometimes she puts the wrong cards down and can't even make three of a kind."

"Do you know her son's number?"

"Mr. Marlowe, Matthew died of polio when he was fifteen. She does have a daughter named Polly."

"In Ann Arbor she told me?"

"Not anymore, Polly hasn't lived there for twenty-five or more years. She only lives about ten miles from here in Farmville. I will call her and send her by. She will know what to do. Byron will also stop by. "

"Thanks, Mrs. Chisholm. I'll be here."

A few times within that next hour Travis went upstairs to check on Mrs. Stanley. She seemed to be resting well. Then, just after seven, a car pulled up in the driveway to the garage behind the old Pontiac. Travis saw a gray-haired woman about fifty-five exit the car and hurry up the steps. Travis opened the door to greet her.

"You must be Polly. No one told me your last name. "I'm Travis, your mother's boarder."

"Yes, I'm Polly Sizemore. You say my mother's ill?"

"She thinks I'm your brother Matthew and I'm fifteen years old. She was tired and I made sure she got to her bed."

"Thanks, Travis. This has happened before and now that it's once too often, I fear we'll have to put her in a rest home.

They call it dementia. She won't be able to live here on her own any longer."

"I'm sorry, Mrs. Sizemore. Your mom's a very nice lady."

Suddenly, there was a knock at the door. Travis opened it and there stood a small man with a full head of snow white hair and a doctor's bag in his hand. "I'm Doctor Chisholm, sir. May I come in?"

Travis directed him in and then the doctor saw the daughter. "Polly. It's been a while. Troubles again with Mildred, eh?"

"I'm afraid so, Byron. I haven't been up to her room yet. Shall we?"

Travis waited in the parlor as Polly and the doctor disappeared upstairs. In about fifteen minutes, he heard their footsteps on their way back down. But when he looked up from his chair, he saw that Mrs. Stanley was leading them down the hallway.

"Good evening, Travis," she said. "Did you have a good day at work?"

"Yes, ma'am. And I picked up that suit for church tomorrow. Do you want to see it?"

"Well, as you can see, Polly is here along with Byron. I didn't expect them. I'll send them off and look at it later."

Polly took a heaving breath and said, "Mom, you're going to stay with me for a few days."

"Well, I'll do no such a thing. I'm not leaving Stanley House for that long."

"I need you to help me with some things, Mom. It would mean a lot to me."

Mrs. Stanley studied a moment and then said, "If you really need me, I can't turn my only daughter down."

"I will look after Stanley House for you, Mrs. Stanley. You know you can depend on me."

"That I can. Okay, let me put a suitcase together. Now Travis, anything you want in the fridge or cupboard you can eat. I don't want anything to go to waste."

"Thanks, Mrs. Stanley. I'll also make sure the house is locked up tight when I come and go."

"And, Travis, since you're house-sitting, don't worry about paying me next week's rent."

"Yes, ma'am. Thanks."

When Mildred Stanley returned upstairs, Doctor Chisholm said, "If you need me to sign the papers for admission, I'll do so." He then turned to Travis. "And she actually called you Matthew, huh?"

"She also thought she had bought that suit for *him*."

"Somewhere in the deep recesses of her mind, she still thinks she has a fifteen year old son. She never got over the trauma of losing him over forty years ago. Now that her mind slips in and out, half the time she thinks he's still living here in this house. You know, one time when I was examining her last year, she called me Bill."

"My father's name," commented Polly. "Sometimes she also thinks of me as somewhere between eighteen and twenty, the last time I lived here. This has been a long time coming and it has now come to an end." Polly then looked out of the parlor window and said, "That's strange. There's an Amish buggy parked out on the street. You don't usually see them this far into town."

Momentarily, there was a knock on the door. Travis answered it and found a clean-shaven young man about twenty two or three standing at the threshold with a piece of paper in his hand.

"Are you Travis?"

"Yes."

"I was sent to deliver this to you." He then placed an envelope in Travis' hand and scurried off the porch to the buggy. After turning the horse around in the street, he clicked his mouth. He and the rig were gone in a flash.

Dumfounded, Travis saw his name neatly printed on the envelope. After opening it, he read the short note.

Travis,

My father and mother would like to invite you to Sunday dinner tomorrow at 1:00 at our home. Our farm is not far from the store. When you come to the store, take a left on that road and go less than a mile. You will see the Oberhauf mailbox on the right. Our house sits off the road at the top of the hill. You can't miss it. Be careful if you plan to walk. I am anxious to have you here with us tomorrow.

Fondly,

Sarah

He could have done a cartwheel off the porch. At last, he would be able to spend some real time with Sarah…under the stern, scrutinous eyes of her father, of course. But that didn't matter. The girl who may very well have become the woman of his dreams was interested in *him*. Maybe even more than just interested.

But, he had promised Mrs. Stanley he would go to church on Sunday. After all, she had bought him a suit for just that purpose. But, Mrs. Stanley wouldn't be there. And now there would be another purpose for that suit.

CHAPTER FIFTEEN

THE AMISH WAY

MOST EVERYONE WAS GETTING OUT OF church that Sunday when Travis left Stanley House for dinner at the Oberhaufs. As a few men and women dressed in their Sunday best were walking from the church house to their homes, Travis did not stand out in his new black suit, shirt and tie. That is until he left the town proper and found himself out on the country road leading to the Amish community called Himmel. After he had made that left turn at the store, he must have been passed by a dozen buggies, each filled with men, women and children on their way home from a meeting at one of their homes. They either met in a house with a large living room or in someone's barn. But Travis also came face to face with families who chose to walk back home from the meeting place.

He was struck by the plainness of a people dressed in common clothing...the married men with their Abe Lincoln beards and straw hats, the women with their calf-length dark blue dresses, white aprons and prayer caps, and the children looking sweet and innocent in smaller versions of the adult clothing. The men rarely spoke, but nodded politely or tipped their hats when they passed by. The women and children were careful to make no eye contact. Travis knew they were merely a people who just wanted to be left alone to enjoy the simple, religious life they had lived for generations. They didn't *look* happy, but somehow he knew they were. The smiles and frolicking of the children reflected that. But would it be the kind of life he would find easy to live, if he so chose? It would certainly be a stark change from the tough streets of New York where people were often pushy, loud and contentious. Even so, could he ever be able to assimilate into such a community, considering he was English? He had heard somewhere that it was possible and had been done before. And if that's what it took to get close to Sarah Oberhauf, then he would do it.

Checking his watch to be sure he was neither too early nor late, he arrived at the Oberhauf mailbox at five minutes till one. The large, white farm house sat majestically on the horizon at the end of the dirt road. Careful not to step in a wheel rut or on a horse patty, he made his way up the hill to the house where he saw Sarah waiting for him on the porch steps. She smiled and waved when he was within a hundred feet and then descended the steps to greet him.

"I was hoping you would come," she said. "My cousin Isaac said he gave my note to a man at the inn and I prayed that he did not stop at the wrong house." She then held out her hand and took his, leading him back up the steps. "You look different today."

"Different good or different not so good?"

"Handsome good," she replied and then flushed for saying it. "I have also asked my friend Mary to join us for dinner and hope you don't mind."

"If she is as pretty as you, then I definitely don't mind."

When they had gone inside, Travis found her mom and dad in their parlor standing with her friend.

"Mother, this is my friend Travis from the town."

Travis waited till she thrust out her hand and then he took it, bowing ever so slightly.

"So this is the young man who seems to be on our daughter's heart."

"Mother, please."

"It is good to make thy acquaintance. Jacob, thee did not tell me he was a nice-looking, mannerly young man."

The scowl was back on her husband's face. "All I said was that he seemed to be a decent man...for an Englishman."

If that was Jacob Oberhauf's attempt at a compliment, Travis would take it.

"And this is Mary," Sarah said.

She smiled and curtsied. "I am pleased to know you." And Travis saw that she was indeed nearly as attractive as Sarah.

"Shall we go to the table?" Deborah Oberhauf invited.

The men waited until the women were seated, then Mr. Oberhauf took his seat at the head of the table. Travis sat on the same side as Sarah opposite Mary and Mrs. Oberhauf.

Sarah's father then folded his hands and dropped his head. "Our Father, most gracious God, we are indeed grateful for Thy bounty of food Thy hands hath provided. Thou art the giver of all life and shower us daily with blessings, both great and small. Bless this food for the nourishment of our bodies as well as the hands that prepared it. We give Thee Jesus all the praise and glory. Amen."

In unison, all repeated *amen*.

At first, no one said anything. The baked chicken platter was passed around and then the bowl of mashed potatoes. The corn, green beans and squash followed. Finally, the yeast rolls. The silence continued as each began eating. But then Deborah Oberhauf opened up the small talk. "Sarah said thee were on thy way to Colorado, Travis. Is that still your plan?"

"Not right away, ma'am. And maybe never. It all depends."

"Depends on what, Mr. Marlowe," interjected Oberhauf.

He wanted to say, 'depends on whether Sarah and I become just more than friends.' Instead, he replied, "It depends on whether things work out for me here."

"And what would that be?"

"My job, the people in Hurley and even the people right here in your community."

"What doest thou want from our people?"

Deborah Oberhauf apparently thought that was too pushy of a question. She brought her disapproving eyes up to his.

"Friendship, sir. That's all," Travis replied tactfully.

"We *are* friends with the English community, Marlowe. We trade with them and enter conversations with them. But the things of their world are of no interest to us."

"Like automobiles, electricity and phones."

"Yes. We do not require such things. All we need is what we grow and make with our own hands. Anything else would be a distraction."

Mary then said, "When we grow up knowing only the Amish way of life, we have no desire to go outside to live like the rest of the world. We place our faith in God and He provides for all our needs."

"Well said, Mary," said Oberhauf.

"And I think I can understand that," replied Travis. "You don't miss anything you've never had."

"That is also well said, young Marlowe."

"Sometimes I wish I could live in a place where material things had no importance." Travis then paused before what he was about to say next. "How is it a man like me could become a part of your sect?"

Oberhauf swallowed the food in his mouth and laid his fork down. "That would not be easy for thee...in fact, rather impossible. "

"For me or for any outsider?"

"Thee must first be a believer. But then thou must vow to leave the life of thy world and all of the material things that will distract thee from thy faith and obedience to God. Then thou must learn our ways from the teaching of the elders through the Ordnung."

"The elders. Are there classes...like school?"

"After the day's work is done, one would meet with our ministers and teachers and study many things...the Amish law, our history and language and the tenets of our religion. But again, most of all, thee must be a believer. Are you?"

"If you're asking if I believe in God and Jesus is His Son, yes. I was confirmed as a Christian when I was a child and then I learned more about the Trinity in Catholic schools all the way up through high school."

"That may be a foundation, but does not mean thee are a true Christian," Oberhauf said. "The Ordnung spends much time educating thee and then after a period of time, thee must sit before the council of ministers and they agree as to whether thy answers to their questions about thy belief are sufficient for thee to come into the order. Of course, there is other education. Thee must learn to communicate in German. Thee must learn to farm and become skilled with thy hands. What skills do thee already possess?"

"I'm very good with my hands. I've never farmed, but have done carpentry work, repaired machinery and worked on loading docks, like I'm doing now."

"Thee must also be of even temperament, but authoritative as a man. Christ is the head of man and man is the head of his family. Thee must never raise your hand in anger against another being. Have thee done so?"

"Father," interrupted Sarah. "Are you not going too far with this questioning?"

Travis looked at Sarah and smiled. "I'm okay to answer that. Well, I can't say I never got into a fight when I was younger, but not since I've matured. I learned to control my temper long ago and spent any frustrations I had through the Golden Gloves."

"What is the Golden Gloves," he asked.

"Youth boxing. I was the junior lightweight champion three years ago in my ward."

Oberhauf 's eyes became more stern than usual. "Thee used thy fists to beat another boy to the ground in sport?"

"I…don't see it that way. We had gloves on our hands and no one got hurt too badly."

The table was quiet for a few moments and everyone seemed to have stopped eating to see what Jacob Oberhauf's next comment would be.

"At least thee art candid about thyself, Marlowe. Thee didn't have to tell me that. However, I see that thou doest appear to be a young man of character and manners. It would take some work with thee. I am not so sure I could give my blessing in recommending thee to the order, however."

Travis placed his napkin on his lap, sat back in his chair and locked eyes with Oberhauf. "Is there someone of authority in the Amish community who I can talk to about become one of you?"

Oberhauf sat without word for a moment, but then commented, "I didn't realize from this conversation that thee were actually serious about trying to become Amish. But if thou art, I can set up a meeting with Bishop Herrmann who addresses such matters."

"And then what is the process?"

"The bishop sits down with the elders and anyone who may be sponsoring the petitioner, after which the person is brought into the meeting to be questioned."

Travis hesitated before asking the question, but then blurted it out. "Would you sponsor me, sir?"

For a short moment, Oberhauf kept his eyes on Travis and then he looked at both his wife and his daughter. Sarah's eyes were wide in anticipation of his response. Deborah Oberhauf gave her husband a slight nod.

"I have not decided, young Marlowe. I think thee will need to prove thyself worthy spiritually. Thy belief and willingness to follow Christ at all costs is first and foremost. And then there is thy motive for wanting to become a part of our community. I am not so sure that motivation is pure. Perhaps it is merely that thee intends to become close to Sarah. Tell me now if that is the case."

"Mr. Oberhauf, I need a life of purpose. I will be nineteen years old soon and have no direction. The Colorado vision might have been more of a whim than a real desire. I'm without a family and I think that coming into the *Amish* order might just fill that void. It's important for me to be around good, honest God-fearing people...to work hard and contribute wherever I can. I've thought a lot about it the last few days and believe this is my direction."

"Thee didst not answer the last part of my question. Does thy motivation have anything to do with Sarah?"

Sarah gave her father a disapproving look in regards to the question, but she said nothing.

"I have talked with Sarah a few times, but have made sure that she was not kept from her duties at the store. I consider her to be my friend. She is the only person my age I've gotten to know. My motivation does have something to do with her. I see that she is a kind, decent and spiritual lady, much different from the girls who were my friends in New York. She is the very kind of friend I have always wanted to have. But that friendship will not distract me and keep me from my responsibilities within the Amish community if I am fortunate enough to become one of you. I hope to acquire more friends, both male and female, just like Sarah."

Deborah Oberhauf stepped in before her husband had a chance to respond. "I have listened to thee, Travis, and thee are obviously a very intelligent young man who has matured beyond his age. Perhaps that was from having a hard life to this point as well as thy religious upbringing and education. I believe thee to be sincere in what thee says. I might be speaking out of turn, Jacob, but I'm sure thou willst agree that Travis is a fine Christian lad."

Nobody seemed to be able to read Jacob Oberhauf's eyes and face as he sat pondering an answer. It was like waiting for the other shoe to drop. Each one of the table occupants, including Travis, sat nearly motionless, hands in their laps and waiting for what they hoped was a positive response from the head of the house.

"I think I am done with dinner, Deborah, and would like a piece of that banana cream pie." He then paused to look at the other four at the table whose faces anticipated a more relative answer. But then Sarah's father surprised them all by saying, "And I *will* speak to the brethren about young Travis here."

Travis smiled, closed his eyes and allowed his head to fall back in relief. "I'm grateful, Mr. Oberhauf. Immensely grateful. I will not disappoint you."

"It matters not whether thou doest or does not disappoint me. But if thou art genuine, I do want to see thee get a chance."

The sun had come out again in Sarah's face and this time she gave her father a tender smile of approval. But then, careful that her father did not see it, she reached to her left and caressed Travis' hand. He squeezed back. Maybe he *did* tap dance a little through his explanation as to why he wanted to join the Amish fold, not telling the exact whole truth. It *was* mostly about Sarah.

Travis did not want to over-stay his welcome since the Oberhaufs did not ask him to spend the afternoon; so, after they had sat for a half hour or so wanting to hear more about Travis' early life, he thanked Sarah's parents for the wonderful dinner and their gracious hospitality. Deborah Oberhauf was still taken with Travis' deportment for such a young man. She would pray that the ministers would consider him worthy to become a member of their community.

Although Travis did not get to spend much time with Sarah, he knew or at least *hoped* there would be many days in the future that he *would*...that is, if he was confirmed by the order of brethren. With a spring in his gait, he retraced his steps back to Stanley House, passing several members of what he prayed would be his new community. When they saw his smile, even the hardest of faces smiled back at him.

But as he continued on, he began to wonder just when it was he would be 'boarded' by the Amish assembly of brethren. The only reservation he had about being taken in by the Amish was the fact that Mr. Kauffmann at Sears would be disappointed he stayed on the job for that short of a time. Travis did promise a commitment in return for Kauffmann taking a chance on him. And then there was Mrs. Stanley, who on any given day might mistake him for her son, then the next recognize him as Travis, her boarder. But then again, what was in store for *her*. He fully expected that if she did return to Stanley House, it would only be long enough for her to gather what she wanted to take with her to a rest home.

Chapter Sixteen

Harvest Moon

That next week was relatively uneventful. The routine continued. Work at the Sears loading dock from seven till three, back to the inn for dinner alone on three of the evenings and visits to the Oberhauf store the other two afternoons to steal a few moments with Sarah. Her father had promised that he would approach the bishop and deacons about setting up a meeting with Travis, but either he had not done so by the end of that week or the order of brethren had not set a day and time that it would happen.

"You'll just have to be patient, Travis," Sarah told him. "My father is a man of his word. He just tells me that things happen on no specific timeline nor with any sense of urgency."

The one day that Jacob Oberhauf was in the store when Travis stopped by, the two men merely spoke to one another cordially without any mention of a meeting. Maybe that meeting would not even happen that year.

That next Sunday morning, Travis found Mrs. Stanley's Bible, put on his suit and walked to the church with the chimes for service. As he had only been to Catholic services in the

Bronx, he was rather apprehensive about attending the Lutheran church at the corner of Main and Central Avenue. Once inside, he saw there was no pedestal of holy water, no colorful stained glass windows and Jesus was not hanging on the cross above the pulpit. The minister had no robe and the congregation was not leaving their pews to receive communion. To him, it was all very mundane. But then it was also a prelude to the kind of service he might experience in the Amish settlement. Sarah had explained, however, that men and women worship in separate rooms of the houses and no musical instruments were played. Pianos and organs were symbols of the secular world and considered distractions to true worship. But whatever religious experience lay ahead for him, he was ready for it.

After a Sunday blue plate lunch at the restaurant on Main, he returned to Stanley House to find Polly Sizemore in the parlor going through some papers in the secretary.

"Hello, Travis, you must have gone to church."

"Yes, ma'am. I hope you don't mind. I don't have a Bible, so when I saw your mother's sitting on the coffee table, I borrowed it."

"I'm glad you did." Her brow then took on a frown. "Mom has spiraled now into what they call a catatonic state. She just sits looking straight ahead and hasn't said a word for several days. I'm afraid this is the beginning of the end for her. But, she's lived a good life these eighty-four years."

"I'm very sorry, Mrs. Sizemore. She has been a kind and generous lady to me…bought me this suit and befriended me in many other ways. She always took time to talk with me in the evenings."

Polly nodded and tears began to well up in her eyes. "The first couple of days at my house she asked where Matthew was and why he hadn't come along. My husband and I plan to admit her to a geriatric facility where she can get good medical care."

Travis dropped his eyes and became somber. "I know she loved this place and it's a shame she'll not be coming back to it."

"We're going to put the house up for sale and have an estate auction on the furniture. That being the case, you will soon have to give up your room. As I know you were kind and caring where it came to my mom the short time you've known her, if there is anything in the house you would like, please ask me about it."

Travis shook his head. "Where I hope to be going, I will not be owning any possessions."

"And where is that?"

"I am attempting to become a member of the Amish sect."

An expression of surprise formed on Polly's face. "Really? Why?"

"It's the people. They've shown me genuine friendship and I have felt very comfortable when I'm around them. And as I have seen so much materialism and the value people place on it, I feel that a simple life in a spiritual environment, even without the conveniences, is what I've been looking for."

"I see. Well, to each his own and I hope that kind of life will make you happy. I know I couldn't do it, but I respect those who live that way."

"I hope to hear something soon as to whether they'll accept me as an outsider, so the timing might be right with my leaving Stanley House."

"Travis, I know you don't want anything from the house, but I would like you to take Mom's Bible."

He smiled. "Thanks, Mrs. Sizemore, but it would be something you might want to hang onto. It is a part of her... part of her mind and spirit that you would have forever."

"I will have my photos of her and my memories and really don't need something that would just lay around collecting dust. Take it, Travis. You said you didn't have one. You'll definitely need it if you move in with the Amish."

Travis paused a moment and ran his hand over the well-worn cover. "Okay then. I will take it and treasure it. Thank you."

"I guess I've done about all I can here for the day. We will contact a realtor tomorrow to put it up for sale. I have a completed Power of Attorney to do so. You are welcome to stay here, Travis, until it does sell. Make yourself at home. Be sure to let me know when you leave for good. And Travis?"

"Yes, ma'am?"

"Don't worry about the rent. You staying here and looking after the place will be payment enough. Mom would agree to that. And here's my number if you need me for anything."

"Again, thank you. You're very kind."

Polly then left and suddenly the house was quiet and lonely again. It would be a long afternoon and the anticipation of hearing back from Jacob Oberhauf or an official member of the order would make the coming days seem even longer.

Travis learned that the brethren who would be interviewing him were consumed with the harvest along with every other member of the community. The apples were right on schedule for early October, but the sweet corn, squash and grapes were late. And now that it was time to harvest them, the work on the farm was even busier. Sarah told him that once the crops were in, the ministers and deacons would be contacting him.

Mid to late October would be a busy canning time for the women. Everything from corn and beans to applesauce and jams would go into the canner. And it was an involved process what with the lid lifting wands and seals, the labeling and bubble freer. That which didn't get stored on the shelf for family consumption would go to sale at the store.

† † †

On the third Saturday evening just after Oberhauf's General Merchandise closed, Travis sat on the bench outside the store and waited for Sarah. Although she was not allowed out after dark, her father said it was all right if he walked her home. And that was a surprise to both Travis *and* Sarah.

But when both father and daughter stepped from the front door, Oberhauf walked to where Travis was sitting and took a seat beside him.

"All right, my young English friend. I have news. Our Sunday service is at Noffsinger's house tomorrow and will conclude at noon. Thee should remember it is where I first found thee on the road. I have been asked to inform thee that the bishop, our community's minister and two of our deacons will speak with thee there."

Travis clicked his fingers and responded with an excited "Great!"

"I don't mind telling thee it may be an intense process, Travis. Thou wilt be asked a great number of questions and thy responses will provide them with insight as to whether thou art worthy. Thy spirituality and devotion to God will be explored as well as thy character. There will be many questions about why thee wants to join the Amish people." He then paused. "And I will advise thee to leave Sarah's name out of it."

Travis smiled sheepishly. "Yes, sir."

"And as I will act as thy sponsor, do not embarrass me, young man."

"I understand. Would never do that, sir."

Oberhauf then held out his hand and Travis shook it. "Now keep my daughter safe on that road as thee are walking her back. The sun has set and it gets dark sooner this time of year. Some of the young hoodlums in their Pontiacs and Mercurys are prone to speeding without regard to people walking."

"I will protect her with my life." Travis then smiled at Sarah.

Oberhauf then went to his horse tied up at the hitch rail and fed her an apple. After attaching the rig to her leather straps, he mounted the buggy seat and with a flick of the reins yelled "Hee-yaah!"

As the light of day faded quickly, the blood orange October moon in its full stage shone brightly on the eastern horizon. When Oberhauf's buggy disappeared ahead of them on the road from sight, Travis took Sarah by the hand. It was a small, tender hand, he thought, velvet to his touch.

They were quiet for a while, both inhaling the sweet, cool fall air and occasionally exhaling a noiseless sigh. Finally, she said, "My father has a rough exterior as you know; but, he likes you. He told me how he believed you to be a respectable young man despite you being a New York City boy; but he wished you were of German descent and had grown up Amish."

"He said that?"

She nodded. "You shouldn't have any trouble with the brethren…that is if your New York accent and slang expressions don't come out."

Travis laughed and squeezed her hand. "I do want to make the best impression. And although I will never be true Amish, I want to be a part of the community and live the Amish way."

She stopped and looked at his face illuminated by the moon. "I hope you mean that and you're not joining our order just because it will make it easier to be with me."

"I've thought long and hard about it, Sarah. I now know that I want this kind of life in the worst way." And then he grinned. "But you, my dear, I consider a bonus."

She grinned, searched his eyes with hers and then leaned in to give him a kiss. This time on the lips. If he wasn't in love before, he sure as heck was now.

The next morning, that pivotal Sunday, when he would be grilled by an assembly of Amish elders that could change the direction of his life forever, he sat in the parlor at Stanley House in deep thought. For sure, this was an opportunity for a new and different life. But, was he not just acting on a whim and could he give up all of the conveniences he enjoyed these first eighteen, almost nineteen years of his life? Electricity, automobiles, the latest music on the radio, the luxury of coming and going as he pleased, and the opportunity to just pick up and travel anywhere he wanted at any time. He knew he wouldn't miss the New York kind of life, but he rather liked this new, small town atmosphere. And after all, was his decision to go Amish mainly because he was just enamored with these people… especially one Sarah Oberhauf who he would see more frequently? If he *were* approved to join the order, he knew that hard work was ahead. And because he *was* who he was, there would be no going back. If he was anything, he was a man of commitment. But what about the Sears job? He had committed to Mr. Kauffmann. Would he not be breaking a promise to a man who had taken a chance on him?

Before him on the coffee table lay Mrs. Stanley's Bible. Actually, it was *his* Bible, now that her daughter had given it to him. Slowly he picked it up and began strumming his thumb over the edges of the gold-leaf pages. It fell open to Romans 12.

I beseech you therefore, brethren, by the mercies of God, that you present your bodies a living sacrifice, holy, acceptable to God, which is your reasonable service. And do not be conformed to this world, but be transformed by the renewing of your mind, that you may prove what is that good and acceptable and perfect will of God. For I say, through the grace given to me, to everyone who is among you, not to think of himself more highly than he ought to think, but to think soberly, as God had dealt to each one a measure of faith. For as we have many members in one body, but all the members do not have the same function, so we, being many, are one body in Christ, and individually members of one another.

The passage not only seemed to describe what was on his heart, but how he envisioned himself as a member of a Godly people. Hopefully, Mr. Kauffmann would understand and not be angry. However, if he were confirmed into the order, would he ask for a delay in joining? Perhaps till the beginning of the New Year? He owed it to Mr. Kauffman. It was the right thing to do. But, was it God's will? Was *any* of this God's will? And if so, did God have His own time table for him?

Suddenly, the quietude of the morning was broken by the chimes at Redeemer Lutheran. As the nostalgic melody rang through the streets of Hurley, the words to the music somehow came back to him.

All to Jesus I surrender; all to Him I freely give. I will ever love and trust Him; in his presence daily live. All to Jesus I surrender; humbly at His feet I bow. Worldly pleasures all forsaken; take me Jesus, take me now. I surrender all. I surrender all. All to Thee, my blessed Savior, I surrender all.

Was the song meant for him? Was it God's way of sending him a message? Travis could not remember the last time he had prayed. Maybe it was when he learned his mother had been killed. He had sat in his room, denying it was so, bargaining with God, *praying* that it was not so. But as he sat in Mrs. Stanley's soft, plush easy chair, he leaned forward and placed his head in his hands. From his heart it came in a gush. A long, deep and earnest prayer. A prayer for direction.

Chapter Seventeen

Third Degree

Travis wanted to show his promptness by being at the Noffsinger house exactly at one o'clock. However, it appeared that the service at the house was not yet over. More than two dozen buggies and horses were still secured to a series of hitch rails in perfect alignment at the edge of the pasture adjacent to Noffsinger's large red barn. The afternoon sun which had long since taken the chill off the morning had warmed the air to near seventy. As Travis settled into a rocker on the porch, he basked in its warmth. From his pocket he took a white handkerchief and wiped the dust from his shoes that had accumulated from his nearly two mile trek. Inside the house, he suddenly heard the voices of men singing a song in words that he did not recognize…German, he thought. When the voices ceased, someone with a deep, guttural voice chanted a prayer and then Travis heard the rumble of shoes on the hardwood floor grow louder as the men and boys began to file out the front door. Several of them carried with them the backless benches they had been sitting on. A few moments later, the women and girls followed. Each of the men eyed the kid in the worldly suit curiously and nodded.

Finally, Deborah and Sarah passed through the door. Both offered smiles, but before Sarah left the porch, she touched Travis on the hand and smiled. "Break a leg," she said and then turned to accompany her mother. It was a comment straight out of the movies; and where she would have heard it, he couldn't guess. But, it made him smile.

Momentarily, Jacob Oberhauf appeared on the porch. "Ah, Travis. Thou art here. My apologies, but our service ran longer than usual. Come inside."

Travis, with Bible in hand, followed the taller man into the Noffsinger parlor where three other stern-faced, bearded men were standing. "Travis Marlowe, I want thee to meet our bishop, Karl Herrmann, our Himmel minister, Nells Strubhar, and Deacon Averill Zehr."

Bishop Herrmann shook his hand first and then the others. "Won't thee have a seat there," Herrmann said in a thick, Bavarian accent.

Travis sat and saw that Jacob Oberhauf also took a seat. "I am a deacon as well, Travis," he said. "I will be sitting in the meeting not only in my official capacity, but as thy sponsor."

"I believe we should make quick work of this, if we rely on Herr Oberhauf's recommendation," remarked the bishop. "So, I will begin. I have been told thy history from Jacob here, Mr. Marlowe. Thou art from New York and of Roman Catholic background. As thee hast expressed a desire to become part of our order, thee must realize not growing up as Amish may present some problems for thee."

"I have thought long and prayed hard about that, sir, but am ready to meet the challenge. I have not had much structure or discipline in my life and have needed it. Neither have I had a family since early on. I need both."

"And thee believes thee can find it with us."

"Yes."

"Then first let's talk about thy faith. I'm not sure that thee would be a true believer, coming from the Catholic Church. We are Anabaptists, believing that we are saved only by the grace of God. We believe in the Trinity...Father, Son and Holy Spirit. Three persons in the Godhead. Doest thou believe that?"

"Yes I do."

"We take issue with the Catholic faith in many ways. We do not believe that Mary is the Mother of God, although she was the earthly mother of the Christ. We do not believe in the infallibility of the Pope. And when we communicate with God, it is directly and not through a priest. You having a Roman Catholic background, is it possible for thee to accept that?"

"I will say these are beliefs I have always struggled with and they are not necessarily part of my Christian foundation."

"I see. Have thee personally accepted Jesus as your Savior and that He alone sacrificed Himself by taking thy sin upon Him?"

"Yes."

"And that it is only through believing He did so, thou wilt ever see Heaven."

"With all my heart."

"Hast thou been baptized?"

"I was sprinkled when I was a baby."

"That is not the same thing. We believe in the sacrament of baptism. Would thee agree to be baptized based on thy profession of faith?"

"I would."

"Doest thou believe in eternal security?"

"I am not sure what that means."

"Let me be clearer," said Herrmann. "Doest thou believe that once thou art saved, thou art saved forever?"

"Yes. I think I believe that."

Strubhar then interjected. "That is not what we believe, Mr. Marlowe. Thee would be not only arrogant, but ignorant to believe that."

"Again, I'm not sure I understand."

"A man can backslide and lose his faith. When he does so, he is not secure with God. He can find himself in hell if he commits more sin by not keeping the commandments."

"Then can I ask you a question?"

"Thee may of course," replied the bishop.

"It seems to me a man would then have to keep getting saved over and over. We all sin...even us Christians. Would it not be redundant to keep going in and out of God's graces? If we accept Jesus as the Savior and believe in Him, doesn't the Bible say we are then saved? If that is not the case, then John 3:16 is nothing but a myth."

"Thou darest blaspheme the scripture, Marlowe?" said Strubhar.

The bishop then held up his hand to Strubhar and said, "I think young Marlowe should not be ostracized for his belief in this area. This does not make him less a Christian."

Deacon Zehr then asked, "How would he then be able to join our religious order if his doctrine in Christianity differs from us?"

Jacob Oberhauf then broke in. "I suggest that if we ask the men and women in our own order what they believe, we might even get different answers as well."

"But, we preach and teach our doctrine to all and we must assume that everyone is of one accord in what we believe."

"I think Herr Oberhauf has a point here," said the bishop. "In thine hearts and in the sight of God we are all Christians. It will be up to Him on Judgment Day whether any of us will measure up. I believe we should end the questioning about our beliefs and concentrate on Herr Marlowe's motives." He paused for a moment. "Travis, thou mayest have heard many of us speaking German, which is our traditional language. We would require thee to learn the language as well. Art thou willing to do this?"

"Yes, sir. Does that mean I will have to adopt all of the thees and thous?"

Oberhauf almost smiled. "No. But, thee would be attending classes with our children who are taught the foundations of both English and German."

"I would go to school with the children?"

"Yes. Thee wouldst work on the farm during the morning and then around two o'clock go to class."

"I have no problem with that."

"Art thou a skilled craftsman of sorts?" asked Zehr.

"I have experience working as a carpenter...actually a carpenter's apprentice."

"Good," said Bishop Herrmann. "We are always in need of repairs to our homes and barns. But let me change the subject and go back to what thee told us in the beginning. Thee said thee needs structure, discipline and family in thy life. Thee can find that most anywhere in thy own world. It doesn't tell me why thee hast come to us, requesting to become a *part* of us."

"I had never thought much about the Amish people, although this is not my first experience with the order. I used to go from New York down to Philadelphia a lot and sometimes would go just west of there to Lancaster County. Sometimes I would visit their stores and watch them go about business in their buggies. I knew they did not have all of the conveniences and because of that had a harsher life, but they always seemed contented...even happy. And when I got to know Mr. Oberhauf and his family, I saw they were rich beyond what most people in the outside world could ever be...even though the outsiders might have more money than they could ever spend. You are a people with good hearts. You live a life of honor and respect. God and family are foremost. Why wouldn't I want to live that kind of life?"

Herrmann nodded and smiled. It was the first time in the meeting anyone had smiled. "I must say, Travis, thee appearest wise and well spoken beyond what I would have guessed considering thy young years. So, doest thou have questions for us?"

"Yes, sir. If I am fortunate to become a part of your community, where would I live? I don't own property nor do I have money to purchase land and build a house."

"That will not be a problem. If thou art confirmed, I have arranged for thee to stay on my brother's farm which is about five miles to the north. His wife died last year and it is only he and his son Seth now. He needs much help and would welcome thee wholeheartedly."

"Thank you. That's kind of him to offer. But the second question is...when you would expect me to physically join you?"

"Anytime thou art ready. It sounds as though thee may even be ready now."

"Well, I'd like to wait for at least another month if that's all right. You see, I took a job with Sears in town only two and a half weeks ago. Mr. Kauffmann hired me when I had no home or references. I work the loading dock. I made a commitment to him and feel an obligation to give him a few more weeks rather than leaving him high and dry. If it were not for that, I would be here tomorrow..." Travis then raised his eyebrows. "That is, if you all agree to take me in."

"I find that admirable, and it says a lot about thy character. I can't say at this time if thou *wilt* be confirmed. This community has never taken in an Englishman and I am not sure if our brethren want to set a precedent. Just as with Mr. Kauffmann, we know little about thee. Only what thee told us."

"I understand. Then when will I hear from you?"

"Herr Oberhauf will advise thee. I know that thou wilt see him soon as thee regularly frequent the store for some reason." He then smiled at Oberhauf, but the smile was not reciprocated.

Travis stood and held out his hand. "Then I thank thee... you for your consideration."

Herrmann nodded. "God be with ye, young Marlowe, whatever the decision."

"Whatever the decision," Travis repeated. And then after shaking the other men's hands, he left.

It seemed like an even longer walk back to town. In a way Travis felt good about the interview with the brethren, but he wasn't sure about Minister Strubhar. Or even his own sponsor, Jacob Oberhauf. If it required a unanimous vote, he knew he wouldn't be in. In his head, Travis argued with himself all the way back to the inn about whether the vote would be yea or nay. The bishop obviously knew about his feelings for Sarah because of the comment he made..."as thee regularly frequent the store for some reason." And then there was his look and smile at Oberhauf. But no one came out and asked the question "Is thy true motive to become part of our order Sarah Oberhauf?" Maybe Sarah's father told the bishop about Travis and Sarah. But as the community *was* close-knit, he wouldn't have been surprised that there existed the same kind of gossip mill as in *his* own world.

Travis did not go by Oberhauf's store on Monday. He *was* a little tired, but he also felt that it might be too soon to make an appearance there the day after his meeting. Actually, the more he thought about it, perhaps he was just afraid to come face-to-face with Jacob Oberhauf for fear of receiving the bad news.

The house seemed even quieter and lonelier than ever that evening. Around eight he walked further down town for something to eat. Nothing was open except the Tasty-Freeze. As he sat eating a hot fudge sundae, he was set to wonder if he would ever be allowed to go into town at all, should he be confirmed. He had seen a few of the Amish in town trading with the English, but as he would be at Mr. Herrmann's mercy as regards transportation, he may not see civilization for a very long time. But if that was the case, so be it. He could get his ice cream at Oberhauf's.

Then another thought struck him. If Bishop Herrmann's brother lived five miles to the north, according to his calculations, the store would be nearly six miles from his new home. Again, time, transportation and opportunity would be factors. He may be seeing Sarah even less. And then another stroke of reality hit him. Would he even make any money on the farm? How would he sustain himself… and where would he get his clothes? He couldn't wear the English clothing. Why didn't he already have these questions in mind to ask in his meeting with the brethren?

Travis did walk to Oberhauf's after work on Tuesday, catching Sarah's eye immediately upon his entry. If the decision had been made about him, he couldn't read it in her face. She smiled, however, like she always did and then in a few minutes she shook loose at the counter and came to him.

"Hi," she said. "I kind of expected you yesterday."

"I wanted to come by, but I was a little tired. How are you?" It was small talk to evoke some type of response from her about the boarding. But then again, maybe her father didn't convey the result to her one way or the other. So, he didn't press it.

"Well, anyway, I'm glad you're here today" she said. "I'll try to get some help at the counter so that we can go outside and talk."

"Thee wilt have to wait thy turn," came a voice from the other side of the aisle.

"Father. I didn't know you were already back."

"Hello, Mr. Oberhauf," Travis greeted. "Does that mean you want to talk to me?"

"It does," he answered somewhat sternly. "Wilt thou come outside with me?"

"The last fellow that wanted me to step outside with him wanted to fight." As quickly as the words were out of his mouth, he wished they weren't. "Sorry, sir. I was just making a joke." Then, he wished he hadn't said *that* as well.

Oberhauf glared at Travis and said, "Let's go, young Marlowe."

Once outside, Travis jumped the gun. "You...have an answer for me, I take it."

"It was a three to one vote, Travis. One dissenter. It must be unanimous."

"Oh," Travis said with a dejected tone. "Well, I thank you for sponsoring me anyway, sir." He then put out his hand. Oberhauf did not take it.

"However," Oberhauf continued. "The bishop liked thee very much and told the lone dissenter that he was over-ruling the *nay* vote. Thou art one of us now, Travis." And then he put out *his* hand.

Travis threw back his head, closed his eyes and grinned. "Thank you, Lord."

It was then a smile broke out on Oberhauf's face...a *real* smile. "Well, I'm not thy Lord, but I *will* take a little of the credit."

"I...I didn't mean to infer..."

"I know, Travis. It was a joke. I can make one as well."

† † †

On the third Friday morning in November, Travis rapped on Maxey Kauffmann's door. Kauffmann looked up over his glasses and seeing it was Travis, he said, "Come in, Mr. Marlowe. What can I do for you? Please sit down."

"Well, sir, I want you to know I have enjoyed working here these weeks."

"Which always translates to 'But, I'm quitting.' Is that correct? Are you quitting me for a better job?"

"It's not like that, Mr. Kauffmann. I know you went to bat for me...hired me when you knew nothing about me except that I was more or less a vagabond."

"So you do have another job."

"No. Not exactly."

"Not exactly? You either do or you don't."

"I'm...going to live with the Amish people...will actually become one of them."

Kauffmann broke out into laughter. "You're kidding, of course."

"I'm serious, Mr. Kauffmann. That's why I'm here and to give you my two week's notice."

"I've never heard such a thing. I know from time to time a lad leaves that bunch wanting to get out into the real world; but, I've never known anyone that wanted to get *in*."

"I'd like to leave at the end of the month, sir."

"Well, I guess if you're all fired up about this, I can't hold you back."

"I do want you to know how much I appreciate you giving me the job. You came through for me when I was down almost to my last dollar."

Kauffmann stood up and extended his hand. "You did a good job for me, son. Good luck to you. And I think you're going to need it. Their world isn't like ours. But I guess you know that."

"Yes, sir."

"You can leave any time you want, Travis. I'm okay with no two week's notice."

"Then why don't I leave next Wednesday. I could use another few days of pay and I'll also need time to clear out from Stanley House."

"How is Mrs. Stanley?"

"Not well. Her daughter has now put her in a nursing home as she can no longer care for herself."

Kauffmann nodded. "I had heard she has dementia really bad. Sweet old lady."

"Yes, she is. Well, you'll see me on the dock till next Wednesday, sir."

"Good. Come say goodbye before you leave. And Travis?"

"Yes, sir."

"If it doesn't work out with those people, you can always come back to Sears. I'll make a job for you."

"I appreciate that, sir. Goodbye."

The next day, after that last Saturday of work, Travis called Polly Sizemore and told her his plans to vacate Stanley house…the day before Thanksgiving.

Chapter Eighteen

Bildung

As he didn't have room in his suitcase for his new suit, he wore it to the store that Wednesday afternoon. When she saw him dressed as she was and with suitcase in hand, her eyes lit up as they always did. This time she came directly to him and placed her hands on his. "This must be the day."

"It is. Today I start my new life. Is your dad around? I was hoping he could take me out to Mr. Herrmann's house."

"He's in the back. I can ask him."

"Well, if he can't, I'll just have to hang out with you the rest of the day."

She grinned. "You sound like that will be a chore."

"The kind of chore I could do forever."

She squeezed his hands and said, "I'll go get him."

Momentarily, Jacob Oberhauf's head appeared from the storage room. "I shall be glad to take thee, Travis. Art thou ready to go now?"

He wanted to spend a little more time with Sarah, but he wasn't going to push the envelope with Mr. Oberhauf. Now that he was in the community, he hoped there would be many opportunities to see her...and not just for a few minutes at the store during her work hours.

"Yes, sir."

"Then I will meet thee at the buggy."

Six miles in a horse-drawn buggy on a country road seemed to take a half day, although it was actually something like forty-five minutes. But during that ride over some very lovely farm country, Oberhauf opened up more than he ever had with Travis, giving him a quick schooling on bringing in the harvest, the myriad of other farm chores and the community's annual come-together on Thanksgiving Day. Tomorrow the celebration would be on the Kegler farm. Each family in the community would bring covered dishes, tea and desserts. The women spend their afternoon in a room quilting while the men congregate in two or three groups to talk about prices at the market, horses and the weather. Travis was alerted that many conversations were in German and to not be discouraged. He would pick up the language in time. Tomorrow, Oberhauf said, he would be introduced to the community who would in turn welcome him wholeheartedly.

Benjamin Herrmann, the bishop's brother, was a hard man with little to say. He had been that way since his wife died two years before. Seventeen year old Seth Herrmann had a 'tough row to hoe' around the farm, according to Oberhauf, and Travis might just be the friend he needed.

At just after five they arrived at the Herrmann farm. "Thee can see that the house and barn need much work. He will probably have thee working with him and Seth bailing the hay in the pasture in the mornings and he will know that thou needest to complete Bildung in the afternoons."

"What is Bildung?"

"Thy education, where thou wilt learn our culture and to speak German. We have many rules about conduct and custom, and thou wilt need to abide by them. Thou wilt also receive spiritual training along with the children. I would then say that if thee wisheth to get along with Herr Herrmann, perhaps thee can offer to make repairs to his house and barn. I must say, he is a good farmer, but not a very good carpenter. Well, this is thy stop. We will see thee tomorrow at the Keglers."

Travis shook his hand and said, "Thanks for your part in getting me here."

"The rest is up to thee, young Travis."

Travis thought perhaps Oberhauf would have taken the time to introduce him to Herrmann, but he clicked his mouth, turned the horse and buggy around and trekked back down the lane to the road. And there Travis stood, suitcase in hand, clad in a suit and feeling like his dad had just dropped him off to some country-fied boarding school.

Seth Herrmann, a blonde kid who was only a few inches shorter than Travis, and having heard the horse's hooves, came out to see who was there. Eyeing Travis curiously, he said, "Who are you?" Another young man who did not fully adopt the Amish manner of speech.

"Travis Marlowe. I guess I'll be living with you and your father."

"I heard something about that. Well, come down to the barn. Father will need to know you're here."

When they had walked the fifty yards down the hill to the barn, Herrmann was just coming out. "Thou art the Marlowe boy?"

"Yes, sir."

"Thee cannot be walking around looking like that. Go in the house and change."

"All I have is a couple pairs of work pants and shirts."

"Thou wilt dress according to our code. Seth has some extra pants that will fit thee. And thou wilt wear a white shirt. Thy room is upstairs across from Seth's. Now go on and get settled. Supper will be on the table at six." He then returned inside the barn.

"You'll get used to him in time. He's not the easiest to get along with, especially since Mother died," Seth said. "I do what he tells me and try to stay out of his way. If he gets cross with you, let it roll off you."

Seth had four pairs of pants...with buttons. He gave Travis two of them that were a little worn and frayed. They fit in the waist, but were about two inches short. He hadn't noticed before, but there were no zippers on Amish made pants. Nor belts. As Seth had only one pair of suspenders, Travis would have to purchase one at the store.

Promptly at six, Mr. Herrmann had dinner on the table. It was a meager supper of ham steak, beans and white bread. No other vegetable and no dessert. There was tea or coffee to drink. Few words were spoken at first, but then Travis opened up a dialogue. "What is the daily routine here?"

"We rise at five and we will work in the fields" replied Herrmann. "Thou art to go to the school at two. Tomorrow is Thanksgiving, however, and we will go to the Kegler farm at noon. The day will get me behind on my work."

"Where *is* the school, Mr. Herrmann?"

"Two miles east on the Albricht farm. Seth will take thee there."

"Do you attend as well, Seth?" Travis asked.

Seth gave him a puzzled look. "I am seventeen and have not attended for over four years."

"Does your school not go to the twelfth grade?"

"The children study for eight years," replied Herrmann sternly. "After that, they work the farm."

"I see. What studies do you have in your school?"

"English, geography, arithmetic, Amish history and values mostly," said Seth. "We also study the Bible."

"Thou wilt only receive the German, Amish culture and Bible studies, Marlowe," added Herrmann. "At least that is what my brother told me. See that thee attends each day until thou art told not to return. When thou art not at school, thou wilt work for me. I will pay thee two dollars a day in addition to thy room and meals."

"Will I have time to go to the store for personal items?"

"I will give thee no more than two hours each week to do so."

"How will I get there? It's over five miles."

"Thee cannot have the buggy as there are times I will need it. But I have three horses. Thee wilt ride the mare."

Travis became wide-eyed and laid his fork down. "But, I've never ridden a horse."

Benjamin and Seth Herrmann glanced at one another. "Then that presents a problem for thee," said the elder.

"Before the sun sets today, I'll have you riding her," remarked Seth.

"Thou wilt also learn to groom her...and the others."

Travis nodded. "Seems that I have much to learn."

Travis was agile and had a good sense of balance. He learned quickly. By dusk he had brought the horse to both a trot and gallop, handling the reins like an experienced horseman. Seth cautioned him not to push the mare since she was nearly as old as he was. Even if she trotted part of the distance to Oberhauf's, he would have to slow her to a walk about every quarter mile. But at least that evening he had two of his questions answered: the mare was his transportation and he would be paid for his work, as meager as it was.

Thanksgiving

By the time the Herrmanns, who were traveling in the family buggy, and Travis trailing on the mare, arrived at the Kegler farm, more than half of the families were already on site, setting up the long picnic tables. Sarah, who was helping place the food on the tables, looked up to see the young man, who she almost didn't recognize, riding onto the grounds with the Herrmanns, sitting tall in the saddle with his wide brim black hat partially covering his face. Trying to stifle her grin with her hand, she caught her mother's eye.

"Very handsome, he is. And I see that thou hast noticed as well."

Sarah didn't answer, but continued her part in setting the food out.

Travis dismounted and went straight to her. "Howdy, ma'am," he said, touching his fingers to the brim. "Right nice day. Isn't it?" After his western-style greeting, he then was set to wonder if Sarah even understood his manner. She had probably never seen a western movie nor did she know who John Wayne was.

"There is a threat of rain, they say, which may ruin our Thanksgiving."

"Either way, mine won't be ruined as long as I get to be with you. Will your family allow me to sit with you?"

"I'm sure it will be fine. Will you not be expected to sit with the Herrmanns?"

"That I don't know. But I already told Seth I'll be spending as much time with you as I can."

"As I told my parents."

"Good. Perhaps later, we can take a walk."

"Yes. In that grove of trees over there is a trail that runs beside a beautiful stream. With all of the people here, we might *want* to break away for a little solace."

"I can't wait."

Already on the table in preparation for the noonday meal was more food than he had ever seen in one place...and that included the buffet at Gerryman's Smorgasbord in Manhattan. There was turkey, ham, beefsteak, venison, corn, a half dozen different bean dishes, relishes, white and sweet potatoes and those wonderful Amish fruit and cream pies. And all of the food was not yet placed.

Children were scampering about the grounds playing their favorite game, Gray Wolf, which was a cross between tag and hide and seek. A circle of five or six year old girls, looking precious in their bonnets, played with their homemade dolls...dolls with blank faces. Travis learned when he visited Intercourse back in Lancaster County that the dolls had no faces because it would break the commandment to have no graven images. Two sets of the men sat in chairs with tables between them playing chess and speaking in German. And although musical instruments were seldom if ever played since they were considered worldly, an ancient man in a white beard sat on the porch playing a fiddle. Travis thought it was some kind of German hymn that sounded a lot like *Fairest Lord Jesus*. It was all very homespun, yet festive.

It was a day when the entire community participated in one of their most treasured holidays that celebrated the bounty...the reaping of the harvest. All blessings from God.

Travis learned much about the Amish people that day, taking account of their customs and dress and observing their behaviors . He saw that the men's suits were all dark, straight cut and had no lapels or pockets, their jackets fastened with hooks instead of buttons. The women wore dark blue or black calf-length dresses with capes and aprons. On their heads they either wore a kind of bonnet to match the dress or a white prayer cap. And ironically, while Travis stood watching the people, Mrs. Oberhauf slipped up beside him and to his surprise, handed him a large box.

"Hello, Mrs. Oberhauf. What is this?"

"Thee must open it and see."

Flipping open the cardboard flaps, he saw that it was filled with clothes. A complete suit, tailored Amish style, two shirts and two pairs of work pants.

"I…I don't understand. Are these for me?"

Sarah, who stood beside her mother, nodded. "Yes. The suit was my father's. As you have noticed his hefty frame, he kind of out-grew it. Mother and I altered it to what we believed your size to be. We made the shirts and pants."

"Take them with our blessing, Travis," said Mrs. Oberhauf. "We knew thee didn't have the required dress. It is sort of our 'welcome to our community' gift."

"I don't know how to thank you. You have been so kind to me." He then took each of their hands, brought them to his lips and kissed them.

"Who is this man kissing my Oberhauf women?" the familiar gruff voice behind him said.

"I…was just expressing my gratitude for your wife's and your daughter's kindness. They put together this box of clothing."

"My old suit!" he said with a degree of expression. "This was my favorite. It fit me…"

"It no longer fits thee, Jacob, and it never will again."

A half-smile came over his face. "Thou art right, Deborah. Thou art always right." He then turned to Travis. "So, did thee get settled in at the Herrmanns?"

"Yes, sir. I will be ready to start work early tomorrow morning."

"Just remember thy training in the afternoon. I made sure that Benjamin knew about that."

"I will be there."

"Well, enjoy thyself today, young Marlowe. And…get thyself some suspenders. I see that thee keeps pulling up thy trousers."

"I will."

It was now time to bring everyone together for the Thanksgiving dinner. Bishop Herrmann stood with his wife, his adult son and daughter, and with Benjamin and Seth Herrmann, calling the people to assemble around him for the blessing. His prayer was long and his voice booming, but all stood with heads bowed in reverence, including the children who amazed Travis with their stillness and sense of obedience. After the multiple amens, the bishop spoke from Psalm 100:

"Make a joyful noise unto the Lord, all ye lands! Serve the Lord with gladness; come before his presence with singing. Know that the Lord, He is God. It is He who has made us, and not ourselves. We are His people and the sheep of His pasture. Enter into His gates with Thanksgiving. And into His courts with praise. Be thankful to Him, and bless His name. For the Lord is good. His mercy is everlasting. And His truth endures to all generations."

Travis slightly touched Sarah's hand with his and said, "I have always loved the Psalms. How fitting is that verse for this occasion?"

"Yes," she replied softly.

Thanksgiving dinner lasted for just over an hour. Travis learned from Sarah that leaving the table while others were still eating is considered impolite; so, even though he had long been through with his dinner, he sat until others began clearing their plates. As the women and girls began to clean up, Travis sat with Seth Herrmann and talked.

"I saw you sitting with Sarah Oberhauf during the meal," Seth commented. "How did you get to know her?"

"From visiting the store while I was living in Hurley."

"How long have you known her? You seem to be more than friends."

"Going on two months." He paused for a moment while watching her clear the tables with the other women. "I'm going to marry Sarah one day."

Seth laughed. "But you are English. It's forbidden for the Amish to marry outside of the order."

"It doesn't matter. Rules or not, she *will* be my wife."

"Her father will never allow it. Neither will the bishop."

"It will happen, Seth. I guarantee it."

"Have you asked her?"

"Before this year is over, I will. I promise you that."

Travis continued to watch her flit about with all of the blithe and grace of a ballerina. Every move she made was poetic. From time to time, he would catch her eye and then she would smile. Finally, when the dishes were all washed and the majority of the women went inside the Kegler house to work on a quilt, Sarah came to where Travis and Seth were standing, leaning on a hitch rail.

"Would you like to take a walk?" she asked. "I'd want you to see the stream beyond the grove I was telling you about."

"Sure." He then looked at Seth. "Sorry to break away, but if it's a cross between standing here talking to you or take a walk in the woods with Sarah, you lose, buddy."

Seth laughed. "Yeah. Don't think I wouldn't drop *you* if I had a chance to be with Sarah Oberhauf."

Other than that evening the week before, when Travis walked Sarah from the store to her house, it was the first real opportunity they had to be alone for any length of time. As soon as they had entered the grove and found the trail, she placed her hand inside his. The wind had picked up some, causing the trees to rock and sway, creating a noise that sounded like murmuring voices in song. Sarah pointed out the different types of hardwoods…the oaks, hickories, ash and maples, shedding more and more of their crimson, burnt umber and gold leaves with every gust. Off to their right, running parallel with the trail, a sparkling stream gurgled and sang over the rocks. It seemed that all of the sounds of nature were coming together to perform a symphony that God had written just for them.

Stopping to sit on a large downed walnut tree, part of which carried over the stream, they didn't speak for a while. They merely allowed nature to speak to *them*. But then they began searching each other's eyes, communicating their feelings of love…love that had come upon them quickly, maybe from the first time they saw one another in the store. Her eyes danced and sparkled like the stream that ran beside them. He leaned in and she allowed him to kiss her, tenderly, passionately, until both of them seemed to be starving for breath.

"You *have* to know how I feel about you, Sarah. You might think it premature for me to say this, but even though we've been together this short time, I have fallen in love with you. I think about you every moment. Sometimes I would even lose my concentration at work and couldn't remember whether I was loading or unloading a truck."

She sat without word for a few moments, leaving Travis to think either she didn't feel quite the same way or thought it was too soon to say the 'love' word. But then she placed her arms around him, drawing him close into her, and whispered, "And I love *you*, Travis Marlowe."

The very words he needed to hear.

Suddenly, from one of those gusty breezes came the rain...a hard rain. Quickly, they gathered themselves up and began running hand in hand from the woods and back across the open field toward the Kegler house. By the time they reached the house, they were soaked. Sarah's beautiful chestnut hair was falling down through her prayer cap and water dripped from the brim of Travis' hat in gushes. When they burst through the back door, a score of people stopped their conversations to cast their attention upon the young man and woman, dripping all over the Kegler kitchen floor. One set of eyes belonging to Jacob Oberhauf seethed with ire and embarrassment.

"Sarah," he said. "Go find thy mother in the quilting room. We are leaving."

Oberhauf said nothing to Travis. His look told Travis what was on his mind. Within moments, they left. Sarah's eyes, those same bedazzling brown eyes that earlier said told him she loved him, were now saddened. She would get a lecture about proper decorum and Travis would be fortunate to see her again anytime soon except perhaps at religious services.

Travis worked hard mornings on the Herrmann farm and then sat with children in the classroom learning more about Amish customs, traditions and protocol. He found German difficult, but it helped to be in the company of Amish people when they spoke it. Seth bounced words and phrases off him in the evenings, which seemed to reinforce what he learned in the classroom. After school, six days a week, with few words being exchanged between he and Benjamin Herrmann, Travis repaired the rotted wood around the eaves of the house and the window sills, replaced the deteriorating boards on the front porch, shored up the chimney on the roof to stop the leak that filtered into Seth's bedroom ceiling, and after stripping the sideboard on the exterior of the house, he slapped on two coats of white paint. He would start on the barn early next year.

The first snowfall on the Sunday before Christmas measured fifteen inches, burying nearly everything. But still, it did not impede the community from attending services, this time at the Oberhauf house. Travis only caught a glimpse of Sarah since the men worshipped in the living room and the women in the large country kitchen. He did not seek her out that day, but did ride to the store one afternoon after his class. She greeted him once more with loving eyes and spent a few moments talking with him. Jacob Oberhauf passed by them, nodded to Travis, but said nothing.

"I thought you might be in trouble after you went home on Thanksgiving," Travis said.

"Not really. He said very little to me. He didn't tell me not to see you, so I guess he's gotten over it."

"I didn't see that we did anything wrong. We just went for a walk and got caught in the rain, that's all."

"I suppose it was just the picture of us coming in together like a couple of drowned rats in front of all the people."

"Yeah, I guess. But regardless, I intend to still keep seeing you as much as I can."

"You'd better," she replied, smiling. "We'll be having another opportunity to spend some time together at our Christmas service. More food and merriment."

"I'll look forward to it. Well, I just stopped by to say that I still love you."

"It's what I wanted to hear. I see you got your suspenders finally."

"Yeah, they're Seth's. His father gave him a new pair for his birthday the first week of December. I can now keep my pants up."

"My father will be pleased to hear *that*." Then having said that, she blushed. "I didn't mean that the way it came out."

Travis laughed. He then placed his hand around hers. "See you on Christmas."

"Christmas it is."

CHAPTER NINETEEN

1948

AFTER THE COMMUNITY'S CHRISTMAS DINNER INSIDE of the Amish community's assembly house where a battery of Christmas carols had been sung to close the festivities, Travis was invited to the Oberhauf house for some ginger cookies and hot cider. Actually, it was Sarah who had pled with her father to allow him to come by for a visit.

"I am not sure where thee intends for thy friendship to go with him. If thou art serious about Travis Marlowe, thou wilt be wasting your time. An outsider cannot marry into an Amish family."

"But Father, the subject of marriage has not come up. I am sure he respects our traditions about that. We are merely good friends who enjoy talking with one another."

"I suspect it is *more* than that in thine hearts, Sarah. Just don't expect too much from thy friendship with him. Thee both will then be disappointed."

"I understand, but I still would like him to spend the afternoon with us. He has no family and I'm sure it is not a very pleasant experience for him to sit around any evening with cranky old Benjamin Herrmann…especially on Christmas Day."

"All right. But he must be gone before dark."

"Thank you, Father." And then she kissed him on the forehead.

For nearly an hour Travis, Sarah and both of her parents sat in the Oberhauf parlor in conversation mostly about his adjustment to life in the Amish order. On the coffee table before them sat the platter of cookies and cider.

"The cookies are excellent, Mrs. Oberhauf. My mom used to make them along with chocolate chip and oatmeal cookies. I have good memories of her. And of days like today. I still have the angel she made for our tree."

"I'm sorry that she left this world so early in life. Was she a Christian as well?"

"Yes. She was a devout Catholic and she insisted my education be in a parochial school where I could learn about God and Jesus."

"I'm sure that experience made learning our religious ways so much easier. There may be differences in the way we worship, but thee received the Christian foundation."

"So, tell us, Travis," began Jacob Oberhauf. "Doest thou feel thee hast adjusted well these past weeks? Doest thou miss anything about the secular world?"

"I'm enjoying the Amish life, sir. Maybe I miss things like Christmas trees and hearing the latest popular music on the radio. Oh, and the sundaes down at the Tasty-Freeze."

Oberhauf smiled. "As thou canst see, we don't have Christmas trees in our homes nor any decorations. We prefer to keep the focus on this day on the Christ child. But, we do give one another just one gift."

"And on that note, we have a gift for you," said Sarah. She then handed Travis a medium sized box with only a plain red ribbon wrapped around it.

He grinned and gleefully pulled the ribbon from the box. "Ah, my own set of suspenders."

"It was Mother who made them for you."

"No kissing this time, young Marlowe," said Oberhauf with a half smile.

"Thank you kindly, Mrs. Oberhauf. Now I have a complete set of Amish clothing, thanks to you. Except my hat, which I borrowed from Seth Herrmann."

"How art thee getting along with him," Oberhauf asked.

"Very well. He is always quizzing me about the outside world and especially life in New York City."

"Many of our young men have that curiosity. Sadly, a couple of them left our order five years ago to join the American military during the war. They never returned. We never heard much about the war, but as the English were fighting in the Vaterland against our people, we did try to gain as much news as we could."

"Vaterland?"

"The Fatherland...Germany," Sarah said.

"My father died in France fighting in that war."

"Then he fought against our people," commented Oberhauf.

"I'd like to think that he died fighting the Nazis and not the citizens of Germany."

Oberhauf looked away for a moment. "Yes. There was a difference of course."

"I meant no disrespect against the people of Germany, but my father was a hero in serving his country. He won the Silver Star."

"I'm sure thy father was a fine man."

"Yes, sir. A great man."

Although the conversation about the war and Germany had not taken a sour turn, Deborah Oberhauf interjected before it did. "Jacob, let's let these young people alone for a while. I'm sure Travis would like to talk with Sarah more than he would us."

"You're right, Deborah. Remember that it gets dark just after five, Travis, and thou wilt have some distance to cover on the horse. It's not good to be on the highway in the dark with all the autos speeding about as they do."

"Yes, sir."

The Oberhaufs then rose and climbed the stairs to the upper floor. When he could hear them no longer, Travis scooted closer to Sarah on the couch.

"I guess I don't have much time to spend with you so I wanted to make the best of it," he said.

She laid her hand on his. "Which means you want to kiss me," she replied.

"Well, yes, that too. But I wanted to also get something out before I lose my nerve."

"Sounds serious."

"It is." He paused for a moment while looking down at the floor. "Sarah, I know now it was no accident that my car broke down on the road back in September and then your father came along to give me a ride. I am dead sure that God had a hand in it. As He directs our lives, I feel He makes things happen for a purpose. He is the One who led me to you."

She smiled and squeezed his hand. "Just the other day, the same thought entered *my* mind."

"Call it fate or God's will, I know He led me to you. And…because the way I feel about you…well, I'll just say it again…I love you. I also think it's God's will that we *remain* together. I know it's been just three months, but it seems I've known you for years. I guess there's no other way to say this except come right out with it. Will you be my wife?"

For a moment, Sarah sat with her mouth open. Then she took her hand from his and dropped her eyes. "As much as I know I love you, you *know* that is not possible. The Ordnung forbids an outsider from marrying within the order."

"But that's just it. I'm no longer an outsider. I've chosen the Amish way and now live in this community."

"But that still may not be enough for my father and the bishop of our church. You're not of German descent. I think that's what the Ordnung requires."

Travis was silent for a few seconds. "Then somehow, we must get around it. I'll not give up on this. Unless, of course, you don't want to marry me."

"I *do* want to marry you, but since as you said, we've only known one another a few months, maybe we ought to give it some time to work on my parents. When they see we're not giving up our deep friendship, we'll get my father's blessing." She then smiled. "And maybe you need to learn a little more German."

"You really *do* want to marry me?"

"I cannot imagine marrying anyone else."

Travis then clicked his fingers on both hands. "Yes!" he exclaimed. "Sie haben mich den gluchlichsten Mann in der Welt gemacht." (You have made me the happiest man in the world.)

Sarah grinned and clapped. "That's very good. You need just a little work on your dialect, but good just the same. You *have* come a long way...and in just a month."

"Next year, sweetheart. I'm going to approach your dad next year. As most Amish weddings happen in the fall by tradition, can we shoot for 1948?"

"If you can convince my father and the elders that you have become Amish enough to satisfy the Ordnung, I'll marry you anytime."

"Wunderbar," he replied. Then taking her head in his hands, he kissed her fervently to seal their promise to one another.

For the next hour they talked about many things...mostly what she didn't know about his life. The mention of his father piqued her interest. And what was his mother like? What was life like in the New York City streets? And had he had other girlfriends before her? If she was going to marry Travis Marlowe, she wanted to know who he really was and who he had been in his former life. By the time he left the Oberhauf house at four-thirty, she had received a full education on her husband-to-be.

Even that small glimmer of hope, hanging on a shoestring that Jacob Oberhauf and the order of brethren would approve of their marriage, sustained Travis through the long winter months of 1948. While waiting for the planting season, he worked hard on the Herrmann barn to shore it up, replacing the deteriorating wood, inside and out, as well as the roof. The stalls and feeding troughs were also repaired. Benjamin Herrmann, who had not even asked him to do any work on his house and barn, was well-pleased with his drive and initiative, not to mention the completed product. That resulted in more smiles and conversation at the dinner table.

Travis and Seth learned much from one another. Seth became Travis' apprentice on the house and barn repairs, and Travis learned more about Amish protocol so that he would not commit any *faux pas* at the gatherings. When Travis and Seth communicated, it was mostly in German. That helped Travis not only learn to arrange the more difficult words and phrases in a sentence, but more readily capture the proper dialect and articulation.

And then it was school every afternoon with Mrs. Yoder. She would assess and evaluate Travis' progress and then turn in a report to the established board of elders that was comprised of people like Bishop Herrmann, Thomas Kegler and one Jacob Oberhauf. As there was no mayor or any specific leader of the settlement, the board met on all matters pertaining to community business. However, only the bishop, ministers and deacons met to address any individual breach of Amish protocol and moral or spiritual failings.

Even though the ground was still hard in February, all three men on the Herrmann farm pushed their necks, backs and legs to the limit tilling the soil for the planting of peas, the earliest crop. In March and early April, quadrants B and C of the farm were plowed for the planting of snap beans, kale and rhubarb. And it was not until late April that the corn went into the ground. By the time planting season was over, Travis' body was hardened and conditioned as it had never been in his life. And that included his short stint as a Golden Gloves boxer. He discovered muscles he never knew he had. And his tanned face from the spring sun made Sarah's eyes light up all the more, when he saw her at services. Then when she sneaked an opportunity to hold hands with him at the socials, she found them to be even more muscular and calloused.

"I'm going to speak to your father about us very soon," he told her at the May Day celebration.

"Maybe you should wait a while longer, Travis. The timing may not be right."

"Okay, but don't be surprised one day when the sun, moon and stars all align and I find the courage to approach him."

"Maybe next month. But let's talk about it first."

Travis nodded. "As you wish, my dear."

June

On that last Saturday afternoon in June, when his work was done, Travis rode the mare to Oberhauf's store for no other reason but to see Sarah. As usual, she broke loose from her duties at the sales counter and came to greet him. This time as they walked to the rear of the store where there were no other customers, it was Travis who stole a quick kiss.

"Tomorrow, Sarah. Tomorrow, I will go ask your father for your hand in marriage. The time is right."

"Are you sure?"

"It's been building up in me all of these summer months and we must tell him before fall comes."

She nodded. "Okay. I'll have a pit in my stomach the rest of today and through the day tomorrow until you meet with him. Of course you'll have to come by the house."

"I'll ask to do that after the service."

"I'm feeling queasy right *now*."

"I'm the one who should be feeling queasy. It's *me* that has to approach him." He then smiled. "But, even though he has a few pounds on me, I think I can take him."

"Don't talk like that. I can imagine you two getting into a scrap over me, but please keep it civil."

"I will be on my best behavior."

She then turned away. "Yuk. I think I might lose my lunch."

Travis took Sarah by the hand. "It'll be fine. You'll see. All he can do is say 'no.' He's not going to toss me off the porch or anything."

"All right. You have my blessing. I think while you're there I might go visit Mary. And if I hear a bomb go off, I'll know where it came from."

At services the next day, after Minister Strubhar ended his sermon, visiting Bishop Herrmann snagged Travis' coat with his fingers and said, "A moment, young Marlowe."

"Yes, sir."

"I have been hearing good things about thee from several sources. Thee seems to be assimilating into our environment quite well. My brother says thou hast made his house and barn look like they did when they were built thirty years ago. He also says thou hast learned to be a very good farmer."

"My carpentry experience seems to have paid off. I enjoy doing that kind of work."

"Then perhaps others in our community could use thy skills. They would of course pay thee much more than my brother can afford."

"He does give me room and board along with that. Even at the two dollars, I've been able to save more than a hundred. My needs are minimal."

"I have also heard from Mrs. Yoder that thou art quite the Bible scholar. Thou hast gathered much insight and helped her bring the same understanding to our children" Then he laughed. "But as to German, she has never before heard the words spoken with a New York accent. Still, it seems thou art mastering the language."

"Ja. Ich genie Be es mehr, als ich dachte." (Yes. I enjoy it more than I thought.)

"Ah. Sehr gut."

Jacob Oberhauf, who was standing close by, overheard much of their conversation. "Come , Jacob," said the bishop. "I was just congratulating Travis on his accomplishments. He has fit in quite well. Shows much initiative *and* promise. I am glad thee personally vouched for him."

"He has actually surprised me. I have watched him turn the corner, as they say."

The bishop laughed again. "I am sure thou hast been watching him for *other* reasons as well, Jacob."

A half smile appeared on Oberhauf's face. "Which reminds me that Sarah and Deborah are waiting for me. Auf Wiedersehen, mein Freund."

"One moment, Mr. Oberhauf," said Travis. "Would it be possible that for me to speak to you this afternoon?"

"Yes. What would it be about? I can spare one more minute."

"It will take a little more than a minute, sir, and I'd like to talk in private."

"Then be at the house at three. Again, what is…"

"I'll see you then, sir." Travis then tipped his hat and walked to where he had parked the mare.

The mare began limping a bit after the second mile on the way to see Oberhauf, which told Travis that he would have to check her out when he returned back to the Herrmann house. As he did not push her beyond a walk, he arrived at his destination at ten minutes past three. After wiping the toes of his boots on the backs of each pant leg, he knocked on the door.

Following what seemed like an unbearably long minute, Jacob opened the door. "Hello, Travis. Doest thou wish to talk out here on the porch or in the parlor?"

"If it's all the same to you, sir, out here is fine."

Oberhauf motioned Travis to one of the rockers and then sat down in the other. "What's on thy mind, son?"

"I think you might have figured it out, Mr. Oberhauf. But, please don't stop me or I might never have the nerve to ask you again."

"I did wonder when the day would come that thou wouldst ask for my blessing to marry Sarah."

"And, it is this day."

"I fully expected it as early as last Christmas. And of course I would not have provided my consent."

Travis' face sank, but he still kept his unwavering eyes fixed on Jacob Oberhauf. "Then you won't give your blessing."

"Have thee even asked Sarah to marry you?"

"Yes, sir."

"And I take it she said 'yes.'"

"She did."

"Here's our problem, Travis. Although I've grown to like thee over this past year and thou hast officially become a member of the Amish community, thou art still not a blood German who was born into this order. Being accepted into our order is one thing; the inter-marriage of an English man and an Amish woman is forbidden."

"I know that, sir. Don't think I didn't do my homework. But If I could get your blessing, perhaps you and I could take it to the board of elders for consideration."

Oberhauf sat rocking and staring into Travis' eyes. For the longest time, he said nothing in response. "Thou wilt have my blessing, Travis. I cannot think of another harder working and dedicated, Christian young man anywhere in our community. Nor could I think of anyone else in our order I would *want* Sarah to marry." He then held out his hand. "I am good with thee, son. Whether the *elders* will be, is another question."

Travis pumped his hand vigorously and grinned. "Thank you, sir. You will make a wonderful father-in-law."

"There several things though. If thee does not promise to do any one of them, I will withdraw my consent. Thee must vow to always love her and protect her. Thou wilt be the man of the house and provide for her and thy children. Thou wilt keep the Father and His Son Jesus Christ at the forefront of thy thoughts, raise thy family in accord with the scriptures and maintain a Christian home, giving praise and glory to God for all that thou hast."

"I promise to do these things with all my heart."

"I'm not through." He then leaned into Travis. "Thou wilt always be faithful to Sarah, never straying and never forsaking her."

"Mr. Oberhauf, such deviances would never enter my mind. She will always be my one and only love. There will never be cause for me to desire another woman."

"Then, we are good here. I give both of thee my wholehearted blessing."

SOUTHERN PSALMS

Part Three

Turn Yourself to me and have mercy on me, for I am desolate and afflicted. The troubles of my heart have enlarged; bring me out of my distresses! Look on my affliction and my pain, and forgive all my sins.

Psalm 25: 16-18

CHAPTER TWENTY

TRINITY

IT SEEMED THAT AS HE SAT on the bench across the street from Trinity Methodist watching the families entering the church, memories of that first year in Hurley and the Amish settlement of Himmel flashed through his mind in merely seconds. Wiping his wet eyes with his sleeve, he couldn't stop the tears. He had disappointed his wife, Bishop Herrmann *and* his adopted community; but had Jacob Oberhauf lived past the third year of their marriage, he would not have just been disappointed, he would have been furious. His words on that day Travis asked for Sarah's hand in marriage suddenly haunted him. "Thou wilt always be faithful to Sarah, never straying and never forsaking her."

The tears were not just from his nostalgic reminiscence of those wonderful early days, but the fact that he had allowed his perfect life and perfect wife slip away because of his own lust and self-centeredness. And now he was left with only his self-imposed feelings of guilt and shame…and the reality of just how far he had fallen.

The church reminded Travis of that Lutheran church in Hurley…not only because one closely resembled the other in structure and style, but because of the chimes. They were playing *Great is Thy Faithfulness*, the same song he heard playing that first Sunday morning in Hurley. The same song he heard at fourteen at his parish church. He dabbed at his eyes again with his sleeve…eyes that tracked along the building's structure all the way up to the spire that sat on the red cedar shake roof. Trinity Methodist was a combination of siding and stucco that consumed nearly the entire block. And most of the blocks in Destiny averaged over two hundred feet long. Root systems from the stately oaks and magnolias had through the years tunneled under the sidewalk, causing it to crumble in places making foot travel dangerous and unaccommodating, especially for the elderly.

A sign at the front of the church grounds advertized the church's name and its minister, Drake Moreau. "You have to hear this preacher," Smokey had told Travis. "Yeah, I go to another church out of town, but if I didn't, I'd be sittin' in one of his pews every Sunday. You won't hear a message any gooder than what he brings. Pure fire and brimstone. You'd think you was in a Southern Baptist church for sure. You come out of there and it might be days before you think of sinning.'" Travis smiled, remembering Smokey's colorful choice of words.

After entering the church, Travis sat in the last pew of a sanctuary that held perhaps four hundred worshippers. And every pew appeared to be filled. A few of the women still wore hats, although the fashion appeared to be ever changing. Every man had on his Sunday best suit, a greater number now being tan or seersucker that felt cooler to the skin in the southern heat than basic black. Travis then looked down at his own rumpled suit, a black jacket with hooks for buttons that *un*fashionably shouted Amish. However, it was doubtful many of the people knew it to be so as they would likely have never had a reason to be around the Amish.

Following an ear-piercing solo sung by a very large woman whose soprano voice made the song sound more like an operatic aria than a hymn, Pastor Moreau took the pulpit. A tall man, perhaps fifty-five, with a graying brown head of hair, projected a baritone voice that resonated throughout the sanctuary without the need for a sounding board or microphone. Quoting from Psalm 105, one of Travis' favorite, he recited:

"O give thanks to the Lord! Call upon His name; make known His deeds among the peoples! Sing to Him, sing psalms to Him. Talk of all His wondrous works! Glory in His holy name; let the hearts of those rejoice who seek the Lord! Seek the Lord and His strength; seek His face evermore!"

Pastor Moreau made his recitation sound like a mini sermon. His delivery was so commanding, even these few words made the hairs on Travis' neck stand up. The man could have been a dramatic actor had he not been called to the ministry. Smokey was right about him.

Perhaps Travis needed such a compelling sermon that he readily engulfed and absorbed Pastor Moreau's message so openly and completely. Moreau spoke of the temptations in the world that can make a man, woman or child be so easily swayed that the whole applecart of one's faith, spirituality and morality can be upset. "Do not be tempted by the pleasures of the world that keep us from putting God and His Son the Lord Jesus first." Travis sat mesmerized for the entire hour of Moreau's oratory. The words hit him hard as though they were manufactured especially *for* him. And although his pangs of guilt and shame resurfaced throughout the message, at the same time, there came upon his soul a healing effect. Moreau continuously reinforced the fact that God was still in man's corner, pleading for him to give up his evil ways and return home to righteousness.

As Pastor Moreau had held his audience once again in a state of hypnotic conviction, it was as though the Holy Spirit of God Almighty hung in a heavenly haze over their heads. For Travis, the pressure of the anvil of guilt that had lain on his chest for more than two months…from when he had first committed adultery…felt as though it had been lifted. He needed this message like a spiritual Vitamin C. Then at last while the congregation stood to sing the closing hymn, he remained in his seat with his forehead pressed against the back of the pew to his front, praying the sinner's prayer.

Following the pastor's eloquent benediction, a few of the men and women sitting near Travis, realizing he was a stranger in their midst, turned to officially welcome him. After shaking their hands and nodding to each with a smile, the next hand extended to him was Pastor Moreau's. It was his last stop before leaving the sanctuary. He was even taller than he appeared behind the pulpit which served along with his deep, rich voice to project a commanding sense of presence.

"It's good to have you here with us, my friend. Are you visiting the area?"

"Well sir, it seems that Destiny was the end of the line when the train stopped here last week. I'm not sure I'll be here long, though. It all depends on God's will."

"And your name?"

"Travis Marlowe."

"Ah, a strong English name."

A sudden feeling of déjà vu swept through Travis. It was the very remark that Jacob Oberhauf had made when Travis first met him some thirteen years before.

"Your sermon was as powerful and uplifting as any that I have ever heard."

"I felt the Holy Spirit within me, especially today. The words of course were those of the Almighty and it is to Him that I give all the glory."

At that moment, a woman, also tall and striking, joined them.

"This is my wife, Catherine. Travis Marlowe, my dear."

Her warm eyes somehow reminded him of Sarah's, which sadly had turned cold and pendant the last time he saw them.

"A pleasure, sir," she said. "You are just visiting?"

"In a way, ma'am. Destiny's a beautiful little town."

"Well, we love it here. Have you taken up residence or passing through?"

"I'm not sure, Mrs. Moreau. The wind blew me all the way here from Indiana. So far the town seems very comfortable."

She laughed. "Just wait till July and August and see how comfortable it is. The humidity alone can stifle a breath."

"So I've heard."

He noticed that she was looking him over. "An interesting suit, Mr. Marlowe. I've not seen that style. No lapels or pockets and the jacket is fastened by hoops."

"It was hand-made for me by my wife."

"Is your wife not with you?"

Pastor Moreau, who seemed to be familiar with the style of the suit, and himself wondering why Travis had been traveling from what might be an Amish or Mennonite community in Indiana, noticed the flush in his Travis' and said, "Come now, Catherine. Don't bombard Mr. Marlowe with your usual battery of questions."

"Well, again, Reverend Moreau, your message really hit home with me. Thank you for serving God and the people of this town."

Moreau smiled and shook Travis' hand. "I hope to see you again next Sunday. If you're still here."

"I'll plan to be here."

As the pastor and his wife began communing with others who were making their way out of the sanctuary, Travis slipped away.

Upon returning to the diner, Travis changed clothes and pulled from the large commercial refrigerator some leftover meat loaf, corn and beans from Friday night's dinner. Reheated, it tasted as good as it did two days before. He capped it off with a piece of apple pie. Smokey bought his pies for resale from Mrs. Devereaux's dessert shop a few blocks away.

Sunday afternoon was the first real time he had had to himself. Actually, he found it a bit lonely, thinking maybe it was because he was so used to the diner being jam-packed with people during the day. But the time alone also gave him an opportunity to focus his thoughts on Sarah and Rachael. They would have just left Sunday service at someone's house and on their way back home for dinner…just the two of them. But maybe, they instead would have that dinner at her mom, Deborah's house. Deborah had not remarried since Jacob's death in 1951, when the cold he caught that winter spiraled into pneumonia. Travis and Sarah had taken over the store that same year, but as Sarah had lost her desire to continue on with it, they sold it to Hanz Eichel, one of the more wealthy members of the Himmel community. That is when Travis began farming the large acreage that was part of the Oberhauf estate.

But the time off on that Sunday afternoon made him feel both relaxed and nostalgic. And when he turned on Smokey's radio, the music playing made him even more melancholy, especially when the program announcer introduced Elvis Presley's new ballad. Was this the same Elvis Presley that was supposed to be Officer Presley's kin?

Immediately, though, sadness found its way back in his heart when the song began:

Are you lonesome tonight? Do you miss me tonight? Are you sorry we drifted apart? Does your memory stray to that bright summer day, when I kissed you and called you sweetheart? Do the chairs in your parlor seem empty and bare? Do you gaze at your doorstep and picture me there? Is your heart filled with pain; shall I come back again? Tell me, dear, are you lonesome tonight?"

While he sat in the same red vinyl booth where he and Dreama had sat talking the night before, he watched the pedestrian traffic as they walked by the large plate glass window. They seemed to have a Sunday kind of energy about them...determined, but carefree as though they had no real places to go. Smiling, contended, almost waltzing in choreographic fashion along together in the afternoon sun, one foot in front of the other. Some were Negroes, dressed to the nines, the women in their colorful dresses and hats, and the men in their white suits and fedoras. The little girls wore ruffled dresses, knee socks and black patent leather shoes. Often ignored and sometimes pushed aside by the Whites, they might act as if they didn't care. It was a way of life. However, Travis knew they did care inside, even though their behaviors didn't show it. But, it was Sunday and they didn't have to work the docks or on the shrimpers. Or the fields. And they were with their families. Life today was good.

Travis had not been around the Negroes since he was a teen in the Bronx. He had almost forgotten about them, having lived for thirteen years with the Amish. But the Negroes in Hurley were a different people than what he remembered in New York. And then in the south they were even more laid back, didn't say much, but smiled politely showing their brilliant white teeth. Some were musicians who played on the streets and in their night spots just outside of town. It was what he imagined New Orleans would be like some fifty miles away.

He then thought about Sissy. She was a happy sort, always singing as she worked, in spite of the looks and rude attitudes of the diner's customers. She shrugged off the fact that as soon as she placed the silverware on the tables, a customer might spill a little water from his or her glass onto the fork or spoon and wipe it thoroughly with the napkin. And when she passed by Travis, she would smile and say, "'Spect he thinks I got the scurvy or sumptin,'"

But then Travis turned his thoughts to Sarah and Rachael again. They did nothing to deserve the horrible sin he committed. His weakness, his betrayal had cost him everything. Everything important to him. The elders, in shunning him, had cast him out as a non-believer. But he *was* a believer. Falling from faith did not make him a non-believer. That's where he differed from the tenets of the Ordnung. Can one be a Christian one day and not the next? He had made that point clear the day he was questioned by the elders. But, then he thought perhaps someday he might take up that question with the man who he had just heard deliver that powerful message.

After he had taken a walk along nearly every street in Destiny, perusing its downtown area, admiring a few of the more stately homes on the east end and shaking his head after seeing the shanties on the poor side of town, especially in the Black west end, he returned to the diner at sundown. Again switching on Smokey's radio, he sat the rest of the evening listening to music he had loved from back in the 40s and the new, more popular songs he had never heard before.

Frank Sinatra and Glenn Miller had been replaced by people such as Ruby and the Romantics and Jerry Lee Lewis. There was more music from that peculiar fellow who sang the song he heard earlier, *Are You Lonesome Tonight*, only these songs were faster in pace with twangy guitar accompaniment. He wasn't sure he liked *Blue Suede Shoes* and *Jailhouse Rock* as much as the ballad. But he did like a real crooner named Perry Como. He sounded like a throwback to the Big Band era. And then there were ads about electronic gadgets and automobiles that were foreign to him. In a way, he felt as though he had been in a coma for a dozen years, then woke up to a new world of technology and to what the people playing the records called music. Finally thinking that much of the music was not worth listening to, he then turned the radio off.

Finding a tablet of paper, an envelope and a pen in Smokey's office, he returned to the booth to pen the letter he had been putting off too long…the letter to Sarah. It would be his first communication with her since he left.

> *"My dear wife,*
>
> *I wish there was a way I could call you, but since there are no phones in any house in Himmel, I guess this letter will have to do. I pray that you will write me back, especially to let me know how you are doing physically and emotionally as well as with the farm. Please let me know about Rachael as well.*
>
> *My words cannot possibly convey to you how sorry I am that I caused our separation. You were angry and hurt the day you compelled me to leave. I felt it best to leave the area completely when you said I was out of your life forever. Maybe I was angry as well. Not with you, of course, but*

with how things ended that day. And then on top of it all, the board of spiritual elders banished me from the order. Maybe it was also my shame that drove me out of town. When I hopped a freight train, I just kept going aimlessly. However, I continuously ask God to forgive me for my actions and ask that you do the same. Although you may never forget what happened, I pray you can find it in your heart to forgive.

I think of you and Rachael constantly. I am sure I fell in love with you the very first time I saw you in your father's store, and have not stopped loving you since. My terrible act with Mary did not happen because I did not love you. It occurred because I was weak, physically and spiritually. It was a selfish act of lust and I have hated myself ever since it happened. As I have prayed for our Father's forgiveness, I believe that He truly has provided it. Now, I ask for yours.

I am in a place called Destiny, Louisiana. After traveling on the Illinois Central off and on for these weeks, this is where the train stopped. I am working in a diner for a very benevolent man. It will be temporary, of course, as it is my intent to start back north soon.

I cannot stop thinking about that day we were married in November just after Thanksgiving. Your father was in my corner the whole way to convince the elders that I was not just English, but truly a man of the order. I learned much from your father and even though he passed into Heaven long before I was ordained into the community's ministry, he was the one who inspired me and took time to educate me scripturally. I especially learned to love the Psalms as he did. I read them every day and find both comfort and solace in them.

It is often I think about our wedding. You were clearly more beautiful that day when we said our vows than any day before. And you became even more radiant as the years progressed. These twelve or thirteen years have been the happiest of my life. And I want those days back. I want you and Rachael back.

If you <u>can</u> possibly find it in your heart to allow me back into your life, I want to be your husband again. I will be there on my hands and knees before you if I must. I know that the elders will not allow me to return to the community, but somehow I need you to be my wife again. If necessary, I will find a place in Hurley to live for a while so that I can be with you and Rachael until something is worked out.

I pray that the time we have been apart has helped your wounded heart to heal and that you will still love me. I have no other need in life but for that love. I also pray that God will continue to provide to you and Rachael His comfort and protection. If you find it in your heart to write me back, you can send the letter to the address on the envelope in care of The Old South Diner, Destiny, Louisiana. God bless.

My eternal love,
Your husband,
Travis Marlowe"

Travis kissed the letter, then sealed it up in the envelope. He would ask Smokey for a four cent stamp tomorrow morning and mail it off. At just after nine-thirty, he turned out the lights, checked all doors to see if they were locked, and then turned in for the night. It would only seem like minutes had lapsed until he heard Smokey slam the back door the next morning on his way into the kitchen.

Chapter Twenty One

Defending Sissy

Travis had just dressed and put on his apron to go to the kitchen where Smokey was already baking biscuits when Sissy arrived for work. She was early…perhaps an hour earlier than usual. But she did not go directly to the kitchen *or* dining room. Instead, she closed the ladies room door behind her.

"Was that Sissy?" Smokey asked.

"Yes," Travis replied.

"She's always here on time, but never this early. How was yesterday? Did'ja go down to Trinity like ya planned."

"You were right, Smokey. Pastor Moreau was hands down the best preacher *I've* ever heard."

"Could be the most respected citizen in the whole town."

"I'll be going back."

At that moment, Sissy came out of the rest room, but did not immediately approach either Travis *or* Smokey. When she stepped from the shadows into the light, Travis could see why she had been reluctant to do so. There was swelling on her left cheek and her eye was nearly swollen shut. More of Joubert's handiwork, no doubt.

When Travis placed his fingers on her elbow, she flinched and groaned in apparent pain. Obviously, he had injured her in several places.

"Why do you put up with this, Sissy?"

Her eyes filled with tears, she replied, "What *can* I do, Travis? The law won't do nuthin.' They say they don't interfere in Black folks' business. And *I* sure can't do anything about it."

"Is there any place you can stay...like a relative's house?"

"He'll just find out where I am and then whoever I stays with might also be in danger. I won't do that. But, you know the worst thing about it? My girl, Tina, she sees him beatin' on me and stays upset. I see her start shakin' every time he comes around."

Smokey, who had overheard the conversation, then came out from the kitchen. When he saw her, he shook his head. "All I know is, he'd better not show his face within fifty feet of the diner or I got a load of buckshot waitin' on him. Come on now, let's get things rollin' this morning.'"

The usual Monday morning patrons filled the dining room within only minutes after Travis opened the door. Notables included Monique Sourette, the hair stylist, along with a couple of her employees; Fred Nicholson, who ran the Western Auto, and Judge Harley Crenshaw from the circuit court. Of course there were the other faithful stool sitters with whom Travis had had discourse the previous Monday, such as the contentious Marty Boucheau and his sidekick, Eddie Anderson. Boucheau was the first to take note of Sissy's weekend injury.

"What's the matter, girl. Joubert use you as a punchin' bag again?" And then he laughed.

Tears welled up in her eyes, but she said nothing in return.

Travis, who had been clearing a table immediately behind him, stopped on his way to the kitchen, leaned into him and said in a low voice, "Come on. Mr. Boucheau. She's had a hard enough time and doesn't need any ragging from you."

Boucheau, whose eyes took on sudden rage, responded as expected. "Mind your own business, bus boy. What're you tryin' to do, run Smokey's customers off? He won't like you interferin' in conversations that don't concern you."

"He won't like you making snide comments to his employees, either."

Boucheau then turned to Eddie. "Ya hear that, podna? What's this place comin' to? Maybe we outta start havin' breakfast over at Connie's place."

Travis went on about his chores without further dialogue with the man, but not before shooting Sissy a glance and shaking his head. It was a shame, he thought, that she had to take physical abuse at home and then endure verbal disparagement in her workplace.

No sooner was this discord over, in walked a distinguished looking man of about sixty five, dressed in a light blue seersucker suit and a red bow tie. Before he was within a dozen feet of Boucheau, his loud, commanding voice could be heard above the white noise of the other customers' conversations. "A good morning to ya, Marty. Eddie." The man then took the stool to Boucheau's right.

"Good Mornin,' Mayor. Hot already out there, eh?"

"Ah, but it's a fine start of the week, anyway. How is Mrs. Boucheau? Is she still down in her back these days?"

"She is. Some days she can't even get out of bed. I'll be takin' her to the chiropractor this afternoon again."

"Well, give her my sincere regards, Marty. And do not fail but have her call Glenda if she needs assistance in any way."

"Very kind of ya, yer honor. So tell me, who do ya think's gonna win this fall...Nixon or Kennedy?"

"I will tell you one thing, Marty. If this country votes in a Catholic and a Democratic nigra-loving liberal like this Massachusetts senator, this country's going to find itself on the brink of another Civil War. The south is not going to condone having a man like that as its President. There will be more Black faces in the government and in public office than ever. And how do you think that's going to set with the good people here in the south?"

Mayor Brent St. Pierre, an icon in Destiny, was a lawyer, a former judge and had otherwise been an influential political fixture in the parish for over forty years. When he spoke, it was not only with profound and succinct diction, but with a touch of theatrical flair. Lifting his head pompously and batting his eyes in true narcissistic form, he always searched the room to assure that all ears were hearing his loud, commanding voice.

Smokey, who was standing over the griddle, said to Travis, "What he don't care about is that almost a third of his constit-chunce in this town are the Negroes. Theys his people, too."

"Is nearly everybody in Southern Louisiana prejudiced against Black people?"

"No. It sure ain't as bad in this state as it is in Miss'ippi or Alabama. Most of the White blue collar workers around here, which is a lot, work shoulder to shoulder with the Negroes on the shrimpers and in the factories. Some of 'em are even pretty good friends. It's the high-falluntin' crowd that thinks theys better and puts 'em down. Thank God they ain't many of 'em in this town. But, I believe the Mayor is soon in for a rude awakenin'.' Things are changin.' I believe soon the gov'ment is gonna pass some acts and laws that'll give the Black people every right the Whites have, and dina-sars like St. Pierre will be out."

"You're pretty politically savvy, Smokey. Unfortunately, I haven't thought or even cared anything about politics for the last dozen years since I've been away from the world."

"That Amish life you had, I believe if things was different, I could get into it myself. I don't give a hill of beans about modern conveniences. Don't have air conditionin' in my house. I work six days a week and hardly ever see the daylight. Don't watch TV or much listen to the radio. The only thing I'd miss would be my pickup."

Travis smiled. Smokey and his pickup.

"It was a good life, those years," Travis commented.

"So, why aintcha back there livin' it?"

"You already know part of the story, Smokey. Someday I'll tell you the rest."

"Someday I'll letcha."

The one face that Travis was *not* anxious to see that Monday was Dreama's. She had been his temptress, but after he refused her and she fell unconscious in a wine-induced stupor, he had left her. He expected that when she woke on Sunday morning, recalling what had taken place, she would either be embarrassed or angry that he had staved her off. That is if she remembered anything about the evening at all. But as she had tried to be the siren, Lorelei, seductively luring him into the breakers and the rocks until he crashed, she had failed. And that, he was sure, would not have set well with her. Smokey had warned him to steer clear of her. It wasn't that she was evil, he thought; but, she was the kind of woman who couldn't or wouldn't be left alone. She needed someone in her life. But if she thought it would be Travis, one thing he knew for sure...it definitely was not going to be him.

At just after three, Dreama came in to start her shift. Taking advantage of the fact that there were no customers in the dining room, and wouldn't be till four, she pulled Travis aside, out of Smokey's earshot.

"Do you have any idea how it makes a woman feel for a man to up and leave her like that? I mis-read you, Travis."

Her words caught him off guard. He fully expected that she might feel a bit uncomfortable facing him that afternoon, but didn't expect her to light into him like a sprinter straight out of the starting blocks.

"I'm…sorry, Dreama. I didn't intend for the evening to end up like it did."

"Then what *did* you expect when a woman invites a man into her house that time of the night?"

"Remember that you had asked me to come see your paintings."

She shook her head and laughed sarcastically. "Are you actually that naïve, Travis? So what *was* it about me you didn't like; or were you just thinking about the woman you left up in Indiana?"

He didn't answer her. After a long moment of searing eye contact on both their parts, he turned heel and walked away. He knew one thing; he would not allow himself another weak moment with her. And then neither would *she* ever lower her self-esteem by again trying to seduce him. For the remainder of the afternoon, they breezed by one another in the dining room, like ships passing in the night with as much distance between them as safely possible. And then, when it was time for her to go home, she shot him a quick glance and said in a rather cold tone of voice, "See you tomorrow."

"Good night, Dreama," he replied softy.

At nine-thirty, Dummy was waiting on the bench under the Mimosa tree in front of the store. The plastic plate Travis carried to him contained chicken and dumplings, mashed potatoes and stewed tomatoes. With the dinner, he placed in the man's hand a hot cup of coffee. There was something strange about Dummy that night, however. Instead of acknowledging the act of kindness with his usual grin and slight bow, the man merely stared at Travis with cold, angry eyes. Travis even thought at one point when Dummy opened his mouth, he was trying to form a word. But nothing came out. It caused an eerie chill to run through Travis' spine.

"Is anything wrong?" he said.

For a moment Dummy just sat holding his plate in his lap with his eyes fixed on Travis.

"Okay. I'm going back in now. If you want anything else, just rap on the door."

There was still no response of any kind.

When he returned to the kitchen, he asked Smokey, "There's something strange going on with your beggar friend out there."

"What do ya mean?"

"He's always grinning and appreciative of the food you send out, but tonight he just took the food, then sat there and stared at me as though he was angry about something."

Smokey shook his head. "That don't sound like him at all. I know he lives a harsh life out there on the street, but he's always let hardships roll off of him. Sometimes with street people, things ain't always right with the mind, ya know. Maybe he was havin' some kinda episode."

"Maybe. But for some reason I don't think so. His face had a kind of evil expression on it. The last time I saw it was on the man's face I had a run-in with on the train."

"And that's another thing I'd like ta know about. I didn't push anything with ya when the police was in here questionin' ya. When we gonna talk about that?"

"One of these days, Smokey, we're going to sit down over a cup of coffee and I'll tell you probably more than you care to hear."

"Well, anyway, I'll keep an eye on Dummy. Strange what you're tellin' me."

After he had laid down on his bed, Travis let his head fall back on his pillow, finding the brightness of the naked bulb on the ceiling glaring in his eyes. Mrs. Stanley's Bible lay open on his chest. It was the Bible that he carried to the altar on his wedding day. It was the same Bible out of which he ministered to the men, women and children in Amish Himmel. How old it was, he didn't know. But its cover was well-worn. The pages were soiled and dingy. And Mrs. Stanley had high-lighted much of the text with a soft red pencil. Ironically, Mildred Stanley passed away on the same day he and Sarah were married.

He then sat up, placed it in his hands, and opened the scriptures to again visit a favorite excerpt from Psalm 139: *Your eyes saw my substance, being yet unformed. And in Your book they were all written, the days fashioned for me. When as yet there were none of them. How precious also are Your thoughts to me, O God. How great is the sum of them. If I should count them, they would be more in number as the sand; When I awake, I am still with You.* And when he thought about Sissy, her community, and man called Dummy, he read from 140, *I know that the Lord will maintain the cause of the afflicted, and justice for the poor. Surely the righteous shall give thanks to Your name; the upright shall dwell in Your presence."*

Then Travis prayed for all of them, followed by his constant prayer for the health and safety of his beloved Sarah and Rachael. He capped his prayers by asking God to touch Sarah's heart that when she read his letter, she would find in herself a way to forgive him and accept him back. That somehow, some way, their marriage would be restored.

The following morning Sissy did not show for work. Although she did not have a phone, whenever she or her daughter was ill, she would go next door to call Smokey. In the four years she had been in his employ, she had not missed but three days of work. Smokey and Travis were able to manage those breakfast hours in spite of Sissy's absence; however, Smokey did reluctantly admit he probably needed to hire another full time waitress to not only better serve his customers, but just in case either Sissy or Dreama was out for a lengthy time. And of course that that would mean an increase in prices. It also might drive his customers down to Connie Walker's restaurant. So, that day, besides performing his dish washing and table cleaning duties, out of necessity Travis had to learn the ropes of *waiting* the tables and running the cash register. But, he had been observing Sissy and Dreama for two weeks and these additional responsibilities were not difficult to assume. To take up the slack, however, Smokey became cook *and* fellow dishwasher.

After the last customer was out the door at nine-forty five, they both sat at the counter having coffee. Smokey pulled out a pack of Chesterfields and offered one to Travis who shook his head 'no.'

Smokey lit up, blew out a long plume of smoke and smiled. "Don't drink, don't smoke, don't cuss. I guess you *are* a Christian boy, huh?"

"Actually, I was a minister to our order, Smokey. I was considered by the Amish elders to be 'enlightened' and called to the ministry almost two years ago. The hierarchy of our order begins with the bishop who is over all three communities and two other ministers; then there is a senior minister over *our* people and a minister in training to take over when the senior minister either dies or is for some reason unable to continue. I guess I was the junior varsity."

Smokey took a drag from his cigarette and smiled.

Travis continued. "My wife and I ran her father's store for a while, and after he died, she gave it up. I then worked our farm. Those were wonderful years, Smokey." He then paused, took a deep breath and looked away for a moment. "I'm ashamed to say I then did something and my wife asked me to leave. I don't know if it's forever. I pray that it's not. One day soon I'm going back, however. But, don't worry, I'm not going to leave you just yet…that is until after everything cools down. I'm banking that she will forgive me and take me back."

"So, what did you do so bad that she booted you?"

"I won't lie to you, Smokey. I committed an atrocity against my marriage. An affair. To this day I can't tell you how or why I let it happen. I was just weak."

Smokey put his big right paw on Travis' shoulder. "Look, boy. I ain't no barber, priest or bartender, but I got a pretty doggone good ear."

"Thanks. Maybe I will go into it one day with you… maybe even over a beer." Travis then smiled.

Smokey nodded and then developed a deep furrow in his brow. He kept looking toward the door. "It ain't like her to miss like this and not call. I don't mind tellin' ya I'm a bit worried."

"You saw her yesterday with the welts on her body. Maybe he got to her again."

"Tell ya what, Travis. While there's a lull around here, take my pickup sittin' out back and go check on her at her house. If she's there, see what's wrong. Then let me know."

Travis swung his legs around on the bar stool and stood. "I can do that. Where does she live?"

"Down on 4th Street in an area called Cabbagetown. It's a yellow house…the only yellow one on the street."

"I think I was on that street when I was walking around town Sunday afternoon."

Smokey's eyes lit up. "You was down in Cabbagetown? Man, you coulda got yourself knifed or sumthin.'"

"I didn't feel threatened. The people walking the streets nodded and spoke. Some very friendly."

"Well, there shouldn't be anybody hangin' around that area this time of the day. But go on and report back as quick as ya can. If somebody comes up to ya and wants to cause trouble, get back in the truck quick." He then pulled a huge set of keys from his belt and added, "It's the one that says Ford on it."

No sooner than Travis jumped into the driver's seat of Smokey's battered pickup, he realized that not only hadn't he driven a vehicle in thirteen years, he didn't have a license. If he was picked up by the police, that may be all they needed to throw him in a cell. However, he was determined to find Sissy. After depressing the clutch and running the floor shifter through all of the gears to gather with the feel, he then turned the key to start the engine. It started immediately but filled the alley with a mushroom of blue-gray smoke. So far so good. After pushing the gearshift into first, he popped the clutch and the engine killed. He then restarted the truck and this time eased the clutch out a little easier at the same time giving it gas. Now moving forward, he still jerked the truck two or three times, before the engine smoothed out. And then after grinding through second gear, he began to get comfortable with his shifting. He hoped he would be bringing the truck back with the transmission still in it.

Once he had traveled through the town proper on Main Street, he turned right onto Banks and in two blocks left onto 4th. After crossing over Whittaker, halfway down 4th on the right he spotted a yellow house. Travis then pulled the truck onto a sandy spot just off the street and killed the engine. Seeing no activity at the house, he dismounted the truck and walked toward the front porch. Before he placed his foot on the bottom step, he caught sight of an elderly woman standing on her sidewalk at the house next door.

"You lookin' for somebody, mister?" she asked.

"Yes, ma'am. Sissy Mumford. Is she home?"

"Not anymore. The am'blance done took her away about three hours ago."

"What happened?" an astonished Travis asked.

"That man of hers, Joubert, laid into her again. I heered them maybe five o'clock. Heered her screamin.' So I called the law. They didn't come. They never come."

"How badly was she hurt?"

"Bad. This time, I think. Real bad. After Joubert left out, I went inside and found her on the floor. She was breathin' but knocked slam out. I finally got the am'blance people here. Don't know nuthin' more."

"I'm not familiar with the area, but do you know what hospital they took her to?"

"The only one what takes Coloreds. Bap'tist over in the next parish. Who are you, anyway?"

"I work with Sissy and we were worried about her."

"Yeah, I know Smokey. He treats her nice."

"How about Sissy's little girl?"

"I have her with me. She's in the house. Been cryin' a lot. I keep her on Saturdays while Sissy's workin.' Other days, I see her off to school."

Suddenly, a car with a loud muffler rounded the corner a half block to the west. It was the same car that Travis had seen in the alley the day he found Sissy with a split lip against the back wall. Joubert. When he screeched to a stop in front of the house, Travis pointed a stern finger at him and yelled, "You! Get out of the car! I want to talk to you!"

His courage fueled by anger surprised even himself, but certainly Joubert. "What you doin' here, peeshwank? White people ain't welcome in this neighborhood."

"Get out of the car," Travis again shouted.

Joubert not only sprang from his car, but he came at Travis in a dead run. Before he could throw the roundhouse punch from his cocked arm, Travis fired a straight shot with his fist directly between Joubert's eyes, splintering the man's nose and knocking him to the ground in a bloodied heap. As Joubert struggled to get to his feet, Travis hit him again with a series of rights and lefts, one of which crashed into Joubert's cheek at the jaw line, instantaneously shattering the bone and sending him back to the dirt. Blood poured profusely from his nose and mouth. This time he did not get up.

Travis stood over Joubert like Thor, fists clenched and hanging at his side. "Now you listen to me, parasite. I don't know what kind of shape Sissy's in right now, but you'd better hope she recovers. And when she gets out of the hospital, I find you've laid another hand on her, the next time we meet I won't be so nice. Understand me?"

Joubert, fighting to keep the blood that was gushing from his nose from strangling him, nodded quickly. But then suddenly from Joubert's mouth Travis heard a strange hiss…something like a puff adder. Travis reached down and grabbed Joubert by his blood-soaked shirt, stood him to his feet and flung him toward his car. After Joubert crawled into the driver's seat, he turned and flashed a diabolical grin. "Ah, but you think this is over, Travis Marlowe. But it isn't. It's just begun. You might have beaten *this* man, but you'll never beat me."

The words were more articulate and succinct than Joubert could *ever* summon. And the voice belonged to someone else. He then laughed and Travis heard the strange hiss again. A chill ran through his neck and spine. He then knew that the being inside of Joubert was not him. Joubert then sped away, laying rubber from the tires of his high-performance Plymouth all the way into the next block.

"Lawdy!" the neighbor lady exclaimed. "I ain't never seen nobody with hands that quick. Good for you. Joubert finally got what he deserved."

"Ma'am, if he does come back here, please call the diner right away, okay? And tell Sissy's little girl that everything's all right now. We'll' go see about her mother."

"I will, mister. Thank you." She held out her hand not expecting Travis to take it, but he did.

She grinned and shook her head. "No, sir. Ain't never seen fists flyin' as fast in my life."

On the way back to the diner, Travis began to shake. Not about the fight, what little there was of it, but that someone or some*thing* had obviously entered Joubert's body…just as Travis had experienced with the old man on the train. A supernatural being. A most *evil* being. The man might have been Joubert at the beginning of the fight, but not the end. And he knew Travis' name. Joubert could have learned it from Sissy the morning Travis found him in the alley, but *what* he said and in the *voice* he said it, "you might have beaten *this* man, but you'll never beat me;" that was a warning from the Evil One or his disciple. And obviously a threat. Satan was definitely at work in Destiny and it appeared he had made Travis his target.

CHAPTER TWENTY TWO

SATAN'S FOLLY

WHEN TRAVIS RETURNED TO THE DINER, he told Smokey about Joubert's assault on Sissy and that she was in apparent serious condition in Baptist Hospital. He said nothing about Joubert accosting him and the ensuing fight. Smokey was furious and said if he didn't have so much work to do, he'd go hunting for Joubert...he and his shotgun.

"By the way, Smokey, what does peeshwank mean?"

"Cajun French word, kinda means runt or maybe pip-squeak. Why?"

"No reason. Just heard it somewhere is all."

Smokey had called Dreama while Travis was gone, asking her in to help with the lunch crowd. He would pay her for her hours. Dreama agreed to come in at eleven. She would fill in not only for the rest of the day, but the remainder of the week.

However, on Thursday after the dinner patrons had dropped off considerably around seven, Smokey sent Travis in his old pickup to Baptist Southern to check on Sissy. For two days she had lain in a coma from a subdural hematoma, but then only an hour or so before Travis arrived, she returned to consciousness. Her head was still wrapped in gauze and both eyes were nearly swollen shut. Still, she was able to make out the smiling but concerned face at the side of her bed.

"Travis," she said feebly.

"I won't ask you how you feel," he replied.

"They say I was out for a long time. I don't even know what day it is."

"Thursday night."

"My baby. Do you know if she be okay?"

"Your neighbor lady, the older woman next door, has her. She's fine."

Tears formed in Sissy's eyes and her lower lip began to quiver. "I hope he don't take her. Miz Armstrong won't be able to stop him."

"I think he has other things on his mind right now...like trying to breathe through his nose."

"I don't understand."

"No matter, Sissy. Why does he keep doing this to you?"

She turned her head and winced from the pain. "He wants to come back and live at the house. But, when he stays there, every time he starts drinkin' and is out of work, he gets real mean. I told him I don't want Tina seein' him like that."

"But he still comes around and beats on you regardless whether he's living there or not."

She nodded, but didn't respond.

"I don't think he'll bother you again, Sissy."

"How you know that? You don't know Joubert."

"Trust me on that. Anyway, Smokey and I will be looking out for you."

"I hope I don't see him no more. I can't take it."

"When will they let you go from here?"

"Don't know. I ain't got no insurance. I guess I'll be a charity case as far as they concerned. But as soon as I'm able to stand on my feet, they'll put me out."

"I don't know. The staff seems like good, caring people. I talked with a couple of nurses on the floor. But, hey, I'd better go and let you get some rest."

"Thanks, Travis, and thank Smokey for me. The nurses told me the flowers over there were from him."

Travis smiled. "He's a good man, all right."

"I know some of the customers give him some grief about me workin' there, but he don't pay 'em no mind."

Travis pat her on the hand and said, "I'll come back to see you again maybe Sunday if you're still here. Heal up and get on back. Things aren't the same at the diner without you."

She nodded and tried to form a smile.

When Travis left the room, he stopped back by the nurse's station to inquire whether the hospital might release her prematurely since she couldn't arrange to pay her bill."

"Not to worry, Mr. Marlowe," replied the head nurse. "It's being taken care of."

Travis was puzzled. "How?"

She looked at Sissy's chart. "By a man named Clinton Woodruff."

"Clinton Woodruff?"

"It says here he owns a business in Destiny. A diner."

He smiled. "Smokey."

"I'm sorry...what was that?" the nurse asked.

"Oh, nothing. Thanks for your information."

A *very* good man.

✝ ✝ ✝

At the end of the Saturday night shift, there was no invitation this time from Dreama to spend the rest of the evening with her. Actually, there was nothing more from her lips, except "See you Monday, Travis."

After she left, Travis stepped out the front door for a breath of air. To his surprise, Dummy was sitting there. He was never there on Saturday nights, according to Smokey. Sometime during the day, he would collect enough change for a bottle of whiskey and consume during the night, waking up on Sunday morning somewhere on the street.

"I didn't expect you this evening," Travis said. "I'll go ask Smokey to put together a plate for you."

But when he turned to go in, he was absolutely stunned beyond belief when he heard Dummy say, "I'm not looking for a handout tonight, Travis."

"You…you spoke. How…?"

Dummy's face took on a sinister expression. Travis was sure his eyes began to glow and his mouth curled up into an evil snarl. "How do you *think* I'm able to speak, Travis? You know this old man has neither a brain *nor* a tongue."

"You! What do you want from me, Devil?"

"Strange isn't it, my son? You talk to your God and he never speaks back to you. But I do now, with a tongue that has never spoken. Isn't that ironic?"

"First of all, I am not your son. My Father is not a snake that preys on and deceives the human race. And He is the one and only true God who doesn't have to take on the form of another human being to speak to me. He communicates with me in other ways. And he answers my prayers."

"He does, eh? You pray that your lovely Sarah will invite you back into your marriage. But it doesn't happen. You haven't asked *me*. Maybe *I* can do something about it."

"You can go back to the pit of hell and leave me alone."

"Or what? Will you get physical as you did with the old man on the train or Joubert Mumford? Will you also assault this old man."

"I'm not laying a hand on you, nor am I continuing a conversation with the lowest form of life in the universe. I am committing a sin at this very moment in doing so. *Now stay away from me!*"

Travis then left the man on the bench. He waited several minutes, however, then looked out the window to see if he was still there. He was gone.

From the kitchen he then heard Smokey's booming voice, "Whatcha doin' at the window, boy?"

It was not the time to tell Smokey what had just happened with Dummy or about any of the obviously satanic phenomenons he had experienced these two weeks. Smokey wouldn't believe him anyway. But there was one person with whom he would speak about it. Tomorrow.

Travis began his Sunday morning with a prayer at breakfast over his bacon and eggs, first for Sissy, then his family and then for God to keep the hounds of hell away from him. Why had Satan singled him out for persecution? He knew his soul belonged to God, so what was the Evil One's purpose in harassing him?

But then he thought about his confrontation with Joubert. Was it purely his anger that caused him to call the man out from his car and beat him to the ground? Or was it Satan who egged him on, causing him to again fail in his actions, thus adding to his list of sins? But, then again, had he become God's own instrument of punishment for Joubert in retribution for his heinous assaults on Sissy?

Now, three times within the past two weeks, the serpent had taken over the mind and body of a human and tried to get inside Travis' head. One man was an itinerant hobo who ended up dead; a second was already an evil sort with the devil in him; but the third, a kindly man, a woeful soul who could not speak, suddenly developed a reptilian mouth and became Satan's unfortunate pawn. Satan's folly.

Travis then closed his eyes to purge all of this from his head and think more pleasant thoughts. Thoughts of home. Was it a glorious Sunday morning in Hurley, Indiana? Was his little Rachael sitting on the front porch waiting for her mom to take her to services, singing to her faceless Amish doll as she remembered her mother doing with her? Was his beautiful Sarah standing in the kitchen sipping the last few drops of her coffee as the warm morning sun beamed through the window, highlighting that small wisp of chestnut hair peeking from under her prayer cap? Was the corn now high from the abundance of rain that had blessed the fields for days on end just before he left? He smiled. God willing, one day soon he would be back there.

At ten-thirty, wearing the same common suit he had worn the Sunday before, his only suit, looking every bit the Amish gentleman farmer that he was, he left for church. It wasn't quite as hot as it had been on other days this time of morning, perhaps because a cold front had come through during the night and lowered the humidity. The residential area downtown near the church was a true southern postcard. Birds filled the magnolias and moss-adorned oaks, singing their choruses of hymns to glorify God. Beautiful bougainvillea vines and climbing roses flourished along the wrought iron and picket fences that majestically fronted the turn-of-the-century homes, homes that had been coarsely weathered by decades of tropical storms. However, in spite of their battered siding, they were still stately and inviting. And then he heard the beckoning chimes of Trinity playing *The Church's One Foundation.*

After thirteen years without hearing any musical instrument played in Sunday services, the rich chords of both organ and piano could be heard emanating from inside the sanctuary and spilling into the street. It was a welcoming sound that reminded Travis of Sundays in his Bronx parish when his mom held his hand as they walked up the stairs of St. John's. The Trinity pews were white of the vintage early Nineteenth Century style, some having small family boxes with doors. The boxes may have been purchased eons ago by the benefactor founders of the church. Perhaps even Andrew Jackson might have sat in one of them. Red, red carpet ran throughout and several of the stained glass windows depicted the biblical scenarios such as the birth and crucifixion of Christ, the Acts of the Apostles and the travels of St. Paul. And behind the pulpit hung a rugged, ten foot high wooden cross.

Pastor Moreau's sermon was another powerful masterpiece, laced with stimulating superlatives and illustrations, every effectual point was delivered succinctly and with articulation. Travis couldn't remember when he had been so inspired. Then after the service, when the congregation filed by Reverend Moreau at the entry door to shake his hand, Travis intentionally held back so that he would be the last to exit the sanctuary.

"Ah, Mr. Marlowe. I am so glad you're back. Maybe you're thinking of making Destiny your home?"

"Well, it certainly is for the time being. Compelling sermon, pastor. I have not heard anyone like you."

"It is the Lord's words that you hear, my friend. I just deliver them."

"And with great vigor, I might add."

Moreau smiled and gave Travis a slight bow, then turned to leave the doorway.

"Pastor," Travis called after him.

"Yes?"

Might I have a few minutes of your time this afternoon, maybe after your Sunday dinner?"

"Absolutely, sir. Would you like to stop by the parsonage…
which is next door there?"

"Yes. What time?"

"How about three-thirty?"

"Perfect. I will look forward to it."

"And I will have Catherine prepare us some lemonade.
It'll be refreshing when the afternoon heats up."

Chapter Twenty Three

Catharsis

After Travis had put down a burger he charred on the small griddle and heated up some left-over home fries, he cleaned up his mess and then took a short nap, leaving his door open. He still had two hours before he was expected at the parsonage.

It was not long and he began dreaming. The face he saw belonged to Joubert Mumford. At first the man just stood in front of him, expressionless, eyes unwavering and hollow. But then fear grew on his face and his mouth opened up in horror resembling the subject in the painting called *The Scream* he remembered from his youth. Suddenly, his eyes turned fire red, then black as coals. Smoke began pouring from the sockets. Blood oozed from Joubert's chest through his white shirt. The body then began to convulse just seconds before it fell to the ground. Travis thought he heard someone scream. But the scream was not coming from his dream. It was from outside the diner.

Quickly, he rose from his cot and scrambled to the door. Several people had gathered in the roadway directly in front of the diner. Travis then went outside to determine what had happened. All he could see in the middle of the road was a man with a white beard and hair lying face down in mangled condition. Dummy. He wasn't dead, but apparently he had been struck by a hit and run driver. There was no car in sight. A pained expression covered Travis' face and he said a quick prayer.

In less than ten minutes an ambulance and squad car were on the scene. Two officers exited the sedan, one of which was Harold Presley.

"Poor old Dummy," he said. "Layin' there in the road like a dad-bum possum. I reckon he'll recover, but his leg is messed up pretty bad."

Before the medical crew put Dummy on the gurney, Presley checked the man's pockets. From his right jeans pocket he pulled a piece of paper...and then he looked at it. Slowly, his eyes then panned around to Travis, who was standing on the sidewalk.

"You boys go ahead and load 'im up and the rest of you disperse. Nothin' more to see here. Marlowe, you stay put. Johnny, you start markin' off the street and I'll join you in a few minutes. I got business over there."

When the ambulance left and people began walking away, Presley said, "Let's go inside."

"Cup of coffee, officer?"

"No. Let's just talk."

After they had sat down at one of the tables in the dining room opposite one another, Presley said, "You know, Travis, the chief thinks you might be some kind of new menace here in Destiny, masqeradin' as a good guy bus boy. Like you blew into town specifi'cly to cause trouble."

"And what do *you* think, Officer Presley?"

"I told him you were just a poor dumb Yankee down on his luck who's only on the run to get away from his wife." He paused. "Now, I'm not so sure."

"What's changed your mind?"

"That man out there in the street and what I found in his pocket. Here." He then placed the piece of paper on the table.

"I'll save ya the trouble of readin' it. It says 'If I'm dead, ask Travis Marlowe why.' Now what do ya think *that's* all about?"

Travis' face registered his surprise. "I have no earthly idea. It was not me who ran him over. I don't have a vehicle."

"I know that. There were a couple of witnesses who saw the car and the driver. Their description don't match you."

"Then how could I be involved and why the message on the paper?"

Presley shrugged. "You tell *me*?"

"All I know about him was that Smokey fed him two or three nights a week right outside on that bench. Last night he was out there and was acting strangely." He paused a moment. "You're...not going to believe this, but he spoke to me."

Presley laughed. "Spoke to ya? Why that man ain't never spoke a word his whole life."

"And, Smokey said he couldn't read and write, either. So how do you explain the note?"

"I don't know, Marlowe. It just seems all the strange happenins goin' on around here, you got somethin' to do with."

"I'm sorry, but I can't explain this stuff. And this note thing...just doesn't make sense. Obviously, somebody else wrote it and gave it to him."

"For what reason? Somebody got it in for ya?"

Travis shook his head, but didn't respond.

Presley then rose to his feet and sighed. "Okay, young man, neither of us got answers. But the Destiny P.D. is gonna try findin' some."

"I wish you luck and then we'll *all* know what the devil's happening around here."

When Presley left the diner and joined his partner out in the street, Travis sat back down and mulled over the last half hour. What started out with a horrific dream about Joubert Mumford, ended in the running down of a harmless beggar who had a note in his pocket that blamed Travis for his malady. The dream, the hit-and-run and the note. What did it all mean? And why was the Evil One still haunting him?

Travis looked at the clock on the wall. Two forty-five. After splashing some water on his face and running a comb through his thick hair, he slipped on his suit jacket and began walking down Main.

"Mr. Marlowe," greeted Pastor Moreau. "Come in. How about a glass of that lemonade I promised?"

"That would be nice."

Moreau led Travis directly into the parsonage study...a bright room where there sat a magnificent mahogany desk flanked by a wall of bookcases containing scores of Christian texts, novels, hymnals and various editions of the King James and Scofield Bibles among other books.

"You have a very nice home, Pastor."

"Well, it's the church's home, but I've been fortunate to live here with Catherine for over nine years. I couldn't expect any nicer place on the salary the church pays me. But our needs are simple and we live within our means. It would not do for a man of my position to live a flashy life. That's why you see that '53 Studebaker in the driveway."

"I can identify with that. All of my life, for one reason or another, I've lived meagerly."

"Well, why don't we sit down and talk about that life. I have always admired the Amish and would be interested in learning more about the people." He then said "excuse me for a moment." Sticking his head outside the study door, he called to his wife, "Catherine, can you bring us some glasses of that lemonade. Thanks, honey. And some of that gingerbread you baked?"

"The gingerbread does smell good. It hit my nostrils as soon as I came in. But sir, would you please call me *Travis*?"

"Okay then, Travis. But I will ask you to reciprocate by calling me Drake. Everyone does."

Travis smiled. "The esteemed figure in the community that you are, I might find it a little uncomfortable."

Moreau laughed and shook his head. "Naw, Travis. I am no more important than the least of anyone in our community."

"Even as powerful a preacher as you are and a man with such immense presence, somehow I knew in this conversation I would find you humble." He could see, however, that the more praise he gave the pastor, the more uneasy he was becoming.

The lemonade and gingerbread then arrived and Catherine Moreau gave Travis a warm smile.

"Now, my friend. Before you begin with whatever I believe is on your heart, tell me who Travis Marlowe is…a little history, perhaps."

For the next fifteen minutes or so, Travis told his story… his youth and teen years in the Bronx, his landing in Hurley and becoming acquainted with the woman of his dreams, and his ultimate acceptance into the Amish order.

"Wasn't it difficult to go from a street-wise teen into a highly-disciplined society where there are no cars, TVs or electricity?"

"Initially, it was a little inconvenient, but after falling in love with not only an Amish girl, but the Amish people, I adjusted pretty well. I married that girl twelve years ago this coming November. Not long ago, I was ordained as the second minister in our community."

"Ah, you received the calling, did you? I am proud to then be in the presence of a fellow man of the cloth." Moreau took a couple gulps of the lemonade and eyeing Travis curiously while he seemed to be chewing on the words of his next question before spitting them out. "So, how does a man like you who lives the wholesome, humble and happy life among the Amish in Northern Indiana end up in Destiny, Louisiana? If there is something you wish not to talk about, that's okay."

Travis laid his saucer of half-eaten gingerbread down and nodded. After a moment of contemplation, he said, "Drake, I threw away that near perfect life and marriage. I was unfaithful to my wife. It was a temptation I did not resist and I have asked God's forgiveness about it every day. You see, in the Amish order, infidelity is one of those unforgivable sins that gets one banished, or shunned as it is called, from the community. There is no going back. And my wife, Sarah, told me to leave. I started to stay so that I could be near my daughter, Rachael, but then made the decision to fall away from everything...at least for a while. I jumped onto a freight car and worked odd jobs all the way south, until I landed here. I guess that's it in a nutshell."

Moreau's eyes were hard to read, but still they had remained steady and warm. "And in your culture, you will never be allowed to return to the Amish order?"

"As I became rebellious in the eyes of the elders, committing a heinous act against my marriage, I had the bitter taste of sin in my mouth...that any words that would come out in their eyes would be hypocritical and even ungodly. I am now, according to the law, a non-believer and unable to enter the Kingdom of Heaven."

Moreau leaned forward from his chair and placed his hand on Travis' shoulder. "The Amish have it wrong, Travis. We all commit sin, but there is no degree of sin in God's eyes that would keep us away from Him. We don't just become non-believers because of our sin. That sin, as I'm sure you know, was already paid for by the blood of Christ long before you were even born. I know from the conviction that you are under at this very moment that you *are* a believer in the Almighty and His Son. We cannot hope to ever get into Heaven based on our good works and trying to be as perfect as we can. We can *never* be that perfect. Yes, you have fallen, but by the grace and mercy of our Lord Jesus Christ, your sins are washed away."

"I know these things in my heart, Drake, and as a minister, I am ashamed to say I soft-sold them to my congregation. I often went against my heart to convey that God reviews our sins against our works and faith, then makes the judgment as to whether we are worthy to enter into his kingdom."

Moreau nodded. "We must all try to keep His commandments. That is the nature and responsibility of being a Christian citizen; but knowing we cannot, God gave us an option…accept that Jesus His Son paid the cost and follow Him or reject Him. The Plan of Salvation is a simple one. Man cannot judge us or determine whether or not we have earned the right to enter God's kingdom upon death. So, you can continue to beat yourself up or you can accept what plan God laid out for us two thousand years ago. You have asked forgiveness you say many times over. But God heard your very first prayer. He has not turned His face away from you, so you can continue to face *Him* with the knowledge and understanding that your slate is clean."

"Again, I do know these things, Drake. Even when I was a younger man and faced the elders that day I was allowed into the order, I told them the very same thing you just reinforced with me. Unfortunately, somehow along the way, I shoved the message aside and found myself conforming to their law." He then settled back in his chair, crossed his arms and stared at the pine floor. "But, I still have a hole in my heart, Drake. My wife and I are as good as divorced under Amish law and I fear she will never let me back into her life. I'll always love her. And I miss both of my ladies."

"I believe I would then be back on the train going north. There must be some way your marriage can be restored."

"Sarah would never leave the order. And even if she did, I'm not sure if she will ever find it in her heart to forgive me."

"Don't give up on her, Travis. Continue with your prayers. God will provide the pathway back, but you must open your eyes to Him and *take* that path."

Travis nodded, but then shifted uneasily in his chair, for a while saying nothing.

"I sense more consternation, Travis. Is anything else bothering you?"

"I'm not sure where to begin, Pastor. It's actually the real reason I came by. What I'm about to tell you will be hard for you to believe and when you hear it, you might think me a liar or even delusional. I haven't told this to another soul since I've been here and feel that you are probably the only person in this town I can confide in."

"I think I have a good idea of who you are, Travis, and can't imagine anything you'd tell me would be too far-fetched to believe."

Travis smiled. "You haven't heard it yet."

"I'm all ears."

"I have seen the devil...or at least experienced his demons."

"Well, certainly the devil is everywhere. He is in all forms of distraction that will keep us from our faith. Yes, vanity, materialism, lust. He tempts us, just as Christ was tempted."

"I don't think I clearly got through to you, Drake. I actually came in contact with him, argued with him and fought him. Face to face, I met him."

As Travis had expected, Moreau looked bewildered. "You...met him."

"Of course you will find that difficult to digest. Okay, it doesn't sound rational. But if you can believe that Satan appeared in actual form during the days of Abraham and Christ, do you not think it possible now?"

"It's not that I think it impossible; it's just that there have been no other confirmations about somebody meeting and talking with the devil in human form. There are some reports of people becoming possessed and then the evil spirit being exorcised from them. But someone coming face to face with Satan? This *is* the Twentieth Century."

"I realize how this sounds, but let me tell you specifically what I encountered."

Travis began by telling him about the hobo on the train and how the man knew things about him he couldn't have known. The demon had admitted possessing the man. It had made Travis so angry and frightened that he tossed him from the train. The next morning the man was found with the pentagram carved into his chest and eyes gouged out with what appeared to be hot pokers.

"Maybe the man was psychotic."

"Possibly, but how could he know things about me when I was a teen, and then later a minister in the Amish community? And of my infidelity?"

Moreau nodded. "I see what you mean."

Then Travis told him about Joubert who suddenly no longer spoke in his Cajun brogue, but with a more articulate dialogue. He too called Travis by name and blasted him with a diabolical warning.

"I know Sissy and am sorry for her. No woman should be subject to what she experienced. But I also understand what you're telling me about your altercation with Joubert. And there is nothing you read into what he said or how he said it?"

"No. I know what I heard from his lips. But last night, I experienced something even more alarming. The man who Smokey gave handouts a few times a week that people refer to as Dummy..."

"Yes, I know the man. A sad, unfortunate case."

"No one had ever heard him speak...until I did last night. Before, he was always just grinning and so thankful for his dinner, but last night his face took on an evil expression and he actually spoke to me in what I would say was a demonic voice, taunting me as well as God."

"Astounding. What specifically did he say?"

"He questioned me as to why God had never physically spoken to me like *he* was doing. He talked about my wife, Sarah, and that God had not arranged for her to take me back in. He knew about my altercation with the hobo on the train and my fight with Joubert. And then just a few minutes before I came here, someone hit and badly injured Dummy in the street in front of the diner."

The pastor suddenly sat upright in his chair and leaned forward. "Oh, Lord, no. The poor soul."

Travis continued. "It *was* unsettling. But, the strange thing that followed was a piece of paper that Officer Presley found in his pocket that read, "If I'm dead, ask Travis Marlowe why." The man could not read, write or speak. So, who gave him the paper?"

Moreau did not have the same look on his face he did before Travis fully got into his story. His look was troubled. "Travis, if what you say is credible...and I'm not doubting you for one moment...why would the devil follow you? If he has settled in this community, why doesn't he confront someone like me who ministers to probably half the church-goers in Destiny? What motive would he have with you?"

"Maybe Satan just plucks people out. Maybe I'm his goat or patsy. But I do know these phenomenons began when I landed here."

"The voices you heard from all these people you believe were possessed. Any commonality?"

"Now that you mention it, yes. Besides sounding diabolical, I actually believe they were all the same voice. They had a guttural tone to them, mocking and taunting, in almost sing-song fashion."

"Interesting," Moreau commented, stroking his chin with his fingers. "If what you told me is true, Travis, and you did not imagine or dream all these things, then it tracks along with some other things happening around here. The police have mentioned there has been increased vandalism in the town where the numbers 666 and drawings of pentagrams have been found on public walls. A few of the beatnik type kids have been wearing crosses upside down, which in itself is concerning. There have been reports in the newspaper about the formation of witches covens and satanic cults. We of course have a history here in Louisiana of certain people who are into voodoo and hoodoo. Not far outside Destiny, there is a kind of commune where the occupants call themselves Broken Birch. Historically, this is an organization of self-proclaimed Satanists and witches who were found to be sacrificing animals." He was reflective for a moment. "Perhaps Satan *has* taken up residence here, and if that's the case, then God help us. I think we should pray about this." He then leaned forward and placed his fingers to his forehead.

"Father, you know my new friend's heart and much has lain on it these past weeks. He has confessed his sins to You and I know You have heard his prayer. He has demonstrated his remorse for his sins, but he believes that evil follows him still. I know Your power and that nothing is impossible for You. If the Evil One has settled in this town, I beseech You Father that You strike the blow against him that will rid the community of the poison he spreads…that You will drive him back into the hell that he deserves. You have given unto us your Son whose sacrifice paid for all of our sins and He is all we need as we combat the dark forces that continue their attacks on each and every one of us. Give our friend, Travis, Your divine blessings…the blessings of mercy, grace and peace. And if there is any way possible that he and his family can reconcile, I know You will make it so. "

It appeared that Drake Moreau was preaching his second sermon of the day as a prayer. It continued on for several more minutes giving praise and glory to God, thanking Him for the enumerable blessings of life, both great and small. Travis soaked up every word like a sponge. But more importantly, as Moreau prayed on, the heaviness in Travis' chest began to dissipate.

"Thank you, Drake. You don't know what your counsel and support mean to me."

"I'm glad that you came by with this information, Travis. Maybe it's a matter I should include in next Sunday's service. Maybe our community needs a wake-up call. Something I'll be thinking about. But just remember, Travis; God is in charge. Always. As a Christian and a minister, you know that. And I feel God may even have had purpose in landing you here. Perhaps he has laid upon you a mission…and Satan knows it. I expect that's why he has made you his business. Stay vigilant and as you do God's will, Satan will *never* be in control."

Travis stood and shook Moreau's hand. "It was good to spend this time with you, Drake. This has been a kind of catharsis for me. I feel more inspired and that I'm about to turn the corner on my luck."

Moreau grinned. "Luck? My boy, it is something I do not believe even exists. For the most part, we are the authors of our own fate. Whatever else happens to us might be thrust upon us by forces we cannot control. But through prayer and faith, we can combat evil by putting on our whole armor. We may get wounded in battle, but even Satan knows we will win the war."

"You are both profound and eloquent, sir. And I feel that somehow, I've been drawn to you and this church. I consider that to be my good fortune. Please thank Mrs. Moreau for the wonderful refreshments."

The pastor dropped his head sharply in a bow. "God bless you, my friend, and I hope as long as you're here, you will make Trinity your church home."

As he walked back to the diner, Travis wasn't absolutely sure Drake Moreau fully believed him about his encounter with Satan or one of his demons personified in the form of human beings. Maybe the pastor thought he had just imagined the voices and their knowledge of Travis' past. Maybe with all of the emotional and spiritual trauma Travis had endured with losing his wife, his ministry and basically his life, he had *indeed* become delusional. But he didn't think that Moreau had discounted all of what he had laid out before him. The pastor did appear to be convinced that perhaps an evil pall may be hanging over the community of Destiny, considering the vandalism, behaviors of the teens and the occult activity. It wasn't that Satan was trying to destroy the town; but, he *was* trying to destroy its spirit and its faith in God.

CHAPTER TWENTY FOUR

MURDER ... AGAIN

IT WAS INEVITABLE. THE *WAITRESS WANTED* sign finally went up in the diner window. Whether Sissy came back to work or not, Smokey knew he had stretched her, Dreama and Travis beyond their limits too long. Although at any one time there may only be twenty five to thirty people in the diner, a few of the customers were beginning to complain about the time it took to get their food, refills of their glasses of sweet tea and coffee, and finally their bill. Regardless of how a few of the more bigoted patrons didn't like having a 'Colored' waitress, Sissy *was* quick and efficient. She catered to them without them having to sit and wait for *anything* or otherwise experience inconvenience. But on a busy Monday morning, when it was just Smokey and his busboy with no waiter experience, service was suffering and the grumbling became louder.

"I be with you in a minute!" Smokey yelled a couple of times from the kitchen. "Travis, can you break loose and hep those ladies?"

To Travis' credit, he was trying to do the best he could under the circumstances. The customers liked his courteous manner and his patience. And they could see what was going on. But he was no Sissy or Dreama. Although he was proficient in operating the cash register from his early days in the Oberhauf store, he hadn't developed the knack of moving from kitchen to table, table to table, and remembering who ordered what. Sissy and Dreama always flitted about with choreographed efficiency and service ran like a brand new engine on a smooth track.

Monday and Tuesday were nightmare days for Smokey and Travis...even considering that Smokey had added three hours to Dreama's work day. But on Wednesday morning to everyone's surprise, Sissy came through the back door just after six.

"No," said Smokey, as Sissy painfully tied the apron around her body. "You git on back home. Yer in no condition to come to work."

She was still a pitiful sight...eyes swollen, although no longer ninety percent shut, and head bandaged. "I be fine, Smokey. They let me go home last night, so I must be in good enough shape to work. And I *need* to get back to work to put food on the table."

"I'll pay ya the rest of the week, anyway. So git on outta here."

"No suh. I can't let you do that. It ain't right. I'm goin' to work. Anyway, I been lyin' on my back in that hospital too long."

Smokey then let out a sigh. "All right. Suit yerself. But I don't want to hear the first groan outta ya." But, he knew he wouldn't.

Before the door opened to customers at six-thirty, Travis took five minutes for a cup of coffee at the counter. As she flit about, he could see that Sissy was in no shape to go though two meal periods, even though Dreama would be in around twelve. "Why don't you take Smokey's advice, Sissy? You don't have to do this. You need time to heal."

"I'm okay...really. Anyway, I don't want to be around the house right now. Tina and me stayed with Miz Armstrong last night."

"Afraid Joubert would be back," he remarked.

She dropped her eyes onto the floor and didn't reply.

"Did anybody see him at the hospital or in the neighborhood the last couple of days?"

"No. Miz Armstrong say she saw his car drive by the house on Sunday mornin,' but that's all. She also told me that you and him..."

"We don't need to talk about that, Sissy. That's water over the dam."

"Okay," she replied, trying to blink back the tears. "You also a good man, Travis."

"Hey, we'd better get cracking here. People will be crowding in here in about ten minutes. And if you need help lifting anything, you tell me." Travis wondered if she would be able to lift the heavy metal pitchers of water and tea.

She nodded and then went back into the kitchen to help Smokey with final preparations for the morning patrons.

There was no mistake about the voice that lifted the heads of the other diners when he walked in. Flanked by Chief Couture and another Destiny officer, Jimmy Boughton, Brent St. Pierre made his grand entrance by shaking the hands of a half dozen constituents on the way to his usual table. "Good to see you, Buddy," he said to the town's flower shop owner. "How is Bessie feeling today?" he bellowed loudly across three tables to Billy Pryor, the funeral director.

"Mornin' out there, Mayor!" Smokey hollered from behind the counter.

"Morning, Smokey," he called back. "How about fixing up special some shrimp and grits with a couple of lightly poached eggs?"

"Ya got it."

Couture then called out to Travis who was cleaning up a nearby table. "Travis Marlowe, how about comin' over here a moment?"

Travis set the deep tray of dirty dishes on an empty table. "Good morning. What can I do for you?"

Couture looked him over for a few seconds. "Still hangin' around, eh? I thought you'd be long gone by now."

Travis shook his head. "No immediate plans either way, Chief Couture."

St. Pierre, who also had his eyes on Travis, sat scratching his head. "Say, didn't I see you the last couple of Sundays down at Trinity? You're the man with the funny looking suit, if I remember correctly."

"Yes, sir. I was there."

"So, what do you think of Moreau?"

"As powerful a preacher and fine a man as I've ever met."

"Maybe so, maybe not. Some people think he comes on a little strong with his hellfire and brimstone sermons."

"Could be that's what the community needs," Travis replied.

St. Pierre continued eyeing Travis thoughtfully as though he were dismantling him, right down to his molecules. "Chief here tells me you were the man who was on the train with the tramp who was found all cut up a couple weeks ago."

Travis nodded, but didn't otherwise respond.

"Since you were probably the last person to see him alive, how do you explain what happened to him?"

"I wasn't the last to see him alive, Mayor."

"How do you know you weren't?"

"The last person to see him alive was the one who killed him."

"The Chief finds it mighty strange that another body was found on Monday butchered up the same way in about the same area where the first guy was found. You want to take it from here, Chief?"

"Yeah, Mayor. The M.O was definitely the same. Eyes burned out, pentagram carved on his chest and knife in his gut. The coroner says he was probably killed sometime late Sunday night. So, Marlowe, where were you Sunday night?"

"Right here, sir. I turned in early around nine-thirty."

"Can anybody verify that?"

"No one was here except me. I assume nobody was watching me sleep," Travis added with a small degree of sarcasm.

"Don't be a smart alec, boy. Funny thing is, this second man killed, you *also* had something to do with."

"What do you mean?"

"Does Joubert Mumford ring a bell?"

Travis was stunned. "It was *him*?"

"Yep. When we went by his house on Tuesday morning, the Armstrong woman next door was out waterin' her flowers. We asked her about the last time she'd seen Joubert and would you like to know what she told us?"

Travis didn't reply. His eyes remained stoic and fixed on Couture's.

"She said you fought with 'im...and leveled 'im. We didn't tell her that Joubert was dead. Figured it would only be proper to tell that Sissy gal first. When we're done here, you tell her we'd like to see her outside. Don't want ta tell her in here with all of Smokey's customers around."

Travis nodded. "I will. So, why are you grilling *me* about his death? You think I had something to do with it?"

"Connectin' the dots, Marlowe. Any second day rookie cop can see the connection. You fight with two people and both end up murdered?"

"I know it looks...well, bad, but I had nothing to do with either death. *Now* what happens? Are you here to arrest me?"

"Arrest you? For killin' a nigra...and a good-for-nothin' louse at that? It weren't no great loss to *this* town. But, there's still the matter of the tramp. We ain't closed that case yet. He was a White man, actually Jewish, but poor or not, he didn't deserve to end up like that. I ain't fully decided whether to run you in, but since I know you were violent with both of 'em, I'd say we could prob'ly make a case. I'll be talkin' to the D.A. about it, so don't go no where."

Travis unhooked his eyes from Couture's and then looked to the far side of the room where Sissy was serving an elderly couple their ham and eggs. How would she take the news? She might be thankful to be free of him; still, he had been her husband and at one time loved him. *And* he was the father of nine year old Tina.

"Is that all, sir?" Travis asked.

"For now."

"Then, I'd suggest you go to the counter and talk to Smokey, before you take Sissy outside to tell her about her husband."

After Couture had taken one of the stools at the counter and motioned Smokey toward him, about thirty seconds later, Travis heard Smokey's low whistle. Subsequently, the Chief then walked toward Sissy, said a few words to her and then he and his officer escorted her outside the front door. Travis then joined Smokey at the counter. Both stood watching through the diner's plate glass window as Sissy suddenly placed her hands over her face and began sobbing.

"What do ya think, Travis? Tears of relief or sorrow?"

"Maybe a little of both."

"Couture thinks you did it. And what's this about you beatin' Joubert up? You never told me that."

"It's not something I'm proud of."

"Well, he did have it comin' and I'm sorry I didn't get in on it. Man, this little town done got like the streets of New York in a hurry. What else is gonna happen around here? I *will* say one thing...it all started when you came to town. Did you bring all this with you?"

Travis gave him a slight smile. "One might think that all right."

"Well, don't worry about it. And I ain't worried about *you*. I know you didn't have anything to do with either of them killins.'"

Travis watched as Officer Boughton escorted Sissy back inside. She was still weeping. "*That's* who we should worry about, Smokey."

Considering Sissy had experienced both physical trauma and now an emotional blow, all within a week's time, it finally seemed that the toll on her had been taken. Smokey and Travis watched helplessly as her emotional fortitude systematically began to break down. Holding her head as tears streamed down her cheeks, she sat at the counter shaking uncontrollably as though she had just been thrown into some kind of seizure. After escorting her back to his office, Smokey, seeing that the town's doctor, Mark Sayville, was just finishing up his breakfast at one of the booths, asked him if he would check Sissy over. "Sure, Smokey."

Once he had examined her and asked her a few questions, Dr. Sayville, then stepped outside of the office and pulled Smokey aside. "She definitely shouldn't be here, Smokey.

I suspect she was released from the hospital too soon, considering her concussion and other injuries on her body. And then getting news like this on top of that could exacerbate those injuries."

"Exassa-what?"

"Worsen her condition."

"I understand that, but why would she give a hoot in hell about Joubert getting' killed? He didn't do nothin' but beat on that poor girl. She oughta be glad he's out of her life."

"Smokey, often, a woman who experiences physical abuse at the hands of her husband confuses that abuse with love. She might even blame herself because he was angry all the time. 'If I would only be a better wife, maybe he wouldn't have to beat me.' She wrongly accepts much of the blame and guilt, believing she has actually *failed* as a wife. 'I know he does these things to me because he loves me.' Whether or not Sissy actually believed these false notions or had cultivated such an unhealthy sense of love for Joubert is only my speculation. But she needs some psychological help as well as a lot of rest to heal from these injuries."

"I *told* her that, but she insisted on being here. And I also told her I'd continue to pay her salary while she was off."

"I would just go ahead and take her home, Smokey, and tell her to *stay* there for a couple of weeks."

"I'll be doin' that all right. Thanks for checkin' her over, Doc."

At noon, when Dreama came in to continue taking up the slack, Smokey told her about Joubert and the way he was killed.

"I'd say good riddance. He was a louse, the way he tortured her. I hope *he* got tortured before his lights went out."

"I'd rather have seen him go to jail," said Travis. "*No* human being should end up like he did."

"He wasn't a human being, Travis," she replied. "*Sub*-human, I'd say. He deserved what he got. Case closed."

"Closed except for getting the person or persons who did it. I'm sure Sissy loved the man at one time."

"If you say so. And just when did you become such an expert on relationships?"

Travis was sure that comment was meant to reflect on his failed marriage, not to mention his abrupt departure from her house that Saturday night he refused her advances. He didn't respond, but looked down at the coffee he had been incessantly stirring.

Sensing his disconsolate mood, she began back-peddling. "I…I didn't mean anything by that. I'm sure you loved your wife at one time."

He glared at her. "I *still* love my wife…and always will."

"But aren't you divorcing?"

"No."

"She's there and you're here."

The conversation was becoming immensely uncomfortable for him…if not too personal. "It's very complicated, Dreama. But listen. I really don't want to continue on with this. I'm not sure how we got on the subject of my wife, anyway."

"I'm sorry. Obviously, there's something painful going on and it wasn't right of me to go there."

He nodded and offered a partial smile. "Maybe we should get back to work before Smokey starts yelling at us."

Not long after Travis turned in that night, a terrifying thought hit him. In his dream those few nights before, he had actually witnessed Joubert's horrific death. A premonition in the form of a nightmare. But who put the dream there?

Did Satan want him to see what he and his worshippers were capable of? What would his dream be about tonight? For more than two hours he lay awake, dreading what he was sure would come another nightmare. But sometime during the early morning hours, his brain finally signed off. And fortunately, that night the dreams stayed away.

Sissy had one more difficult day to go through. Joubert had no other family except her and her daughter. When the coroner finally released the body the next morning, there was no funeral. But, she and her daughter were present at the gravesite when he was buried that Saturday in a pauper's grave. A grave on which was placed a fifty dollar marker containing only his name and date of death.

† † †

On Sunday, Pastor Moreau's sermon to the Trinity congregation had a different slant. Departing from his usual uplifting and motivating message about God's unconditional love and benevolence, they instead heard a message about "the evil pall that is hanging like a poisonous cloud over your beloved town of Destiny. There is a growing cancer among us. Satan is at work in our very community, spreading his malodorous stench of evil. And if we do not become vigilant and arm ourselves with the weapons of faith and prayer, he will continue his calamitous mission of dissuading you against your belief in God and the Lord Jesus Christ." He went on to warn his people that Satan might begin with a single person and then through that person, the entire town could become infected. Even people of faith would begin falling like dominoes. "As Paul said in Ephesians 6, if it were not possible for Satan to attack and wound us, why should we then need to put on the whole armor of God?"

A rather alarmed congregation did not respond well to this message of gloom and doom. Although Travis nodded his approval as Moreau carefully but dramatically pounded out his message, Travis noticed that quite a few heads were turning toward one another...the men's faces flashing expressions of disapproval and wide-eyed women holding dainty handkerchiefs over their mouths.

Following the sermon, a few of the men had a couple of words with Moreau as they left the sanctuary, but Travis said to him, "It was needed, Pastor. The people *need* to be aware of what appears to be happening here."

"You were very convincing last Sunday, Travis. I believe what you told me. God help us all, but I now know there are truly evil forces at work. I prayed about it and God put this message on my heart. When next Sunday, after our people hear more about Satan's presence and the possibility of demonic possessions actually occurring, I probably couldn't be elected dog catcher if I ever decided to go into politics."

"But a man with your presence and reputation in this community, *will be heard.* Destiny needs a crusader like you...a voice crying in the wilderness. This time, the voice warns of something *evil* coming our way."

"Well," Moreau replied with a smile. "I know I have *one* supporter in this crusade."

"I will be here next week, Pastor."

Sissy was back to work that Monday, in spite of Smokey's protesting. But, her wounds appeared to be gone...both physical and emotional. The smile Travis had seen that first day he sat down for breakfast was back. Even Marty Boucheau's curt and condescending attitude toward her didn't faze her. As horrid as it was, maybe Joubert's death *was* a blessing. A cancerous tumor had been removed and she could now go about her life in safety. The humming and singing were back as she worked with Smokey in the kitchen, much to his annoyance. But still he smiled, knowing that his dependable little firefly was back.

CHAPTER TWENTY FIVE

THE BIG EASY

TRAVIS HAD COUNTED THE DAYS SINCE he sent his letter to Sarah. Although he had no idea as to how long it took for a letter to go from south to north, he estimated four days. If Sarah waited a couple of days before writing him back…that is, if she would at all…enough time had already passed. Maybe she *meant* it when she told him she never wanted to see him again. And that likely meant *any* form of communication.

He had been slugging away at his job from five-something in the morning till sometime after ten at night six days a week. It was suddenly early July and other than Sundays, he had not had a day off. Good-hearted Smokey, realizing that Travis had been looking a bit drained that Friday night, told him to take Saturday off. "And here's an extra twenty."

"Hey, thanks, Smokey. But that'll leave just you with Sissy in the morning and Dreama in the afternoon. And this place fills up at breakfast as well as for the low-country boil tomorrow night."

"Well, I got news about that. I hired two people this week…a woman named Jane Lowry, as a part-time waitress, and a kid about sixteen or seventeen by the name of Stevie

Ray somethin' or other. Jane's husband died recently and she needs to supplement her social security. Both will start tomorrow."

"That's great. What will Stevie Ray 'something-or-other' be doing?"

"He'll be your assistant."

"Does that mean I'll be management now?" Travis asked, grinning.

"Sure. He'd be somethin' like your apprennus."

"I'm suddenly moving up in the business world."

"Yep. But don't git the big head over it." Smokey then laughed.

"I'm not sure I know what to do with a day off. If I *don't* get out and do something, I'll just be spending the day in my apartment back there. I might as well be at work."

"Boy, you ain't learned to have any fun in your life, have ya? You can pack a lunch and take my pole out to Baker's Bridge Lake. Spend a relaxin' day fishin' with some of my buddies. Or how 'bout this? The bus leaves outta here around eight in the mornin' for the Big Easy...Nawlins. Go see that town. You might have so much fun there, ya might not wanna come back."

"Which is why you hired Stevie Ray."

Smokey laughed again. "Go do it."

"Maybe I will. I had actually planned a trip there when I graduated from high school; but, when I had to leave my granddad's apartment, I started spending what little I saved to begin living on my own."

"Then go. But watch ya self, though. They's a revelin' crowd. Lotta hard drinkin' goin' on. But you'll also hear some pretty dadgum good music in some of them joints."

"Okay. You talked me into it. Where does the bus leave from?"

"The bus station on Main at Puryear's Drug Store. Cost ya a buck fifty to ride. Now go git ya self some shut-eye. I'll clean up here."

† † †

About two dozen people loaded on at Puryear's, three of which were children. Most were Negroes dressed in their colorful Sunday best. Travis settled in the next to the last seat on the left side of the bus. Beside him at the window sat an elderly Black man with a short-brimmed brown hat and a face of hard-life wrinkles.

Sharply at eight, the driver, dressed in a gray uniform and cap, closed the door. Travis looked at the other passengers around him. All were Negroes. And they all were looking at him. A few had smiles on their faces; a woman in a large-brimmed hat and a couple of the men nodded. Then it dawned on him as he continued to look around the bus; all of the White passengers had taken up the front half of the bus. Because he had joined the Black people in the rear, that was the reason they were staring at him. Even having just spent a dozen years in an Amish environment, he knew about Rosa Parks and her stand five years before in Alabama. And had the people around him not heard about the Supreme Court decision, rendering such policies of segregation unconstitutional? Maybe it was their way of saying 'we realize we can now sit anywhere we want, and we *choose* to sit in the back.'

At three minutes past eight, the bus pulled away from the drug store. It was not long until the terrain changed from small city store fronts to open country farmland to sugarcane and rice fields and finally to the swamps and bogs of the bayou from where thousands of tree remnants protruded. A kind of gothic beauty unlike anything he had ever seen before.

Travis then closed his eyes and settled back in his seat to relax the remainder of the trip. He had had enough sleep the night before, but was still tired from what proved to be an exhausting week. But, although he had put his body at ease, his brain would not relax. Images of dead men's faces suddenly began flashing through his mind...first the face of the train hobo, then that of Joubert. And then he wondered about Dummy. He hated the fact that he had never learned his real name...and then was set to wonder if anyone else in Destiny knew it. If he died, what name would go on his tombstone? A man without a name, without a life and without a friend. Except for a few benevolent souls like Smokey. God bless Smokey.

And then when he pondered the whole diabolical scenario, it all seemed just too surreal. All three men had apparently become possessed by a demonic spirit...that is unless he had somehow imagined it. Two of them butchered and one mysteriously nailed by a hit-and-run driver. But there was one thing for sure...the note in Dummy's pocket had Travis' name on it. *That* was real. And some demonic being had placed it there. Would Satan's persecution of him continue? Would there be more deaths? And were the people carrying out these sacrificial rituals on human beings members of a satanic cult or actually possessed by the devil themselves? So many questions. But the biggest question of all was...why was *he* in the middle of it all?

Finally, when he opened his eyes, Travis was able to void all of these mental pictures of the underworld from his brain, and he once more concentrated on the Southern Louisiana landscape. Right about that time, the bus then entered a massive bridge system that crossed several miles of waterways and tributaries of Lake Pontchartrain, giving Travis cause to wonder how such a magnificent engineering feat could be accomplished. Far ahead on the eastern horizon, the tall buildings and spires of New Orleans came into view. Less than fifteen minutes later, the bus entered the city limits, and after a few blocks, subsequently pulled into the bus station on Loyola.

"All right, people," bellowed the driver. "From here you can pick up the streetcar. The St. Charles Line will take you on downtown and then you can pick up the Canal Street or Riverfront trolleys. A quarter and you can ride all day long. The bus leaves from here back to Destiny and points west at four and then again at ten. Don't be late or you'll be spending the night. So, welcome to The Big Easy. It ain't a bad deal if you like to drink, have a mess of good gumbo and listen to some cool jazz. Everybody off here."

Travis figured on riding the Canal Line for a while to see some of the homes in the suburbs and then get off in the heart of town to take in the flavor of the city. From there, he would walk to the French Quarter and the Mississippi Riverfront. The cable cars, with their mahogany seats, brass rails and naked light bulbs in the ceiling, were a must to experience for any tourist. Clamoring along a network of tracks on streets shared with automobiles, they were definitely the means of getting around town. As Travis sat by the open window on his car with his arm extended down the side of the coach, he was in awe of the massive, century old live oaks that stood like faithful guardians over shotgun style Creole cottages supported by brick piers and magnificent Greek Revival and Renaissance Colonial homes with twenty foot columns and wrap-around verandas. Into the city proper, the car clanked past colorful souvenir shops, blues bars out of which poured a pulsating blend of music he had never before heard, lively arcades and quaint hotels over which loomed second story balconies with ornamental wrought iron railing. The city was simply a plethora of fascinating sights, sounds and smells.

After jumping off the street car, Travis began walking to the French Quarter. His mother, who had visited New Orleans a few years before he was born, had once told him about the magnificent St. Louis Cathedral with its stately spires...and it was everything she said it was. The centerpiece of Jackson Square, taking up the entire block between rue de Chartres and rue Saint-Pierre, Cathedral-Basilica, with its baroque style décor and gloriously-cast stained glass windows, was by far the most magnificent church Travis had ever seen. He spent more than an hour going through the sanctuary, taking long, mental pictures of its ornately painted ceilings, the statue of Joan of Arc and the gilded work called Sacrifice of the Lamb of God that hung over the altar. From this moving, even piteous experience inside the church, he conjured up memories of the day his mom sat with him in the second pew on the right at St. Peter's just after getting the news about his father's death. She held his hand while she prayed silently for over a half an hour. The sanctuary at St. Peter's wasn't nearly as big or ornate, but that day at Cathedral-Basilica, as he sat in its second pew on the right, the atmosphere somehow seemed the same.

For the remainder of the afternoon, using all of his five senses to the fullest, he peered inside store front windows at purple and gold feathered masks worn during Mardi Gras, ran his fingers over a large brass *fleur de lis* on a stone wall, listened to the music of sweet clarinets and moody saxes pouring into the streets from jazz bars, drew in the savory aromas of freshly-baked beignets, and sampled rich, creamy pralines from Beaudary's. And then there was the busy-ness of working people on the go, the tourists and more tourists, the noisy cable cars and exhaust fumes from the taxis. Although the size of the city definitely didn't compare with the area in which he grew up, it still all took him back...back to the streets of New York more than fifteen years before where from the ethnic delis the aroma of pastrami and sweet breads enticed his olfactory glands. Where the drivers of yellow and checkered cabs blew their horns incessantly. Where hot dog vendors and street hockers seemed to be on every corner. But this city...this big, easy city carried on as though nobody had a care in the world... and the world was one big party.

However, there were other experiences he found *not* so exciting, such as the stench of liquid garbage flowing onto the sidewalks from the bars, and seedy, inebriated characters with bloodshot eyes stumbling into him, one of which spilled his entire cup of beer onto his clean white shirt. Homeless street people seemed to be on every block, hitting on him for change. And then there were the two young women in skimpy dresses who openly propositioned him.

As the sun was slowly disappearing from behind the spires of the cathedral, his stomach then reminded him that all he had put in it was a beignet from the Café du Monde and a sample of praline. At one of the corner vendors, he woofed down a shrimp po'boy and then set out for the Mississippi riverfront. As he sat on a park bench near the dock, he asked a man with a watch what time it was. Five minutes till eight. He watched as a long line of tourists completed boarding the riverboat Natchez, after which its obnoxiously-loud blare of a horn suddenly startled him. And then he spied the couple standing at the dock's railing, watching the boat's departure, smiling and occasionally gazing into each other's eyes, obviously so much in love. For a few seconds, he closed his eyes and drew in the cool, evening Mississippi River air, to capture a memory of a young Amish woman and a young man hoping to one day become Amish, sitting on the trunk of a fallen tree by a stream. Her eyes laughed and danced as he told her funny stories of his childhood. His heart throbbed with ever deepening love, so wildly that he wondered if it might explode from his chest. Where had that most perfect love gone? How could he have allowed his life with Sarah Oberhauf to slip away? And how could he have been so weak as to fall into another woman's arms?

But, his eyes *and* ears were suddenly opened by the first notes of an alto sax beginning a torchy melody of a song he had never heard. He recognized it was what they called 'blues,' but as beautiful as it was it had an almost sinful aura to it. The notes were from a young man with long hair and a short-cropped beard who had set up at an adjacent bench during the moments that Travis had his eyes closed. The horn's case lay open beneath his feet where passersby who might have enjoyed his melodious offerings would drop coins. As the man played, the haunting mephisto-like music seemed to invade and infect Travis' brain like some soul-eating cancer. After the last, almost mournful note had echoed away, the man looked at Travis. However, his look then became more of an uncomfortable stare, cold and unwavering, sending a chill through Travis' spine. But then he remembered that many of the 'street' people that he had encountered as a teen in the Bronx were troubled people...some even demented.

Suddenly, the man spoke. "You don't appreciate my music?"

His words stunned Travis, but then he replied, "Uh...yes. It was good. You have a very nice sound."

"You don't think it merits a few coins in my case? Perhaps a couple of dollars? You of all people should take pity on the poor."

Travis then stood, reached into his jeans pocket and dropped two quarters in the case. In a way, he felt intimidated, but then again, he did enjoy the man's music. And then the man's words rang back to him. "What do you mean…'you of all people?'" Travis asked him. "If you think I'm a wealthy man, I'm not. The saxophone in your hands is worth more than anything I own."

"But you obviously have a job and money in your pocket. And me? I make enough in one day playing my music for people like you to buy a sandwich. You sleep in a bed. I sleep on a bench." The man then looked inside his case and scoffed at the quarters. "Fifty cents, eh. You can't spare more than that?"

Travis became incensed. "I won't be coerced by your words to give you any more. Thanks for the song…but goodbye."

The man's eyes suddenly turned venomous. "Doesn't the God you worship demand you do better than that? What you do to the least of the least, you do to Me…"

"So, you know my God. You seem to be able to quote His words."

"Yeah, I know your God, minister."

Travis took a step back and glared at the man. The same chill…the chill that went through his spine when he heard the demons speak through the hobo, through Joubert and then Dummy…was again going through his neck. "You refer to me as 'minister.' Why?"

The musician laughed. "Don't pretend you don't know me." As he rocked his head, first to the left and then to the right, his eyes remained glued to Travis' face.

"I *don't* know you. I've never seen you before today."

"Of course you do. I've invaded your dreams. You have seen me wearing other faces. As a matter of fact, faces that belonged to people who are now dead."

Angry adrenaline pumped through Travis' system and he kicked over the instrument case, spilling a score of coins onto the pavement. "You! Why do you continue persecuting me?"

The man laughed again and then picked up his saxophone to play a popular spiritual in the streets of New Orleans... *Just a Closer Walk With Thee*. After the first few bars, he stopped. "Will you now walk with *me*? I have sought you out, but you continue to fight me. You know that I am the true one...the one your soul craves." He then continued with the song.

Travis flew into a rage and slapped at the saxophone, causing it to jam further into the man's mouth, splitting his lip. Blood oozed onto the vagrant's white shirt. Suddenly from fifty feet away a voice rang out into the night.

"Hey, you! What are you doing to that bum?" The voice belonged to a large-set police officer who began hustling toward them from the vicinity of the railroad tracks.

Realizing that if he stayed around, he would be facing assault charges, Travis bolted toward the west along the sidewalk by the river. Behind him he heard the officer's voice bellowing, "Stop right where you are!" But he also heard laughter from the demonic being he just left. And as he ran into the night throughout a series of streets, further intermingling with the crowd, he finally saw that he had outrun the officer. But here and there from street musicians on nearly every block, he heard the same musician's song, *Just a Closer Walk With Thee*, played over and over by trumpets, trombones, more saxophones, seemingly in mockery of him *and* the song. He began running again, not knowing where he was or what time it was, having lost his map. He now had no sense of direction. After covering a dozen or more blocks, crossing Poydras, Cardonelet and Dauphine, he thought he should turn right. He then encountered more streets that he didn't remember walking down, like Bienville, St. Louis and Rue Toulouse. And then to his utter dismay, he found himself back near the riverfront. He had somehow gone in a complete hour-long circle. Helplessness and even terror suddenly gripped his mind. The streets were no longer filled with revelers and it seemed that the dark had turned the city into a hell-pit of evil creatures with hideous faces and glowing eyes that lurked in the alleys, followed him, called out after him for money. Was it his mind playing devilish tricks on him or were they real? Had Satan's band of demons followed him and converged in force on these New Orleans streets to further haunt and taunt him? The faster he ran, the wilder his imagination grew.

Finally, he saw a bank building with a large clock that read nine-fifty two. He had less than ten minutes to make the ten o'clock bus. Knowing that it was impossible to get to the station by ten, he hailed a taxi. "The bus station on Loyola," he said after getting into the back seat. "And please hurry."

So, 'would the taxi driver also be some kind of personified demon,' he asked himself. But when the driver spoke, he merely asked Travis, "You in town for some fun tonight?" His face was friendly and voice, actually normal. Travis smiled with relief and replied. "Just in town for the day and going back to Destiny."

"Destiny," repeated the cabbie. "My grandmother lives there. Do you know Hattie Jenkins?"

"No, I've only been living there a few weeks."

"I need to go see her one day soon. Nice little town, Destiny."

They passed a street corner where there was a clock on a pole. Nine-fifty nine.

"Is it much further? The bus will leave in only one minute."

"Just two blocks, sir."

"How much is my fare?" Travis asked, rummaging through his pocket.

"It's a buck ten now...maybe a buck fifty by then."

When the taxi came to a stop in front of the station, a bus was still stopped at the stand. The lighted message over the windshield read *Destiny-Houma*. Quickly, he shoved three dollars into the cabbie's hand, said "Thanks" and then hit the pavement running. But when he was within thirty feet, the bus began pulling out.

"Stop!" he yelled after it. But it continued on.

Exhausted and drenched in sweat from having previously run several blocks, he once again cranked up his tired legs and sprinted after the bus, faster than he had run since he was a teen on the St. Mary's High track team. Three blocks later, when the bus had stopped at a light, he caught it. Just as the light turned green and the bus started pulling away again, he began banging with his fists on the folding doors. The driver stopped the bus abruptly and opened the doors. With an exasperated look, he said, "All right, git on."

After handing the driver two ones and getting his fifty cents back, Travis looked down the aisle to find the bus half-full. Finding the long bench seat in the very back unoccupied, he practically fell onto it to catch his breath. When the bus was well on the way out of the city, the warm night air flowing through the windows did little to cool him down. However, after about ten minutes, he began to relax and then settled back in his seat to reflect on his day and evening in the Big Easy. What started as a good day, ended up as a nightmare...a nightmare that was all too real. Any misgivings he had about his continuing diabolical experiences *not* being real were now behind him. But why was Satan terrorizing him? He was small potatoes in the world...a small speck of matter in time. But then a new thought hit him. Maybe the winning of his soul was *not* the devil's real plan. Maybe Satan was trying to stop something that God had planned for Travis. If Satan scared Travis off…all the way back to Indiana…then he could complete the plan that he had for Destiny. Satan could then prove to God that he was just as powerful as He was, tearing down the moral and spiritual fiber of the town, and barring whole communities from accepting God's plan of salvation. And then other places like Destiny all over the world would fall prey to Satan…fall like dominoes.

For the remainder of his trip back to Destiny, Travis laid his head between the seat back and open window, allowing the ever-cooling air to fill his lungs. There was no more contemplation as to whether or not an evil force had him in its crosshairs. He was sure of it now.

Travis stepped off the bus just after eleven-thirty and then walked the seven blocks back to The Old South. After a cool shower in his make-shift quarters, he turned in. Maybe Monday he would talk with Smokey about him moving to an apartment or rental home, now that he had enough money for a first month's rent. However, Smokey's pay was meager and unless the rental place provided gas, electricity and water in the deal, he would probably be spending his entire month's pay just to have a roof over his head. Then again, if and when he heard back from Sarah, and if she opened her arms to him again, he would immediately be seeking the quickest mode of transportation back home to Indiana.

Chapter Twenty Six

Sounding the Alarm

As his body had extended itself in an entirely different way the day before on the streets of the Big Easy, Travis woke early Sunday morning still tired and sore. And too weary to get up to check the time on the dining room wall clock, he rolled back over to sleep a little more. However, as his stomach told him it was time to get up for some bacon and eggs, his bones still ached for another hour of sleep. But then his brain finally sided with his stomach and reminded him that he needed to get moving so that he wouldn't miss the Trinity service.

After donning his ageing suit, he then told himself his Saturday off would have been better served had he skipped the New Orleans venture, stayed around town and bought a new Sunday suit. Not only were the old Amish coat and trousers beginning to look shabby, he stood out like a sore thumb among his fellow parishioners. It wasn't that he wanted to be in fashion, but he was a bit tired of people coming up and asking him about the suit. "Is that a new fad?" one woman asked. And then a rather smart alec teen approached him after the last service and said, "Interesting suit, daddy-o. Where did you get it…at the Salvation Army?"

As Travis settled into his pew, this Sunday fourth back from the front on the right side, Pastor Moreau, who was already seated in his chair behind the pulpit, nodded to him and smiled. Following his lengthy invocation came the morning hymn, the offering and then the operatic contralto with the heavy vibrato singing *His Eye is on the Sparrow.* And then Drake Moreau dug in with both feet and came out swinging with Part II of the previous Sunday's alarming message.

"My friends, when I ended my service last week, I was approached by several of you who told me that my message may have been a little too frightening for our children and maybe I shouldn't be preaching on the devil and his destructive power. That maybe I over-stated the fact that I believe there is some kind of spiritual plague hanging over Destiny like a demonic fog. But, my friends, I am only preaching what God has laid on my heart. The fact is, we *do* have a colossal problem in our community. It may not be obvious to you, but there is a diabolical underground at work, orchestrated by the devil himself, to draw you into his web, unsuspectingly, unwittingly, according to his battle strategy. As he started the war on Christianity, millenniums ago, he has now made the community of Destiny his new battlefield. There is an undercurrent of Satanism afoot that goes beyond the voodoo and hoodoo practices that have been common in Southern Louisiana. This is a new age, a new world kind of conspiracy that is aimed at our children which brings with it the ingredients of sex, alcohol and music containing lyrics of the demonic world that fuel misconduct. Satan's sentinels are always out and about, waiting for the chance to be impressionable in the most subtle ways. But lately, we have seen evidence that he and his demons have taken on a personification, actually entering the minds and bodies of Destiny's citizens..."

There was a sudden murmur throughout the congregation as husbands and wives again looked at one another. A half dozen people immediately excused themselves to their fellow pew sitters, stepping by them to leave the sanctuary.

Moreau continued. "Satan's quest is to capture the minds, souls and even bodies to begin establishing his worship kingdom. Believe me, folks, this is all too real. He wants to gain a foothold on America, on the world, with all people, so why not set wildfires of rebellion and establish cults that perform sacrificial rituals. We've seen the increase in Darwinism, Atheism and Satanic worshippers, whose course it is to disciple, be deceivers, attacking and spreading seedbeds of evil that infect the Christian infrastructure of churches like ours."

Travis saw that several more couples were walking out and he wondered if the place would be empty once Moreau completed his sermon.

"My friends, I pray that you will take what I am about to say to you in the spirit that it is intended…a spirit of love and concern. But, the attitude and behavior of our own church seems to have changed. More and more of our own congregation seem to be questioning the truth and validity of the scriptures. I see it coming out in our adult Sunday school and in random conversations. It is as though a pall of agnosticism is hanging over us. In the past two months, attendance has dropped. Even among the most faithful attendees. The spirit in this very church seems to be faltering. I can feel in my bones that we are no longer the faithful, God-fearing people we once were. It used to be that I could converse with our town people about Jesus when I see them on the streets, in the barber shop and at the diner. But, the light of the Lord that used to be on their faces is no longer there. Our children and our teens seem to be finding more mischief to get into…

fighting in school and on the playground, teen drinking and being caught fornicating in parked cars. There is increased vandalism and burglary. We must now even keep this very sanctuary locked as someone has come inside and stolen our brass candlestick holders and chalices.

"The only way we can combat the evil that has invaded our community is pray. Pray hard and trust in the Lord Jesus Christ. As Jesus Himself cast out the demons from the poor souls two thousand years ago, we must find out where they are here and pray them away. But it will not be easy. The persuasive nature of the Prince of Darkness is strong and overpowering, especially to the weak in faith. As I said last week, my friends, as he is like a blood-sucking leech, well before he attaches himself to our minds and bodies, we must put on that full armor of God. Satan has the power to control us all…even the most devout of Christians. As the Bible warns us, 'Some will fall away from the faith, paying attention to deceitful spirits and doctrines of the demons.' In First Peter we are told that 'your adversary, the devil, prowls like a roaring lion, seeking someone to devour.' Even we, my dear friends, are not immune to this ancient disease…a disease for which there is only one remedy. Prayer."

And then Pastor Moreau broke into a long, impassioned prayer that lasted more than fifteen minutes. Afterward, when Travis looked up, clearly half of the congregation was missing. But, just before the service ended, the closing hymn was sung…and it struck Travis in the chest like a lightning bolt. As soon as the organist formed the first notes of the song he had heard in mockery the night before, *Just a Closer Walk With Thee*, Travis felt like running from the sanctuary himself. If the song wasn't just an ironic coincidence, had Satan now also invaded the holy sanctuary at Trinity? The night before, Satan had somehow made the song sound as though it belonged to him. Through the musician he had asked, "Will you now walk with me?" Was it the devil's purpose that it be chosen especially for Travis as the closing hymn? No, Travis told himself. It was pure coincidence.

Several of those who had stayed to the end of Moreau's sermon, shook his hand at the door. They were not only faithful to the pastor, but were fully in sync with his message. "I knew something evil was afoot, Drake," said one older man. "People been actin' strange for more'n six months. Not only have I noticed the queer looks on their faces, people just act hateful. Other people seem like somethin' has sucked the life outta them. I don't know. You might be onto somethin.'"

And then there approached an older lady in a Mamie Eisenhower pill box hat who remarked, "I've been hearing about these murders, Drake. How two men got cut up and eyes put out. Like some devil cult did it. And then I saw one of those five point star things with a circle around it painted on the overpass out on Tucker Street."

"A pentagram, Doris."

"Yes, I reckon that's what I saw. A pentagram. I despise what's going on around here Drake and bully for you in bringing it to everyone's attention. I hate all those people walked out of the service. Some are my friends."

And then again, the last hand that Drake Moreau shook belonged to Travis. "It was needed, Pastor. Sorry you lost a few today. Some people only want to hear inspiring, uplifting messages full of proverbs and don't even want to *hear* the name Satan. I expect they think he is just some mythical creature that has no place in a sermon."

Moreau nodded. "This community needs a mirror held before its face, to understand just how it is being affected by what we both know is a demonic crusade on the devil's part."

"I stand with you, Drake. I'm not a voice that anyone wants to hear, but I will echo your message wherever and whenever I can. I am even more so convinced that the phenomenons I have experienced are Satan's warning for me to leave town. You see, I know now that I was sent here to somehow help stop the spread of Satan's cancer. And he has revealed himself to me in human form to try scaring me off."

"Interesting that you tell me that, Travis. Perhaps God *did* send you down here to us to not only be His Paul Revere, but His battle captain." He then embraced Travis. "Let's fight the fight together, my brother."

† † †

An Arresting Development

Travis began his Monday as usual popping out of bed as soon as he heard Smokey, his 'alarm clock,' clattering pans in the kitchen. By the time Travis had cleaned up and dressed, Smokey had wheeled out the meats, eggs and the prepared batters of pancakes, waffles and biscuits from the industrial-size fridge. Travis then started up the coffee urn, fired up the grill and set out the sweet rolls and donuts in the large glass container. Sissy came in at six and by six-thirty when Travis turned the door sign to *open*, everything was ready for the onslaught of breakfast patrons.

"So, where are your two new employees, Smokey?"

"Stevie Ray will be in at eleven-thirty ta make life a little easier for ya. You two can split things up the way ya see fit. Now, old Jane will start at four-thirty and go till nine. I reckon as possessive as Dreama is about her job, she may not like anyone crowdin' her. But, she *wanted* some relief. Now let's see how another woman in her turf sets with her."

In the middle of the breakfast hours, about eight fifteen, Travis spied three men at the door, Chief Couture and two serious-looking men wearing black suits, skinny black neckties and granite faces. When Couture saw Smokey behind the counter, he gave him a finger summons. Smokey wiped his hands on his apron and came out to meet the men in the center of the dining room.

"Mornin,' Chief. Did ja bring some out-of-towners in for breakfast?"

Couture shook his head. "Nope. These fellers are from the FBI and they're here to take Marlow into custody."

"What for?" exclaimed Smokey.

"Government business. How 'bout tellin' him to come over here. We don't mean to make a scene."

Smokey walked to where Travis was wiping down a table and said, "Those guys over there are Feds. They say they want to take you in."

Travis narrowed his eyebrows. "What for?"

"Beats me, but I sure as the devil intend to find out."

When Travis approached the men, Couture said, "Let's step out front, Marlowe." He then lightly took Travis by the arm and led him to the door. The agents followed with Smokey on their heels. There wasn't a scene, but all necks in the diner were craned to what was going on.

Once outside, the older, taller agent asked, "Are you Travis Marlowe?"

"Yes. What's this about?"

"Turn around and put your hands on the wall."

"Why? I've done nothing."

"Do as I say!" the agent barked.

Slowly, Travis turned and did as ordered. The agent then ran his hands over his pockets and on the insides of his legs.

"Okay, turn around."

"You need to tell me what's going on here," Travis said in a tone that reflected his ire.

"We need to talk, son. Let's go."

Smokey then stepped up and asked, "Where you takin' him and what are ya arrestin' him for?"

The agents ignored the question and proceeded to lead Travis toward the unmarked government car.

"I have a right ta know what this is about. *I'm his employer!*" yelled Smokey after them.

The shorter, much stouter agent shook his head and then put Travis in the back seat of the sedan.

Smokey continued his rant. "I know what this is about, Chief. This bein' election year, St. Pierre wants to save his job. Puttin' somebody behind bars will be a feather in his cap."

Couture looked back at him, but said nothing.

But, as Smokey continued to protest, all he could do was watch helplessly as the car pulled away from the curb and quickly disappeared down Main.

Travis, who was sitting in the back seat with Couture, then opened up on them. "Okay, officers, I've had about enough of this. I demand to know where you're taking me and why."

"We're goin' to the station house where these agents will be questionin' you," replied Couture. "Now keep your mouth *shut*."

After the sedan had covered about eight blocks toward the center of town and turned off Main onto Barrow Street, it came to a stop in the parking lot of the Destiny Police Department. The agents then led Travis inside and Couture showed them to the interrogation room. Once situated in the room, the taller agent sat opposite Travis, leaning over the small table between them, and Couture and the other agent stood off to the side against the wall.

"I'm Special Agent Jim LeFevre and the man standing with the Chief is Special Agent Mike Nelson. We are dispatched from the New Orleans field office. We have a warrant for your arrest. You are charged with the murder of one Joubert Mumford, a Negro male against whom you made threats, assaulted and then brutalized before killing him Sunday week."

"Wait a minute. I was already questioned by Chief Couture about that and was under the impression I had been cleared."

Couture then interjected. "Marlowe, I had an obligation under the law to put these murders out on the blotter...to all law enforcement includin' the Bureau. Your name obviously went up as a suspect. I guess since Joubert was Colored and all, and got hisself butchered up like he did, old J. Edgar musta got interested."

LeFevre continued. "The Bureau has a new task force dedicated to the investigation of hate crimes on Negroes and Jews. Based on the information we have received, it appears this could be one of them. I'm going to ask you a few questions, Marlowe. You've probably heard them before, but your responses will determine whether we drop the charges or have you arraigned in Federal court for the murder."

"Before you begin your questioning, sir, I think you should know there was another man who was found tortured and murdered the same way, and he was a *White* man."

"And from the information we received, you also had some kind of altercation with *him*. You had fought with both men and the next day, each was found with eyes burnt out, pentagrams carved on their bodies and finally a knife wound in the abdomen that ended their lives. Where were you the night Mumford was murdered?"

"If it was earlier in the day, sitting in the diner listening to the radio. I think I then turned in early."

"So, basically, you can't prove where you were. No one else saw you."

"That's correct. You have to understand, there is no way I could be capable of such heinous acts, Agent LeFevre."

"Then let me explore your history a little. First of all, let me see some identification."

"I...don't actually have any. All I carry is a money clip."

"What do you mean? Everybody has an I.D. A driver's license or some other form of identification."

"I don't own a car or drive anymore. I used to have a Social Security card, but it's been a long time since I've seen it."

"What *is* the number?"

"I don't remember."

"We will have you fingerprinted in a few moments. So, what kind of record will we find?"

"You'll find nothing. I've never had my fingerprints taken before."

"How old are you?"

"Thirty one."

"Thirty one and you don't have a driver's license."

"Are you an alien?"

"You're asking if I'm from another country?"

"I'm not asking you if you're from another *world*, Marlowe."

"No. I was born in America and have lived in this country all my life."

"I think you're lying about the driver's license and Social Security card. And I think you're hiding something. "

"For the past thirteen years, I have lived under the Amish order. They don't drive cars nor elect Social Security."

"Amish, huh? Where?"

"Indiana."

"Where in Indiana?"

"Near a town called Hurley."

"We can check that out and will."

"Fine. Then do that," Travis replied sharply.

"If we contact the Hurley Police Department, what will we find out about you?"

"Nothing…I promise you. Anyway, they don't know many of us Amish."

"Do you have a family?"

"A wife and daughter."

"Where are they?"

"Back home in Indiana."

"You're here and they are there. Why?"

Couture jumped in. "He says he and his wife split up."

LeFevre scowled. "I want *him* to answer the questions, Chief." He then turned his eyes back to Travis. "You left them and came to Louisiana…landed here after jumping off a box car."

"I did."

"Why did you leave your family and then end up here?"

"I just wanted to get away…far away. At least for a while."

"Why did you split from your wife?"

"That, sir, is personal. I won't answer anymore questions about my family. But, I do think my leaving was probably the biggest mistake of my life."

"Until you came here and killed two people."

"I killed no one, sir."

"The Chief here says you may have been involved in another crime…the hit-and-run of a town beggar."

"No, sir. Again, I have no vehicle and only know about it because it happened directly in front of the diner where I work."

"Then, how do you explain the note found on him blaming you for the incident?"

"I can't, sir."

"Did you ever communicate with him before?"

"A few times. I took food to him when he showed up hungry."

"If you were kind to him, why would the note in his pocket infer that you might somehow be causing his death?"

"I...I don't know. Unless somebody had it in for me."

LeFevre shot Couture and his partner a glance. "And why would somebody have it in for some new guy in town who works as a bus boy?"

"I can't answer that. But, it's the only possible reason I can give you."

"You fought with Joubert Mumford the day before he was killed. You beat him pretty badly from what I hear. You obviously had a lot of anger in you that led to a display of violence. And that's one step away from murder."

"I was defending myself and the honor of the young woman I work with."

"Mumford's wife. I know the story. You got so angry with Mumford, like you did with the man on the train, and decided to finish the job. You committed unspeakable acts on the man, humiliating him *and* mutilating him. Payback for what he did to his wife."

"No, sir. It ended in the street where we fought."

LeFevre smiled wryly. "Joubert was a large, muscular man. How did you manage to take him down?"

"I used to box. When I was a teen, I was the Golden Gloves champion for my age and weight class in the Bronx."

"A New Yorker. I thought I detected the brogue."

Agent Nelson, who was leafing back through several pages of notes he had written, broke in. "Let's talk about this Amish thing. What kind of work did you do in that community?"

"At first, I worked in my father-in-law's store; then after he died, my wife and I sold the business and I began working our farm. I also served the last couple of years as a minister."

"You were the minister of the community?"

"I was the youngest and newest of three ministers who taught and served the men, women and children. The eldest is the senior minister and he officiates at most of our Sunday services and at weddings and funerals. I worked mostly with the children."

"Hmm. A minister who left his wife and lost his position in the community. Sounds like some unpleasant things happened. Were you excommunicated?"

"I'm ashamed to say that I was shunned by the elders."

"I take it that's pretty much the same thing."

Travis didn't respond.

"Agent LeFevre laid out the reason you assaulted Joubert Mumford and then decided o go back and finish the job. I have a second theory."

"What?"

"Let me first ask you this: have you ever been a member of the KKK?

"No."

"Have you ever been associated with the Neo-Nazis?"

"Absolutely not."

"You lived in an all-White community. The Amish are German people, aren't they?"

Most orders of the Amish and Mennonites are direct descendents of the Deutsch, the True Old Order called the Swartzentruber."

"So, the Amish being German, or Aryan if you will, would consider Negroes and Jews to be impure and subservient races. A Black man was slaughtered, we know. But did you also know the man on the train found cut up the same way was

Jewish? The name in his wallet was Rosenthal. Obviously not one of the more successful Jews." He then chuckled. "Maybe this superior race ideal was pounded into our head all these years by the Krauts you lived with. You encountered these people and thought you'd commence to rid the world of two disgusting animals. But why the pentagram and mutilation? Did you fall into some kind of satanic cult?"

Travis jumped to his feet, knocking the chair to the floor behind him. "How dare you accuse me of being not only a racist, but a devil worshipper! Is this an interrogation or a witch hunt?"

Nelson walked over to Travis, up-righted the chair and shoved him back down in it. "Sit there and don't get up again, Marlowe. You wouldn't be the first of your kind that cracked due to some kind of toxic faith brain washing."

"What do you mean…my kind?"

"You Christian types…zealots."

"You make it sound like Christians are fanatics or members of some kind of cult. I take it *you're* not a Christian, Mr. Nelson."

"You're all a bunch of weak-minded people who use your religion as a crutch. *And* you've got blinders on about the real world."

LeFevre stood and pulled Nelson aside. "That's enough, Mike. You're out of line here. Just ask the man the questions and hands off his faith. You know better than that."

"Hey, I was just trying to get him riled enough to come after me. This guy's got a temper…we've already seen that."

"Get out, Mike. You're not in this interrogation anymore."

Nelson gave him a searing glare, snatched up his notebook and then left the room.

"I apologize for Agent Nelson's behavior, Marlowe. There was no reason to besmirch one's religion; however, religion aside, when you add it all up…your assault on two men, one

Jewish, one Negro beginning with the night of your arrival, you have no alibi for the night Mumford was murdered, and you get angry. Whatever happened to turning the other cheek? You, a minister, fighting with people."

"Only when provoked. There's such a thing as righteous anger in my faith." He then paused before asking, "So, what happens from here?"

"I'm asking Chief Couture here to lock you in one of his cells for suspicion of murder...two counts. We'll have to place charges on you under the circumstances. I'll be running your fingerprints and checking with the Hurley police. If there's no record on you, that doesn't mean you get out. Too much stacks up against you."

"So you actually think I'm a kind of psychopath who could commit such crimes that obviously is the work of Satan worshippers or crazed practitioners of voodoo."

"I don't know what you're capable of, Marlowe. Who knows *anything* about you?"

"I'll tell you who...my wife and daughter, the elders in the Amish community, and Smokey Woodruff."

"Get yourself a lawyer, Marlowe. If you don't have the money, there's always the parish public defender."

"And how long do I sit while you carry out your investigation of me?"

"Could be days...could be weeks. If you did do these crimes, I suggest you use the time to think about your options. Come clean and it'll go easier on you. Maybe in doing so, you can save your life."

"There won't be any confession to something I didn't do, Agent LeFevre. Maybe you should make better use of your time by searching for the real killers."

"We've *got* our man, Marlowe," said Couture. "Take our advice and avoid the gas chamber."

CHAPTER TWENTY SEVEN

VISITORS

IT WAS LIKE SOMEONE WAS PILING on. Maybe even God. Travis had thought he was at his low ebb that day he walked along the road to Hurley, after Sarah had told him to leave and after the elders shunned him from the order altogether. Now he was sitting in a cell with dirty concrete walls, a hard, urine-stained bunk, a grungy sink and a nasty toilet. The storage room Smokey let him use seemed in comparison like the Holiday Inn. As he sat on the bunk with his back against the wall, he allowed the events of the last two months to travel through his brain in chronological order, like the proverbial snowball rolling down the hill, enlargening and gathering speed until it crashed at the bottom…which was where he was. The bottom.

"God in Heaven," he said to himself. "Why is all this happening to me? If it is a test, I've failed. I admit it. But haven't I paid enough for my sins? Have I not asked a hundred times for your forgiveness? Am I a present day Job? And if so, you know that I do not have his fortitude. I surrender. I give up. Just show me what you want me to do and I will do it. Give me but a morsel of hope I can build on. I'm all out of faith."

By automatic reflex, when in such spiritual need, he reached down beside him for the Stanley Bible. But then he realized he was not in his room at the diner. He felt naked without it, as though his right arm had been separated from him. It was the one friend to which he could turn for daily ecclesiastical counsel. Without it, he would be suffering the spiritual D.T.s.

At one-fifteen, Harold Presley brought him a lunch consisting of a ham and cheese sandwich and cold French fries from Connie's. It didn't even smell good. He shoved it away and sat back down on the bunk.

"If it's anything to ya, Marlowe, I believe you when you say you didn't kill those men. I got a keen sense about people and you ain't the type to butcher up and kill like that. But, I'm just a small fish around here and my opinion don't count for nothin.' Now Chief? He's fully convinced you're the murderer and he'll do his best to see you punished for it. But, it's a Federal deal, now."

"I appreciate you telling me that," Travis replied. "I guess I need someone in my corner right about now."

From another part of the building they suddenly heard Couture calling. "Harold! Come back outta there and tend to this girl!"

When Presley answered the call, he found Couture standing with Sissy Mumford.

"She's here to bring Marlowe a basket of food from Smokey. Inspect it thoroughly and then take her on back."

"They ain't no knives or guns in here, if that's what you're lookin' for," Sissy said.

"Don't offer me any sass, girl. Check it out thoroughly, Harold."

"Just a plate of food and…a Bible. That's all," said Presley."

"Let me see that Bible."

Presley handed it off to Couture and the Chief grasped the Bible by the spine and shook it."

"You think I hid a file in there or somethin'?"

Couture glared at her and threw the Bible back into the basket none too gently. "Git on with ya. Got two minutes, girl."

As Couture watched Sissy leave the room, he said, "Go with her, Harold, and watch her."

Presley led Sissy into the hallway and then stopped at the first of two cells. "Visitor, Marlowe."

Travis pushed himself off the bunk and smiled. "Sissy."

"Smokey done sent this food to you, Travis. They's some ham and yams, some bread and piece of chocolate cake. He say he'd be by sometime tonight, maybe when he quits work."

As the basket would not slip through the bars, Sissy slid the plate underneath the bottom of the door. "He sent you some sweet tea, too."

"Tell him thanks, Sissy. I didn't much like the innkeeper's lunch." He then smiled at Presley.

"Before I leave, Travis, I gotta ask you somethin.' I hear the people talkin' all around me about you killin' Joubert. You didn't, did you? 'Cause if you did, that's okay. I mean... nobody needs to kill nobody; but Joubert, he needed to go away in the worst way."

Another voice emerged from the hallway. There was laughter attached to it. "It was the worst way, all right," said Couture. "Marlowe there gave you your wish."

Travis ignored Couture. "No, Sissy. I didn't kill Joubert or anybody else. I swear to you I didn't."

"And I believe you, Travis. I know you fought with him and he got the beatin' he deserved. But, I really didn't believe you could cut on a man like they say he was found." Tears then began rolling down her cheeks. "When they gone let you outta here?"

Couture again. "He ain't *gettin'* out.They're gonna get the goods on him before it's all over and one day soon he'll be sittin' in one of them chairs where cyanide pellets start droppin.'"

Sissy put her hands over her face. "That's horrible!"

"I'll be all right, Sissy. The truth will come out and the real killer or killers found."

She nodded and wiped he eyes. "I 'spect I be getting' back. I'm gonna stay a while and help Smokey until Dreama comes in. You rest easy, Travis. God, He be lookin' after you and I'll say a prayer for you."

Later that afternoon, Travis was reading various scriptures from The Acts about the Apostle Paul's imprisonment when he saw the friendly face on the other side of the bars. Smokey had taken a few minutes off just after seven to leave Dreama and Jane to 'mind the store.' Jane was a good cook in her own right and showed him earlier in the supper hour how she could manage the grill. In Smokey's hands was the same basket Sissy had carried, but now containing fresh red shrimp from the gulf, corn on the cob and new potatoes. Since Chief Couture was out and about, Presley didn't bother inspecting the basket.

"Thanks for coming, Smokey. And thanks for giving Sissy my Bible along with the lunch."

"Yeah. And that's another reason I know you didn't commit any murders. Somebody who reads the good book like you do…well, he don't have it in him to kill anybody. So, they treatin' you all right?"

"So far. It looks like the Feds are the ones who intend to see me prosecuted for those two murders. Something about racial hate crimes. Like I intentionally came down here to seek out Negroes and Jews to kill. They're building their case as we speak."

"The Yankee gov-ment is now goin' overboard when it comes to crimes against the Coloreds. They think the south is still persecutin' and hangin' the Blacks. There might be a few bad apples out there who have it in for Coloreds and Jews…like the Klan; but most people around here are treatin' 'em fine. I reckon it's the older people whose daddies fought for the Confederacy that's kept this prejudice thing goin.' It gets handed down through generations. For the most part, Washington is still punishin' the south. They think we's still fightin' the Civil War, I guess."

"But, the war was over nearly a hundred years ago."

"My daddie used to tell me the war wasn't fought over slavery. The northerners think the south was full of *Gone With the Wind* type plantations and everybody owned slaves. The fact is, only about four percent of landowners owned slaves. Most farmers were too poor to buy 'em. The war was mostly over the way the gov-ment dictated who the south could trade with and the ridi-clous taxes they would have to pay at the ports. As far as Color? I never knocked down any Negro man because of his skin. A man's a man, and I think most people around here feel the same way. Oh, a few like Boucheau and even the mayor got prejudice in their bones. But hey, how'd we ever get on this subject anyway? Let's talk about how we gone get ya outta here."

"I'm for that. I guess I need to contact the public defender."

"I can hep ya with that. I know Tom Barfield pretty well. Good man. He'll dig in for ya. But I don't know the Federal judge. I think he'd be outta Houma."

Travis nodded. "I know you'll help me by word of mouth anyway you can. Say, how did the Jane lady and Stevie Ray work out today? I didn't get an opportunity to meet either of them."

"Jane's gonna be good. She cooked over at the high school for years before her husband, Calvin, died. Now Stevie Ray, I don't know about. He don't have your gumption and kinda lopes around. When you get back, I'll let you tend to 'im."

"*If* I get back."

"Oh, you will, son. I gotta feelin' they'll be droppin' the charges. Well, I need to git back there. And I'll be talkin' to Couture to make sure you're treated right." He then stopped before leaving and shook his head.

"What's the matter, Smokey?"

"I almost said I have to get back and check to see if Dummy's out front. Poor guy. He was always grateful for what he got. Kind of like me feedin' an alley cat. Sure do miss the old varmit. He's been comin' round for years." He shook his head again.

"I didn't take a plate to him but a half dozen times, but he did seem like a decent human being...the wretched soul that he was." Travis didn't choose to go into the *two way* conversation they had had the night before he was run down. It didn't matter anymore. "But, we act like he's dead. He didn't..."

"Naw. He did get out of the hospital, but I ain't seen him. A couple a guys came in for breakfast yesterday and said they seen him down around the courthouse on crutches. He weren't gettin' around though."

"Maybe we'll see him again."

Smokey grinned. "You still think he said somethin' to ya?"

"I know he did."

"Well, okay. If you say so...but hey, I gotta go. Have a good'n if that's possible."

"Thanks for the visit, Smokey. Somehow I knew you'd be by today."

Smokey then turned and walked away, raising his hand in a farewell wave.

Travis watched the big man as he lumbered back through the door to the station room and was out of sight. He knew he had never nor would probably ever have a friend like Smokey Woodruff.

It was a long evening for Travis. He read from the Psalms until there was no more light from the sky filtering in his barred window. He then lay awake until Officer Presley looked in on him at midnight. "I'll be leavin' now, Marlowe. We got Lennie Blake comin' in for the night shift. Chief will be here at eight and will see that somebody sends out for breakfast."

"Can he make it the diner and not that Connie's place?"

"See what I can do about that." He then grinned and added. "Now don't go anywhere."

After Presley left and turned out the hall light, Travis' cell was dark. However, the light of the moon and stars helped him see enough to move around, brush his teeth and use the toilet. After stretching out on the bunk, the night seemed to magnify the pungent odor of sweat and urine that had long since been absorbed by the mattress. When he finally closed his eyes, he pictured himself lying beside Sarah on their soft mattress with clean, fresh-smelling sheets. Feelings of anguish and self-pity soon took him over. When he re-opened his eyes moments later, he found them moist and he dabbed at them with his sleeve. The moon, nearly in its second stage, silver and bright, looked down on him through the barred windows high upon the wall. It was the same comforting friend that filtered its rays through his bedroom window some fifteen years before in his Bronx apartment the day his mother died. It was the same sweet friend that fell onto his shoulders as he sat rocking his baby daughter the night she had the croup. And he smiled realizing that at that very moment the same gentle moon was spreading its glorious rays over the farmhouse and fields back in Indiana where Sarah and Rachael were sleeping. It made it all the more difficult for him to fathom the predicament he found himself in. Maybe tomorrow somehow, someone would realize that Travis Marlowe was the wrong man behind bars.

Perhaps an hour later he finally fell asleep. But, then, he realized he wasn't in the cell any longer. He was lying on his back in a field of cool grass. To his horror, he found he had been stripped of his shirt and his hands and feet were tied to metal stakes pounded firmly in the ground. He saw the moon again, now full and at twelve o'clock high. When he turned his head, first to the left and then to the right, he saw them. The flickering fire in the chimney reflected off their black robes while they danced and chanted. Hoods covered their faces and he could not readily make out whether they were male or female. However, two of the twelve he could see had no faces at all…like Rachael's doll. And then suddenly, a dark human form appeared over him, blotting out the moon. It was a man. The man then threw back his hood and revealed his face…a face having deep, penetrating eyes that shown like black diamonds, and a mouth that was turned up at both ends into a sinister smile. It was the same face that he saw on the musician at the New Orleans Riverfront. In the man's right hand was a fiery red poker and in his left was Travis' Bible that had been set afire. The man then dropped the burning pages onto the ground and brought the iron to within inches of Travis' face.

"You have refused to see the truth, Travis Marlowe. Now you will no longer see at all."

"No!" Travis screamed out.

It seemed like only minutes after the horrid nightmare when the morning rays of sun streamed through the bars and opened his eyes. But he opened them slowly as he feared they had been turned into fiery coals. The dream was *that real*. His heart was pounding and he was drenched in sweat. Slowly, he sat up and placed his back against the wall. Why had such a dream come over him? Was it another premonition of an event to come? His dream about Joubert's death came true. He shuttered thinking about it. But that's all it was, he told himself. Just a dream.

The first thing he noticed before getting out of bed was that his neck and back hurt from the sagging mattress. If he had to sleep on that bunk many more nights, he may just end up an *orthopedic* nightmare. *But,* if he had to endure any more such dreams, he feared one morning he might never wake up again.

After splashing water onto his face from the basin and brushing his teeth, he sat back down on the bunk with his Bible. Although he needed something uplifting and encouraging from the *Good Book*, as Smokey had called it, his Bible ironically opened to Psalm 88. And at the very top of the text, he read verse 6:

You have laid me in the lowest pit, in darkness, in the depths. Your wrath lies heavy on me, and You have afflicted me with all Your waves. You have put away my acquaintances far from me. You have made me an abomination to them. I am shut up and I cannot get out; my eye wastes away because of affliction. (Verse 13) But to You I have cried out, O Lord, and in the morning my prayer comes to You. Lord, why do You cast off my soul? Why do You hide Your face from me? (16) Your fierce wrath has gone over me; Your terrors have cut me off. They came around me all day long like water; they engulfed me altogether. Loved ones and friends You have put far from me, and my acquaintances into darkness.

He thought about the dream again. There was something familiar about its location…but he couldn't put his finger on it. Maybe it would come to him.

When he thought it was around seven, considering where the sun was in the sky, the door from the station room opened. A young man in uniform, perhaps nineteen or twenty, entered carrying a breakfast tray. "Good morning, Marlowe. I'm Lennie Blake. Presley told me you wanted this to come from Smokey's, but the city contracts with Connie's for the prisoners' food. It smells pretty good, though…bacon, eggs, toast and coffee." He then slid the tray under the door.

"Thanks," replied Travis.

"So you're the man who is supposed to have butchered up and killed those two men."

"Which I didn't."

"Oh, everybody we put in here says they didn't do the crime. But, I have to admit, you don't *look* like a murderer."

Travis smiled while opening up the container of coffee. "What does a murderer *look* like?"

"I don't know. Maybe rougher looking, evil eyes… different from you, I'd say."

"Thanks for your vote of confidence. At least I have *somebody* wearing a badge on my side."

"I didn't say I was on your side. I'm not the judge or on the jury. But, I hope to God you didn't kill those men."

"If you'll *talk* with God, maybe he'll convince you in some way I truly didn't kill them."

"Maybe I'll do that. Well, I'd better get back. My shift will be over soon. The Chief will be here in a few minutes."

Blake did seem like a nice young man to Travis and he wondered why someone like Couture would have put the kid on the force, as timid and personable as he was.

Travis took one bite of the eggs and rubbery toast and was fully convinced nothing that bad would ever come from the Old South. He wasn't hungry anyway and slid the tray back under the door. The coffee he took with him back to his bunk.

Travis found it a long, lonely morning. None of the officers came back to check on him. At least someone would be bringing him lunch...even if it *was* from Connie's. And since Agent LeFevre had said it would take several days to perform their background investigation on him and determine whether there was enough evidence to take to the U.S. Attorney, he would not see them anytime soon. Maybe he *would* be the guest of the Destiny P.D. for longer than he figured.

His lunch did come at 12:30 and he actually found the tuna salad sandwich and chips edible. But maybe it was just because he was hungry.

Then at 2:30, the door from the station room opened again and through it waltzed Dreama. Officer Merle Harkins escorted her in. "You have ten minutes, Miss Van Horne." He then closed the door after him.

When she reached the cell bars, she said, "Can you believe it? The letch actually tried to search me." She then fluffed up her hair. "Oh, Travis. I can't believe they actually arrested you. Everybody knows you didn't murder Joubert Mumford."

"Everybody but the law."

"Well, listen. The reason I'm here is to tell you I have a friend...a lawyer over in Morgan City who's well respected. His name is Tommy Barfield. I know you probably can't afford him, but he does do some public defender work every once in a while."

"Thanks, Dreama. I'm open to anything to get me out of this place."

"Can I bring you something from the diner before I go on shift?"

"I'm okay. They brought me a sandwich earlier."

"From Connie's, I understand. Don't worry, I'll get Smokey to put together a good dinner this evening."

Suddenly, the door opened and Officer Harkins re-appeared.

"It's not been ten minutes, you know!" she barked.

"Marlowe, you must be the most popular dang jailbird we ever had. There's somebody else out here," Harkins said.

No sooner was that said, another familiar face appeared in the doorway. "Ah, Miss Van Horne, I believe. I see you've come to check on our friend as well."

"Hello, Mr. Moreau. I was just leaving."

"Not on my account, I hope."

"No. I just have to get to work. Bye, bye, Travis. I'll call Tommy later on." She then squeezed his hand through the bars.

When she had cleared the door, Drake Moreau said. "I just don't think that young lady likes me. I witnessed to her in the diner a couple of times and she broke away from me like I had the plague."

"I too found that talking with her about God scares her off. But, Dreama's a sweet lady and will do anything for you."

"I'm sure," replied Moreau.

"Thanks for coming by, Pastor. I guess you didn't expect to find me cooped up like a canary in a cage, did you?"

"I should say not. I just found out about it this morning. One of our deacons is a friend of Mayor St. Pierre's. He told me the FBI had caught Joubert Mumford's killer and maybe that of another man. You don't *look* like a killer, my friend. Should I have feared for my life when you visited me?" He then chuckled.

It also brought a partial smile to Travis' lips. "I can't tell you how good it is to see you, Drake."

"I have thought about your predicament all morning as well as the supernatural experiences you have had. And I remain amazed about the trouble that has befallen you."

Travis smiled. "And all morning, this song has kept running through my head, *Nobody Knows the Troubles I've Seen*."

Moreau laughed, but then his face turned somber. "And I too have experienced some troubles as a result of my last two sermons to the church. You saw that clearly half of the congregation walked out on me. I can't tell you the number of calls I've received from very concerned members. Some think I have gone off the deep end while others just believe that my warnings about the evil, perfidious happenings in our community are merely attempts on my part to *scare* people into salvation. A few also told me their children are now frightened and one parent even said that their eight year old daughter knows the devil is living in her bedroom." Moreau then looked away, breathed a deep breath and shook his head. "It is not my purpose to scare children and I am terribly sorry if that has happened."

"I wouldn't worry about it, Drake. People have to know what is going on around here. I'm sure they've heard about the murders and are aware of the diabolical symbols painted on buildings and overpasses. It's the nature of people to turn a blind eye and put their heads in the sand rather than face reality. But, in a way, I feel responsible. I brought these things to your attention…"

"And opened *my* eyes. I'm not so sure *I* wasn't one of those ostriches you were talking about. But, we together have been the alarmists that this community needed."

"Does there seem to be a kingpin in this undercurrent going on…someone who seems to be influencing others in your congregation?"

"Strange that you should mention that, Travis. My own associate pastor, Christopher Rudman, had some words with me. He as much said I have alienated our congregation... maybe to a point where people will soon leave our membership in hordes. I thought he above all people would be supportive. But, he hasn't been in the church but a few months or so. Maybe I've never really gotten to know him. But, I'd say the most vocal and most influential dissenter is the Mayor himself...St. Pierre. Interesting that he also only recently became a member, but he has tried to buck me at every turn...not just in my sounding the alarm about this demonic fog, but in other church business. I've had the impression that he's using his position to gain a foothold in the church."

"Why would he want to do that...to cause friction, which often leads to the splitting of a church body?"

"I have always thought of the man as power hungry. He is not only the Mayor, but his family owns most of the land the town businesses sit on. He is a trustee of our largest bank. And he is feared by most because of that power."

Travis nodded. "And when he comes into the diner, he flaunts himself to everyone around him so that people can recognize that power. What you're telling me is that if Destiny had a president or king, he would be it."

"He's been a public figure for more than twenty five years, but mayor for eight. I doubt he will be defeated this next election. Some have run against him in the past and have been trounced...not only at the ballot box, but end up sorry they ever challenged him."

"It's he that has been pushing your police department to get the evidence on me for these murders." Travis then leaned into the pastor. "And on that note, sir, I have to ask you...have you at any time ever believed I was guilty of those murders?"

"Never, Travis. I was aware they occurred, of course, but in getting to know you, it has never crossed my mind that you could ever be capable of murder...even after hearing that you were a suspect."

"I know that some of Smokey's business has dropped off since the word's gotten around about me these past few weeks. I guess people have been afraid to be around me. But Smokey has never said anything to me. Nor would he ever *can* me."

"Smokey is the kind of man I'd like to have as a member in our church. *He* would be the positive influence that our church body would need."

Travis nodded in agreement. "Not to change the subject, Pastor, but I've been thinking the past few days as to why I've been accosted by Satan and his demons. At first I thought he was just taunting me about my indiscretions. Maybe even trying to disciple me and turn me against God. Because he was already here and using Destiny as his playground, when I came along he might have found it amusing to irritate and provoke me. But now, I'm almost convinced that he sees me as a threat and thinks, along with you, I'm here to stop him. Maybe it's his way to scare me back to Indiana."

Moreau then reached in through the bars and placed his hand on Travis' shoulder. "Do you really think that? That maybe God sent you here to impede Satan's quest of spiritually devouring this town?"

"Not only that, but I think He led me to your door to start a crusade against the devil. Satan intends to poison the souls of this town and every town like it in this country. The large cities are already under his spell and control. It's the small God-fearing towns and the heartlands of America that he wants control of."

Moreau thought for a long moment. He then took Travis by both hands and said, "I think this is the moment for prayer, my son. Will you allow me to pray over you?"

"Of course."

"Father God, I come to you again in the name of Your precious Son, beseeching you to use Your omnipotent power to cast out the demons that continue to haunt the very soul of Your servant, Travis. And if it *is* truly his calling and mission to interfere with Satan's goal of devouring this town, help him…and me…to expose the devil for not only *who* he is, but the crux of his plan, as well. I further pray that you will give Travis and me together as Christians and brothers–in–cause the spiritual tools and armament to somehow intercede into that plan. Moreover, I pray that You will extract Travis from this hellish dungeon and arrange that all the charges be dropped. Give us both the strength and courage to continue this battle against the Evil One and open the eyes of our town to his diabolical plan. Keep this despicable adversary from scattering his poison over this community and drive him back to the pits of hell from whence he came. And beyond that, I ask that You spread the warmth and presence of Your Holy Spirit over this town to once again bring our good people to their knees in praise of no one but You. I pray these things in the name of Jesus our Savior. Amen."

During Moreau's prayer, Travis began to not only feel a release of his anguish, but the Holy Spirit engulfing him, sealing him off from the world as though he were inside some impenetrable protective bubble. Then after his amen, Travis leaned down and kissed the hands of his brother and friend which were still tightly clinched around his.

For a long moment Moreau stood at his side of the bars looking away. Travis thought he caught a tear in the pastor's eye and he watched him swallow an obvious lump in his throat.

"Is something wrong, Drake?"

Moreau smiled. "Well, you being behind these bars *is* obviously wrong of course; but for some reason my mind just took me back to a very sad time in my life."

Travis cocked his head to one side and narrowed his eyes. "Something you can talk about?"

"Not readily...but I thought maybe I'd tell you anyway. Catherine and I have not always been by ourselves. We...had a daughter. Her name was Amelia. A beautiful child full of life... sweet, spunky and hair as fair as golden fleece. When she was twelve she developed rheumatic fever. We had her in several hospitals, tended and nursed her at home, and then held her hand as she ultimately weakened and went home to be with the Lord. My very faith was tested and I became angry with God that He took her. I was at the lowest point in my life. And now seeing you in here at perhaps *your* low point, maybe that's why I have suddenly been compelled to think about her at this moment." He paused for another moment and then smiled. "She would have been about your age now."

"But then of course you ultimately reconciled with God."

"Through intense prayer and with Catherine's counsel, yes. She was very strong through our ordeal. For a while my sermons suffered, but my flock stayed with me. Time heals, Travis. You will find that to also be the case in your marriage. You both have grieved for a different reason from mine. But I pray the marriage will not suffer a death such as I and Catherine have suffered with the loss of our child."

"I'm so very sorry, Drake. I can't imagine what it would be like to lose my Rachael. I don't even want to think about it."

Moreau nodded while digging his right hand into his coat pocket. From it he pulled out something shiny gold. He then took Travis' hand and placed the metal object into his palm and closed his fingers. When Travis opened his hand, he found a cross about the size of his little finger attached to what appeared to be a two inch long plate. A bookmark.

"It was Amelia's," Moreau said. "We pulled it from the last page that she read...the second chapter of James. I think the last year of her life she knew she was dying and told us she wanted to read the Bible from Genesis to Revelation." His eyes glistened again. "She was one book shy of her goal." Wiping his eyes, he said, "I want you to have it."

Travis shook his head and shoved his hand with the bookmark back through the bars. "I can't accept this, Drake. It has to be a sentimental keepsake for you and Catherine."

Moreau smiled. "It *has* been, but it's time it goes to someone else...someone who seems to have the same spirit as she did. Someone to whom I hope it will bring luck."

"No, Drake. I..."

"Please."

Travis bent back his fingers and allowed the tips of them to massage the outline of the cross. "All right," he replied in almost a whisper. "I will cherish it."

"And when you finally make it back to your wife and daughter, I would like you to place it in Rachael's hand... in the hand of another sweet soul."

Now tears formed in Travis' eyes and he choked back a lump of his own. "She will love it. Thank you, Drake. I will tell her Amelia's story."

"Well, I must go now before the deputy throws me out of here. God will place his angels in charge over you, Travis Marlowe. Don't worry. The eyes of those who intend to prosecute you will soon be opened and you will be vindicated."

"Thank you, Pastor. And I look forward to the day I'll be back in one of your pews hearing one of your profound sermons."

"They are not *my* pews, my boy. And as I told you before... neither are my words. They are God's."

When Drake Moreau left the jail, a pall of sadness came over Travis for some reason. Maybe it had to do with self-pity, but he thought it had more to do with never having a true spiritual friend in his life to talk with. And now the people he admired the most in Destiny, Smokey Woodruff and Drake Moreau, he could not be around.

Settling back on his bunk, he thought about Sarah again. He then remembered that *she* was his other spiritual friend. She had been his prayer partner *and* confidant for more than twelve years. And he could not be with *her* as well. For some reason it brought back the memory of that day in 1958…that Sunday when Bishop Herrmann attended the Sunday service that he and Sarah sponsored at *their* house. After Minister Strubhar had closed his sermon out with a prayer and the men sang *Blest Be the Tie That Binds*, always in acappella, he approached the bishop to divulge that he knew he had received a calling to the ministry. The bishop then laid his large hand on Travis' shoulder and said, "Somehow I thought thou wouldst one day come to me to tell me that. I have followed thee these years and know that thou hast been a ravenous student of the scripture. I also know that many have sought out thy counsel. Thou hast led many of our devotions and I have seen the spirit of God in thee. I am happy about this Travis and will call together an ordination meeting of the district's ministers and deacons. I am sure Minister Strubhar here will support thee and sponsor thee for ordination. I would like to see more youth taking up the ministry so that when dinosaurs like me and Strubhar die off, our order will be in good hands."

Travis leaned his head back against the cell wall and tears came to his eyes. Bishop Herrmann had gone to bat for him from the very beginning, leading the way for his induction into the Amish order. And he had officiated at his and

Sarah's wedding. And now, Travis was a disappointment not only to Herrmann, but all of the people whom he served as a minister. He couldn't blame anyone else. Only *he* had done himself in. His punishment was continuing, he thought. Maybe he *deserved* to be sitting in that cell.

SOUTHERN PSALMS

Part Four

Deliver me from my enemies, O my God; defend me from the workers of iniquity, and save me from bloodthirsty men. For look, they lie in wait for my life; and the mighty gather against me, not for my transgression nor for my sin, O Lord. They run and prepare themselves through no fault of mine.

Psalm 59: 1-4

Chapter Twenty Eight

Lamentations

THE WEEK DRAGGED ON AND THE FBI had not returned to the Destiny Police Department with their evidence to further Travis' case...as far as he knew. The boredom, dread and anticipation of learning *something*, *anything* about his fate were taking its toll on him. There were days he didn't shave or even pray. Most mornings he slept without either touching his breakfast or lunch, mainly because he didn't sleep at night. One of the things he missed was the town itself. Although it was only on Sundays that he was afforded the opportunity to walk about town, he loved the fresh air and the sweet aroma of the jasmine and gardenias that clung to the fences. However, he could only *hear* the life outside his window...people calling to one another on the street, the sound of vehicle motors and an occasional horn, and even the garbage truck when it set its empty dumpster down. Sounds of the world.

When the officers did bring him his food, one might try to make small talk. None of them...Blake, Boughton or Harold Presley...were ever condescending or obnoxious. If things had been different, any one of them might have even turned out a friend. The face he didn't see that week, or even *wanted* to see, was Couture's. Unless Couture finally came with the key to let him out.

He did look forward to either Smokey or Dreama coming by with the day's dinner. It was Dreama who brought the large dish containing Smokey's tasty catfish, some clams, corn on the cob and a baked potato, still warm. She smiled as he devoured it the best he could, using the plastic utensils. It was the first food he had that day and he was famished. He gulped the sweet tea after every other bite and within fifteen minutes it was all gone.

"Tommy Barfield will be here first thing Monday morning, Travis. I explained to him what was going on and he said he couldn't believe they threw you in here with the flimsy circumstantial evidence they had, then not provide you with proper due process. He says he will 'go the full boat' to get you out of here next week."

"I pray you're right about that, Dreama."

"Well, you rest easy tonight and hopefully we'll see you back in the diner next week. Gotta run, now. I'm meeting up with some friends later."

"Thanks for thinking about me in here."

"Don't mention it. But when you *do* get out of here, you and I need to sit down to have that little talk about Travis Marlowe, man of mystery."

"Perhaps we will, Dreama. I hope you have a good evening."

She moved to the bars, touched two fingers to her lips and planted them on Travis' lips. "Shave. You look like a bum." She then smiled, turned and called out to Harold Presley to let her out.

Saturday was an especially long and boring day. He only knew it was Saturday because of the Friday night catfish special from the night before. Moreover, the anticipation of meeting with Dreama's lawyer friend made the day seem even longer...and there was still Sunday in between. He did shave, because Dreama was right. Although there was no mirror over the basin or in the shower down the hall, in running his hand over his scraggly face, he *felt* like a bum. For twelve years as a married Amish, he did have a lower beard. But that was different. He kept it neat and well-trimmed...and it looked good on him.

Sissy was back with an early afternoon lunch, which she dropped off on her way home. "I been thinkin' about you a lot this week. Been prayin', too. You gone get outta here and soon, Travis. I hear Smokey talkin' with that police chief the other day...and not too kindly. He say if he need to go to the gov'nor hisself, he'll get you outta here. Smokey, he was mad as I ever seen. I don't think the way they left it that the Chief will be back in anytime soon. That be okay with me. And that goes for his KKK friends too. Now here's some good meat loaf and white bread you can make a sandwich from. You rest up today and know we all thinkin' of you down at the diner. Stevie Ray, bless his little heart, ain't never met you, but is rootin' for you too."

And then that Saturday night when Smokey came by at ten with some leftover peach pie and ice cream that had melted just a tad, he saw that there was something else in his hand. An envelope. "Thought ya might like to have this before ya hit the sack. I think it's what you've been waitin' on, Travis boy."

Travis' heart leapt in bounds. It was a letter from Sarah. Who else? He was almost afraid to open it. Would it be short and to the point that any future they had together was futile or was there some way they could be a family again under the circumstances? He knew it couldn't be under the Amish order. She would have to consent to leave the order and take up a more secular, less structured life with him.

"I knew how dark it is back here and you wouldn't want ta wait till tomorrow to read it, so I brought ya this flashlight."

"You're a real friend, Smokey. I don't care if you *are* my boss, you're still one of the truest friends I ever had."

"Ah, git off that mushy stuff and eat your pie. The ice cream'll be milk if ya don't. Well, best git back. Have a good'n, boy. I'm still workin' on people ta git ya outta here." And then he was gone as quickly as he came.

After wolfing down the pie and runny ice cream, Travis sat nervous as a cat anticipating what Sarah's response might be, running his thumb and forefinger over the edge of the envelope until it was nearly as sharp as a knife's blade, all the while afraid to open it. Eventually, he tore the flap away and pulled the contents out, immediately seeing there were two and a half handwritten pages. After flicking Smokey's flashlight to *on*, he began reading:

"Dear Travis,

I really didn't know what to expect when I received your letter. For all of these weeks I had no knowledge where you had gone, but am glad that you are safe.

Although nothing has changed with our situation, I do want you to know I have missed you. Even though I can never forget how you betrayed our marriage, I do forgive you. I have never stopped loving you. When you left, yes, I was angry and hurt; however, over the course of these weeks, my yearning for you has caused that hurt to quell some and if there is a way you can come back to be with Rachael and me, I want you to do that.

I am not saying we can be husband and wife again, although on paper we remain so. I will also never leave my Amish people. It is not a matter of choosing the Amish over you; it's just that this is the only way of life I have known. It is right for Rachael as well.

Mary was also shunned and she has left the order. She is living in Hurley because she wants to be close to her parents here. She and her husband are in the same status as us. There can be no divorce, but they will just not live together as husband and wife. It is a harsh decision all the way around, but according to our ordinances, it is only the right decision.

It would be good to see you again. You have been a part of my life since the day you walked into my father's store. I don't know what can be worked out between us. I also do not know whether the Amish council would ever relent if you came home and convinced them you have remained a believer. This is the most difficult situation I have been able to endure and I'm afraid I do not have the answer.

If you want to come back, as you say you do, and you still love me, perhaps we can work things out. But, do not expect that things will be as they were. They will not.

Rachael cries for you every night and I just keep telling her to have faith that she will be seeing you soon. I too will be looking for you to return to Hurley as soon as you can.

Sarah

The entire time he was reading her letter, Travis' heart was pounding. Slowly he laid the flashlight down and then clasped his hands together. "Thank you, Lord. If it be possible at all, please allow it to happen. Break me loose from the chains that bind me and make it possible for me to return home where I belong. You have provided me the first glimmer of light that I have had since coming here, and I pray that it is just the beginning of good things to come for both Sarah and me."

Moments later, while still smiling, he went to sleep. It was the first full and peaceful night of sleep he remembered having since he arrived in Destiny. And this night there were no dreams.

On that Sunday morning when Travis woke, the smile was back. Blake came with his breakfast from Connie's around seven-thirty and he didn't even mind how the biscuits and gravy tasted. In fact, he rather enjoyed the meal. Around ten-thirty he heard the peal of Trinity's bell reverberating throughout the downtown area. Although the barred window was too high for him to look out, he could see that it was a lovely day with deep blue morning skies for a change. It also meant that the humidity was low and it wasn't going to be as hot as usual. His lungs craved to breathe in just five minutes of fresh air. His legs ached to walk even one block of Destiny's streets. And his spirit longed to hear once again the true, unimpeachable and uncontradictable word of God through the dynamic voice of His faithful servant, Drake Moreau. When the bell had finished calling Trinity's faithful to worship, the carillon's chimes rang out one of Travis' favorites, *Come Thou Fount*. It then took him back those thirteen years to Hurley, Indiana, when one Sunday he put on that nice new suit Mildred Stanley had bought for him, subsequently answering the call to worship beckoned by the chimes of Rehoboth Lutheran. And then he remembered how he sat in the sanctuary hearing nothing the minister with the monotone voice had to say because of the sweet face of one Sarah Oberhauf that kept invading his brain. But that was then. And now, because of what she had told him in her letter, his hope of ever seeing her again had been restored. How he missed her. And Rachael. And he *would* return to them as soon as he was released from jail.

Would he give Smokey his two week notice or just pack his meager possessions and take the first bus north? Of course, he'd be sure to stay off the trains.

As the chimes continued, he sang the words to the song, as he did many times with his Amish brothers. It was kind of like singing one of David's Psalms:

"Come thou fount of every blessing, tune my heart to sing Thy grace.
Streams of mercy never ceasing call for songs of loudest praise.
Teach me some melodious sonnet sung by flaming tongues above.
I'll praise the mount I'm fixed upon it, mount of Thy redeeming love.
Here I raise my Ebenezer hither by Thy help above.
And I hope by Thy good pleasure safely to arrive at home.
Jesus sought me when a stranger wandering from the fold of God.
He, to rescue me from danger interposed His precious blood.
O to grace how great a debtor daily I'm constrained to be.
Let Thy goodness like a fetter bind my wandering heart to Thee.
Prone to wander Lord I feel it, prone to leave the God I love.
Here's my heart, O take and seal it, seal it for Thy courts above."

It was a great Psalm with which to begin his morning.

The day went slowly. There would be no good food coming his way this Sunday since the Old South Diner wasn't open. Tomorrow would provide him even more hope when Dreama's friend, Tommy Barfield, arrived at the police department with demands that he be released. He wanted to see Barfield blast Chief Joe Couture…and the FBI agents, when their time came. Hope. *Faith* and hope. They were the only weapons he had against the system.

He thought it had to be sometime after midnight when he began dreaming again. Trinity's chimes were again calling as he climbed the steps toward the door that led to the sanctuary. He was late because the congregation was already singing. But as he was entering, every head suddenly turned in his direction. Keeping their eyes on him, they continued singing the song. A song he had never heard. Even in his dream…even in the safe confines of the church walls, he became unnerved. For some eerie reason, he knew that those sitting around him were not regular church members, but people with some kind of diabolical agenda. Momentarily, the singing ceased and the people lifted their hands upward in the direction of the altar. Suddenly, the large purple curtain over the stage ripped in half and a beautiful man-like creature with wings dressed in a black robe came forward. As many in the congregation began to chant praises, others swooned. And in a tongue Travis had never heard, the creature shouted *Ego sum solus verus deis. Inflecto tenus mihi!* (*I am the only true god. Bow down to me.*)

The being then dashed the ten foot wooden cross onto the altar and splintered it into several pieces. As the chanting grew louder, the walls of the sanctuary began to crack. Blood ran from the cracks, turning the carpeting an even deeper crimson. The people then turned to Travis and placed hands on him as though he were being ordained.

It was the shrillness of all the sirens that woke him, not only startling *him*, but a rat was sent scampering from his cell and down the hallway. Obviously, there had been a terrible car accident somewhere. Another night of interrupted sleep. Of course, he didn't mind being awakened from yet another horrific dream. For several minutes there continued to be multiple sirens and the noise of speeding vehicles along Main Street. A terrible accident indeed. It was probably an hour before his brain signed off again.

When he opened his eyes, he had no idea what time it was. It was light outside and he was a bit hungry, so he figured it must be seven-thirty or eight o'clock. While he waited for his breakfast, he opened his Bible to Psalm 18. It was not only an uplifting chapter, but one that he hoped would clear his mind of the lingering nightmare he had about Trinity.

I will love You, O Lord, my strength. The Lord is my rock and my fortress and my deliverer; my God, my strength, in whom I will trust; My shield and the horn of my salvation, my stronghold. I will call upon the Lord, who is worthy to be praised; and shall I be saved from my enemies.

So, where *was* the breakfast...the rubbery sausage, the cardboard toast and the tasteless eggs? He called out once and then a second time, but there was no answer from the station room.

It now had to be late morning when he finally heard loud voices in the squad room. That lasted about fifteen minutes and then the door opened to the hallway. Officer Boughton appeared with a large-set, blond-headed man with a square jaw and three-piece suit.

"Mr. Marlowe?"

"Yes."

"I'm Tom Barfield, attorney and public defender from Morgan City. A friend of mine called me and said you needed some help."

"All I can get, sir. Pleased to make your acquaintance." They then shook hands through the bars.

"Well, outside are two G men and we just went round and round about you. I have a piece of paper here in my hand from the circuit court that's hopefully going to get you out of here. Those people out there have absolutely no tangible evidence that warrants holding you for these murders." He then turned to Boughton and said, "Open up the cell, Officer."

The officer pulled out his key and turned the lock. When the cell door swung open, Travis said, "Just a moment." He then retreated to his bunk and picked up his Bible. Holding it up, he said, "The bread of life."

When the three men entered the station room, three other men sat waiting...Couture and Agents LeFevre and Nelson. Barfield placed his hand on Travis' shoulder and moved him toward a chair opposite the agents and then he sat down. "All right, gentlemen. After taking this man's fingerprints and performing your investigation, what did you find out?"

"No indication of any record, Mr. Barfield."

"Uh, huh. No record. I assume you also did a police check in the town he came from. Where was that, Travis?"

"Hurley, Indiana."

"Hurley, Indiana. And what did you find there?"

"The police believe he is someone from the nearby Amish community. Apparently, he had never been in any trouble there."

"Amish. Which accounts for the fact he had no driver's license or other identification. He's just a clean-living, ordinary citizen of a religious community."

"Who proceeded to argue with and assault two men who ended up brutally murdered, counselor," commented Couture.

"I understand he was merely defending himself, Chief. So, do you have evidence that placed Mr. Marlowe at the scene of those murders?"

"That doesn't mean he didn't kill them," said LeFevre. "That doesn't mean a thing."

"It means *everything*, agent. You have no proof of his involvement. All your evidence is only circumstantial. He was found with no knife or any other weapon. He has no car. How did he get way out there in the woods where they found Mumford and the Rosenthal hobo…more than six miles out there?"

"We believe he didn't act alone," interjected Nelson. "Proof of that is what happened last night. We think he must be part of some cult whose business it is to kill as an act of sacrifice."

"And what happened last night?" asked Barfield.

Couture spoke up. "A murder was committed at Trinity Methodist."

Travis' jaw dropped. "At Trinity? What? Who?"

"The Pastor…Moreau. After preaching his Sunday night service."

"*Oh, God, no!*" Travis exclaimed.

"He was always the last out…but he never *came* out. His wife Catherine thought he may have met with some deacons afterward or was counselin' someone in the church study. About eleven, when he didn't go home to the parsonage, she went into the study and found him. It wasn't pretty, Marlowe."

Travis sat with his head in his hands and a rush of tears filled his eyes. "How?" he sobbed.

"Somebody came in and stabbed him in the chest, then smeared his blood on the wall, forming the image of a pentagram. Afterwards, they entered the church and repositioned the large wooden cross above the altar."

"Repositioned?"

"They hung it upside down. It's considered an insult to Christianity." Couture then chuckled "…like giving Christianity the middle finger."

Travis thought he was about to vomit. He closed his eyes and the picture of a slain Drake Moreau entered his brain. He imagined the body lying in a pool of blood on the carpet. "It…

it must have been horrible for Catherine to find him. I can't believe it." He then glared at Couture with seething eyes. "You and your people have been spinning your wheels trying to prosecute *me*. Yet you allow these demons to run about killing people. You're either too incompetent to find them or you don't care what's happening in this town. I guarantee you one thing; you'd better go looking for these people, because if you don't, *I will*. And that goes for you Federal goons as well."

Couture leaned across the table into Travis. "And then what, Marlowe? More assaults? More people endin' up dead? Don't threaten me and don't take matters into your own hands. You're still not out of the woods on these other murders, you know."

"Yes he is," said Barfield. "And if you agents don't drop these charges right now, I will be back here in two hours with the circuit judge's order for his release. Then Mr. Marlowe will be filing suit against the U.S. Government for false arrest. And as for you, Chief; hear me. I'll personally see to it you won't even finish out your term."

"I still think…"

Agent Fefevre interjected. "The charges are dropped, Mr. Marlowe. You're free to go."

Travis nodded. "Could I please have a cup of water, please?"

It was Tommy Barfield who bothered to go to the water cooler to draw a paper cup of cold water when none of the officers made a move.

"Thanks." Travis gulped the water and after his wave of nausea had passed, he said. "I mean it. You'd better be out there beating the bushes to find these people or the hounds of hell will not be able to stop what I put into motion."

Barfield then touched him on the shoulder and said, "It's time to go, Travis. Let's go before things escalate here." Turning to LeFevre, he said, "My card, Agent. I'll expect the formal dismissal papers on my desk in three days."

LeFevre nodded.

"Watch yourself, Marlowe," Couture called after them.

Tom Barfield then wheeled around and pointed a stern index finger at him. "There had better be no harassment of this man, Chief, or you *will* hear more from me."

Couture did not respond. Although, considering his power and ego and the fact that he was not easily bested, he knew Barfield was closely connected with the Governor's office...and he meant what he said.

Once outside the building, Travis shook hands with Barfield. "I...don't know how to thank you, sir. I will pay you..."

"Today I'm acting as public defender, Travis. The parish pays my salary. My regards to Miss Van Horne. Tell her I'll be calling her one day soon."

When they parted company, Travis found a nearby park bench on which to sit. His legs were so weak, he didn't think he could walk. As he looked down the street over the magnolias and oaks at Trinity's spire, the tears came again. And then suddenly what he had eaten the evening before came up. Passersby may have thought the poor man regurgitating on the street was either ridding himself of last night's booze or had some kind of stomach virus. He didn't care. His friend was gone. Butchered and lying in a pool of blood for his wife to find. It would be enough to drive *anybody* mad to find such a grisly scene, much less a loving wife.

No. He would not immediately return to Indiana and Sarah. Not just yet. He had to somehow avenge Drake Moreau's death. He had to see the end of these demons or cultists or whoever these devil worshippers were. He owed it to his friend. He had brought to the pastor his knowledge of Satan's presence in Destiny and of the diabolical happenings. His friend was dead because of him. And with God as his one and only ally, he would somehow bring death to Satan's plot.

Chapter Twenty Nine

Conversations

AFTER A WEEK'S INCARCERATION, HE WAS free. But that freedom meant very little in comparison to the anger and sadness Travis was feeling about the brutal slaying of his friend and mentor. And as he walked the dozen blocks to the Old South Diner, he would be passing by Trinity. From a block away, he could see the throng of church members, curiosity seekers with cameras, news media and police authority on the sidewalks on both sides of Main Street. A few of the mourners were weeping and patting their eyes with handkerchiefs or just staring at the church in disbelief that their beloved pastor had been murdered. In front of the church was parked a long, black Lincoln Travis thought might belong to the funeral home; but as he edged closer through the crowd, he saw the license plate. It was a State of Louisiana tag with the number 1 on it. The Governor, no doubt. Travis knew that Drake Moreau had not only been a religious icon in Southern Louisiana, but a counselor and confidant to past governors, congressmen and business leaders.

As he found a place across the street on a stone wall that belonged to a rather stately home, he was again given to ponder the evil had set in like a demonic fog over this sweet community. It was obvious to him, and now him *alone*, that there were two diabolical scenarios simultaneously occurring: first, Satan and his demons had taken control of the minds, mouths and bodies of at least three poor souls in an attempt to taunt, harass and drive Travis from the town. As Travis was now certain that God was planning to use him in some way to expose the devil and his mission to devour Destiny, Satan knew about it even before Travis hopped onto that box car. And he was pulling out all stops to thwart him. Secondly, Satan was also fueling the cult, which in his name, was carrying out the ritualistic, sacrificial murders of human beings. Of course, the only killing that didn't fit into the equation was Drake Moreau's. But the pastor had in no uncertain terms warned his congregation about Satan's presence in the community and issued a call to arms to act. In doing so, he had become both a nuisance and impediment to Satan's plan. Moreau had to go and the devil knew just the people to carry out his murder. Now, only Travis stood in his way.

Travis lifted his eyes high above the crowd until they reached the cross atop the spire. "I'm ready to fight you, Lucifer. I am now only one man; but, I want you to know one thing...God is with me. And you are going down."

Gathering himself up from the wall, Travis slowly trudged on toward the diner. He knew that his emotional pain would not soon go away, but the mission was at hand. Somehow, someway, he had to see the end of the demonic plague that had struck Destiny. However, he had no idea where to start. But he knew that God would either reveal to him how it could be done or actually *place him in position* to stop the advancement of this demonic sickness.

Travis figured that if he walked directly in through the front door of the diner, he might cause a commotion. All eyes would immediately be thrown on him and the tongues would wag. After all, most people knew that it was the diner's busboy that had been arrested for the murders of two men. And just when *was* he released? Was it *before* Drake Moreau was killed?

Easing into the restaurant through the back door, it was his intent to stay in the storeroom for a while. Someone would still eventually see him anyway, but the distraction that ensued would not be all at once. Moving stealthily down the hallway, he ducked into his room. As meager as a makeshift apartment as it was, it was a welcomed sight. His bed, which was little more than a cot, would still be more comfortable than the station's bed…and it would not reek of sweat and urine.

It was early afternoon and he was hungry. However, the thought of putting any food into his stomach made him nauseous again. He thought he would just go ahead and take a shower and change clothes; then, when the lunch customers thinned out, he would make himself known to Smokey and Sissy.

No sooner had he showered, shaved and redressed, the door to the storeroom opened. A young man about eighteen wearing an apron appeared and asked, "What are you doin' back here?"

Travis finished buttoning his shirt and replied, "I live here. You must be Stevie Ray."

"Yeah…and you're the guy Travis. I thought you were in jail."

"Not anymore."

A look of alarm suddenly covered his face. "You escape?"

Travis managed a smile and shook his head. "No. They dropped the charges."

"Well, Smokey heard something back here and told me to check it out. Thought you might be a burglar. He was about to bring his gun."

"Good that he didn't. There's been enough dying in this town."

"Yeah. I heard about that preacher. My mom goes to that church. Bad deal."

"Tell Smokey I'm back here and not to worry. I'll filter in a little later."

"Okay, boss. Well, good to meet you."

"Same here."

It wasn't thirty seconds when Travis heard a rap at the storeroom door. "Travis, you in there?"

Sissy.

He opened the door and she then threw her arms around him. "You're back!"

"I am."

"How did you escape?"

He chuckled. "Why does everyone think I escaped? They let me go."

"Oh, good thing. 'Cause if you did escape, I'd find a way to hide you."

Travis smiled. "I know you would." It was good to see her face again.

"You comin' out?"

"No. Just tell Smokey I'll show my face when people are out of here. Maybe in an hour or so. I'm just going to sack out for a while."

"You rest easy, then."

Travis needed some *spiritual* food as well. This day, without peace in his heart, he was angry with God. Why had He taken such a loyal servant…a man set on fire with truth…a man who loved sharing the gospel of Jesus Christ with his flock…a man who like David, also was surely a man after

God's own heart? Opening his Bible, he leafed aimlessly for something that would be uplifting, yet bring him comfort. So, he turned to Romans 5 for the counsel of Paul.

Therefore, having been justified by faith, we have peace with God through our Lord Jesus Christ, through whom also we have access by faith into this grace in which we stand, and rejoice in hope of the glory of God. And not only that, but we also glory in tribulations, knowing that tribulation produces perseverance; and perseverance, character; and character, hope. Now hope does not disappoint, because the love of God has been poured out in our hearts by the Holy Spirit who was given to us.

Travis lay back on his pillow and closed his eyes. As he repeated the words of Paul over and over...*we have peace with God through our Lord Jesus Christ...*he could feel the heaviness being lifted from his chest. The words fed and nourished him; and as they did, his nausea also dissipated. Perhaps now, he *could* eat something.

When he eased his way down the hallway, he could see the clock on the wall read one forty-seven. Only two customers were left in the dining room and Smokey was trying to talk the lollygaggers out the door. After he had done so, he locked the front door, as he always did till four, and turned toward the kitchen.

"Ah, Travis. Stevie Ray told me you were back there. So, they let you go, eh?"

"Dreama's lawyer friend, Mr. Barfield from Morgan City, beat them down. The Chief put up an argument, but the FBI agreed they couldn't hold me."

"I'm glad *somebody* came to his senses. Say, I'm real sorry about the pastor. I know you'd been goin' there and had talked to him a few times. This world done gone crazy. I can't imagine what kind of animals coulda done a thing like that."

"He was probably the most spiritual man I ever met…and he was killed because he was sounding the alarm about all of the demonic things going on around here."

"Yeah. A woman from his church that comes here for breakfast pretty often told me this mornin' that for a couple of Sundays Reverend Moreau had been fired up about the devil and how his band of demons have moved into Southern Louisiana. They was takin' over people's minds and stealin' souls. Said he had proof of what he was sayin' and practi'cly demanded people to follow him and hunt down the devil worshippers who was committin' these murders. She said he had people so riled up yesterday, she thought they was gonna tar and feather him and ride him out on a rail. He said he was goin' after the devil people, if the congregation was with him or not." And then he lamented. "I guess they got to him first."

"Does anyone know when his funeral will be?"

"They say the coroner won't release his body for a while. Also, the State Police and Louisiana Bureau are in there now and won't be through with their investigation for some time. I 'spect it will be later this week or maybe next. Say, you look a little pee-ked. Ya need somethin' to eat?"

"I could use something and maybe a coke. My stomach's been a little tied up in knots."

"Then let me fix ya up a bowl of pintos and cornbread. It's always good for what ails ya."

"Okay. Maybe I'll instead have a glass of milk with that."

As he sat at the counter nursing the bowl of beans, he watched Stevie Ray washing dishes at the sink. Travis didn't want to think highly of himself, but he knew he worked twice as quickly as Stevie Ray. The boy was taking an inordinate amount of time with each dish and piece of silverware. Travis wondered if he would even be done by the time the doors reopened for dinner. Momentarily, Smokey came out to the counter and shook his head. "Slow as molasses, that boy is. But at least he was helpful while you were in the hoosegow, and he don't complain none. Glad yer back, son."

"I'll work with him to speed up his pace."

"That goes for clearin' and wipin' down tables, too."

Dreama was in for her shift on time and her eyes clearly lit up when she saw Travis. Giving her a wry smile, he said, "Yeah, they let me out and I didn't escape. Your attorney friend was ready for the FBI and gave both the agents and Couture a mouthful. They didn't as much as put up a fight. By the way, he says he will catch up to you."

She hugged him and then sat down beside him at the counter. "Told you he was good."

"And I'm grateful that you called him. I would still be sitting in the cell if it weren't for him."

"I cared enough to send the very best," she said.

"Hallmark, right? I heard that commercial on the radio a couple of weeks ago. Anyway, I owe you."

She placed her hand on his. It was an innocent touch this time. "I know this has all been tough on you. Getting arrested for something you didn't do and then your preacher friend dying like that."

"They got to him, Dreama."

"Who did?"

"The same demon cult that killed Joubert and the tramp from the train. Pastor Moreau was a man of God, ordained by God, to minister to this community."

"You really *are* a religious nut. More so than I thought. I think I'm beginning to understand why you walked away from me like you did. You and I are at opposite ends of life."

"I guess I've always been a very spiritual person. Unfortunately, I haven't been a very *pleasing* person in the sight of God."

"We're not all that different, you know. I'm a very spiritual person, too; just not on the same plane as you."

"You could be. God's message of love is out there for everyone, no matter who we are or what we've done."

She then removed her hand from his. "But how about those people you say killed the minister? Is there any room in your God's heart for them? If they killed one of His people, I'd say He'd be pretty ticked off about it."

"They will get what's coming to them...unless they repent and accept Christ. One way or another, their judgment will be in the next life."

"Ah, the Heaven and hell myth."

"I'm sorry you think it's a myth, Dreama, but trust me... it's all very real. Eternal life with God or eternal damnation. Everybody's choice. Are you willing, at the end of your life, to take that chance?"

"Wherever you *did* come from, my dear Travis, you certainly got brainwashed."

"I'm sorry you feel that way, Dreama. I'm very solid with my Christian faith *and* who I am."

"And what has it gotten you? Your wife is no longer in your life; you were arrested and thrown in jail; and one of your admired friends was murdered...and you have nothing but the clothes on your back. Some life."

"Yes, but it *is* a life. And I thank God every day he allows me to have one."

"Like everyone doesn't have one? You need more in that pitiful life, Travis. If you hang out with me, I'll show you what living is all about. As a matter of fact, a bunch of friends and I are getting together to play some cards over some beer and wine. I know that you being Mr. Goody Two Shoes, you won't do the wine, but it's all very innocent. We don't gamble or anything. We just have a few laughs is all. And you *definitely* need to laugh."

"Thanks, Dreama, but I don't think so. And I think the last card game I played was when I was a kid...rummy, I think."

She laughed. "Boy, you *are* a real square. What happened to you? Were you abandoned as a child, then adopted by some nuns and raised in a monastery? You don't drink, play cards, fool around...what is it with you?"

"You know, this might be a good time for that talk about my life you were wanting to have. I..."

Before he could get anything out, Smokey approached them and sat down on an adjacent stool with a cigarette between his fingers. "You don' all right, now? You know you don't have to work today. Just take it easy."

Dreama then jumped in. "Travis was just about to crawl out from under that secret rock and tell me his life story."

"Travis, boy, you don't have to tell anybody anything you don't want to. I know you're a good fella and just because this nosy gal here wants to open you up like a can a peas, don't mean you hafta tell her anything."

"Yeah, I know, Smokey. But I guess I owe it to you all around here to let you know a little more about me...not that it's all that interesting."

At that moment, Smokey's newly-hired waitress, Jane Lowry, entered the diner.

"Jane," called Smokey. "Come over here and meet Travis."

Jane was sixty-ish with silver hair and probably looked seventy. A very conservative-looking lady, compared to Dreama, that is, she wore a light pink, poplin dress that was made for waitressing, kind of like a uniform. Dreama had always refused that waitress look and preferred wearing more fashionable clothing.

"Hello, Travis. I have heard them talking about you."

"Jane," he replied nodding.

"You seem to be a most interesting gentleman from what I hear."

"It appears I *have* ruffled a few feathers in this town. But it will be good working with you."

"Likewise."

"All right, Travis. Let's hear your story," Dreama said. "I'm sure Jane would like in on it, too."

"His story?" Jane asked.

"There really isn't much to it. And I don't want Jane to get a bad first impression of me."

"How bad can it be, considering what I already know about you...big religious guy that you are?"

"All right. Be prepared to be bored."

For the next fifteen minutes Travis provided his co-workers a capsule of who he was...the early years in New York, the new life he started in Hurley, Indiana, his first association with the Amish and the girl with whom he fell in love. He told of his acceptance into the Amish community as one of them and then his marriage. Rachael was born soon after and then less than two years ago, he was ordained as the community's junior minister.

"You? A preacher?" exclaimed Dreama.

"A minister," Travis repeated.

"Did you know about this, Smokey?" she asked.

"No. I knew he was Amish, but it don't surprise me none he's a man of the cloth.

"So, how did you get here?" Dreama asked.

Reluctantly, he then told them that his marriage had failed because of an indiscretion, on which he wouldn't elaborate. He left home and finally worked his way down the Mississippi, ending up on the box car in Destiny at the end of the line.

"And you said your life wasn't interesting. So, why did you leave entirely? Your daughter's there."

"I won't go into that, Dreama. I'm just not proud of something I did. I've regretted it every day I've been away."

"Son, we've all done things we ain't proud of," Smokey said. "Don't beat yerself up about it. I know you're a good man and now that I've found out you're some kind of preacher, I got the utmost respect for ya."

Dreama added, "Yeah, what's done is done, so you now have to start thinking about yourself. You need to start enjoying your life. You started a new life way back when, so you can do it again."

"But, I want my *old* life back. I want my wife's forgiveness and to be a father to my little girl again."

Smokey tapped out his cigarette. "Sounds to me you need to pack yer stuff and git on the first bus outta here back to Indiana. That's where yer heart is, boy. I knowed ever since ya got here that you were missin' somethin' in yer life. Now it all makes sense. That girl will take ya back. Time heals…you know that. I bet that woman misses you as much as you miss her."

"You're right, Smokey. And this time yesterday, I was all but on that bus as soon as I would be released from jail. "

"But?"

"But, I have some unfinished business to take care of first."

"What kind of business?"

He then looked at all three of his listeners. "It's just something I have to see through. I don't even know what or how."

Each had puzzled looks on their faces.

"Okay, I'm with ya, Travis. Stay as long as you need to. But don't make that young woman in Indiana wait too long."

"Would it be okay with you if I *did* go back to work today? It'll help take my mind off things."

Smokey nodded. He then said in a low voice, "Go school that young'n in there in the kitchen about speedin' things up. I'd like to have clean plates on the table by dinnertime."

Travis smiled. "Will take care of it, boss."

When Smokey returned to the kitchen, Jane said, "Well, I must say it was interesting getting to know you. I didn't expect to hear your life's story when I walked in. Frankly, I didn't expect to see you at all."

"Again, I look forward to rubbing elbows with you around here, Jane."

"Literally," she added.

The coroner released Drake Moreau's body to Pryor Funeral Home on Thursday. There would be a wake in the parlor of the parsonage Friday evening from six to eight and the funeral would be on Saturday at the church at two, officiated by Trinity's Associate Minister, Christopher Rudman. Travis would ask off for the funeral.

Smokey let Travis off for an hour for the Friday night visitation as well as for the funeral. With a *retrained* Stevie Ray now more efficiently and timely cleaning tables and washing dishes, Smokey could allow more time off from work.

There was a long line of mourners standing on the sidewalk of the parsonage waiting to get in, many of whom Travis recognized having walked out on the pastor's sermon the Sundays he had visited. How hearts turn fickle at a time of one's passing, he thought. A half hour later, he had worked his way to Catherine Moreau whose eyes were understandably swollen and red. However, her head was lifted high and she had a warm smile for everyone…especially for Travis.

"Mr. Marlowe," she greeted. "Yours was the face I needed to see tonight. Drake talked so much about you. He said he had a nice conversation with you when he went by to see you at the station. He said you were wrongly accused and would appeal in every direction to get you out of there."

"I can't tell you how sorry I am, Mrs. Moreau. He was by far the most spiritual man I ever knew and I was privileged to call him both friend and counselor."

"Someday I'd like to talk more with you about the dreadful series of events going on in the community. Drake lost his life over them. He tried to warn everyone..." And then she wept bitterly.

Travis squeezed her hand and noticing that other mourners behind him were becoming impatient, he said. "I will say prayers for you, Mrs. Moreau. And one day I will come see you and we can talk further."

She regained her composure and smiled through her tears.

While working his way back through the crowd toward the door, he could not help but over-hear the flowing dialogue. They were a much different congregation from the people who walked out on Drake Moreau during his powerful sermons of warning. The sermons that scared the children. But now, they couldn't deny the resident evil within their community...and the reality that Satan's influence was everywhere. And it wasn't just Trinity's people who were shocked, outraged, frightened and even horrified. The news had spread like a wildfire not only throughout the State of Louisiana, but the entire country. It was on page one or two of every newspaper. And it wasn't just that a prominent pastor had been murdered, but the horrendous way it was carried out. A religious icon had been stabbed, his blood smeared in the form of a pentagram on the wall of his study, and the church's cross hung upside down in the sanctuary. And to Christians everywhere, it was the ultimate affront to God Himself.

At noon on Saturday, when he had Stevie Ray fully set to task, Travis showered and yet again donned his only suit...the Amish one, basic black with no zipper on the trousers or buttons on the coat, with a new white shirt and black tie. Smokey was sure the church would be 'bustin' at the seams' with people beginning about one, so Travis had 'better git there early.' On the way to the church, Travis passed by store fronts on the south side of the street...the Ace Hardware, Kreske's Five and Dime and Christina's Dress Shop. Amused at the name of the only beauty shop in town, *Making Waves*, he came upon a shop called Madam Marie's Gallery and his eyes immediately became fixed on a painting in the window...a painting of a familiar subject.

As the tingling bell on the door signaled his entry, a woman about forty-five with long dark hair and wearing a red, peasant-style dress, stood from behind the sales counter to acknowledge him.

"Good afternoon. I'm Marie. May I show you something?"

"Not really," Travis replied. "But, I was curious about the painting out there in the window."

"Which one?"

"The landscape scene...the one with the chimney where a house used to be."

"Ah, yes. It is a numbered print by Brandon DuMont, a local artist. There were only fifty prints made. I think I only have three left."

Travis remembered seeing numbered prints in Hurley of Amish and Mennonite subjects by its local artist, Isaac Neurbren. He had painted barns, carriages and Amish families on their way to services. Jacob Oberhauf had even placed some of them in his store. And although it went against the strict Amish custom, Neurbren had painted faces of the Amish people. Jacob had taken a little heat from a few of the Amish for displaying paintings because of the graven images.

"I've seen a similar painting of that location…an original by a lady named Dreama Van Horne."

"Ah, my friend Dreama. Yes."

"I work with her at the diner."

"Such a sweet young woman. I love her," Marie said. "Are you settling in the area? I haven't seen you before."

"I'll just be here for a short while longer, then back to Indiana."

"Indiana. I was there once. Nothing but flat farmland where I was."

"My farm has a little roll to it."

"I'll bet it's nice. So, about the print…"

"It has a uniqueness about it. A field lying in a fog with a chimney faintly showing through. It has a kind of ghostly look about it."

"And for good reason. The area is called Devil's Tea Table. The chimney is all that remains to this day of an old house where a Wicca used to live."

"Wicca?"

"A witch. Her name was Junie Bargeron. Probably the most famous if not notorious of all of Louisiana's women, except for maybe Madam La Laurie over in New Orleans. She lived there about seventy years ago and supposedly died in a fire that burned down the house."

"Supposedly? Didn't they find the body?"

"Oh, they did find it. Burnt to a crisp. But then people started seeing her after that, flitting about the countryside in her long, flowing black gown. That's the way she dressed when she would come into town."

He laughed. "So, she became a ghost."

"There have been very accurate accounts by credible, respectable people of seeing her for many years. Even now, hunters and trappers swear they see her on nights when the moon is full. I don't know how believable they are, though. People tend to exaggerate around here and make up stories about seeing her."

Travis smiled. "What was she doing when she died... mixing up some kind of potion and burned the house down?"

Marie shook her head. "It was like Salem all over again. Her Wiccan practices were chastised by the community and a band of Christian town folk accused her of performing satanic rituals. They came with torches and set her house on fire. She refused to leave and, well, you know the rest."

"A pity."

"Yes. Unfortunately, well-meaning people who perform a little black magic from time to time are still ostracized and persecuted for their beliefs and practices."

"Just as Christians have long undergone such persecutions for *their* beliefs."

"People should be left alone to worship whoever or whatever they choose, especially in a land that guarantees the right to do so," she added.

Travis was not sure how a question about a painting in the store-front window led to a discussion about worship freedom, so he decided to change the subject.

"How about you? Are you a long-time resident?"

"All my life. About twenty years ago I bought this place. It was a run-down butcher shop, but I cleaned it up, got the smell out with scented candles and incense, and started selling local artists' works on consignment. In no time at all, it caught on. I still don't make a *great* living, but you'd be surprised what a couple of original works went for last year. The Yankees that come down here love paintings of swamp critters and street scenes of musicians on Bourbon Street in New Orleans."

"I was just there a couple weeks ago. Interesting city, but I felt really out of place there."

"It's not for everyone. I go there a couple times a year, but personally, I like life in small towns like ours and the bayou country."

Suddenly, Travis heard the two bongs of Trinity's bell announcing that it was one-thirty.

"I'd better go," he said. "But I enjoyed talking with you."

"You didn't tell me your name," she said.

"Travis. Travis Marlowe."

"Well, come back again, Travis, whenever you want to spend some money." Her blue eyes danced to the music of her laughter. "But, come back even if you *don't* buy anything."

CHAPTER THIRTY

THE BEAST AMONG US

ANOTHER LONG LINE OF PEOPLE WAS still edging slowly into the sanctuary by the time Travis arrived at the church. In fact, by the time he found a seat, he ended up in the balcony in the next to the last row near the organ pipes. Two faces he recognized well up front were those of Mayor St. Pierre and Chief Couture. However, most faces belonged to the regular members...people he had seen before. He was fortunate to have gotten inside, considering many didn't. Officer Harold Presley had cut off the line after there was no room for anyone to stand in the aisles.

A low murmur of voices permeated throughout the sanctuary for nearly twenty minutes. As he waited, Travis noticed that the wooden cross had been fully removed. He wondered why it hadn't been re-hung right-side up. Finally, a large-set woman who Travis had heard previously began her operatic solo with organ accompaniment of *Beyond the Sunset*. At precisely two o'clock, the chimes began to sound as a path was cleared in the aisle for the Pryor brothers to wheel in the coffin that contained the pastor's body.

As soon as the coffin was set in place on the altar and the spray of red roses was placed on its lid, Catherine Moreau began to sob. As it is always contagious, other women began weeping openly as well while a few of the men dabbed at their eyes with initialed, white handkerchiefs. A deacon then read from 2 Corinthians: "*Blessed be the Father of our Lord Jesus Christ, the Father of mercies and God of all comfort, who comforts us in all our affliction so that we may be able to comfort those who are in any affliction, with the comfort with which we ourselves are comforted by God.* And from John 14: *Let not your hearts be troubled. You believe in God, believe also in Me. In My Father's house are many mansions. If it were not so, I would have told you. I go and prepare a place for you and if I go and prepare a place for you, I will come again and receive you unto myself, that where I am, there you may be also. And you know the way to where I am going. Thomas said unto him: Lord we do not know where You go, so how can we know the way. Jesus said unto him, I am the Way, the Truth and the Life. No one comes to the Father but by Me.*"

The Lord's Prayer was then sung, this time by the Trinity choir.

At half past the hour, Christopher Rudman took his place behind the pulpit. As he stood looking out over the congregation, he paused for a moment, seemingly in dramatic flair, and then lifted his hands into the air.

"My dear friends. We have come to this place to celebrate the life of Trinity's pastor, Drake Moreau. I fear I cannot even come close to providing you with a service that this man could deliver with such eloquence and passion. As he stood behind this very pulpit for more than thirty years ministering to Trinity's faithful, we are saddened to realize that his body now lies before you, broken and lifeless. A great voice has been silenced for all time." He then paused for several moments and scanned his eyes over the congregation. The eyes were now piercing, even stoic. "I have to ask you, however; does it make any sense to us as to why this God would allow Drake Moreau's life to be taken so brutally, a soul that served so dutifully. How can one possibly understand that it was His will? This God of love. If He is the God of love, then why does He allow such heinous crimes to be committed on His most faithful?"

These opening words ripped through the sanctuary like barbed wire. They were certainly not the words of hope and consolation that the people had expected. They were lacerating words that not only proved painful for Catherine Moreau, but questioned the very sovereignty of God. Was Rudman angry with God or was he intentionally being blasphemous? For the remainder of the message, there was little said about the life of Drake Moreau…such as that he was a man of God who loved Jesus…and loved his family. There was no reference to the fact that the people's pastor was now in the bosom of Jesus, singing praises to God on high. There was no scriptural foundation for any part of his message or any mention of the embracing comfort of the Savior in times of grief. Rudman's words were instead angry and offensive, filled with rage and vehemence…ending only ten minutes after they began.

When Christopher Rudman turned from the pulpit and then abruptly disappeared through the side door of the sanctuary, the congregation sat with mouths agape. The man who would replace Drake Moreau had disappointed them at a time when they needed to hear words that praised both God *and* their beloved pastor. It was as though Satan himself had shown up, entered the body and mind of the associate pastor and then spat his poison into the ears of the congregation. Travis was set to wonder...if Rudman was *not* the devil, or had the devil *in* him, then what was his motive?

While the organist played *Breathe on Me, Breath of God*, the pastor's body was wheeled out the side door of the sanctuary. Then, after Catherine Moreau was escorted out on the arms of two deacons, the congregation began to file out as well. Most shook their heads and talked among themselves with immense animation. Travis heard words such *horrible* and *disgraceful*. And then when he had reached the entry door, he heard one of the deacons say, "There is no way Chris Rudman will deliver Drake's graveside service," while the other replied, "If he even shows up."

Travis did not go to the cemetery, not just because he had no means of transportation, but his heart was sick. The contemptible words of Christopher Rudman had been an insult to the memory of Destiny's great preacher *and* a personal affront to his wife. And as the deacon had expected, Rudman did *not* show at the gravesite. Drake Moreau would be buried without a minister's last words. Travis later learned that it was Deacon Jerry Carlisle who delivered a proper graveside eulogy.

At just after three, Travis returned to the diner through the alley door, going directly to the storage room to change out of his suit and to ponder the afternoon's disappointment. Picking up his Bible, he leafed through it trying to locate the words that would soothe his troubled soul. Nothing he found seemed to work for him. Finally, frustrated and just plain mentally tired, he laid his Bible aside and closed his eyes.

It was now fully apparent...the Beast had its grip on Destiny, Louisiana. His presence was now being experienced by Trinity's congregation, whether they realized it or not.

All they knew was their pastor had been brutally murdered and their church house desecrated by somebody that either had it in for him or was part of the satanic cult. Moreau had warned them; but even now, would the people associate his murder with the devil and the demonic plague he told them existed? Travis feared they may still not be convinced that there was a demonic underground of satanic ritualists who was offering up the highest form of sacrifice...that of the human kind...to their god, the Prince of Darkness himself. Their heads would remain in the sand.

Travis thought he would just close his eyes for a few moments and then get back to work. But a deep sleep took him over and he was out for more than two hours. At some point in his sleep, he began dreaming. In this dream, he saw a flickering light through some trees that drew him into the woods. At first, he thought it was the campfire of a hunter or trapper, but then as he drew closer, he saw the huddled figures of a half-dozen people on their knees before the fire, their hands and faces touching the earth. For a moment, he stood transfixed, wondering if they were just trying to keep warm or were they in fact worshipping the fire.

Suddenly, another figure appeared seemingly out of nowhere, dressed in a white linen garment and arms stretched out in welcome. His face was beautiful and he had engaging eyes that seemed to pull him helplessly, but wantonly toward him. A soft glow of light fully encompassed the man's body as he floated gracefully, effortlessly through the trees. He then turned and beckoned the hooded figures behind him to raise themselves from the ground and come forward to worship him.

Travis wondered if the man was Jesus, as his face was similar to the idealistic images he had seen in artists' renditions. And were the demonic figures in the background now realizing

His power and sovereignty over them? As Travis continued to move toward the figure, he somehow knew that he had been in a similar dream before…the horrific dream where he had been staked to the ground. And he also recognized the landscape to be the serene place in the painting he saw at Dreama's house and in the window at Madam Marie's. In the fireplace of the chimney, searing embers from the burning wood popped and cracked, sending a plume of white smoke filled with red hot ash into the evening twilight, its wispy haze laying in the tops of the trees like a ghostly fog.

The Jesus figure then pointed to yet another figure lying on the ground, arms and legs tied to stakes. The man's face showed immense anguish and he seemed to be screaming; yet he had no voice. Blood began to pour from his eyes resembling red tears. Beside the man's torso was a large knife with a gleaming blade stuck partially into the ground.

Travis then moved to the man and try as he did to resist, he was compelled to pull the knife from the ground and raise it high into the air to drive it into the man's chest. He then looked back at the Jesus figure who then gave him a nod. Bringing his eyes back to the horrified man's face that lay before him, Travis then recognized him…Drake Moreau.

Travis again looked back at the man and shook his head in disobedience. But then to his own horror, the figure's face was no longer that of Jesus. The eyes were now fierce and piercing; the face, evil and venomous like that of a cobra. Even in his dream, Travis realized that Satan can take on the appearance of something or someone beautiful, enticing his victims and deceiving them into believing that one's choices and actions will always be good and right.

"No!" Travis cried out. "I won't do this!"

Suddenly, as if on command, the hooded figures began closing in on him, chanting satanic verses. As he stood paralyzed in fear, they laid hands on him. Even as he resisted, it was as though a powerful hand had taken hold of his wrist, forcing his arm downward in one powerful stroke, burying the blade in the minister's chest.

"No!" he cried again. And then he woke.

Satan had again invaded his subconscious. It was at that moment that Travis somehow knew there would soon be a crescendo…a climax in this whole diabolical scenario that would involve him. The dream was Satan's warning. Either leave at once and let him carry out his plan, whatever that was, or face death.

Suddenly, there was a tapping on the storeroom door. "Travis," Smokey's voice called. "You in there?"

Travis jumped up and opened the door.

"I thought I heard somebody yell out," Smokey said. "I didn't know you were back. Wondered what happened to ya."

"Sorry, boss. I was just so tired, when I laid down to rest a bit, I guess I fell asleep."

"And you need it, son. Go on back in and lay down."

"No. I'm coming out for work. You need me and I need *it* to help clear the cobwebs from my brain."

Travis had not planned to attend the morning service at Trinity the next day. But then that Saturday evening during the low-country boil, Travis overheard Trinity members Bennie Taylor and Marsh Brennan talking about a memorial service led by Deacon Carlisle…a true ceremony of praise that had failed to come off at the pastor's funeral. They said further that Rudman, who had left the church immediately after his miserable sermon, had been accosted by several other deacons at his home and told to step down. He was also asked to leave the church entirely. They said Rudman sneered, made a few off-color comments and then showed them the door. They couldn't imagine what had happened to the man to change him. An apostate if they ever knew one. But, good riddance, they said.

So, Travis changed his mind. He *would* be there. And if things went to plan, by the early afternoon of that Sunday in late October, 1960, he would have forced the devil's hand.

✝ ✝ ✝

Travis needed a good breakfast. As he only felt like nibbling a couple pieces of the shrimp the night before, the plate of sausage, two eggs and toast was what his stomach needed. After showering and dressing, he closed and locked the front door and began walking down Main in the direction of the church. This morning there were no chimes from Trinity's carillon. But the birds cheerfully offered up their own music.

Travis imagined it would be a most somber service beginning with a profound eulogy and then perhaps a series of recollections by people of the life of Drake Moreau. There might be some that wanted to share with the congregation not only their love for the man, but perhaps even some light-hearted stories about him that would evoke smiles and laughter.

When everyone was seated and a dark-haired lady in a colorful dress had just finished playing a medley of Drake Moreau's favorite hymns, Jerry Carlisle, senior deacon at Trinity, took the podium.

"My friends, this is a morning for celebration...celebration of the life of our own Drake Moreau." So far so good, Travis thought...as well as everyone else. "Today, our beloved pastor of thirty-two years is in the presence of our wonderful savior Jesus Christ, singing praises to God and his glory. Although we are saddened for having lost our brother to this world, we rejoice in the fact that he is now home. There is no pain, no trouble, no heartache where he is. It is the place to which we all aspire to go, for it was promised to us. Drake Moreau was God's faithful servant all the years he was a Christian and he touched in some way each and every one of us. We remember so often how he loved to quote from the Psalms, his favorite one being: *I love the Lord, because He has heard my voice and my supplications. Because He has inclined His ear to me, therefore, I will call upon Him as long as I live.*

"That epitomizes Drake Moreau. I never saw him down, because if ill winds ever set in, he never failed but to call upon the Lord." He then looked down at Moreau's wife. "Catherine, we all loved Drake." And then he chuckled. "We all didn't agree with him one hundred percent of the time, but we always respected him."

That remark prompted Travis to recall how disrespectful clearly half of the congregation was the day he saw them walk out.

"And at this time, I want to encourage others within our throng to offer any praises or recollections about this honorable man you may have. So, who will be first?"

A tall, elderly and gaunt-looking gentleman in the front row then stood and said, "He sat with my Esther for two days on her death bed, never taking anything but water, holding her hand and praying. He was there for me when she died. He was a true friend and I will always love him until the day God brings me home." He then sat down. A few of the women began to weep.

"I have a story about Drake," said a plump woman about sixty-two or three halfway back on the left side. "My Hank and I were two of the first people he married. Right after we said the 'I do's' we all went to the reception over at the old

Janakus building...you know, the place that burned. Well, every time I got to dancin' with Hank, Drake would come up and tap him on the shoulder to break in. I believe I had more dances with him than I did my new husband." She then looked at Catherine Moreau. "Of course, that was before you came on the scene, Catherine dear." The mood had swung with this story and laughter permeated throughout.

There were several more stories offered up by long-time members and friends which served to elicit both tears and laughter, and then at a point when no one else stood to further eulogize their good friend, the tall, dark-haired man in the strange suit finally stood.

"Yes, sir," said Carlisle. "You have something to offer?"

"I do sir," replied Travis. "You don't know me, except for Mrs. Moreau, but I have been in your community for several weeks now..."

As Travis was speaking, he heard a man behind him say in a low voice, "That's the guy from the diner who was arrested for those murders."

"My name is Travis Marlowe, and although it has little to do with what I have to say, I am an ordained minister in my home community in Indiana. My background is Amish and I was pleased to serve in my order as the youngest of all the ministers in the district. But, after I came here to Destiny, the church I wanted to attend was Trinity, mainly because of what I heard about Drake Moreau. I've attended three services here and each time sat transfixed in awe of Pastor Moreau, listening to his eloquently-delivered, God-sent messages. I visited with him in his home and he returned that visit only a week ago. On each occasion, I received both his counsel and blessing. And in just that short period of time, we became close friends. He was one of the most beautiful spirits I have ever met.

"Now, this is where I hope it is not inappropriate for me to speak about something that some of you have believed controversial. But, this will be my only opportunity for my voice to be heard in this community, since you, the Trinity congregation are the backbone of this town. You heard his message and for the most part, you rejected it as myth. Pastor Moreau and I literally spent hours talking about this blight with which Satan has infected this town..."

Deacon Carlisle then interrupted Travis. "Mr. Marlowe, this is neither the time nor venue for you to bring up such unpleasantries. Yes, some of us thought Drake had gone too far with his idea about the devil and his band of demons suddenly making Destiny its home."

"This is *absolutely* the proper time to continue the crusade that the pastor started, Deacon Carlisle. You all have seen the pentagram and 666 markings and graffiti on buildings. Even on your Confederate monument. I have heard officers in your police department speak about the crime statistics sky-rocketing a thousand percent just in the past two months..."

"Yeah," shouted a voice behind Travis. "While you were in the town's jail charged with murder. We know about you."

The congregation then began a murmur that escalated to such a volume where the deacon had to call order. "Friends, friends, we are out of control here. Mr. Marlowe, are you now through?"

"No, sir. I would like to continue if the congregation will bear with me."

Another gentleman then spoke up. "He's disrupted this service enough already, we might as well see what he has to say."

"Thank you, sir. Yes, I *was* charged with the murders of two men, both ne'er-do-wells. However, the charges were proven groundless. That business is over, sir. But, you have to know something...something that may sound bizarre to you. I don't know how to convey this except to just blurt it out. I...have seen the face of the devil..." The murmuring began again along with some laughter. "Hear me out, please. Not only has Satan fueled the activities of a cult that is practicing ritualistic human sacrifice, but he has personified himself in human form. In taking over the bodies of two men, the devil has personally accosted me, warned and taunted me on several occasions. And then when these two men ended up butchered and murdered in ways too shocking to describe to this church..."

"Please stop." A very prim, well-dressed lady, Eugenia Carter, every bit of eighty if she was a day, was now standing, chin in the air and eyes resolute. In a meek, but articulate voice, she said, "Sir, you dare intrude on this solemn occasion, saying frightening things in front of our young people and placing notions upon us that this community is under some kind of demonic siege. You expect us to believe that you have even come face-to-face with Satan in human form. This is not two thousand or five thousand years ago, and this is not some science-fiction movie we find ourselves in. What purpose do you have in telling us this rubbish and even if it were remotely true, what would you have this congregation do about it?"

"I'm only here to warn, ma'am...and as your pastor instructed you, to put on the full armor of God. Protect your families and see what your children are into. I am further convinced there may even be people among you who may be of influence to the church and who could be part of this satanic cult. In Mark 12, we are apprised that evil spirits do exist inside human beings. He says they can travel even to the inside of the church. In Colossians, we learn about underworld beings with super-human powers.

The devil knows who is weak enough to be pulled into his web of evil and deceit. The occult has its own unique lure by giving its recruits the power to feel a part of the supernatural world. Your children with their impressionable minds are especially vulnerable..."

"I'm sorry, Mr. Marlowe," said Carlisle. "That has to be enough. No one wants to hear any more of this. You..."

"But, I do," came the voice from the front row. Catherine Moreau slowly came to her feet. "I will stand with Mr. Marlowe. I am confident what he shared with my husband, he truly experienced. Drake was savagely murdered by this band of devil worshippers, whoever they are. He was right about this evil in our community...and he paid with his life for attempting to incite this very congregation. They are very real and I am convinced no one could commit such a brutal act except under the influence of the devil. For some reason Satan has chosen Destiny, Louisiana as his playground. But we in turn can make it a *battle*ground, seeking out this occult by getting the word out around town. Talk it up. Find out who they are and turn them in. Challenge anyone you see who wears the upside down cross or a witches' cloak. We have heard the stories from men who hunt and trap. They have seen the hooded people in the forests around the fires and have heard their chants. But we have turned a blind eye about all of it. We ignored the news about the men whose eyes were put out, whose chests were engraved with pentagrams and who were then killed. Will you also ignore the way your pastor died? How these people mocked our Lord Jesus Christ *and* ridiculed Drake. I'm sorry if I don't have a humorous or praise-filled story about Drake to tell today. We all know the stories and they are wonderful...all of them. I can stand here and tell you that this community has never had as its citizen a greater man than Drake Moreau. But today, I stand with Mr. Marlowe whose only real opportunity to tell his story was at this memorial service for Drake." She then turned to Travis. "Sir, you have me in your corner just as much as my husband was with you. I will do whatever I can to spread the word about this satanic invasion of our community. And I challenge everyone in this room to stand with me and listen to you. The beast is among us. Beware the beast."

Travis smiled at her as she sat down. "You said what I came here to say, Mrs. Moreau. All that I will add is that we must all keep Jesus in our hearts, resisting all temptation, thwarting Satan's attempt to not only secure that foothold in your community, but take control of our very souls. If Jesus lives inside of us, the devil will let us be. Both cannot live inside us at the same time. It is written."

When he had sat down, the large room was quiet. No one said a word. There was not even a cough. It was as though the air had been sucked out of the sanctuary. Finally, Deacon Carlisle, looking rather lost and bewildered, appeared to be searching for words. "Uh…well, my friends, I uh…think we will ask Betty to close our service on the keyboard with another of our beloved pastor's favorite hymns…uh…how about playing for us *How Great Thou Art*."

Whether or not Travis would be dismissed as some misguided sap by the skeptics and doubters, he would be a topic of conversation for days to come not only among Trinity's faithful, but throughout the town. Would they heed his words? And those of Catherine Moreau, the woman they loved and trusted? After the people had given their words more thought, in merely a couple of days they would most likely be forgotten, if not rejected from the get-go.

Until there was another murder.

CHAPTER THIRTY ONE

THE BUZZ ABOUT TOWN

HIS MISSION OF CONVEYANCE COMPLETE, TRAVIS felt that after standing before the most influential people in Destiny, his warning would get around...one way or another. Was this dish washer's cautioning merely a fool's folly or now that they thought about it, perhaps there *had* been some reasons for concern? But for Travis, as his foreboding speech was over, he felt that a huge weight had been lifted from him.

For the remainder of the afternoon, while listening on one of the good stations to the likes of Percy Faith, Ray Charles and Connie Francis in the rundown of what the DJ called the Top Forty, he penned a short response letter to Sarah.

"My dear Sarah,

I was overjoyed when I received your letter. Just the possibility that we could again be together, some way and somehow, has given me so much hope. There is nothing more in this world that I want than to be with you and Rachael. I will go to every length to see that it happens.

Without going into detail, I must tell you that I have been about the Lord's business here in Southern Louisiana. There are some pressing concerns within the town on which I know that God has set me to task. With this unfinished business, it may be a few more days before I can leave the town. But, once I do, I will be home as quickly as I can. I am confident we will be able to work things out, given our situation. As I love you, I also felt the love you have for me in the words of your letter.

It grieves me to know that Rachael has been crying for me. Please tell her I love her and that her father will be home soon to tell her stories of his travels. Tell her I will also bring her something special when I come.

I have continued to wonder how we could arrange a conversation by phone, considering there are no phones in Himmel. Perhaps you can go into Hurley to call me some day. It should not take more than two or three dollars of coins to do so. The phone number here at the diner where I work is DE-59849. Just to hear your voice would be like listening to the most beautiful music I could ever imagine.

I don't have much more to tell you, but as I have managed to save what meager pay that I have received, I am enclosing eighty dollars. I hope that it will help with the finances.

Please pray for us as a family as I have done incessantly. I know God wants us to be together again. He sanctioned it more than a dozen years ago and then gave us a beautiful child. Keep the faith, be safe and trust God. Soon we will be back together.

> *Your loving husband,*
> *Travis Marlowe"*

The next morning, as Travis and his apprentice, Stevie Ray worked feverishly clearing and cleaning tables, then scrubbing plates and pans in the large sink, Smokey tried to keep up with the orders while Sissy contended with the patrons. The breakfast crowd was unusually large on this Monday morning, sometimes stacking up and waiting beyond the front door. At first Smokey didn't realize why. But after over-hearing some of the customer dialogue, he learned that his senior dishwasher had caused quite a stir at Trinity Methodist. Although many of the patrons that morning were members at Trinity and had heard him speak about devilish things, along with Catherine Moreau, the phones must have lit up on Sunday afternoon around town. Who *was* this Amish character and why did he land in Destiny to end up standing before them with such a foreboding tale? As he moved about the diner engrossed in his work, they eyed him, put their heads together and gossiped, still refraining from having any direct contact with him. A person of immense oddity and uniqueness, he was continuing to pique their curiosity.

"You made quite an impression at church, I hear," remarked Smokey. "What was that all about?"

Travis laid a new set of dishes in the sink for Stevie Ray and replied, "About what I know to be going on around here."

"You actually stood up in church and told them the devil had moved in here and took over? Where'd you git such a notion and why am I just hearin' about it?"

"I don't know. I guess I was afraid you'd think I was some kind of kook."

"Like everybody out there does, eh. Well, anyway, your little talk at the church brought a ton a people in this morning.' I ain't complainin' about that."

Sissy, being so busy that Monday, didn't have but a few words for Travis; however, she was all smiles with him and nodded as though she was definitely on board with him, the spiritual person that she was. Jane came in at noon to overlap between Sissy's and Dreama's shifts. Being so new and having not gotten to know Travis, she had nothing much to say either. Travis did ask her to drop his letter to Sarah in the mailbox after she left work.

When Dreama arrived at three, she *definitely* had something to say. "Wow, preacher man. Destiny's new citizen has sure made a name for himself. I find something interesting about you every time I turn around."

"So, you too think I'm a nut case."

She laughed "I'm not sure who or *what* you are. But I still think you're a nice guy who needs a friend."

"Yeah. I think I'll *definitely* be needing one. People don't warm up very well to strangers who go around sounding the alarm about the devil coming to Louisiana."

Dreama slid onto one of the counter stools and took out a cigarette. After lighting it she spewed out a long plume of smoke. "About that…maybe you should back off this devil thing. I had no idea you were going around spreading this kind of junk. Are you not sure it's something you imagined or dreamed up?"

"I guess you probably heard through the grapevine most everything I said to the people over at Trinity. I'm not the only one who has been sending a warning to the community. Pastor Moreau had been preaching on it for several Sundays and obviously it got him killed. The satanic cult that murdered the other two men most certainly killed the pastor who apparently was calling too much attention to the diabolical happenings in the community."

"I guess coming from him, the important religious guy that he was, he made the people start thinking about it. It's no secret where I am on this religion hogwash. I just don't pay it any mind. We are masters of our own fate and who or what we worship and where we end up after we die is our own business."

"I'm sorry you think that, Dreama. Is there any way I can sit down with you someday and tell you about God and His Son Jesus...who by the way are very real? I want you to hear the truth."

"The truth?" She then laughed. "This is the truth, Travis, you and me sitting here. Talking. Communicating with one another. This is reality. How can I believe in something I can't see? You show it to me and maybe I'll believe it. But right now, all I believe in is little ol' me, this place and the miserable paycheck I get from working here."

Her rejection of the Truth and her refusal to open up her heart and mind to God disturbed Travis. It was not only because they had become friends, but she was yet another soul who would be lost. And even one soul lost was too many. Would there ever be a time when she would have a change of heart? He would not give up on her.

It was now mid-week and as Trinity's community was still in mourning for its pastor, the police were no closer to solving his murder. Or the murders of the other two men. All they knew was that with the similarities of the M.O., they were obviously committed by the same cult of killers. There did appear to be more presence by the State Police, who began increasing its patrols of the town and parish. And the Louisiana Bureau of Investigation had been in town asking people questions about anything strange they might have observed. A small task force of the LBI had been combing the woods near where the bodies of the train hobo and Joubert had been found. Although they had been found in different locations near the Thibodeaux Bog, there was evidence they had been murdered somewhere else.

The press was also in town covering the pastor's death, not just because he was a prominent religious icon in Southern Louisiana, but that it occurred within the hallowed walls of the pastor's church. That made it sensational, tabloid news. Unfortunately for Travis, the press also descended on the Old South Diner to try catching an interview with the itinerant Amish restaurant employee who seemed to have an explanation for the murders. First, Channel 5 out of Baton Rouge set up with their reporters, microphones and cameras in the parking lot outside. Then a day later, reporters from the New Orleans based *Times-Picayune* entered the diner looking for Travis. It was all clearly disruptive to Smokey's business. When the reporters did manage to corner Travis for an interview, customers began leaving their tables to gather around, so that they could hear the dialogue and perhaps be captured themselves on camera. However, Travis declined any interviews. "I'm sorry. I said what I needed to say at Trinity Methodist last Sunday. Some of these other folks who were there can fill you in. It is not my intention for all of this to become a circus. I have brought to the attention of this community everything they need to hear. So, please don't ask me any more questions. Anyway, I have to get back to work."

All of this media attention on the town had not only put Destiny, Louisiana on the map, but served to turn Travis Marlowe into an instant celebrity. Customers even began inviting him to their tables to engage him in dialogue; however, he politely resisted, telling them he had a job to do and needed to be about his business. Although the frenzied activity was a boon for Smokey that week, he still looked out from the kitchen at Travis with disapproving eyes.

Travis, realizing that when Smokey didn't say much, he was not pleased, was apologetic on that Friday between the lunch and dinner hours. "I'm sorry, boss. I didn't envision any of this would ever happen. Maybe I should just quit and find another job in an obscure location."

"No. Forget that notion. This will all die out in a couple of days and things will return to normal. But who'd a thought a few words outta your mouth would cause such a stir?"

"Yeah. Who'd a thought," Travis said to himself.

Travis was now getting impatient and wanted to go home. Whatever was going to happen, he prayed God would *make* happen. If he was to be impactive in all of this, something needed to come to a head very soon. And he didn't know what. Or how.

Saturday night when Travis stepped out front around eight to catch a breath of fresh air away from the cigarette smoke, he was surprised to find Dummy sitting on the bench under the tree with a crutch in his hand. As he was apprehensive about the man, considering the last time they communicated, Travis was not sure if he would engage him. Would he again take on the demon's face and spew out a new battery of taunting words? Travis searched the man's eyes and then when he saw how helpless they were, he realized the old Dummy was back. The man began to smile, but said nothing. Travis suspected Dummy probably had no recollection at all about the demon entering his body.

"How are you doing now? It's good to see you back. Sorry about your accident."

The man's eyes glistened. He nodded.

"Wait right here and I'll have Smokey get you something to eat."

Dummy grinned and nodded again, then Travis went back inside.

"Your friend's back out front, Smokey," Travis said.

"What did he have to say?" And then Smokey guffawed.

"Very funny. Nothing this time."

"I'll work somethin' up and take it to 'im myself. Will be good to see the old boy again."

That next Sunday, Travis did not attend at Trinity. For some reason, his heart wasn't in it. His friend and mentor was dead. The associate minister, Rudman, was long gone and good riddance there, and Deacon Carlisle would again be leading the service. Travis was good with just having a nice salad and re-reading Galatians. Over a bowl of bread pudding, he listened to the EZ station from New Orleans. Pat Boone was writing *Love Letters in the Sand*, Gogi Grant was feeling *The Wayward Wind* in her face and Patti Page was visiting *Old Cape Cod*. It was soothing music and their voices were smooth and tender. But then as his eyelids were becoming heavy from the combination of the music and carbohydrates in the pudding, he decided to take a nap. The clock on the wall read one-fifty and if he caught just a couple of hours, he could then take a late afternoon walk after the temperature cooled.

As he watched them again through the trees by the light of the flickering flames burning in the open chimney, they stood in the circle around the man lying on the ground. He was stripped to the waist and even in Travis' dream, he knew what was coming. There were twelve in number this time, again wearing black robes and hoods beneath which were blank faces. They joined hands and chanted verses of an unknown origin in monotone voices. Their victim's mouth was open as in a scream, except nothing came out. "Stop!" Travis yelled out.

The blank faces then turned all in unison toward him. He ran and they began to give chase. His brain told him to run faster, but his feet bogged down in the mire of the swamp. Realizing they were closing rapidly on him, he stopped and turned to face them. He had a gun in his hand, but when he pulled the trigger, the bullets spit out like rubber, traveling only a couple of feet and falling well short of his pursuers. Suddenly, he felt a hand on his arm…and then another. They then began forcing him back to the open field where the fire was now fully blazing in the chimney. He felt its warmth on his face.

But then he suddenly woke and drew in a deep breath to calm himself down. His heart beat like a kettle drum and he once again found himself drenched in sweat. Opening his eyes to the darkness of the room, he lay wondering. Wondering just when it was the dreams would ever stop?

His last couple of dreams had told him the location of the two ritualistic murders. He had seen the site in both Dreama's painting and the one by DuMont in Madam Marie's window. There could be no other place. But how could he tell the police this? They would ask how he knew the location unless he himself had killed the men there. Then he would say that he saw it in his dreams. Dreams? They would scoff and laugh, dismissing him only as the kook who claims he has seen the devil.

Travis arose, still tired…actually *worn out* from the dream. And when he went to the dining room to check the time, he saw that it was only two-fourteen. He was sure he had been asleep two or three hours.

After a cup of coffee, he was just about ready to take that walk when the phone rang. He had heard it ring several times on any given day, usually answered by Smokey or Dreama, but it was the first time it ever rang on a Sunday.

"Hello," he answered.

He could tell someone was on the other end, but the caller did not reply.

"Hello," he said again. There was still no voice.

"All right, who is this?" he finally asked sternly.

"Travis?"

His heart felt like it did a flip. "Sarah...Sarah, is that you?"

"Yes."

It was a strange feeling to speak with her over the phone. In all the years they were married, he had never done so. He had never had reason to do so.

"Oh, but it's great to hear your voice. I've missed you so much."

"I got your letter yesterday. Thanks for the money. I could use it these days. Are you still coming this way soon? You said you had some pressing business there where you are."

"I want to leave here and be home by Thanksgiving if possible. It will be only proper to give the man I work for some notice. He is a good man and has treated me well these weeks. Have things been good with you and Rachael? I have worried about you a lot."

"We both have been healthy, although Rachael developed a cold last week. I think she's about over it. I have had good help with the farm during the harvest. The corn did not bring what it should have, as the market price is way down. We also lost two of our cows just after you left. One was Tess. I loved her."

"I'm sorry, Sarah." He paused a moment. "I think about you every day, you know, praying that you and Rachael are safe and healthy, and praying that our marriage will be restored."

"I know. I pray for us as well. I pray my heart will soon be over what you did. Prayer has helped ease my hurt quite a bit."

"I can't begin to tell you how sorry I am. Your forgiveness is all I have wanted."

"As I told you in the letter, I do forgive you," she said. "I'm now working hard on the forgetting part. I went to see Bishop Herrmann the other day and asked him about any possibility that you can rejoin the order so that we can live as husband and wife. He told me that the Ordnung was very clear about one suddenly becoming an unbeliever because of a grievous sin. But, he did provide a glimmer of hope. He said he always liked you and if you came home and petitioned the council to remove the shun, he would consider supporting you. However, you would never be restored to your position as minister. You would also be required to show good faith by going through intensive spiritual training, proving to the council of brethren that you are a true believer who will keep the commandments."

"I have *always* been a believer. You and I have talked about that part of the Ordnung with which I didn't agree. My true Ordnung is God's word…and his promise of salvation by believing in Jesus Christ. I have been saved since the day I accepted Him and nothing, not even Amish law, can change that."

"And I am with you on that, Travis. But you will also have to demonstrate your faithfulness to me and to our marriage."

"I promise before all that is holy that I will be a faithful husband."

She was quiet for a moment, and then she said, "It will be difficult getting Minister Strubhar to support you."

"I'm sure that will be the case. He was always the first, and sometimes the only one to dissent when it came to decisions about me."

"I've always thought he was just a big stick in the mud, anyway." And then she laughed.

It was good to hear that laugh.

"The operator just said my time is up," Sarah said. "I hope you will be back here soon."

"As soon as I possibly can. I love you, Sarah, and I always will. You…"

And then he heard the dial tone. The operator had ended the call.

As he walked along Main and down Magnolia by the church, it seemed to him at times that his feet were not even touching the sidewalk. Now that Travis had heard Sarah's voice and had told him that she was looking for him to come home soon, it was as though his heart had suddenly unclogged itself from the guilt and shame he had felt these months. The heaviness was off his chest and it actually seemed he could breathe easier.

Circling back around to the courthouse, he then saw just beneath the Johnny Reb statue, a familiar form sitting on the bench. Dummy. His crutch lay beside him on the ground. As he closed in on him and their eyes met, Travis saw there was not the usual grin on the man's face. At first, he was set to think that perhaps the demon had returned in the man, but when no evil eyes took form nor vile, deriding words spat from Dummy's mouth, Travis became perplexed. The eyes were instead sad and hurting. Dummy then lifted his arms as though he wanted help and his mouth opened as though he were trying to form words.

"What's wrong, friend? Do you need a meal?"

Dummy shook his head emphatically. But he continued gesturing with his arms and hands, making no sense at all to Travis.

"I don't know what you want," Travis said. "Is there any way you can let me know what it is you need?"

The man shook his head slowly, mouth still agape. He couldn't talk and he couldn't write anything down. He was pitiful.

"I'll be glad to take you back to the diner to get you something."

Then Dummy merely dropped his arms and looked down as though he had given up trying to communicate with Travis.

"Are you in pain and need to get medical help?"

There was no response. No nodding or shaking of the head. He simply crossed his arms and became still.

"Okay. You know where I am and I'll be there all evening."

Travis then began walking away, but paused to look back at the man. Dummy's eyes were now back on him...helpless, pathetic eyes...eyes that for some reason appeared to have given up on life. It nearly broke Travis' heart. But all he could do was keep walking.

.

CHAPTER THIRTY TWO

WARREN LIPPERT

IT WAS A TYPICAL WEEKDAY MORNING of work that next Tuesday for the diner crew. The usual customers were seated at their usual places in the booths and at the counter. There were no reporters or camera crews, sensationalists or curiosity seekers crowding in on top of everyone. Bouchard and his sidekick were talking about the fishing they had done out on Pontchartrain on Saturday. Mayor St. Pierre was deep in a conversation with one of the town councilmen, Burt Gastineaux , about the Mayor's opponent who didn't have a chance in Hades of winning next month.

At nine something, Chief Couture and Officer Presley came through the door and immediately slid in beside of St. Pierre and the councilman at the booth on the far end of the diner. Travis was busy clearing the table adjacent to the booth while Stevie Ray was washing dishes in the kitchen.

"Mayor, bad news this morning,'" began Couture. "A road crew found another body up off Highway 30 near the railroad overpass. Cut up like the others and eyes gouged out. The man had a large gapin' chest wound, probably from a knife."

Travis' ears pricked up and he stopped what he was doing.

"Any I.D. on the man?"

"No. No need for it. It was Dummy."

Travis nearly dropped his tray of plates. In doing so, he attracted the attention of Couture.

"I guess you heard what I just told the Mayor, eh Marlowe?"

"I did."

"And I suppose you know nothin' about *that* killin' either."

"Absolutely not. I will admit I did see the man when I took a walk downtown Sunday afternoon. He was sitting on a bench near the Confederate soldier."

"Well, you're the one who's been talkin' up this demon cult out there. You know so much about it, why don't you tell the Mayor and me what you know about it."

"I don't know anything about it except that the M.O., as you police call it, suggests the murders have to be the work of satanic ritualists."

"I think that's a bunch of hoo-haw, Marlowe," Couture replied. "There's no evidence of any such group of people doing that stuff. It's the work of some psychopath...something we've never had in this area. That is before you came along."

"You don't need to go there, Chief," Travis said. "You lost that argument to a very good lawyer a couple weeks ago. But, anyway, I'm sorry to hear about the man. He was a regular around here and a friend of Smokey's."

Presley nodded. "He might have been a derelict, but people in the town kinda looked after him. He mighta been as much an icon as Reverend Moreau, only at opposite ends of the totem pole."

"Old Dummy," said St. Pierre. "I probably put five thousand dollars in that man's cup over the past thirty plus years. He was a town fixture all right. A lot of people will be mighty upset."

"When was he killed?" asked Travis.

"The coroner says maybe Sunday night or early Monday morning," replied Presley.

"And how did he get that far out of town?" Travis asked. "He could barely walk anywhere."

"Somebody obviously scarped him up and drove him out there sometime between when you saw him and dark," said Couture.

"So, with all these poor unfortunates turning up dead, what are you police doing to catch these killers?"

"We're lookin,'" Couture replied indignantly. " But don't you concern yourself with what we're doin.'"

"Yet, another man turns up dead. And what are you doing now? Here asking *me* what I know about it."

Couture scowled. "You're mighty smart alecky for an ignorant dish washer. You tend to your pots and pans and we'll tend to our police business."

Travis did not dignify Couture's last remark with a response. Instead he walked away without word. Presley slid back out of the booth and followed him.

"Hey, son. You need to take a step back with the Chief there. He ain't someone ya want to mess with."

"Then he should stay off my case."

He nodded. "I know. All I'm sayin' is just stay away from him."

Travis set his dishes down on the counter. "What's your assessment about these killings, Mr. Presley? You seem to be a pretty level-headed officer."

"I gotta agree with you, Marlowe. This ain't the work of just one sick human being. It's gotta be some kind of cult... like you say, devil worshippers. All the signs point toward it. I guess you didn't see me, but I was sittin' way in the back at Trinity that Sunday you got up and talked. You made a lot a sense that day."

"I appreciate you saying that. So, why aren't you convincing the Chief about this?"

Presley leaned in and said in a low voice, "Because he is a hard-headed so-in-so and wants in the worst way to pin these murders on you. He thinks you're makin' up all this stuff about a cult to throw the attention off *yourself*. But, I know there's no way you coulda done these murders. You don't even have a means of transportation ta get you way out there where the bodies were found."

"I appreciate your vote of confidence." Travis then looked back at Smokey who was steadfast at the grill. "He's going to be upset when he hears about Dummy."

"By the way, Marlowe. After all these years of him bein' just plain Dummy, when the LBI ran his prints, we found out they were on file at the VA. He was a veteran of World War I. Sergeant Warren Lippert, U.S. Army. The reason he couldn't talk was because he was gassed at Meuse-Argonne."

"A veteran. I'm sure the VA will provide him a nice marker. And now there'll be a name to go on it . Warren Lippert. I wish I had known that."

"I'll do my best to make sure the entire town knows it."

"Officer Presley. As I feel I can talk to you, I want to ask you something. What's common about all of these murders?"

"You mean the obvious...the pentagrams carved on the bodies, the eyes put out...what else?"

"All of them have occurred on Sundays...Sunday nights to be exact. It's as though this cult is intentionally committing these acts on the Sabbath...the Lord's Day. It is not only an affront to God, but an intentional sacrilege."

"Now that you mention it...you're right."

"And I want to give you a clue about something else. I think I know where these murders have actually taken place. And they're not being committed where people have found the bodies."

"How do you know that?"

Travis sighed. "Don't think I'm loony, but I've had several dreams about the killings. And the scene of the murders is quite vivid in the dream."

Presley grinned and shook his head. "You're right. It would be hard for me to place any substance on somethin' comin' out of somebody's dream. But go ahead. I'm game. Where?"

"There's a painting in Madam Marie's store window of a foggy field with a lone chimney on the horizon. The area is ironically called Devil's Tea Table. On it used to be a house owned by a witch and she was burned out. The killings are happening there. I'll bet a month's pay on it."

"Yeah, I know the story. Every kid has heard about it growin' up. I don't rightly know where that place is, but could find out. Now, if I take this dream story to the Chief, he'll laugh me out of the station."

"Maybe you can keep a lookout for activity in the area, anyway. Have the LBI put people out there."

Presley let out a puff of air from his lungs after taking in all of what Travis told him. "Let me think about it."

"I'll then ask that you don't think too long."

Travis thought he saw some tears in Smokey's eyes once he had told his boss about Warren. Smokey then took a break and sat down at the counter with Travis for a few moments. For a while, he was quiet and reflective. But then he said, "I used to sit out there and talk to Dummy, goin' on for maybe ten ta fifteen minutes while he scraped out the food on his plate. Of course, it was a one way conversation. I'd say somethin' about what was goin' on around town and he'd nod. He knew what I was talkin' about, 'cause he prob'ly knew more what was goin' on around town than that mayor out there does. It sounds strange, but we did communicate." He then took a drag of the cigarette he had started. "I remember the day he brought me one of them ben-yays from down at the bakery. He knew how much I enjoy them things. He took money somebody else gave him for a bottle to buy that ben-yay." Smokey then dabbed at an errant tear with his index finger. "Why would some crazy kill that innocent soul? He never hurt *no* one."

"Did you know he was a veteran of the First World War?"

"No. But it don't surprise me none. Fact is, when ya look out in that street, ya just don't know what people's background is. A guy like that gets stepped on like a bug sometimes, and then ya might find out he was a Medal of Honor winner or somethin.'"

"I took a walk Sunday afternoon and saw Warren in the courthouse park on a bench. He acted strange, Smokey, and was trying to communicate with me the best he could. His eyes spoke to me, but I didn't understand them. He flailed his arms at times like he was trying to make a point, but I just couldn't decipher what was on his mind. He did look frightened, however; and now that I think about it, did he know something was about to happen to him?"

"I don't know that I believe all that omen stuff…like people have some kinda ESP. But, you could be on ta somethin' with this theory of yours about the cult."

"It's an evil lot that's murdering these people, Smokey. Instead of sacrificing goats and chickens, they're offering up to the devil the highest form of blood sacrifice…human beings. *Now* do you see why I've been on this crusade? These Satanists have to be stopped."

Smokey nodded, but didn't say anything in response. He merely tamped out his cigarette, squeezed Travis' right shoulder with his powerful hand, and then returned to the kitchen.

The town of Destiny was now in an upheaval. The man they knew as Dummy...the man they kidded, gave coins and an occasion dollar bill to, and considered a town fixture much as they did the Bonne Aire House and the Johnny Reb statue, was the newest victim of some psychotic miscreant. The other two men who were murdered didn't much matter... although there may have been some marginal concern about some crazed serial killer or devil gang on the loose. Maybe there *was* something about that dish washer's story down at the diner. Maybe there *was* a pack of devils out there whose ritualistic killings were far worse than that of any voodoo cult known to practice its religion in the Louisiana back country.

Destiny's appreciation for the man they called Dummy was even more magnified once the people learned that he actually had a name. Not only that, but he was a veteran of what was called the *War to End All Wars*. On the Friday before All Saint's Day, Warren Lippert was given a funeral by the town...paid for by the town. Anyone who was able to get off work was there. Even people, who in Warren's life never even acknowledged his existence, were there weeping as though they had lost their best friend. At his graveside service, the Baptist minister, Archie Camp, read from the Psalms and gave a stirring mini-sermon in Warren's praise. And, the American Legion was there to fire their volley of three rounds, after which their bugler sounded Taps.

On that Saturday, the talk over the breakfast and lunch tables at the Old South was mostly about what the police were *not* doing to protect their town. The citizens weren't particularly worried about themselves or their families, considering that the killer's or killers' targets appeared to be the "lower-life people, like the tramps and Negroes."

"But what about the preacher?" asked Brace Greenwood, the First National Bank's President. "He was not of lower class."

From across the table Chamber of Commerce member, Tom Haverty replied, "I'd say because he preached those sermons about the 'demonic plague,' as he called it, he was a threat to the mission and resolve of the cult."

Greenwood then leaned toward his tablemate and said, "Then I would say that young fellow over there cleaning up the table should be looking out for himself. He not only brought to the town's attention the existence of this satanic presence, but he himself is not exactly one of the town's upper crusts, if you know what I mean."

And then Travis over-heard a couple of what they called 'good ol' boys' at the lunch counter talking about the killings. One of the men said, "It don't make sense all this killin' goin' on in a respectable, God-fearin' town like Destiny. If the devil wants to attract some followers, maybe he oughta be lookin' out in Hollywood or in New York for his souls."

"Naw," said the other. "I'd say he's already *got* them people in his pocket. He don't need to do any marketin' in those places." Both of the men then laughed.

Travis was not amused. It was no laughing matter. Four people had been brutally murdered. And considering how poorly these good ol' boys themselves were dressed, perhaps *they* may one day also be mistaken for derelicts and plucked from the street.

That afternoon, before the Saturday dinner hour began, Travis sat talking with Dreama in one of the booths by the large plate-glass window while Jane helped Smokey with preparing the evening's low country boil. After some small talk about goings-on around the town, Travis said, "I've been thinking about the painting you did...you know of the field with the chimney?"

"Why, Travis, I didn't realize you were such a lover of art, being cooped up in that Amish village of yours. What about the painting?"

"Where is that place exactly?"

"Oh, maybe a dozen miles out in the country near Kornigay Bog."

"I saw a similar painting of the same place downtown in Madam Marie's store. Looks like a pretty place. Maybe you could drive me there some time...maybe to have a picnic."

"A picnic? Sounds very romantic, Travis dear."

"Only to eat and commune with nature," he said. "Maybe some fried chicken, pecan pie and a lot of fresh air. Would do me good. I think I need a break from this six day a week sweat shop."

"Well, since Sunday is the only day we could do it, how about tomorrow? I can come by and get you about three and we could be back here before dark."

"Good. Let's do it."

It wasn't so much Travis was anxious to get out of the diner for a nice afternoon in the fresh air to commune with nature as much as his need to investigate the site that had haunted his dreams. Was it actually where the murders took place or were his dreams just suggesting it because the painting was stuck somewhere in the abyss of his unconscious? Perhaps on the sly he could find evidence there of ashes in the fireplace, holes in the ground where stakes had been driven, pieces of rope and a lot of footprints. He was no detective by any means, but *somebody* had to check out the site. He was almost convinced that Harold Presley wouldn't say a word to any of his cohorts as to the location of the place. But if Travis did discover any evidence of sacrificial rituals at the site, he would then have good ammunition to take to the police.

But, then he wondered, if it *was* the place where the murders were carried out, would Dreama and he be in any danger if the hooded demons suddenly returned? After all, each of the murders did occur on a Sunday night.

CHAPTER THIRTY THREE

ARMAGEDDON

AN EARLY THUNDERSTORM ROLLED THROUGH AROUND eight on Sunday morning, each clap and subsequent boom of thunder shaking the diner as though it was being shelled by an artillery barrage. Although Travis had never experienced battle, he assumed that might be what it would sound and feel like. However, the accompanying deluge of rain quickly moved north from out of the gulf, and by nine, the sun was out in all its glory. But, although the rain had swept out, the atmosphere still remained moist. Even in late October, when the landscape finally heated up at midday, the humidity could be oppressive.

Travis was looking forward to this day...eating a good breakfast, attending morning worship to hear the new interim pastor at Trinity and a late afternoon picnic with Dreama Van Horne...totally innocent of course. Although he was sometimes bored on Sunday afternoons, a day of solace was still welcomed. It was good to have a day of leisure after six straight grueling days of work, five AM till closing, that not only included a continuous flurry of activity, but listening to customers' collective conversations that often escalated to peak decibels.

At ten minutes till eleven, as the carillon chimes played *The Church's One Foundation*, Travis, attempting to slip into the sanctuary unnoticed, sat down on the back right-side pew. But a few of the parishioners who had seen him come in and recognized him, smiled and nodded. Two gentlemen sitting in front of Travis whose eyes seemed to always be scanning the sanctuary for familiar faces, turned around to shake his hand. One of them even remembered his name. "Mr. Marlowe, it's good to see you back here today. We hope to *keep* seeing you."

Although Travis had been at first scorned by the people when he stood that Sunday to reiterate Drake Moreau's message of warning, there were two reasons they had ultimately found favor in him. First, everything he and Moreau had told them had now started to make sense, even though some still refused to accept the supernatural component of the warning. But most now believed there was indeed some kind of a satanically-inspired cult out there somewhere offering up humans in sacrifice. It wasn't just the work of one crazed killer. And then secondly, when the news frenzy occurred two weeks before and TV and newspaper reporters had tried their best to interview Travis, it had made him something of an instant celebrity.

As he looked around the sanctuary, Travis saw that nearly every pew was jammed full of people with more coming in. There still may be some curiosity seekers attending who were not members, mainly to hear any additional talk about Satan and how he and his band of demons were taking over bodies. But most of the church's regulars were there to hear Andy Devereaux, the newly chosen interim, who might just be Trinity's new minister.

He was a young man, perhaps just a little older than Travis, with sandy hair and a brilliant smile. As the choir sang *No Greater Love* with piano accompaniment, it seemed that

Devereaux's engaging eyes met every face in the sanctuary. If he had not said one word, by his smile and good looks alone, Travis believed the minister might have already won every heart of Trinity's membership. During the song, Deacon Carlisle leaned over from his chair and said something to Devereaux. The minister then nodded. When the choir had finished their special, Devereaux then quickly rose as though he was a swimmer off a springboard and went to the pulpit. Stretching out his arms before the people, he began, "Dear Christian friends, and especially those of you who have yet to accept the Lord Jesus Christ as your Savior, I welcome you to the House of God. This is a place for healing and this is a hospital for sinners. The Lord God is pleased that you are here and so am I. My name is Andy Devereaux and I am from Baton Rouge. My lovely wife, Karen, sits on the front row there with our three sons, Matthew, Mark and Luke. If we have one more boy, I expect his name will be… well, I sure you can guess it. If we have a girl, we might be stumped for a name. Maybe Joan."

The audience laughed. So far, they were good with him.

"I graduated from LSU…Geaux Tigers…and…" That registered an applause along with a couple of cheers. "…and I went to seminary at Southern. But other than that, the only additional thing you need to know about me is that God comes first in my world, followed by my family. And it is my solitary mission in life to tell everyone I meet and every soul that hears me preach, about the saving grace of Jesus Christ. He is the Way, the Truth and the Life. Know it, practice it, eat, drink and sleep it. He is the only way you will ever see Heaven in the afterlife…and oh what a joy it will be when we get there. Can you imagine, praising the Lord God every moment of that afterlife? Being in the presence of the One who created the universe and all life in it?

"But, before I begin my message, I think it is only fitting to touch just for a moment on the subject that has haunted this church and this community for the past several weeks. Yes, I am well aware of what happened here and how this malodorous fiend with whom we Christians are at war continues his presence even as a plague. The mood and complexion of this church have been immensely affected by the horrific events that have taken place. Dialogue still flows like the river in the town's shops and restaurants, and on its park benches, where people express fear and alarm about this diabolical force…and whether Satan himself dwells and abides herein, as some have suggested. But understand that from the beginning of human existence, the devil has always taken up residence among us, whether literally or within us as the great tempter he is. That has always been his quest…to get between you and God. Yes, he is present in this community. I haven't learned enough about the specifics of goings-on to formulate an opinion about him actually taking over the minds and bodies of human beings, but he is present just the same. There has never been and never will be a time when Satan does not exist in one form or another in this world…until that glorious day when Jesus comes again and Satan is soon to be bound and cast into the fiery pit of his own hell." The applause began again and continued for several moments.

"But whatever is going on in your community, one thing is imperative…that we all remain strong and steadfast in our faith and resist temptation. Our job as Christians is to spread the gospel of the Lord Jesus Christ to the world. You see it is not just up to me, and people like me, to get the truth out there. Don't be ashamed to tell others the good news…at the barber and beauty shops, to the produce guy at the store and to the man on the street who *has* nothing. Yes, after you tell that man the good news, and he believes it, he will have more riches than all of the kings who have ever lived. Our faith and belief will be made apparent to this devil; and our prayers will drive his black spirit from this very land. As your beloved pastor and one other courageous soul have spoken out against these iniquitous forces, so shall we all, exposing them wherever they hide. Now, my friends, that is all I have to say about this obvious plague on your community. I'm not telling you anything you haven't heard before."

Andy Devereaux's sermon thereafter spoke on the obligatory responsibilities of a Christian...a sermon so powerful that all ears and eyes were steadfastly glued to his captivating voice and manner. Had Trinity found another eloquent Drake Moreau? Was there yet another fearless voice behind the pulpit who would challenge the evil that continued to brew in Southern Louisiana? The nods and amens of the audience certainly reflected their approval.

After the benediction, all of the people stood fast until Devereaux made his way down the center aisle and stood at the double entry doors. Since Travis was seated so far back in the sanctuary, he was the second person to shake the minister's hand.

"Ah, Mr. Marlowe. I'm glad you are here."

"How do you know me, sir?"

"Deacon Carlisle pointed you out before the service began. And I had heard about you anyway. So you are the voice that has been crying in the wilderness."

Travis smiled. "I am pleased that you continued the message so that the church and the people in this town will not relent. Everyone needs to stay vigilant and lookout for their loved ones, especially the children. They are so vulnerable and impressionable."

"So true. I'd like to talk with you sometime. That is, if the church decides in favor of me. We are still in Baton Rouge for now."

Travis then leaned in toward Devereaux's ear. "And *you* must be vigilant as well. As these people must be stopped, at such time you become the church's pastor, they will also try to stop *you*...just as they did Drake Moreau. But, God forbid."

Devereaux nodded. "Understood, my friend."

At four o'clock, Travis was still sitting in the booth by the big window waiting for Dreama. As she was seldom on time for work, he didn't think much about her tardiness. But, then again, he figured she would be looking forward to enjoying a nice afternoon in the woods sharing dinner and good conversation. However, when five-thirty came and went, Travis started getting apprehensive. At seven, he finally gave up on her and grilled himself a ham and cheese sandwich, washed down with some sweet tea.

It was when he had cleaned up his mess in the kitchen and started walking down the hallway, he heard a knock on the back door that led to the alley. She had a key, so why would she be knocking? Anyway, it was dark and the picnic was officially cancelled hours ago. When he unlocked and opened the door expecting Dreama, he said, "Hey, what happened to..." Suddenly, something struck him in the forehead with such a force, he temporarily lost consciousness. When he opened his eyes seconds later, the first thing he felt was the pain and buzz in his head. But as his right cheek was lying on the cool pavement, he then realized someone had knocked him down. And then two or three people began picking him up by his arms and legs. When he began struggling to break loose from them, one of them kicked him in the side. Instantaneously, he heard a rib snap and he cried out in pain.

"Get him up," a man's voice bellowed.

When they had brought him to his feet, he took several swings at them, connecting with someone's jaw. But then he felt another blow to his head and the last thing he remembered was being shoved into a van.

Travis blinked open his eyes to the night sky. The moon was bright and full just off the eastern horizon. Still dazed and in pain, he just couldn't quite comprehend where he was. A faint smell of wood smoke piqued his nostrils and upon trying to draw in a deep breath, the sharp pain in his side cut it short. And then when he tried to get up, he found that his arms and legs would not move. A faint flicker of orange light off to his right allowed him to see that his wrists and ankles were tied with ropes to stakes. The sharp blades of cool grass made his back feel itchy and crawly. He had been stripped to the waist. Fear seized him. He was suddenly now dreadfully aware that his nightmare had become all too real. He was lying in the field Madam Marie referred to as Devil's Tea Table. *And like the other poor souls, he would soon be offered up to Satan in sacrifice.*

Suddenly, three figures in black approached from the direction of the chimney and stood over him. Even in the moonlight, he could not make out their faces...faces that were partially concealed by the hoods they wore.

One of them said, "He's regained consciousness."

"Good," said another.

"Who are you?!" Travis shouted.

"You know who we are. Maybe not by name. But you know me. You have made it your business to pursue me and my disciples the moment you jumped off that train. So, here I am in the flesh. What will you do now?"

"In the name of God, release me now!" Travis yelled.

The man laughed. "Where *is* your God? We don't see

Him." The man claiming to be Satan then turned and looked at a half dozen other hooded beings. "Aboc! Hudac! Isis! Have you seen his God?" He laughed again. "How about you, Shaddai, and you, Cados? Is there anyone here to save him?"

Each of them shook their heads.

"Travis Marlowe, you see before you disciples of the Black Mass, each of who will carve a piece of your flesh until a perfect Baphomet is formed on your chest. It is the Order of the Nine Angles. Just thought you should know that before you die. You will then belong to me. I am the Lord of Darkness. The one who you *really* have worshipped all your life. Before I am done, you will profess your belief and faith in me. You may call out to your God to relieve you of your pain, but He will not hear you. He has been dead for centuries. It is I who rule this world and the afterlife. As a last resort you will call out my name and beg me to end your life."

Travis smiled and then conjured up a wad of spittle, letting it fly into the face of his adversary. The man then lifted back his hood and the face of Christopher Rudman appeared.

"Well, Mr. Rudman…I won't call you 'reverend.' How long have you been masquerading as Satan? Was it you who ended Drake Moreau's life?"

Rudman smiled and then turned to his followers. "And so, let it begin."

Travis lifted his head so that his chin touched his chest. He then turned it toward the chimney that held the now roaring fire. When Rudman stopped short of the furnace, nine other figures followed him, subsequently forming a circle around him. In each of their hands were large knives with blades that gleamed orange in the refection of the fire. Each then dropped to their knees and laid their left hands on the cloak of the man who would be Satan. In monotone voices, they chanted in unison, "Before the almighty and effable god Lucifer and in the presence of all demons of hell who are the true and original gods, we renounce any and all past allegiances to the false Judeo-Christian God Jehovah and his foul, odious and rotten Son. We proclaim Satan Lucifer as our one and only god." Then taking the blades of their knives, they buried the tips into their palms. Finally, they extended their hands high above their heads toward their leader, allowing the trickle of blood to run into his garment. "We praise you, Beelzebub, god of this world, god of darkness."

As they knelt, Travis observed Rudman touching all of their heads as if to bless them. "Esiarp natas, rof eh si dog." Travis ran the words backward in his mind. Suddenly, from their mouths they chanted unintelligible words. Some of them shrieked, some moaned, while others uttered hideous, guttural phrases.

An aura of impending death suddenly overtook Travis. Where were Heaven's warriors to intercede and release him? Had God finally forsaken him, rendering His just and final punishment on him for his sins? But God was a forgiving God who accepts deep, heartfelt repentance. Didn't Jesus' sacrifice take care of his sins?

And then he remembered David's words from Psalm 54. Looking deeply into the night sky beyond the stars, he cried out softly:

"Save me, O God, by Your name, and vindicate me by Your strength. Hear my prayer, O God. Give ear to the words of my mouth. For strangers have risen up against me, and oppressors have sought after my life; they have not set God before them. Behold, God is my helper; the Lord is with those who uphold my life. He will repay my enemies for their evil. Cut them off in Your truth. I will freely sacrifice to You; I will praise Your name, O Lord, for it is good. For He has delivered me out of all trouble; and my eye has seen its desire upon my enemies."

One of the figures then slowly broke away from the others

and moved toward Travis with knife in hand. As the figure leaned over him, he could see that she was a woman. And then he saw her face. *Dreama.* Touching one finger to her lips, she said, "Be quiet." As he gasped in fear of what was coming, he saw the blade come down. But to his amazement, it did not touch his chest. Instead, he was surprised to see that the blade first sliced through the rope securing his right wrist...then his left. And then she cut the ropes from his ankles. Her hand reached down to help him up, jerking him to his feet. Dreama then motioned for Travis to follow her to the tree line.

They had not covered more than twenty yards until Rudman discovered them running. Pointing in their direction, he shouted, "Stop them!"

As they tore blindly through the trees and brush, first Dreama, then Travis, they could hear the quickening crush of twigs and crunching weeds made by the feet of their pursuers. Beams of light swept through the forest perhaps thirty yards wide, indicating the cult members had spread out in their search. Suddenly, they heard the booming voice of Rudman calling out, "Dreama. Give him up now or you are dead right along with him."

"I'm sorry, Travis," she whispered. "I never thought it would come to this."

"Keep moving," he replied. He then grabbed her by the hand. "We're changing directions. If we go ninety degrees, they'll sweep by us."

After veering off to their left, they crossed a stream and found a fallen oak to jump behind. Travis had guessed correctly. The pursuers continued on their straight-away course and passed them by. All of them except one. As the beam of a single flashlight continued to scan the woods, it ultimately fell onto their position. As if he was equipped with radar, the hooded figure then climbed over the massive trunk and landed within five feet of the crouched figures. That's when Travis sprang onto the man, knocking him back against the log. After picking up the heavy, metal flashlight the man had dropped, Travis brought it down hard on the man's head, twice, eliciting a pitiful groan. When he was certain the man was not moving, Travis shone the beam of light in his face. It was Chief Couture. Shocked at his finding, Travis then searched beneath Couture's robe until he touched the Chief's revolver. After shoving it between the bare skin of his abdomen and his trousers, he grabbed Dreama's forearm and jerked her toward him.

"All right, Dreama, start talking. Why are you mixed up in this?"

"It's a long story, Travis," she sobbed. "It all began for me about seven years ago. I was kidnapped, raped and impregnated by one of them."

"Who?"

"Mayor St. Pierre."

"St. Pierre?"

"Yes. My parents thought the father was a boy I'd been dating. They threw me out and I found a place to live until I had the baby. What I didn't know..." She then began to weep, bitterly.

"What, Dreama."

"...that St. Pierre was part of this order. When I was ready to have the baby, they took me forcibly from my apartment and brought me to this place..." She was then crying so hard, Travis could hardly make out what she was saying.

He then put her arm around her. "It's okay. Let it out."

After a few moments, she found her breath to continue. "They cut my baby from me, Travis," she blubbered.

"*Who* did?"

"One of them was a surgeon named Berger over at the

hospital, who was also a friend of St. Pierre's. And then they… they offered up my baby's little body to sacrifice and cut out his heart…" And that was all the further she could go.

Travis pulled her into his chest and let her cry. "I'm sorry, Dreama. I just can't imagine…"

They were silent for a while and then suddenly two beams of light swept back in their direction. "Get down," he whispered.

About the time the two figures were passing by, Couture stirred and groaned. Travis then struck him in the head again…this time with the butt of the revolver. It was a sickening thud. Apparently, Couture's groans were heard by the pursuers who shined their flashlights in the direction of the log. Travis clutched the revolver and waited to see if they would converge on the fallen tree. However, when the men heard nothing further, they continued on. Satisfied they were gone, Travis turned back to Dreama.

"Are you okay, now?"

"Yes," she replied softly.

"What I don't understand is, why did you stay with these people after they took your baby?"

"They told me that if I didn't or if I went to the police, they would kill me. Of course, it wouldn't do me any good to go to the police…" She then pointed to Couture. "Up till recently, I only came here on All Saint's Day with them. We only sacrificed fowl and other small animals. All Saint's Day is when Satan comes to lead us in worship."

"And Rudman is Satan?"

"Not really. We do not know which form Satan will take. We have seen him in strangers. But tonight, as with other nights, he entered Christopher's body. He has done so several times before because he is the most knowledgeable and devoted of all of Satan's followers in Louisiana. "

"Were you present at the other human sacrifices such as Joubert's and Warren's?"

"Yes, I am ashamed to admit it. But, believe me. I did not participate in the murders."

"And Drake Moreau's murder?"

"No. That was all Rudman and Couture."

Travis looked down at Couture and wanted to hit him again, but he was still out cold.

"How many human sacrifices have there been?"

"They have occurred on many Sunday nights over the past four years...maybe thirty or forty. Generally, they burned the bodies where they killed them and spread the bones and ashes all over Devil's Tea Table. But it is only recently that Rudman wanted to leave the bodies intact in other places. He wanted them to be found with the pentagrams carved on them...to make a statement. Satan has said that his kingdom is at hand and that more frequent sacrifices are necessary as a show of faith. It is usually the poor, the vagrants and the Negroes who have been taken. As we have followed the ancient order called the Friends of Hecate, who practiced human sacrifice in the Sixteenth Century, the poor unfortunates are kidnapped from the streets and hobo sites. They are considered as being somewhere between the animal kingdom and human race...sub-human, he called them. Because they are derelicts, they are generally not missed; but then if they are, nobody cares."

"How did this...this cult begin?"

"It carried over from the KKK. Way back about ten years ago, St. Pierre was what they call the Imperial Wizard, I think, and then it took on a completely different focus. But still, they chose to snag the down-and-out Coloreds from off the street to sacrifice."

Travis shook his head in disbelief. Besides Couture and Rudman, what other notables are members of this country club?"

"Well, St. Pierre *was*, but he's been too busy with politics to continue with this sadistic little hobby. The doctor who cut my baby from me died a couple of years ago." She then raised her head above the fallen oak and lamented, "My friend, Marie Andrepont, from the art store is also out there tonight. There are just two of us women in the order. Others you may have seen at the diner, but may not know their names."

Travis shook his head. "I can't believe it. It's all very horrid...loathsome."

"I only know that I have been caught up in this too long. And if we ever get out of here, I'm going to the FBI...even if it means I go to jail. I don't mind losing my freedom for what I've done."

"There is one thing you *don't* have to lose, Dreama."

"What's that?"

"Your soul. If you reject this cult, as you say you have, and accept the true God and His Son, Jesus Christ, your soul will not only be saved, but your life will change. Heaven is real, Dreama. Unfortunately, so is hell. It's your choice."

She shook her head. "I just don't know if I can believe in your Jesus. I know that Satan is real, because I have seen him. In the form of many people. Jesus has never materialized to me, so how can I believe in someone I have never seen?"

"There is a passage in the Bible that goes something like, "Blessed are those who have not seen Me, yet believe in Me." We Christians believe through our faith in God and Jesus Christ. Can you not do this as well? Can you not now confess your sins and say the sinner's prayer with me?"

Dreama shook her head, but then began to cry again. "I can't. I don't know why, but I can't."

"You can do this, Dreama. Open up your heart and say the words. Go ahead."

She stopped crying and then laid her forehead into the fallen log. She was quiet for what seemed like twenty or thirty seconds. And then Travis heard her whisper. "Dear God. Hear me. Forgive me of all these bad things I've done. I've helped to take human lives and I'm sorry...so sorry. I do accept Jesus. I do..." And then there was a choking in her voice, followed by a long groan. Travis shined the light on her face. She was in some sort of agony, grimacing in pain. Behind her he then saw something move. Rudman. He had somehow slipped in on them and thrust his knife into Dreama's back. Rudman then quickly pulled the knife from her body and raised it to in turn drive the blade into Travis.

Travis cocked the hammer of the revolver and pulled the trigger. The simultaneous flash and report from the gun were both blinding and deafening. The bullet slammed into Rudman's chest. For a moment, Rudman just stood with his eyes burning into Travis' like a laser. "This...isn't over." He then groaned and dropped to the ground.

"Yes it is," replied Travis.

Within seconds, when the swarm of lights then converged and began to move toward Travis, he fired the other five rounds from the revolver. Two voices cried out as he saw their flashlights fall to the ground. When the other pursuers began fleeing, a series of brighter spotlights suddenly fell upon them.

A voice then bellowed and echoed through the woods. "All right, all of you stay where you are. This is the police."

Travis watched as more than a dozen figures converged quickly upon the remainder of the cult. "Hey," he called. "Over here. I've got a badly wounded woman with me."

As the police officer cautiously began making his way to Travis' position, not knowing whether the voice he heard was from another cult member, Travis cradled Dreama's head in his lap. "Travis," she whispered. "I...I'm sorry. Please forgive..." She then exhaled one long, last breath and closed her eyes.

"Dreama. *Dreama*," he called to her. But she was gone.

Travis then lifted his head to the tops of the trees. "Father," he prayed. "I have witnessed that this woman accepted your Son as her savior. I ask in turn that you accept your daughter, Dreama, into your kingdom."

Travis knelt by her body for a few moments longer. His tears fell on her face. "I'm sorry, Dreama." He settled back against the fallen tree and stared at Rudman's dead body, trying to get his brain wrapped around the fact that he had just pulled the trigger on a gun that took a man's life. Suddenly, the silence was broken by a man's voice calling out.

"You there behind the log...present yourself!" Officer Presley. "This is the Destiny Police and with me are deputies from the parish sheriff department. Stand up so I can see you."

Travis dropped the revolver and did as instructed.

"Marlowe!" exclaimed Presley. "Is that you?" He continued moving toward Travis.

"Yes."

"What in blazes are *you* doin' out here with these people?"

"They took me forcibly from the diner and staked me out on the ground to kill me." He then pointed down to Dreama and Presley shined his light on her. "Dreama was also mixed up in this cult. But, she helped me escape and we ran to where we took a stand here. One of these other men you see here killed her."

Presley then directed his light to the other bodies and let out a whistle. He didn't readily make out their faces. "Who *are* they?"

"The associate minister from Trinity, Christopher Rudman, is this one. I guess he was the high priest of this devil cult. He found us hiding here and then came up and stabbed Dreama."

"Rudman, huh? Never liked the man, anyway. Looks like he's got a hole in his chest. Somebody shoot him?"

"I shot him."

"Where did you get the gun?"

"From this other man here." Travis then turned him over. "Chief Couture."

"Holy cow!" exclaimed Presley. "*He* was one of 'em?"

"He was. I clubbed him with Dreama's flashlight."

Presley then pushed his cap back on his head. "Couture. I'd a never believed it. He dead, too?"

"No, I don't think so…but he's going to have a whale of headache when he wakes up. But, how did you know…?"

"I thought a lot about what ya told me and I guess the light finally came on. I called my deputy friend from the sheriff department and we decided to come check this place out. When we got to the field where the chimney was located, we saw the fire in it. It weren't long when we heard all the yellin' and then picked up the beams from their flashlights." Presley then put the beam of his light back on Dreama's face. "I can see those other two bein' involved in somethin' like this…but Dreama? What a waste."

"She saved my life, Officer Presley. And if there's any way possible, I'd like to see her name left out of your report."

"How do I do that? She's *dead*. She's here. I can't cover that up."

"Just…think of something."

Presley nodded. "I'll try. Okay, come with me while I go see who all we've rounded up over there."

"Can I have a moment with her?"

"Sure. Take your time, son."

When Presley made his way back to where the deputies had the remainder of the cult sitting in a circle, Travis placed his light again on Dreama's face. If he didn't know any better, he would otherwise have thought she was asleep. She was beautiful...even in death.

"You gave up your life for me, Dreama." He then raised his head again to the sky. "Father, as she stands before you, please remember that."

Chapter Thirty Four

Denouement

The Lord is my light and my salvation, whom shall I fear. The Lord is the strength of my life; of whom shall I be afraid. When the wicked came against me to eat up my flesh, my enemies and foes, they stumbled and fell.

Psalm 27:1-2

OFFICER HAROLD PRESLEY CALLED THE PARISH coroner's office and the hospital ambulance service to give them directions to the area known as the Devil's Tea Table. Not only were there two bodies and a man with a busted head to evacuate, but two other men who were wounded by Travis' bullets. Presley then gave Travis his jacket to help warm him since the night air had cooled considerably and he was bare-chested. His pant legs and shoes were also soaked from crossing the stream by the fallen oak.

"You go on back with Officer Boughton, son. He'll drop you at the diner and I'll be comin' by first thing in the mornin' to get your official statement. Don't say anything to anyone until you hear from me. Except, I guess you can tell Smokey when he comes in early tomorrow. He'll want to know about Dreama."

"Thanks for showing up with the posse, Officer Presley. I'm glad you listened to what I had to say."

"Go get yourself some rest now, Travis. You uncovered a dangerous bunch of people. The town of Destiny owes you big. You tried to tell everybody and got put in jail for it." Presley then looked down at Couture. "I'll be glad to see this guy put away. A real disappointment, he is. And he did his best tryin' to falsely pin those murders on you. He'll get what's comin' to him."

Officer Boughton then led Travis from the woods past Devil's Tea Table toward his squad car. The fire was nearly out in Junie Bargeron's chimney. The moon was now high and bright enough to illuminate the entire meadow. As he and Boughton made their way across the field, it grieved Travis to realize they were walking over a graveyard of human ashes that perhaps went back a dozen years and more than thirty murdered souls. And then even if the authorities *did* find bone fragments, there was no way to ever identify who they were or even how *many* there were. Known but to God.

Travis showered and put on clean clothes in the store room, but did not bother to sleep. It was after three in the morning and he figured 'what was the use.' As he stared at himself in the mirror it seemed to him that the image looking back at him was someone else. Although the blood had been washed away from his hair and face, his forehead was badly bruised and swollen. His eyes were bloodshot and glazed over. He looked as though he had aged ten years.

After stepping into the dining room, he turned on all of the lights in the restaurant and went to the kitchen to make coffee. He wanted to sit for a while to contemplate what he would tell Smokey about Dreama's death. Smokey would be coming in for work in two hours and Travis did not want him to hear about Dreama second hand. The details of the horrid night had to come from *him*...not from the police and not from the coroner.

He made the coffee and then sat for nearly an hour with his hands around the cup, taking only a few sips. It wasn't long and the coffee turned cold. His war was over. At least he hoped it was. He had set the charge and Drake Moreau had lit the fuse. Between the two of them, Satan's plan had been blown to bits. He hoped that since Satan had lost his warriors in battle, he then had no recourse but to pull up stakes and take his malevolent mission elsewhere. It had taken him years to methodically and patiently plant the malignant seed that sprouted his nest of followers. Fueled by his supernatural presence, a racist brotherhood had spun off into a deadly cult practicing human sacrifice. They had in effect traded their white hoods for black ones. Thanks be to God they had been broken up.

But as he sat further meditating on this insane night, another matter sorely pressed on his heart. He had taken a man's life. No matter that it was out of necessity. He still killed a man...and that sickened him. But, if he hadn't, Rudman would have killed *him*. However, Travis also feared the worst about the man's soul. Although only God truly knew the man's heart, to the world Rudman had died in sin, giving his praise to Satan. But then again, what if Rudman had become possessed by Satan, as did the others; would God then still hold him accountable? Travis knew full well that the devil cannot possess a believer and that's what bothered him most. Try as he did, he just couldn't reason himself out of thinking that the man was most probably now in hell.

But then changing the gears in his brain to ponder the events of these frenzied weeks in Southern Louisiana, he could not help but believe that God had placed him on that train moving south to take up His mission. Whether it was an opportunity for him to atone for his sins, so be it. He had sounded the alarm, summoned the people, and ultimately fought the good fight. Had his tenacious endeavor driven Satan from the community? Had the demonic fog that plagued the town for months, even years, dissipated? Was there finally a sense of denouement for Destiny? He prayed that the battle was truly over. God had used him as His resource; but Travis wanted none of the credit. He hoped that most or all of it would go to Drake Moreau and ultimately, Harold Presley, who had rounded up the demonic nest of rattlesnakes that had allied itself with the devil. There might have been plenty of cudos to go around for everybody...but, in the end, the victory belonged to God.

Travis was still sitting at the counter at five ten with the same cup of cold coffee in his hand when he heard the back door open. When Smokey saw the lights on, knowing that Travis was already up, he bellowed, "Travis, did you already unlock the back door? Not a good idea at this time of the morning.'"

Travis looked down at his cup and shook his head. The door was still unlocked from when he opened it ten hours earlier to his kidnappers.

"Sorry, Smokey," he called back. "Won't happen again."

Smokey's face then appeared out of the darkness of the hallway and he turned toward the kitchen. "Smells like you made coffee already. Good."

"I didn't put on the large pot, Smokey. Just made a cup for myself a couple hours ago."

"Couple hours ago? Couldn't sleep?"

Travis paused a moment and then said, "Come on out here and sit down, Smokey. We need to talk."

"Got no time for that, boy. We can talk later or while we're puttin' breakfast together."

"Come sit down, Smokey."

Smokey then came out to the counter and said, "Look, son..."

"*Now*, Smokey."

"Okay, I give up. What's goin' on?" When he approached the other side of the counter, he exclaimed, "Whoa, what happened to your head?"

Travis slid his cup of cold coffee away and then fixed his eyes on Smokey's. "I don't even know where to begin."

"Talk ta me."

"It's about something that happened last night. Dreama..."

"What about Dreama?"

"She's...dead, Smokey."

Travis then saw Smokey's knees buckle. His face broadcast his shock. "This ain't some kind of sick joke, is it, Travis? If it is, it's not funny. It's not like you..."

"It's no joke, Smokey. It's true. You're aware of the killings that have been going on. It was found out that the cult of devil worshippers were indeed carrying out the murders. A false preacher from Trinity Methodist, Christopher Rudman, was the cult's leader. Unfortunately, it was discovered Dreama was also caught up in that cult. Rudman killed her last night out in the Kornigay's Bog area."

Smokey sat down on a stool on the other side of the counter. His legs would no longer hold him. Dropping his head into his right hand, the big man started to shake. From his jeans pocket he pulled a red bandana handkerchief and covered his wet eyes. He sat without a word for a few moments and then lamented, "Ah, Cher. What did you do? Why you be mixed up in that bunch?"

"Sorry, Smokey. I know how you felt about her. The other part of this is, I was there with her when she died."

Smokey looked up. "You...you were involved in..."

"Not like it sounds. They wanted to get me off their case. Last night several men came here, hit me on the head and drove me out to a field several miles from here. They were going to carve me up like they did the others. I was staked to the ground while they danced around and chanted praises to the devil. Dreama broke away from them, cut my ropes and we took off. The cult gave chase and cornered us. That's when Rudman, their leader, slipped up and stabbed her in the back. She died in my arms."

"Good God," Smokey lamented. "I just can't believe all this." He thought for a moment and then added, "But, how did you get away from 'em?"

"Before she was stabbed, another of the cult stumbled onto us. I hit him over the head and took his gun. After Rudman stabbed Dreama, he then came at me, and I shot and killed him."

"Good for you, boy. Did ya find out who the other man was?"

"Your police chief...Couture."

"The Chief? Another thing I can't believe. I hope ya killed him, too."

"I don't think so, but he may have a broken head."

Smokey laid his head on the counter. "Dreama. She was almost like one of my daughters...Sissy, the other one."

"Sorry, Smokey."

They were both quiet for a few moments and then Smokey said, "We ain't openin' today. I don't think either one of us will have our heads in our jobs. Anyway, it wouldn't be right for us to be open. When Sissy gets here, I'll send her home." His head then went back into his hands. "Do ya know what they did with Dreama's body?"

"The coroner was to take it."

"Her mama will be devastated. I never met her, but Dreama always talked about her."

"I miss her already...but the good news is, she's with God now."

Smokey gave Travis one of those 'are you sure about that' looks, but didn't respond.

"Do me a favor, Travis, since we won't open today, besides our *closed* sign, put another sign out there so people won't be knockin' on the door. Make it read somethin' like 'Closed today. Death in family.' People will respect that and won't bother us."

"Will do, boss."

At a little past seven, Sissy arrived for work, singing some song with which Travis was not familiar. Before she grabbed her apron, Smokey stopped her in the hallway and briefly told her about Dreama. He didn't go into much detail.

"Oh, Lawdy above. What is this town comin' to?" She then sat down in one of the booths and started weeping. Travis slid onto the seat across from her and handed her a napkin.

When Sissy had let out all of her tears, Travis asked, "Are you okay, now?"

She nodded. "I didn't see her much, except comin' and goin' as we was on the different shifts. But she always treated me nice. Workin' at the same place together, I always felt like she was kind of a sister."

"I became fairly close to her as well."

"Poor ol' Smokey. What he gone do now?"

"It was good that he hired Jane. I expect she will take over Dreama's shift. But Dreama was so good with the customers. Smokey had a lot of supper regulars because of her...especially men."

"She was a good lookin' woman all right." Sissy then smiled through her tears. "Not as good lookin' as me, though."

Travis smiled back at her and clasped his hands around hers. "I agree."

Smokey then came out to where they sat and stood looking out the window. It was still dark, but the eastern sky was beginning to illuminate. "The weather people said it might rain today."

It was what someone might say when there was nothing else to say.

Sissy then went home, and when Stevie Ray came in, Smokey sent him home as well. All he said to the lad was that they would be closed today. He didn't have it in him to again explain why.

"You should go as well, Smokey," Travis urged.

"What would I do? No. I'll stay here and piddle. I might make up a new batch of ribs this afternoon for tomorrow."

"I guess we'll be sitting here then, looking at one another," Travis remarked.

"No. You'll be needin' some sleep, boy."

Travis shook his head. "I wouldn't be able to sleep if I tried, Smokey."

"Then go out and spend a little of that money I been givin' ya. I know you need some clothes."

"I might. But Officer Presley was coming by here sometime today for my statement. I'd better just stick."

"Suit yerself. Well, I'll be back in the kitchen doin' that piddlin'. Ya still ought ta sleep some."

"I'll be all right sitting here at the counter. I'll make us some more coffee in the meantime. If you don't mind, I'm going to turn on the radio. It'll help change the sorrowful air in here."

All morning until the early afternoon, customers kept coming up to the door. They would read the sign, perhaps peek inside to satisfy their curiosity, and then turn around. Jane then came to the door just before eleven and tapped on the glass. Travis let her in, briefly told her about Dreama's death, which also elicited some tears, and then she left.

But then at two fifteen, there was another knock at the door. It was Harold Presley.

"Came by for that statement as I said I would, Travis."

"Some coffee and maybe some lunch?"

"Just some coffee will be fine."

For more than an hour, Officer Presley, the new acting Chief, scratched out notes on a legal pad as Travis told him in explicit detail about the previous night's horrific moments. Presley stopped him on occasion to clarify specific points. Travis also spilled the beans about the Mayor's former association with the cult and the killing of Dreama's baby. Presley was flabbergasted. When it was over, Travis asked him about what his official report would convey about Dreama.

"I already talked with LeFevre at the FBI and Lieutenant Curt Johnson at the State Police. I might have been a little vague about Dreama. I just said that both of you had been assaulted and taken to that place out there. Rudman and Couture, who were headin' up this murderous bunch caught you two after you broke away. You clobbered Couture with a flashlight and Rudman stabbed Dreama to death. And just like you said, when Rudman came at you with the knife, you got Couture's gun and killed him. That's the best I could do. But when Couture finally comes out of his coma, if he does at all, the truth about Dreama might come out."

"You think Couture might die?"

"Don't know. You hit 'im pretty hard."

"What about Mayor St. Pierre? From what I told you, will you have enough on him?"

"Don't know that either. I guess that'll all be construed as hearsay...unless we go ahead and arrest him and you stick around to testify against him. It might mean you'd be tied up here for months...maybe a year. You *do* want to go back to Indiana, don't you?"

"I do indeed."

"I expect those cult members we rounded up will sing like little birdies to keep themselves from the gas chamber. They'll incriminate both Couture and Rudman. Maybe even St. Pierre, if some of the original members are still with 'em."

"I want to see St. Pierre go down; and if it means me staying here to testify as to what Dreama told me before she died, I'll do it."

"Well, it won't be the same thing as a death-bed confession. She told you about St. Pierre before Rudman stabbed her. But, we'll get evidence on him about his association and I'll personally see he goes down. Never liked the man, the rat-nosed snake that he is. But, listen. My advice to you is to leave Destiny as soon as you can and go back to that family of yours in Indiana. The town of Destiny and the Louisiana Bureau will see that justice is done."

Travis smiled and shook Presley's hand. "You're going to make a great Chief, sir."

"If the town wants me."

"They will, I'm sure."

"Hear that?" Presley said, leaning his ear toward Smokey's radio. "That's my cousin Elvis' new hit. *It's Now or Never.*"

The two of them sat without word until Elvis' sweet ballad was over. There might have been a tear in both of their eyes.

"My cousin's tellin' you somethin', Travis. Now or never. Go home."

"As soon as I can, Officer Presley."

"Call me Harold, Travis. Everybody about town does."

Travis smiled as Presley stood. "See ya, Harold. Thanks."

Presley donned his cap and gave him a two-finger salute off its brim. He then left the diner as Travis locked the door behind him.

† † †

Smokey reopened the diner for business as usual on Tuesday morning, but to a flurry of open dialogue among its customers about the capture of the murderous cult operating in the Kornigay Bog area. "And did you hear that Chief Couture was one of them? And acting Chief Harold Presley actually got a warrant from Judge DeBauchier to search Mayor St. Pierre's house. Was he mixed up in that cult?"

On Thursday the diner was closed again. A sign had been posted in advance on Wednesday. Dreama's funeral was at two o'clock over in Bayou Cane where she was from. There were only a handful of mourners attending. Tommy Barfield was there. Travis and Smokey were the only people from Destiny to attend both the funeral and the graveside service. When her coffin was lowered into the hole, the big man shook with grief.

And then it was on the way back to Destiny in Smokey's old pickup that Travis informed him he would be going back home soon. He said he'd like it to be the Monday of Thanksgiving week.

Smokey nodded without saying anything, and again, Travis thought he saw another tear in his eye.

"I hate to leave you like this, Smokey, but it's time for me to go home."

"I understand, boy. I expected you'd be gone long before now."

"I'm concerned about your staffing, though. Losing Dreama and then me."

"I'll make out. Got Jane and she's workin' out good. And you trained that Stevie Ray boy to where he's picked up a lot. We'll get by all right. Just..."

"Just what?"

"Just hate ta see ya go. Never had a boy. And I kinda felt that if I ever did, he'd turned out somethin' like you."

Now the tear was in Travis' eye. "That means a lot to me, Smokey. And I don't mind saying, you've been like my dad."

Smokey turned his head away from the road toward his door glass. "Need to stop all this mushy stuff, Marlowe. Don't want either one of us to start boo-hooin.' There was enough of that at the funeral."

And that was the last thing said by either one of them the entire way back to the diner.

That Monday morning of Thanksgiving week, as his bus was to leave at nine-thirty, Travis sat waiting in the kitchen in his now frayed and worn Amish suit while Sissy picked up the breakfast food orders from Smokey and Stevie Ray whisked about clearing the tables. Travis was blessed to have worked at the Old South and even more blessed to have worked with such a wonderful bunch of people. As he looked out into the dining room, he envisioned the sweet, young blonde woman standing at one of the booths, stopping to talk junk and flirt with the old men. He still missed her and probably always would. He would miss them all. He would especially miss the big lug of a man who on Travis' first day in Destiny not only gave him a job, room and board, but as close to a father's love as he could ever imagine.

On her break, Sissy came back and sat with Travis while Smokey continued to work around them. She immediately began to cry. "You was good to me, Travis. You treated me like I *was* somebody. I ain't never gone forget that."

Travis smiled. "You *are* somebody, Sissy. You always will be."

"Well, anyway," she snuffed. "You always made me feel that way. I'll be missin' you five minutes after you're gone."

Travis clasped her hand into his. "And I'll be forever thinking about *you*. You're going to be fine, Sissy. Life will be good for you from here on out."

She nodded and snuffed back her mucous. "I actually think it *will* be."

Travis then checked the clock on the wall. "I have to go." Turning to Smokey, he added, "Thanks for taking me in off the street, my friend. You helped me find my way."

Smokey didn't respond. He just continued flipping the bacon on the grill.

"Put down that spatula and give me a hug, old man."

Smokey did lay it down, but said. "You know me. I ain't the huggin' type." He then stuck out his huge right paw.

Travis did not shake with him. Instead, he leaned in and wrapped his arms as far around the man as he could. "And I ain't the hand-shakin' type."

"All right, all right, git on outta here." He then took a reflective moment. "You did somethin' good for this town that a lot a people will never realize. I'm proud of ya."

Travis then pointed his right index finger toward the ceiling. "No. *He* did. I was just His helper."

At just before nine, on his way to the bus station, Travis was passing by Madam Marie's closed art shop. He paused to look at the Brandon DuMont painting of a serene-looking landscape that depicted a field lying in a bank of fog somewhere in the Louisiana countryside. It was eerie, but at the same time beautiful. Faintly discernible in the painting was a chimney standing hauntingly alone on the horizon. To the innocent eye one would think a house belonging to some sweet family had been lost to a fire or decay somewhere around the turn of the century. The painting may be bought some day, maybe in auction, and would grace someone's living room wall, never knowing that its subject held gruesome, dark secrets.

And then as he continued on, Travis heard on the next block the melodious chimes of Trinity sounding the nine o'clock hour after which its carillon played one of his favorite hymns, as though the town of Destiny was sending him off with a gift...*O Victory in Jesus*. As he passed by the large stately House of God and yet again admired its towering spire that could be seen all over the city, a verse from the psalmist entered his brain:

I will extol You, my God, O King; and I will bless Your name forever and ever. Every day I will bless You, and I will praise Your name forever and ever. Great is the Lord, and greatly to be praised.

The Greyhound was waiting for him on the corner by the drug store. Once it finally left, it would take the remainder of the day and night to reach Louisville. There Travis would change buses and be on the road nearly the entire next day before reaching Elkhart. From there a local bus would then take him through Goshen and into Hurley.

Being just a little early, he took a window seat halfway back on the bus. At nine-thirty sharp, the bus pulled away with perhaps twenty-five other Destiny citizens, most of whom would have gotten off along the way before nightfall. One of them was a smallish, elderly lady with hair as white as a swan wearing a colorful, paisley dress and a wide-brimmed white hat. She smiled at him, but said nothing.

As they passed the last series of the town's store fronts, he thought about Smokey's parting words to him. "You did somethin' good for this town a lot a people will never realize." And those that did, he thought, would soon forget.

He smiled and closed his eyes to allow all of the faces from the Old South Café to appear in the eyes of his mind. He knew he would never see them again. And the reality of that saddened him. From his coat pocket he took out Amelia Moreau's shiny little bookmark and once again ran his fingers over the shape of the cross. Closing his eyes, he tried to imagine what she looked like, but could only see the face of his nine year old Rachael. It would be the only present he would bring to her from his travels. He would likewise encourage her to begin reading the Bible from cover to cover just as the bookmark's former owner did. He would help her with the difficult words and explain any part of the text she didn't understand. Eyes still closed, he pictured that scene…Rachael sitting on his lap and Sarah sitting nearby, smiling while crocheting a doily.

"Going far?" his seat partner asked, startling him a little. Travis opened his eyes and turned toward her. "Going home."

"Where is home?"

"Indiana."

"That 's far."

"Yes it is."

"Where abouts?"

"A little place you've probably never heard of called Hurley. And just outside of there is my home, Himmel."

"Himmel. Sounds kind of German."

"It is."

"And that translated means what?"

Travis smiled. "Why, Heaven, of course."

Praises for Lee Martin's Mystery Novels

The Third Moon is Blue

Exciting and thrilling, this is a marvelous mix of psychodrama, romance and loss. Lee Martin really paints a picture well.

Readers Favorite---

The Third Moon is Blue took me back to a time in early adulthood in a way no other book has ever done, partly due to the locale, but also because of the way in which he relates the story in vivid detail.

Glenna Fisher---

The Third Moon is Blue is a great read! Lee Martin has given us a little of something for everyone...an air of intrigue and mystery, a riveting, emotional story of heartache and fear, a life-like depiction of courage in war...and in life. It's all woven together with a love story for the ages...

--James C. Crutchfield
Bethany Baptist

Wolf Laurel

First of a great trilogy. Lee Martin introduces us to Bruce McGowan in this first of three wonderfully-intriguing books with McGowan as the protagonist. Once you meet McGowan, you won't stop reading until you've finished the third book (*A Hateful Wind*) and beg for a sequel.

Andy Black---

The Six Mile Inn

Lee Martin is a master story-teller, making Lavinia's story a compelling page turner. If you enjoy stories woven around actual events, and like a little romance, murder and suspense with a great cast of characters, give this book a try. Definitely worth reading.

Reader's Choice---

The Valiant

Mystery novelist COL Lee Martin continues to excite his audience with his latest release of "<u>The Valiant</u>". I have read most of his books, but "The Valiant" is by far my favorite. In baseball terms, Lee Martin has hit a standup homerun. "The Valiant" is an intriguing mystery novel that includes a silent hero, a spunky, blonde librarian, and a cop that doesn't quit until he gets answers to his questions. The Valiant will keep you on the edge of your seat to the very end. This is a book you'll find hard to put down.

Marc Morris---
The Talmadge Group

I could not put the book down. You'll keep trying to anticipate the next twist. If you're my age, it might even conger up some memories of the past.

Bill Deck---

The novel is a work of a mature author, well in control of plot and structure. Clues are distributed carefully to keep the reader alert and interested throughout. In terms of characterization, the main protagonist is well-defined and believable. The crime story aspect is particularly successful, keeping the reader guessing until late in the work regarding the identity of the culprit. The 'happy ending' is pleasing and emotionally satisfying. It was nice to encounter what many Europeans would consider a positive-minded American finish. Such a denouement is rarer here.

Dr. Sharon Fuller/ Dr. Roy Fuller---
Angers, France

CPSIA information can be obtained at www.ICGtesting.com
Printed in the USA
LVOW11s2001090814

398251LV00001B/1/P